She  ger
and the .... ne.
Would old Applethwaite be discharged if his part in it
came to Edward's attention?

No, she must give the devil his due. Edward was
fair. He would blame Adelaide, not the gardener. Even
to her, he was more decent than might be expected; he
gave her the same pin money he allowed his daughters.
She was able to order books or embroidery silks or
whatever other trifles she wished without asking his
permission or begging him for money. Leonora
ordinarily took care of buying her clothing for the year,
when she went to London with Edward. If she did so
from fear of embarrassment rather than kindness, the
end was the same.

But oh, she hoped the visitor did not report their
meeting and bring her half brother's wrath down on her.
And what if he had been seriously injured after all? She
could cry with fury and dismay. With an effort she
suppressed the tears, all but a few, and freed one arm to
grope in her pocket for her handkerchief. If her brother
sent for her, she must not appear to have been weeping.

Where was her handkerchief? It had been in her
pocket when—

Oh. Oh, no. She had taken it out and blotted the
cut. In her haste, she must not have put it back. Now it
would be evidence against her. She clutched Tabby
more closely, and her friend licked her chin.

A Peculiar Enchantment

by

Kathleen Buckley

A Peculiar Enchantment

Cover Art by *The Wild Rose Press, Inc.*

The Wild Rose Press, Inc.
PO Box 708
Adams Basin, NY 14410-0708
Visit us at www.thewildrosepress.com

Publishing History
First Edition, 2022
Trade Paperback ISBN 978-1-5092-4616-8
Digital ISBN 978-1-5092-4617-5

Published in the United States of America

Dedication

Because of Meret, the model for Tabby, and with heartfelt thanks to my excellent editor, Eilidh MacKenzie.

Chapter 1

Lamburne Chase, Wiltshire, England, July 1741

Adelaide bit her lower lip savagely as she hugged her only friend, who slitted her green eyes and purred. Sometimes it was the only way to relieve her feelings and then only in private. She made it a point of honor never to show anger, hurt, or any discomfiture before her half brother and his family and servants. Curse Thomas, the second footman.

He had been the one; she knew it by his oblique glance as she had returned from yesterday's early evening walk. With the family at supper, there was no chance of encountering one of them in the gardens. Nor was Thomas quite able to conceal his smirk. She discovered the reason when she reached her suite and found Tabby gone. After searching everywhere she could hide or be concealed in her bedchamber, dressing room, and parlor, she repeated the search in the library, morning room, reception chamber, any one where her family were not. She sought out the butler and housekeeper. They promised to return her cat if it were found.

How dare they call her "it." Adelaide thanked them in a colorless voice. To show anger or anxiety would be fatal. She added, "Tabby keeps my rooms free of mice and rats. Whoever returns her to me shall have a guinea." That captured their attention. She told the footman at the front entrance as she whisked out the door. Whoever had stolen Tabby (but she knew that smooth-faced Thomas was guilty) would not have taken her out that way, but Tabby might circle the house, looking for a way in. Her heart thumped painfully: *if she could.*

Some called Tabby her familiar. Such nonsense would not have caused Thomas to abduct Tabby; he was not some credulous country fellow. The footman did nothing unless it benefitted him; he would not have committed this latest affront unprompted. No, his crime had probably been suggested by someone else. Not her half brother, who ignored Adelaide as much as possible. His wife would think herself above conspiring with a servant. The instigator could have been either Charity or Sophia, both of them safe from any punishment for their cruelty unless she were able to mete it out herself.

If the fellow had not stolen Tabby, the contretemps would never have occurred and they would not be in danger. Whyever had Edward's guest been standing under the tree so late? He might have been killed, and it would have been Thomas's fault, though she would have been blamed for it. If she were sent away as her sister-in-law had once suggested, what would become of Tabby?

In the pale light of dawn, Tabby nestled in her arms, none the worse for her experience, though she might have died and Adelaide would have died before she stopped searching for her dear friend. Her family's taunts and petty slights she could ignore, but the attack on Tabby went too far.

Now they had breakfasted, they were both ready

for a nap. If only Edward did not summon her to demand an explanation. Her only hope was that the man—had she been told his name? She thought not—had been too far gone in drink to remember what had happened. Or perhaps he would be ashamed to admit to wandering in the park so late.

She had not cared or even thought about the presence of a visitor in the house until she found Tabby imprisoned in a bag hung in an oak. The burlap bag hung high above her head. Relief warred with terror until she recalled she did have another ally than Tabby, after all. On her infrequent meetings with the old gardener, he was kind to her for her late mother's sake.

Neither of them had seen Sophia's beau when Applethwaite brought out the ladder. The tree's thick trunk concealed the guest, either standing still and lost in thought, or perhaps lying on the ground, overcome by drink. Otherwise he would have heard their approach. Wouldn't he? Though they had not been talking or making much noise, an hour before she had been calling Tabby as she walked through the trees. When she saw the bag in the oak, she had gasped and called and Tabby had answered. As fast as she had run to fetch Applethwaite, it had taken minutes to rouse him and explain, and more time for him to dress and carry the ladder to the tree. Perhaps the man had arrived during that interval. Not that it mattered except for the sequel.

Applethwaite had wanted to climb up, protesting Adelaide should not risk herself on a ladder. She had insisted. For all that he was old and lean, he weighed more than she. Besides, he left the climbing and heavy work to the young under-gardeners now. Strong as he was, his bones might be brittle and break easily. She won the point by saying she could not steady the ladder for him as he could if she climbed. He grumbled but gave in. Just as well: if he had fallen, he might have been badly injured and his hobnailed boots might have done her niece's suitor serious harm. Yet even his minor injury might be her undoing.

When she cut the rope suspending Tabby's sack, the branch under her feet gave way with a sharp *crack!* Applethwaite barked an oath and the next thing Adelaide knew, he was helping her to stand, muttering, "Be you sure you b'aint hurt?" At the time, she denied any injury though now she ached in several places. She was more concerned for Tabby. But the bag had come down on the leafy twigs near the end of the branch whereas Adelaide had fallen on the thick, bare portion, the ground, and Whoever-he-was.

Once she had retrieved her knife to free Tabby and convinced the gardener she would not swoon, he moved the fallen branch off the visitor and bent to examine him. The man was insensible. Applethwaite suggested taking him back to the house. Kneeling, she put her fingers on the side of the visitor's neck above his neckcloth and found a pulse. His breathing was steady and the cut on his forehead did not appear serious. His breath smelled of brandy. Thank God! If the gentleman had been seriously injured, she would have had to agree with Applethwaite at whatever cost to herself. Perhaps he would take Tabby in if…

She did not like to leave her brother's guest lying out in the night, though the air was warm, but she had Tabby and Applethwaite to consider. If her victim had only been stunned, she might have been able to help him up, but an unconscious man far gone in drink was beyond her ability. Applethwaite could have supported him, but she could not allow him to bring the victim to the house, where getting him to his bedchamber would court discovery.

Applethwaite left off arguing only when she pointed out the hazards and promised she herself would summon whatever servants were on duty if the man could not be roused. He reluctantly agreed; apart from his loyalty to her, he dared not risk losing his employment at his age.

"Lord Gervase's stirring," the gardener muttered.

"Is that his name?" she asked as she wiped away the trickle of blood on his pale forehead. Tabby pressed against her side.

"Ay. Some Frenchy name, as well. A marquess's son."

A memory of servants' gossip overheard came to her. "Lord Gervase Ducane. You should go now."

Nevertheless, he waited until Ducane showed signs of regaining his wits before he betook himself and the ladder back to his little cottage. Adelaide licked her forefinger and used it to wash off the remaining traces of blood before giving Lord Gervase's brow one final pat with the clean part of her handkerchief.

Luck seldom favored her; she had best expect to be called to her half brother's study. She would change out of her casaquin and petticoat which were crumpled, grass-stained, and snagged in places by twigs or splinters. Such a pity they had been spoiled. She liked the convenience of being able to dress without the help of a maid, sometimes difficult when she had no maid of her own. She would send a request to Mme. Bernard, who knew her preferences, to make her another jacket and skirt. The state of her clothing hardly mattered as so few saw her, but she did feel happier when well dressed.

Almost anything but blue, which made her look like a corpse. "Don't you think so, Tabby?"

She put on her unfitted old *contouche*, looking for any sign of bruises where they might show. Charity or Sophia would titter, "So clumsy," if they saw her, or whisper, "Madelaide." If she napped in the apricot sacque-back gown, it would wrinkle, but Edward was unlikely to notice while he berated her. She locked the door and lay down on her side. Tabby, purring, crossed the bed to curl up against her stomach.

She could not avoid thinking of Tabby's danger and the accident and worrying about its outcome. Would old Applethwaite be discharged if his part in it came to Edward's attention?

No, she must give the devil his due. Edward was fair. He would blame Adelaide, not the gardener. Even to her, he was more decent than might be expected; he gave her the same pin money he allowed his daughters. She was able to order books or embroidery silks or whatever other trifles she wished without asking his permission or begging him for money. Leonora ordinarily took care of buying her clothing for the year, when she went to London with Edward. If she did so from fear of embarrassment rather than kindness, the end was the same.

But oh, she hoped the visitor did not report their meeting and bring her half brother's wrath down on her. And what if he had been seriously injured after all? She could cry with fury and dismay. With an effort she suppressed the tears, all but a few, and freed one arm to grope in her pocket for her handkerchief. If her brother sent for her, she must not appear to have been weeping.

Where was her handkerchief? It had been in her pocket when—

Oh. Oh, no. She had taken it out and blotted the cut. In her haste, she must not have put it back. Now it would be evidence against her. She clutched Tabby more closely, and her friend licked her chin.

Chapter 2

Ten months ago, he had made the long journey to Blacklaw on receiving word of the birth of his brother's first son. 'Twas a momentous event, after eleven years of marriage without a male child. Gervase celebrated with Robert, both of them overcome with drink and joy. The effect on Gervase's position had not occurred to him, and he suspected it hadn't crossed his brother's mind either.

Two months ago, the marquess summoned him to the family seat. Ordinarily Gervase spent a month or so at Blacklaw later in the summer: to be sent for was a rarity. Robert's greeting was restrained, which was unlike him. Later, alone with Gervase in his study, he rotated a quill between his fingers. Finally he raised his eyes and began, "Now that I have an heir of my body…"

Ducane thought about his situation for days. Reluctantly, he applied to his mother for advice, as his father had often done. Her ruthless practicality was as austere as her parlor, and no warmer.

"I could buy myself a commission with the remainder of this quarter's and all of next quarter's allowance. Robert would advance it if I asked. I ride well and am skilled with pistol, musket, and smallsword." At eighteen, a life of adventure as a brother of the blade might have appealed.

The Dowager Lady Blacklaw contemplated him with more attention than she had paid Gervase since he had suffered an extremely sore throat, mistaken for scarlet fever, when he was ten.

"I cannot think you well suited to the military life when you have become such a town creature in the last few years." She sat for a time without speaking, then sighed. "You have spent little time at Blacklaw since Robert's marriage and cannot be expected to know, though you might have guessed, that a lady who has given birth only four times in ten years is not a good breeder."

"But now she's had Charles—"

Alison, Lady Blacklaw, waved a dismissive hand. "All very well, but she may not bear another boy, and young children sometimes die. The first year is the most dangerous, but once they survive that, there is smallpox, other diseases, and childhood mishaps of all sorts. You might find yourself Blacklaw someday. It would not do to come into the title in your later years with no heir of your own, and in the army you might have the misfortune to die before you begot a son."

He had not given much weight to her objection. After all, there were one or two cousins in the line of succession. No, the sticking point was that he doubted he could afford more than an infantry lieutenant's commission. Any further advance would depend on his own merits and luck, with no money to purchase higher rank. To be a lieutenant at his age, and likely for the rest of his life, would be demeaning. He would also be poor.

"If you marry well, you could continue to live as you have been, amusing yourself as gentlemen do in town, and with the advantage of a house, a wife, and more money, if you choose wisely. Wedding would provide you with some direction, as well. 'Tis all very well for a young man to idle about town, but it is past time you should marry. I trust you will select someone who can undertake the role of marchioness if necessary."

"We must pray Blacklaw secures the succession. I could never fill my father's shoes. Or Robert's, either."

The dowager marchioness tilted her head thoughtfully. "You would do very well as marquess, Gervase. Your father spent near as long training you as he did your brother. I own I was surprised you turned into such a town beau. But you would soon find your feet if worse came to worst. You are quick-witted and deal well with others. Robert is still not at ease with tradesmen and the marquessate's business connections."

She proposed he court the Earl of Lamburne's daughter: the second son of a marquess was a desirable mate. "It would be a good match on both sides. The earl's family would like a connection to a marquess or a duke, especially one popular at court, as your brother is. While Robert publicly disapproves of your friendship with Prince Frederick, the prince is heir to the throne, so we will still have a friend at court through you in the future. Though of course we hope the day of the prince's ascension is far in the future," she added piously.

If she encouraged the match with Lamburne's daughter, it was because she knew the size of the dowry, that the girl was suitable and available, and that her family would be in favor of it. The dowager marchioness was part of a large circle of similar women who maintained a busy correspondence, which his father had once wryly called "the Monstrous Regiment of Women," a description that made his mother laugh merrily.

He had agreed to consider the girl. Before his stay at Blacklaw ended, his mother had written to Lady Lamburne's mother, Lady Agnes Portland, one of her correspondents, to broach the subject delicately.

He should have looked for a girl with a dowry as soon as he took up residence in town ten years ago. But he had already been too old to find shy or prattling misses interesting, and he was not attracted by them in any case. Nor did he care to think of himself as a fortune hunter, which he would be, as he had no property or income apart from his heir's allowance. The matter had not seemed pressing then.

The young ladies seeking husbands seemed shallower and more irritating with each passing year. A widow would have done, but some were as foolish as the girls, and the ones who had property or money were either much sought after or had no interest in acquiring a second husband. He had let the matter slide, thinking he would eventually meet someone he could imagine marrying.

As he strolled toward his rooms lost in these thoughts soon after his return to London, Eustace Wilkes hailed him.

"Ducane, wherever have you been hiding? We haven't seen you for weeks, my dear." Wilkes executed a graceful twirl of his walking stick. The maneuver almost tripped a maidservant scurrying past on some errand.

"I've had family matters at Blacklaw to attend to. Do you mean to visit your brother in Surrey? London is already a wasteland for the summer." A good thing, too, as he did not crave company.

"Going to Feake's place first. A bachelor gathering; no young ladies there, thank God. Are you?"

"No. I'm promised to a house party."

"By your glum tone, I conclude your mother thinks it time you married."

For a fellow who looked as if he had no thought in his head but the latest fashion and the freshest *on-dit*, Wilkes could be annoyingly percipient. Or mayhap talk was already circulating that Ducane was no longer Blacklaw's presumptive heir.

"She's right."

"We all come to it sooner or later. Though I mean to hold out until I find a lady as particular in her tastes as I," he added.

"Do you think you can?" Ducane inquired, laughing. Wilkes was the only man he knew who was more finickal than Jenkins, his own manservant.

"Alas, I doubt it. Shall we look in at White's?"

"One cup of chocolate and a little talk there always seems to lead to drink, gambling, and the bagnio. As I'm setting off in the morning, I think I must decline the pleasure."

"Ah, well. I don't care for coach journeys when I'm cup-shot, either. Good hunting."

Ducane ate a solitary supper and spent the evening reading the *Meditations* of Marcus Aurelius, hoping the old Stoic could persuade him to a better frame of mind.

****

After two days at Lamburne, Ducane questioned

12

his mother's judgement. Coy, flirtatious, breathtakingly ignorant of all but fashion and gossip, Lady Sophia would be insufferable as a wife. To him, at least—she might suit some other man well enough. Fashionable couples might lead separate lives, but still, at times one would have to endure one's wife's presence at dinner and in bed, if nowhere else.

Jenkins sighed almost imperceptibly when Ducane dismissed him without preparing for bed, envisioning his master's clothing scattered on the floor, no doubt. His manservant should know he was not so untidy. He would leave his garments over a chair. Jenkins could tend to them tomorrow.

Tonight, Ducane felt in need of solitude, darkness, and country air. The rest of the house had retired. He himself was not ready to sleep, unaccustomed to country hours. Instead he slipped out to stroll and settle his mind. Watch the stars, and see yourself running with them, Marcus Aurelius advised.

Was he desperate enough to marry the Earl of Lamburne's eldest daughter? Watching the moon climb above the trees, he weighed his alternatives. At seven-and-thirty, with an education which fitted him for no profession, they were limited.

In theory, he conceded his mother was correct that a provident marriage would solve his problems and aid his family. He should not wait longer to beget sons. While he did not covet the earldom, everyone knew of some lady left in near-poverty when a distant relation inherited her late husband's title. His mother was unlikely to suffer that fate, given his father's sensible arrangements for his widow's maintenance and her own investments. Still, they had to consider the tenants' welfare if the property passed to other hands. An heir new to the position and estates would not remember Granny Fernsby giving him cheese tarts or old Rummage teaching him to ride his first pony.

Yet he could not welcome the prospect of having a wife who would offend him with her whims and demands. The most formal marriages called for more intimacy than he could easily tolerate with a lady who giggled, dressed badly, or fell into distempered caprices. A sensible, biddable lady would be acceptable, but army life might be preferable to marrying Lady Sophia.

He had enjoyed a connection with one widow who was intelligent and suitable, had she possessed even a small fortune. But she had no children despite having been married eight or ten years, and he suspected she would not be willing to trade her freedom for a husband. He needed a lady he could respect or at least tolerate and who was well-dowered. Where was he to find one?

The conversation with his mother lingered in his mind, too. Did she really hold so good an opinion of him? Ducane would never have guessed it, or that his mother knew so much about his activities, as he had taken lodgings on moving to London, rather than live in Blacklaw House. Most young men led aimless lives in town. He was not young. A bachelor of his age was more likely to be a man o' the town, as they called it: a rake, dissipated and idle.

The moon and night sky provided no answers. He paused under a tree some distance from the house. What the devil was he to do?

Chapter 3

The next he knew, he was flat on his back, staring up at the dawn sky through branches. What—? He must have lain out all night, accounting for the dampness of his clothing. How much had he drunk last night? He seldom drank deep: impossible to present an elegant figure when bowsy. Granted, he had taken more than usual, but surely several glasses of wine at dinner, a glass of port afterward, and two glasses of brandy later were not enough to make him fall down dead drunk. And he'd had a cup of tea in the drawing room after the men joined the ladies, before the brandy. More likely, he had simply sat down and dozed off as the result of drink and a great many troubling thoughts.

He struggled to his feet, sick and with an aching head, and stood for some minutes leaning against the tree. It could scarcely do his coat and breeches more harm than they had suffered already from earth and grass and dew. What the devil had happened? His head hurt, both the back, where his gingerly exploration discovered a lump, and his temple. His fingers came away from the latter bearing a trace of blood.

Judging from the sun's elevation, it might be six in the morning. He had dismissed his valet at around eleven the previous night and gone out to walk in Lamburne Chase's park to clear his head. "Chase" was an appallingly apt name for the estate where he was the quarry.

When someone spoke near his shoulder, he twitched in surprise and turned so quickly the world spun for a moment. His hearing was acute, but his brain, still slightly pickled and busy with worrisome reflections, had ignored his ears.

"Be you well, sir?" The elderly fellow peered at him—some sort of outdoor servant, in a much-mended leather coat.

Was he? Curst if he knew. "Yes, of course." He cast around for an explanation of his state and noticed a sizeable tree limb nearby. "Ah…a branch seems to have fallen and, er, felled me."

" 'Pears to ha' grazed you on the way down, sir." The gaffer laid a gnarled, calloused forefinger to the left side of his own forehead. "Terrible sorry. I come to take it down if 'twas broke and like to fall as I was told, but it were too quick for me. Will you be needing an arm back to the house?"

"No, I'm not hurt. Thank you for inquiring." Ducane groped in his pocket for a coin for the man's trouble.

"I'll be away, then. G'day to you and thank'ee."

As the gardener ambled off, Ducane wondered why he had not brought a ladder and a saw if he had meant to cut the branch. Surely it would have been less work to come prepared rather than to have to go back for his tools. He could almost imagine the old man as Robin Goodfellow, who would not, of course, be carrying a saw because wasn't iron a charm against evil spirits, witches, and the like? Or so his old nurse had maintained. Mayhap, as the fellow was elderly, he meant to send some younger man to deal with it if necessary. Servants and tenants had their own ways of doing their work, and their masters were well advised not to interfere as long as it got done.

The tree limb at his feet looked healthy, and the broken end was quite thick. No gust of wind should have brought it down. The night had been still when he went out. Down the branch most certainly was, however, and he had a cut and a sore head to show for it. As he moved to gaze up at the place from which the limb had broken away, a scrap of white on the ground caught his eye. It was almost hidden under some twigs. Bending to pick it up brought on another wave of dizziness and made his head throb.

The handkerchief was a lady's: small and edged in lace, stained with blood. Strangely, it was without monogram, though it bore the image of a leaping cat in one corner, finely executed in silk thread. This one was white.

This one? Somehow he imagined it should be black. Why was he thinking of a black cat?

In some besotted dream, a cat screeched. Images flickered in memory: a black cat's face over his own, or a lady who was a cat, bending over him to soothe his forehead, murmuring enticingly. She was weirdly attractive and at the same time disturbing. If he had agreed to go to her chamber to eat bacon or kippers, what would have become of him? Would his fate mirror the myth of Hades and Persephone, with him as the captured mate? Or was it one of Mme. d'Aulnoy's *Tales of the Fairys*? The morning took on an air of the phantasmatical; he had strayed into fairyland. He must have drunk more than he realized last night. He'd had a sharp blow to the head, too. The combination accounted for the bizarre dreams and fancies said to result from a fever or from taking laudanum.

Who carried a handkerchief without a monogram? His hostess, Leonora Setbury, Countess of Lamburne, lacked whimsy or a sense of humor, for that matter. Sophia, whom he had been meant to court, was pretty, spoiled, and lacked the subtlety the cat embroidery implied, whatever that might be! The younger girl, Charity, was a spiteful little cat; he had heard her make malicious remarks about neighbors and servants. She seemed unlikely to have taken a cat as her symbol unless she did not comprehend how revealing it would be.

He shoved the handkerchief into his pocket and trudged toward the door at the side of the house. As the day was so early, he should be able to reach his bedchamber unseen. Bad enough the gardener had seen him disheveled and damp, his hair straggling free of its ribbon, when he prided himself on always being point-device. Even his mistresses never saw him so thoroughly untidy. In the future, he would stop at one bottle of wine and no more than a tumbler or two of brandy.

He really must extricate himself from this scheme of his mother's.

Chapter 4

He woke abruptly when his valet brought his chocolate no more than three hours after he had thrown off his clothing and collapsed into his bed.

Watching Jenkins gather the garments he had dropped on the chair, he remembered that on his return from the grounds, the fire had already been made up. Whatever had the maid thought, finding his bed unused? Not that he cared for the opinions of a servant…except that it would lead to speculation as to whose bed he had been in, if it wasn't his own. Were his aching head and stiff joints not punishment enough? And a certain feeling of unease, as well, its origin impossible to trace.

The valet inspected the grass stains and dirt on his coat and breeches, his expression pained. Ducane sympathized; he was near as finicky as Jenkins about his wardrobe. "Is that Friday face necessary, Jenkins? Surely the grass and dirt can be brushed off when they are dry."

"The dirt will probably brush off without staining, but the grass stains…" He sighed. "On so light a color, it may be impossible to remove them." Then he held up Ducane's stockings and gazed at them as sadly as if he had lost a beloved family member. A twig had torn one of them. "Seventeen shillings the pair, sir, and none to be had this side of London."

"What, not even in Marlborough?"

"Not of your usual quality, sir."

"Ay, a pity and a shame, Jenkins, but let me hear no more of it." He did not want to be reminded of the horrid episode. "I do have other stockings, do I not?"

"Would I forget to pack enough stockings for you, my lord?" He tutted.

Ducane had been sitting up in bed, sipping his chocolate. Not until he turned his head to answer the pressing question of what he would wear to breakfast did Jenkins see the left side of his face.

"Sir, you are injured." His valet sounded as appalled as he had over the state of the clothing, which was rather flattering. Jenkins snatched up a hand mirror from the dressing table and hastened to his bedside. "Only see, Lord Gervase."

A three-inch-long crust of blood marked the cut. "I suffered a mishap while walking in the park. What, did you think I'd been rolling on the ground with some country lass?"

Jenkins ignored the question, going to the washstand to moisten a cloth. After holding it to the wound and then carefully wiping the dried blood away, he said, "I do not think stitches are needed."

"Good God, I hope not!"

"You do have the beginnings of a bruise, I fear."

Wonderful. He would appear at dinner cut and bruised, with no acceptable explanation. "There's no help for it." Perhaps it would give the Lamburnes a disgust for him, which would be an easy way of ending his stay.

"It is well closed, so it may not scar, my lord." Jenkins tactfully did not inquire how he had received the injury. He was probably imagining Ducane falling down drunk, which stung as it came close to the truth. Unfair, too, as he had not done so since he was a callow pup, long before Jenkins knew him.

"If it does, I shall imply I received it during a duel. Or no, in a scuffle with a footpad. That's better."

"A footpad here?"

"Well, no. The challenge will be providing an answer today, for I suppose someone will comment upon it. I'll say I ran into a tree while strolling in the park last night."

"Very good, sir. The peacock-blue suit for dinner, I think, sir, unless you prefer the ice blue?"

"The ice blue." It was his least favorite, ordered against his better judgement because both Jenkins and the tailor recommended the color. He could not afford to replace it on finding he did not grow fonder of it. Today its chilly color reflected his feelings about a long meal spent with the earl's family, followed by the interminable afternoon and evening. No hope of taking some exercise out of doors, either. While he slept, clouds had rolled in, bringing a steady drizzle. He might be able to plead a headache, given the bruise, and retire to his chamber between dinner and supper.

"I found this in your pocket, sir. What shall I do with it?" Jenkins held a stained scrap of linen by one corner as if it were a dead rodent.

Shards of memory pricked at him. There had been the tantalizing cat woman, who had only been a dream. But he did recall finding the handkerchief after he woke in the dawn. How had it come there?

The linen bore a brown stain, like dried blood. He had a wound which had bled. The obvious conclusion

21

was that some female had blotted the cut, and his sodden, stunned brain had transformed the reality into a tale of enchantment. Part of his dream was rooted in fact; the handkerchief's presence proved that much. If he could place any belief in what he recalled, the female had been no servant or rustic, judging from her speech. Did the Lamburne girls still have a governess or a companion to chaperon them? In his experience, women of that sort were self-effacing and utterly correct. Still, one might have been walking in the park for some reason, and such a one might feel she had to give aid to an injured man. She would not want it known lest she lose her position. Ay, that made sense and rendered the world normal once again.

"Put it aside for now. I don't know whose it is, and I don't like to inquire in case it belongs to some lady or maidservant who slipped out to meet her spark. We can hardly send it to be washed, as the laundry maid would tattle to others about a blood-stained handkerchief." To inquire of the family, he would have to explain more about his accident than he wished. Certainly the female who had dropped it was not one of the Lamburnes.

Jenkins confined himself to "Hmmm" and whisked it away.

****

She woke from her morning nap to sharp rapping. Her heart lurched; as she had feared, Edward knew. She hurried to open the door without waiting to put on her shoes, to find it was Leonora's maid.

"Lady Lamburne wishes you to join her in her parlor, Lady Adelaide." The woman looked Adelaide up and down, making it perfectly plain what she thought of a crushed gown strewn with cat hairs and the absence of shoes. "I'll tell her you will attend her shortly." She did not wait for a reply or to be dismissed.

Was this about last night? Had the fellow—some marquess's son—been more hurt than she realized? Had he not roused and returned to the house, or had he taken a chill?

Heart pounding, she buckled on her shoes and covered her untidy hair with a cap before trudging to the other wing. If she had encountered any footman, he would have mistaken her for the condemned prisoner she felt like.

"Addie," Leonora said without greeting her or looking up from her petit-point embroidery. The piece was intended for a fire screen; too bad she had not asked someone with talent to draw the sketch. Leonora's human and animal figures were always out of proportion. Also the unicorn's horn was pointing to a place that would cause men to suppress smirks. Adelaide compressed her lips to hide her own unseemly mirth. Lady Lamburne did not notice. "I don't know if you are aware we have a guest."

She had been vaguely aware of a guest, though no one had actually informed her. From overheard servants' gossip, she knew about a gentleman coming to court Sophia. In a sense she had met him, too. "I believe I heard some such thing, Leonora," she mumbled. Her voice was rough from having spent hours calling Tabby.

"In several days, we will have more guests. 'Tis to be a house party. Knowing how uncomfortable you are in large groups and with strangers, you will wish to remain in your rooms. They will depart on the nineteenth and twentieth."

Certainly she felt ill at ease when visitors were told she was slow or odd or given to peculiar humors. "Oh, dear. Many people?"

"Twelve couples, the Catlins' son who is down from Oxford, our own family, and Lord Gervase Ducane. A few are known to you, others are not. If you attended, the numbers would be uneven. The talk will all be of fashion and of the beau monde. You would not enjoy yourself."

"Oh, I would not like that. Tabby and I will entertain ourselves, I suppose." As they always did.

"That would be best. You may go."

She scurried out of Leonora's parlor. The room reminded her of a mouth: the draperies and upholstery gum-pink, the walls white. In its confines, Adelaide wondered if this was what a mouse felt in a cat's jaws. Once in the wide, well-lighted passage, her pace slowed. A footman stationed at the stairs gave her a startled glance. She was striding, which accounted for his surprise. Part of being invisible was to move like a skein of finest silk in the wind. Too late for that! Adelaide swept past without a word or look. She did not give a groat for his opinion.

No footman stood at the door to the old part of the house; of course not. For once she was glad; her face would reveal too much this morning. How dare her sister-in-law dismiss her as if she were an erring maidservant.

Yet Leonora's manner had been no more dismissive than usual. Adelaide had shrugged off worse treatment in the past when one of the family had noticed her despite her best attempts to be inconspicuous. As a rule, no one cared enough to insist she be present in mind or body. Her old governess had advised her to ignore her family's slights, and Adelaide had done so, too fearful to do anything else. When Edward or his sharp-faced wife called her ugly or clumsy or stupid, she had crept away to hide in one of the less-used rooms or in the park, if the weather were warm. Easy enough to do when she wasn't in the schoolroom with her governess. Still, eventually she had armored herself against criticism and petty cruelties and also learned to make herself invisible. If they did not notice her, she was mostly safe from their gibes.

There were some disadvantages. Did the servants simply forget her existence or was no maidservant being punished for some petty mistake or transgression? Food at least had not been a need. She and Tabby had foraged for breakfast in the pantry when they came in from the park. They did not mind serving themselves; the food they got by raiding was often preferable to boiled mutton or the fattier or more gristly bits of some roast joint. The absent or late hot water and chocolate were irksome, however.

She had been hiding like a mouse for years. Her heart pounded as she marched along the shabby passage toward her mousehole. Only a day ago, she would have let pass Leonora's dismissal of her. The absence of her chocolate and wash water, the late, almost cold meals, the footmen's failure to make sure the sconces in the passage were lighted in the evening: for years she had shrugged off slights as if she deserved them. Her half brother and sister-in-law treated her as less than a poor relation in their house, worse than poor old Lady Muriel who had lived with them for a time. The very servants were insolent and flouted her.

She had tried to convince herself that if the visitor's injury was minor (except for the cut on his forehead), no damage had been done. She had been mistaken. She and Tabby had been harmed. Her brother's household had finally gone too far, turning fear and apathy into smoldering rage.

Thomas had stolen her cat away and left her to die if Adelaide had failed to find her. She pulled the key out of her pocket to unlock her door. She would secure it every time she left her chamber now for Tabby's safety, but that was not enough. She must prevent further outrages, or Thomas and the others would grow bolder. If something happened to Tabby—she could not bear to think of it. Burning this miserable pile of pretense and misery and masonry was less unthinkable. If Thomas had murdered Tabby, she would have killed him if she hanged for it. She would not care.

She dropped onto the window seat beside Tabby who was gazing out through the diamond-shaped panes at the trees in the park and the low hills beyond. *I will tolerate no more.* The question was, how to put an end to it? Some idea would occur to her or an opportunity would arise, or she would create one.

Someone scratched timidly at her door. When Adelaide called, "Come," the new scullery maid stood there mutely, holding a jug of wash water. It was welcome, though she should have received it earlier.

The maid entered hesitantly and scuttled to the washstand with the jug. To send Adelaide the lowest female servant to attend her was another calculated insult. Today the affront rankled.

The girl spoke without looking at Adelaide. "Her ladyship said as you'd want to change your gown."

This was unexpected. One might have thought it a show of concern, but more likely Leonora had been offended by Adelaide's wrinkled gown and disheveled hair. She had probably told her own maid to make sure someone was sent to tidy her despised sister-in-law. This girl in her faded gown must have been the one most easily spared.

"That was thoughtful. I do need to change. What is your name?"

"Jenny Talbot, my lady."

"Did you break a dish or not scour the pots well enough to suit Cook?"

"I don't know, my lady, only I'm new and I don't know all my duties yet. Mistress Jones was right put out this morning. She reckoned as his lordship stripped half the meat from a roast chicken left over from yesterday's dinner to give to his terrier bitch, that's to whelp in the next few days."

Adelaide and Tabby shared a reminiscent moment.

Jenny, still unsure of herself, confided she was grateful for the opportunity to act as a temporary lady's maid. The poor child would never rise to such a post: too countrified, freckle-faced, and plain.

But if anything startling had occurred overnight or this morning, she should have heard of it in the servants' hall or kitchen. Impossible to ask directly. In response to a casual question, Jenny talked about the coming house party. No need to worry about the mishap with the guest, then.

Her curiosity about the visitor had been tepid until she found him while searching for Tabby. Well…fell on him. Who would have thought such a thick branch would give way under her? Fortunately, she had already cut the rope that suspended the bag from the limb above the one on which she was standing. It was too bad the man had been scratched, but on the other hand, if he had not been loitering in the park in the middle of the night, she and Tabby would have fallen very hard and perhaps been injured. As it was, Adelaide had bruises and a painful hip and shoulder from having turned as she fell, so as not to land on Tabby.

At least the suitor had not died or taken to his bed with an ague or cold. She did wish she could assure herself that he would not talk about his midnight accident.

Tabby lay on the coverlet watching Adelaide wash her hands and face after Jenny helped her take off her *contouche*.

"Will you change your jumps for a corset, my lady?"

She meant to tell the girl to fetch out her old plum-colored gown. Then a notion struck her like a flash of lightning. She always enjoyed the sight of those brilliant, destructive lashes of the gods. She glanced at the pretty clock on the mantle. Forty minutes until dinner. There was a way to begin her revenge. She spoke before she could think better of it and lose her courage.

"Yes." She seldom wore a corset because she could remove the jumps without help. The wait, after seeking out the nearest footman to send for a maid, was usually tedious.

"I will go down to dinner today," instead of having a tray in her parlor, the food not hot, and usually only the least-favored dishes. Appearing at dinner when they had Sophia's suitor present would break up her family's peace of mind, which might be dangerous, but perhaps it would also send a message.

Did the guest have any memory of their encounter? He had been drunk. Most men drank, often to excess though the prevalence of disgusting habits did not render them more acceptable. He might have forgotten her. Still, if he had remembered and mentioned their encounter, Edward would already have summoned her. This way, she would be able to discover his condition for herself. If he did recognize her, at least she would no longer be waiting for Edward and Leonora to hear of her behavior. If they did—Her friend sat up and blinked at her, recalling Adelaide from her reflections.

Her announcement had surprised the maid. New as she was, she must know Adelaide seldom joined the family for meals. After a perceptible hesitation, she asked, "What will you wear, my lady?" She may have supposed Adelaide had nothing better.

"Go look in my dressing room and then tell me what you think I should put on. A lady's maid often gives her opinion."

As a rule, the family did not dress elaborately for the meal when they were in the country. From servants' gossip, however, she knew her sister-in-law and nieces had been gowning themselves as carefully as if they were dining in town with a marquess instead of in the country with a marquess's second son.

She could do the same. There had been no more seasons for Adelaide after that one disappointing introduction to the beau monde. The next year when the family went to London, Adelaide remained at Lamburne with Lady Muriel, an elderly, bewildered relative of Leonora's. No one else had been able—or perhaps willing—to take the old lady in when her only son died, leaving her without resources or a home.

The poor woman had lived quietly at Lamburne largely ignored by Leonora and Edward. She had a suite in the family wing, and her own old maidservant served her meals. She ate with the family only occasionally and never when there was company, as much by her own choice as by theirs. In one of her more lucid moments, she had informed Adelaide that she did not care to embarrass herself by dropping food on herself, "which is, alack, far too likely with my poor sight and shaky hands."

Adelaide sometimes read to her or simply chatted with her. If the old lady's mind had not been so slippery, she might have been an ally. As it was, on her good days, she told wonderful stories of life half a century ago and passed on delicious gossip from the court of William and Mary. She had not absorbed the family's hints and warnings about Adelaide and smiled fondly at her whenever she thought of it.

As the family prepared for departure to town the following year, Leonora ascribed Adelaide's remaining at home to reluctance to leave the old lady. In fact, no one had suggested Adelaide should accompany them, and if they had, she would have declined anyway.

To her surprise, Leonora had continued to order clothing for her. If the matter had been left to Lady Lamburne's discretion, Adelaide suspected she would have received few new garments and those not fashionable. No one told her why the lovely gowns and accessories arrived every year, so she could imagine the scene as it might have been in a play.

Setting: Mme. Bernard's establishment

Lady Lamburne: That will do well enough, I believe.

Mme. Bernard: But what of the Lady Adelaide, milady?

Lady Lamburne: She has not come to town this year. She now prefers to remain at home in the country with an elderly relative.

Mme. Bernard: Yet still she will need the clothing, n'est-ce pas? There are les beaux in the country as well. She will visit friends, no? To look like a poor relation...*An eloquent shrug of madame's shoulders.*

Lady Lamburne (lips thinning): I had not considered that possibility. You are correct, Madame Bernard. She will need gowns, though not as many or as elaborate as for a season in town. And I suppose I must order her a new habit. She rides near as much as a gentleman. *A sigh.* Perhaps I will order for her another day as I have not time now.

Mme. Bernard: If she is still of the same *taille de la robe*, I can choose fabrics and have suitable garments made up and also order the habit, to spare your ladyship the effort. I remember well the Lady Adelaide's preferences and what colors become her so-striking contrast of complexion and hair.

Lady Lamburne: Oh...*A slight frown.* It would be more convenient. Yes, I leave it in your hands. Will my rose *robe à la française* be ready by Monday?

"My lady?"

Distracted by her little daydream, she had not noticed the maid waiting, returned from the dressing room.

"What do you think, Jenny?"

"They're all lovely, my lady, and perfect for you. The green would bring out your eyes, but Lady Sophia means to wear green. I'd say either the red or the gold."

Adelaide said, "The gold satin."

"Ooh, a lovely color, Lady Adelaide. Just right for you. That green Lady Sophia fancies don't suit her at all."

"Thank you, Jenny."

Later, she sat at the dressing table, trussed into a corset, gowned, scented, and her hair arranged. Her reflection in the glass frowned back at her, almost her first uncontrolled expression in years. She might be ugly, old, and odd, but she was a gentlewoman and today she looked it.

"Is some'at wrong, ma'am?"

"No. You've done good work, Jenny. I'm obliged to you."

After dismissing the girl, she made one more addition to her toilette and proceeded to the drawing room.

Chapter 5

Ducane approached the drawing room anticipating another tiresome dinner with his hosts. Lord and Lady Lamburne, Lady Sophia, and Lady Charity were already present. The Lamburne sons, one on vacation from Eton, the other from Cambridge, were staying with friends for a month. He supposed they'd been got out of the way for the purpose of arranging Sophia's betrothal without distractions unless they were hell-born boys who might give Ducane a distaste for the family.

Perhaps he'd only assumed he had been invited to a house party. This gathering was entirely too intimate, unless they thought the betrothal certain. Had his mother given the earl and his lady to believe he was sure to offer for Sophia?

Predictably, Sophia exclaimed about his injury and tittered at his explanation. No one else commented. Everyone knew men in their cups stumbled and injured themselves. The Lamburnes' assumption he had been drunk chafed.

Today's conversation seemed unlikely to vary from that of the previous two days. The countess asked if he were acquainted with several ladies and gentlemen who were distantly related to her. Lamburne aired his opinion that crime was rampant and not enough felons were being hanged. Lady Charity giggled. Lady Sophia peeked over her fan and fluttered her eyelashes at him. Boring people, full of their own consequence, the sort on whom, in London, he might have exercised his wit the way he practiced with his smallsword.

Could he introduce some topic other than the weather, the scenery, and the earl's illustrious ancestors or his lady's famous connections? Not politics, because of the ladies. The theater or books, perhaps. He had his chance when talk momentarily flagged.

"Did you see Peg Woffington in *The Constant Couple* when you were in town?"

His question went unanswered as the door opened and a woman swept in like a brisk wind. Four faces turned to stare. Sophia and Charity, previously whispering to each other on a settee, fell silent. The newcomer paused, surveying the frozen group. Their response to the arrival of a woman of no particular beauty who was well past her first youth struck him as remarkable. Ducane rose and awaited an introduction, suddenly nervous. Whoever she was, she brought with her an air of mystery or mayhap excitement. His heart beat a trifle faster.

The earl stood belatedly. "Addie. We didn't expect you."

Ducane heard the tension in his voice, and a thread of apprehension ran through him for no reason he could understand. Who the devil was she?

"Good afternoon. Lamburne, I believe I have not met your guest." Her voice was a pleasant contralto. Night-black hair was neatly pinned up over her unremarkable face. Ducane inwardly saluted her taste in the choice of her little linen and lace cap. It was exactly calculated to be neither what a very young woman might wear nor to be an old maid's. Her eyes were green and slightly tilted.

Ducane had heard green eyes compared to emeralds, a color not often found in anything but that gem. This lady's eyes certainly did not resemble the stones in her necklace, earbobs, and bracelets. Instead they made him think of the murky green of woodland ponds, shot through with golden streaks, really quite striking.

She smiled benignly. Ducane thought he had seen just such an expression on the kitchen mouser's lips when it was full of cream.

The earl's complexion had shifted from ruddy to pale. "Ahhh…Ducane, may I present my half sister, Lady Adelaide Setbury?"

As he made a leg elaborate enough to express his respect and pleasure, he heard one of the girls whisper to the other, "She must be having one of her good days." The words had been meant for his ears.

Lady Adelaide curtsied and smiled at him with a trace of real amusement. She chose a high-backed chair near Ducane and seated herself without fussing with her gown, a robe à l'anglaise of heavy amber silk. Perhaps it was a favorite although not in the latest style, for its color was perfect for her. But most ladies would have had the gown altered to bring it into the current fashion if they did not replace it instead.

"Addie, Lord Gervase Ducane's brother is Blacklaw. The marquess, you know."

Ducane heard the warning in the earl's tones and wondered again at the disquiet in the room. A family of mice finding a cat in their midst might act the same in the seconds before they ran for their lives.

"How pleasant for you, sir," Lady Adelaide observed.

Not what ladies usually said when they learned he was a marquess's brother. Could she be laughing at him? He responded to the sally as he would do among his usual circle in London.

"I'm not sure I agree. My brother seems to enjoy being a marquess, his lady doesn't mind being a marchioness, and I think my mother is rather fond of her own title. To be merely a brother is no great thing, particularly when one has no responsibilities to the marquessate except to avoid scandal."

"That would certainly be a drawback. Life must be rather meaningless without responsibilities."

A startlingly perceptive remark: how had she come by that knowledge? Lamburne's family included one interesting member.

"I do not go into society much, sir, and regret I do not know in what county the marquess's family seat is located."

Lady Lamburne's question crossed Lady Adelaide's comment. "I trust you informed Lowe you mean to dine with us, Addie?"

"I did." Lady Adelaide showed no sign of discomfort at the interruption.

Behind her fan, Sophia murmured "Maddie" to her sister.

Ducane replied, "It's in Northumberland, Lady Adelaide, though Blacklaw is not near anything you are likely to have heard of. There are several lesser properties scattered around, in Essex, Kent, Berkshire, and Scotland. The first three all have better weather than the family seat. The fourth, needless to say, does not."

The lady acknowledged his flippancy with a faint smile, the only one who did. Before Ducane could attempt to draw anyone else into the conversation, his hostess forestalled him.

"You must not monopolize our guest, Addie," Lady Lamburne said sharply. "You were saying earlier, Lamburne?"

"I believe Lord Gervase was mentioning a play when my half sister entered."

"Was I? I wonder what it can have been? Oh, *The Constant Couple*, of course. Did you and your family see it when you were in town for the Parliamentary session?"

The countess moved to the sofa near Lady Adelaide.

The earl raised his voice. "We did, though my lady does not quite approve of females in breeches roles. I will say the Woffington wench filled hers very well," he added.

As he spoke, Lady Lamburne leaned forward to hiss, "Did I not ask you to confine yourself to your rooms?"

Ducane caught the words despite her lowered tone. Out of the corner of his eye, he saw Lady Adelaide shrink from her sister-in-law almost imperceptibly. He had fallen into a nest of vipers. Excepting Lady Adelaide, who seemed to be the only one with good manners. He turned and smiled at her encouragingly.

The earl began to question Ducane about his pastimes in town, all too evidently aware of his lady's ill-natured comment and gamely trying to hold Ducane's attention. Ducane smiled and answered obligingly.

"Yes, Leonora, you did."

"Well, then, why are you here?"

When his host paused for breath, Sophia began chirping about the play, or rather, the noble or notorious people who had also been in the audience. "Only imagine! The Prince and Princess of Wales were present, very merry."

Lady Adelaide's tart reply was audible in spite of her niece's commentary. "I wanted to meet Sophia's prey...beau, I mean. Oh, do you think my presence will discourage Lord Gervase from offering for Sophia? I hardly think it, if he is épris. Sophia is so very pretty, how could he resist her?"

Though of course my real interest is in her dowry.

Lady Lamburne preened slightly at Adelaide's praise of her daughter, which might have been her sister-in-law's intent. He had heard the faint satiric twist in Lady Adelaide's remark if Sophia's mother had missed it. He had not been so well amused in months. Adelaide Setbury had claws.

"Please try to conduct yourself like a lady for the next few weeks." Lady Lamburne returned to her original seat, a throne-like chair that matched the earl's.

Did they think him so desperate for a rich bride that he would overlook their bad manners? Or did they think he wouldn't be offended or wouldn't hear them? Mayhap the latter; he did have keen ears.

Even the family's evident intent to distract him from Lady Adelaide failed to prevent a momentary lapse in conversation during which she remarked, "Perhaps I can order a copy of the play's script. Harry Wildair sounds very amusing, particularly as a breeches role."

What was there in that to make Lady Lamburne clench her hand on her fan?

Dinner was fraught with emotional currents not generally found in polite society. Or perhaps any society. Admittedly, he had spent little time outside his own class. Mayhap in a gang of arrant rogues one would find the same tense silences, sidelong glances, and unsuccessful verbal forays. There the situation might include knives and charged pistols. All very uncomfortable in spite of alleviating his boredom. Her family addressed little speech to Lady Adelaide. Fortunately the lady and he were unaffected by whatever mental tempests roiled around them and kept conversation going.

Lady Adelaide had read a great many plays without having seen a single one. She was particularly fond of Elizabethan and Jacobean drama, of which her favorite was Webster's tragedy, *The White Devil*. She also enjoyed Shakespeare, the tragedies rather than the comedies.

He described the most admired actors and actresses and their most famous parts. An inquiry as to what novels she liked produced a moue.

"Whichever ones come my way."

Lady Lamburne spoke. "I do not approve of most novels for young ladies. It gives them notions."

Her sister-in-law was hardly a young lady. One would think she might be permitted to read whatever she would.

"I quite agree," Lady Adelaide replied, to his surprise. "Too often the female characters are weak and foolish. They are victims and never fight back.

Particularly in uplifting novels."

Talk eventually became general, though not sparkling with wit. He was still the only one to include Lady Adelaide, who made a courteous effort to toss the ball to the others. Though perhaps she was not totally without malice when she asked Lady Charity how her harpsichord practice went.

Not well, to judge by the girl's blush and sullen "Well enough."

While Lamburne rambled on about the problems of land ownership (lazy tenants, low crop prices, poachers), Ducane's mind wandered. The laden table held too many dishes, and they were far too elaborate for what was essentially a family dinner for six people. Ostentatious and spendthrift.

Lady Sophia was nineteen and missed beauty only by a rather pointy nose inherited from her mother and a pout. Lady Adelaide appeared to be at least thirty and was definitely plain. She did possess a trim figure, and her face arrested the eye. *Jolie laide*, the French would say. *Jolie Adelaide?* He had pieced together a great deal about her from a few words. She had not seen *The Constant Couple* because she had gone to London with the family only once, for her first season. Lady Sophia's gloss on this, delivered in an aside to Ducane, was "My aunt is something of a recluse. She is awkward in company, so she stays here."

Or was simply left in the country. Unless she preferred to remain, given her family's discourteous treatment. He had never seen such an open display of ill will toward a relative and with no discernible cause. The lady hardly seemed like a recluse. Perhaps she was shy in large groups, behavior he saw in many young girls in their first season.

The countess dragged the conversation away from her husband's discussion of estate matters by asking about the scenery around Blacklaw Hall.

"Hilly, my lady. Hillocks not worthy of the name of hills, low rolling hills, higher hills, and the Cheviots, which are relatively significant, though not to be compared to the Highlands of Scotland."

"North Britain," the earl interjected.

"Call it what you will, that part of the island north of the Borders is so distinctly different from this part of the country that it might as well be a separate nation. Even when they speak English, one can understand only two words in ten. They have their own money and their own laws. To me, that makes a foreign country."

The earl's fork stopped halfway to his mouth. "Surely you can't be a Jacobite."

"Hardly, sir. I daresay most Scots aren't, either." The Stuart claimant, even if he was a Catholic, would have been a better choice than German George or George II and would have spared the country Robert Walpole's vulgar Whiggish tendencies. Ducane spared a moment's rueful amusement for his own inconsistency: his family's roots were among the Huguenot Protestants in France, which should give them some common ground with the Whigs.

But life was not tidy; four or five generations back, his forebears had served the Crown, first under Queen Elizabeth, then under James and both Charles I and eventually Charles II. Under Cromwell, they had chosen no side and thus avoided imprisonment and confiscation of their property. They were aristocrats to their bones. The Ducane who left France shortly before the St. Bartholomew's Day Massacre had been the fourth son of a count. *Et voilà.*

"I take it you have visited Scotland, sir?"

"I have, Lady Adelaide. 'Tis not far from Blacklaw, after all. Edinburgh rivals London for society and intelligent discourse." Though the Act of Union had done the Scots no favors, so far as he could tell.

Her half smile, which he would have dismissed as meaningless in another, conveyed approval, though how he knew, he could not say. Ducane returned the smile with interest.

Sophia shattered the moment with a question about Vauxhall Gardens. When he had exhausted that topic, not nearly as soon as he would have liked, Lamburne interrogated him about Blacklaw and the marquessate's properties. Clumsy, as he must already have informed himself of Blacklaw's wealth and holdings.

While the countess asked whether he was acquainted with their particular friends, the Duke and Duchess of This and the Marquess of That, and their neighbors, the Bolger-Evelyns, Ducane gave thanks that Lamburne Chase lay far from Northumberland.

Ducane played his part in the dinner table exchanges by rote. Only Lady Adelaide's occasional verbal forays required thought. In a group consisting both of noblemen and tradesmen, the only ones who mattered were the former. At this table, the difference was not rank but similarity of mind and manners. He admired Lady Adelaide's acting ability, as good as Covent Garden's best, for she never displayed offense or hurt at the barbs aimed at her. And in the space of a dinner, he felt he knew her better than he did Sophia after two excruciating days in her company.

Charity started to recount some local lore, something about cats, and was cut off by her mother's icy, "Charity, Lord Gervase is not interested in rustic nonsense."

The more he saw of the Setburys, the happier he would be to bid them farewell. He understood the desperation of some poor creature caught in a trap. Did anyone among his acquaintances in town have an unmarried, well-dowered sister or cousin?

The ladies withdrew, leaving Ducane and Lamburne alone with a bottle of port. After a few disjointed remarks and considerable throat-clearing, the earl uttered, "You must wonder about m'half sister. No harm in her, none at all. Difficult like all old maids. She avoids company as a rule. Take no notice of her. You probably won't see her again for days, if then."

"She seems a pleasant lady, and though we have exchanged only a few words, she speaks like a woman of sense."

From his fit of coughing, Lamburne's port must have gone down the wrong way. When he recovered, he muttered, "Glad you didn't take offense. Won't see much of her anyway."

Does he mean, if I marry Lady Sophia? That eventuality was becoming less likely by the moment.

They did not linger at the table. Of course not, when his purpose for coming to Lamburne Chase was to become acquainted with Lady Sophia.

As the footman opened the door, Ducane heard Lady Adelaide's pleasing contralto.

"The set was my mother's and no part of the Lamburne heirlooms. I am sure my brother will show you the inventory of those if you wish." He entered to see her aiming a basilisk-like gaze at Lady Lamburne.

Lord Lamburne spoke hurriedly. "My sister is correct. But I did not know you had the emeralds in your possession, Addie."

"My mother's jewelry was left in my trustee's care. He sent me this when I came of age."

The earl's brow furrowed. Ducane missed whatever he might have said when the younger girl whispered to Lady Sophia, "Why must she choose today to make an appearance?"

The comment was perhaps more audible than Lady Charity intended. Her aunt either failed to hear or courteously chose to ignore the question.

Ducane filled the awkward pause with some inconsequential question about the county.

Chapter 6

That evening no one explained the absence of Lady Adelaide from supper, leaving Ducane to be entertained by Sophia's inanities and the family's attempt to pretend Lady Adelaide out of existence. Afterward, he listened to Sophia's uninspired performance on the harpsichord (evidently neither of the girls was musical), followed by a game of whist. The evening was endless. The next few weeks loomed like purgatory before him.

He reflected that there was much to be said for keeping country hours as he retreated to his bedchamber. Jenkins helped him out of his clothing down to his shirt. Wrapped in his banyan, he sat down to write to the dowager marchioness. Jenkins remained to fuss over his clothing: brushing the coat and breeches, scrutinizing the waistcoat for stains or pulled threads, consigning his handkerchief and neckcloth to the bag of things to be laundered.

As Ducane uncapped the bottle of ink, Jenkins murmured, " 'Tis an odd household, sir. Not friendly at all."

This was an unusual remark from his valet, who ordinarily confined himself to the subject of clothing and accessories. "I would have said, rather too friendly, myself."

"That's the family, I reckon, my lord. They want you for Lady Sophia. She must not have took in town.

It's the servants, I meant. They stop talking when I enter the servants' hall."

Ducane looked up from the sheet of paper at thin, fretful Jenkins with his pursed lips. He was very good with everything to do with attire and grooming. For the first time, Gervase considered that he failed to pay enough attention to his manservant's value as a source of information.

"That is not the case in other houses we've visited?"

"Servants know their masters' secrets but are expected to keep them. But in other households, there's more joking. Some bickering over position. And the way they treat that poor little scrap of a scullery maid! She's new and maybe don't know her job as well as she should, but it's not what I'd expect. In good houses, the servants are like family."

Ducane regarded his manservant thoughtfully. "Jenkins, are you warning me against the Lamburnes?"

"I would not take it upon myself to give an opinion of any sort about a gentleman or his family," Jenkins said primly.

"You'll be relieved to hear that I also have reservations about them."

"Indeed, sir. Will you want the claret-colored suit tomorrow or the green?"

"Whichever you recommend, Jenkins."

From Gervase Ducane to Alison, Dowager Lady Blacklaw
Lamburne Chase, 2 July 1741
Madam,
I trust I find you in good health…

May I inquire whether you personally know the Setburys? After several days in their company, I am not favorably impressed. Have you heard of any rumors about them? And can you think of any other lady who might do as well as Lady Sophia? I shall not end my visit early, which would be unforgivably discourteous [though he might pray for the end of the world to arrive and cut it short] *but I do not think I will ask Lamburne for Lady Sophia's hand.*

Yr. most obedient son,
G. Ducane

Thus far, being struck by a falling branch while drunk and spending part of the night unconscious on the damp ground was one of his better memories, and he still had almost three weeks before he could thank his host for his hospitality and leave.

Chapter 7

The surge of fury which prompted the action almost failed her at the sight of Edward and Leonora's expression when she entered the drawing room. The mere threat of their displeasure was enough to render her mute as a rule. She had surveyed the room in that moment of frozen terror. If she dined in her chamber and did not show herself for the duration of the visitor's stay and the house party, they would continue to ignore her. Even now she could beg their pardon and flee back to Tabby and her sanctuary. Everything would go on as before.

How would that end, with no friends in the house but her cat? For five or six years, she had had Lady Muriel's company, until her death left Adelaide unexpectedly saddened and alone. If she gave way now, would she end as poor Lady Muriel had, an annoying burden, kept out of sight as much as possible, if not actually locked away? *I already am.*

Even so, her courage faltered until the visitor rose. Did he remember seeing her last night? His eyes had widened slightly when she entered the room, but was it memory or no more than admiration for her emeralds? They were very fine. Or even friendly interest, a response to which she was unaccustomed.

Evidently the family had not mentioned her existence. Knowledge of a relative who was difficult, reclusive, awkward, and unreasonable (not to mention the other thing) would deter most men from offering for a young lady. They must have assumed she would obey Leonora's order to stay out of sight. Why wouldn't they? She so seldom came out when she might encounter her loving family.

How would Edward explain her, now Sophia's beau had met her? He would surely wonder why his host had not mentioned her previously. Would owning to an eccentric half sister be preferable to the scandal of her mother and her own birth? As a child, she had slipped through the house unnoticed and heard the servants' chatter, both about her papa's second marriage and Edward's reaction. Ducane was not much older than she, so perhaps he had never heard the talk.

The question was worrisome. Fortunately, her old governess's lessons came to her aid. She did not lose her composure as the anger that set off her drawing room invasion sank back to its customary level. While her fury at Tabby's danger had been the main charge, the priming charge was Leonora's dismissal of her, as if she were a child or penniless dependent. She was neither. Adelaide knew to the penny how much her half brother received to maintain her, and she doubted she cost him more than half the amount, even with the annual cost of her clothing and pin money.

Lord Gervase's exquisite manners and frivolous conversation had steadied her. To Adelaide's relief, now not solely because she feared disclosure of that regrettable incident, he was none the worse for his adventure and made no reference to it. Naturally not, as it would not reflect well upon him, even if he were not too courteous to embarrass a lady.

She had noticed when she ministered to the cut on his temple that his body was neither slender nor bulky as many men became after their youth. By touch and by moonlight, he must be a sportsman, though without being vulgarly brawny, a happy medium in her opinion. His face was unremarkable, neither handsome nor plain. Conscious, his bearing, manners, and humor gave him undeniable charm.

He dressed with finicking nicety. He might be a fop, though he lacked the affectations of that set as she had observed it during that London sojourn. She had seen a few men whose every action was graceful, rendering them elegant in a way that had nothing to do with being handsome or ugly. None of them had noticed her, of course.

Ducane did. How astonishing to meet someone who had not already judged her based on her family's words. Leonora had likely convinced everyone in the neighborhood to believe her a recluse, given to strange whimsies, and perhaps feeble-minded. On Sunday if she attended the service, most bade her "good day" when they saw her, then ignored her while they spoke with Edward and Leonora and the girls. Mayhap most did so out of embarrassment or for fear her oddness would rub off on them. She once heard the vicar praise Edward for bringing her to church when many kept relatives with wandering wits or strange behavior out of sight as much as possible.

Her foray into the family's territory had been meant only to pay them back for the attack on Tabby and Leonora's arrogance. The result was unexpected. Once she was in the drawing room and had shown herself seemingly normal, the family could do little.

Indeed, they had treated her much better than usual. They could not get rid of Adelaide without unseemliness.

He treated her as he would any gentlewoman to whom he was introduced. In its way his behavior was as illuminating as Mistress Henderson's instruction had been. Under her influence, Adelaide had stopped believing her family's calumnies although she continued to accept them, because she had no choice. Lord Gervase's acceptance and amusing conversation had given her confidence when anger failed her. Did he really see her as an ordinary genteel spinster, no stranger than anyone else? *How remarkable.* Odder yet, he had once or twice seemed to be offended by the others. Edward and Leonora might have missed the faint signs of his disapproval. They had far less need than she to be aware of people's reactions.

When Leonora led the ladies from the dining room, Adelaide resisted the temptation to drift away toward the stair. She had won a single battle. Unless she continued the campaign, that victory would be thrown away.

As soon as the tea tray arrived and the footman departed, Leonora attacked. Adelaide had been surprised she had not broached the subject before dinner. Either she had been too shocked by Adelaide's appearance or the commonest good manners held her silent.

"Where did you get that necklet, Addie?"

She had replied without difficulty, and the arrival of her brother and Lord Gervase prevented what might otherwise have been Leonora's tirade.

A very satisfactory day. Tomorrow she might let

Edward and Leonora recover from their shock and pique until, say, just before supper. Or perhaps not. For the future? She had not made up her mind; all must depend on events. She would attend the wedding if it took place at Lamburne. What a pity the poor man would have a mean-spirited goosecap for a wife if he did marry Sophia. Lamburne and his lady acted as though there was no question about a betrothal. Adelaide hoped it was wishful thinking.

If she could go away, separate herself from her family, would everyone she met accept her as ordinary? She surrendered the tempting idea with a sigh. Boys ran away to sea or to take the king's shilling. She lacked those escapes in spite of having far greater resources in theory. When her thirtieth birthday drew near, she had written to her trustee, who had also been her guardian until she came of age. Although she had received at least one letter a year after that date, she had never met him.

Thanks to Papa's foresight, her dowry and the sum that provided Edward money for her maintenance were safely invested. Most fathers would have left a child's future in the hands of her nearest male relative. Had Papa named Thaddeus Tate her guardian and trustee because he feared he himself would die before Edward was of age and did not trust the man he had named as Edward's guardian to deal fairly with Adelaide? Or was it because he knew Edward bitterly resented her? The scandal was still fresh then, after all.

Mr. Tate's letters had never been patronizing, leading her to hope he would consider thirty sufficiently old and on the shelf to allow her the funds to live on her own. In this she was mistaken. While he had the greatest respect for her discretion and her intelligence, he wrote in reply, an unmarried lady should live with her family. To do otherwise would cause talk detrimental both to herself and to her brother, her sister-in-law, and her nieces and nephews.

With no employment available to her and no money beyond the pin money Edward provided, she would starve by the side of the road if she left Lamburne. Worse, Tabby would share her fate or, if she were lucky, survive by catching mice and squirrels and birds, in danger herself from larger predators. The thought of Tabby starving or in the jaws of a fox brought tears to her eyes. As she wiped them away, Tabby caught her hand in her soft paws and licked it.

After supper, she sought out Applethwaite to ask if he knew what had become of her handkerchief. He had not found it when he cut up and took away the branch. Then the wind came up, bringing a soaking rain. The little linen square had surely blown away. If it had been picked up, someone would have mentioned it, unless the finder was one of the lower servants. An under-gardener, a footman, or maid out for a stroll or an assignation might keep it. A male servant might give it to a girl he was courting. She or the maid lucky enough to find it would pick out Adelaide's design and substitute her own, and put it away for her wedding, perhaps.

The lost handkerchief was the least of all the fears that beset her. If found, nothing connected it to Ducane's accident, except the blood, which might have been washed out by the rain. Or the stain could easily be explained as a hand pricked by a thorn. She spent enough time walking in the park that she could have dropped it almost any day. She had far greater problems to worry about.

Chapter 8

The following day continued gray and damp. Lady Lamburne assured Ducane he would like to see the portrait gallery. Sophia came, too, following demurely behind him and her mother. The countess recited the names and histories of the Lamburne ancestors, none of them remarkable for accomplishments or service to the Crown. The hovering presence of Sophia at his shoulder made concentration difficult.

A few portraits were excellent, more interesting for their execution than for the sitter. Some were of far less merit. Some were old, dating back to the time of Henry IV in one case. The Lamburnes were lucky to have them, even if the quality of the painting was not outstanding.

"…and here is our family," she said, stopping before a group portrait of the earl, countess, two boys, and Sophia and Charity.

"A very attractive composition, my lady." Beside him, Sophia preened. Something pricked his curiosity. He glanced back at the four portraits to the left: the previous earl, a group of his wife and children, then the current earl and the picture Lady Lamburne had indicated.

Where was Lady Adelaide's likeness? Or her mother's? Adelaide was not illegitimate. He could not imagine Lamburne and his lady acknowledging a bastard sibling, nor would she be referred to as "Lady Adelaide." He filed the thought away for future investigation.

He did not see her at dinner. When Lady Adelaide had not appeared by the time they entered the dining room, the countess's relief was palpable. The rest of the family discoursed in as spritely a fashion as they ever had in his limited experience, which was to say, not very. Lamburne exerted himself to entertain Ducane, but as the only topics to interest both—politics and international events—were unsuitable in mixed company, the effort was unsuccessful. Lady Lamburne interrogated him about parish matters at Blacklaw. All he could say in response was that his mother had been active in good works in their neighborhood, and now she shared the duty with his brother's wife. Ladies Sophia and Charity sulked.

The afternoon crept in its petty pace, to quote MacBeth. Evening was better, as Lady Adelaide appeared and provided some leaven to the gathering. He learned that she was fond of riding, spoke French like a Parisienne, and admired the Stoic philosophy. Sometimes he caught a hint of amusement in her eyes when her sister-in-law made a more than ordinarily foolish statement. At one point, her gaze met his and Ducane had to school his expression to blandness.

After taking tea with the ladies, Lamburne proposed a game of billiards. Billiard tables were to be found in a number of coffee houses in London, but Ducane had not encountered one in a home. It occupied half the space in the library, revealing more about the earl than his host could have guessed. Ducane could only deplore reducing a library to bring in a billiard table. Not all gentlemen would disapprove; some of his friends had fathers who considered reading unmanly. Not as bad as a female reading and having opinions, but not desirable. He knew men his own age who thought the same. They were mostly country gentlemen whose interests ranged no further than their acres, their stables, and their kennels. No one among his friends remarked on his liking for books. He rode as well as any gentleman and had won a reputation for being too dangerous with both a sword and a word to risk offending. No one wished to be the butt of one of his Latin epigrams.

Fortunately, Lady Lamburne suggested Lord Gervase would prefer to enjoy a musical evening. The earl, who had apparently forgotten the purpose of their guest's visit, hastily agreed. "Some other time for a game, hey?" he muttered to Ducane.

Ducane had been ignorant of his mother's friendship with Leonora Lamburne's mother. He had probably met the earl and countess at some insufficiently select affair, but if so, they had made no impression on him. Their sort would never otherwise intersect with his own circle. None of the earl's family were clever, witty, or charming (except Lady Adelaide). They had no influence at court, and Lamburne and his wife were very much on their dignity, like jumped-up merchants. The upper level of the beau monde would tolerate one or two of those faults. The sum of them sank the Lamburnes. He was no longer surprised the earl would settle for the impecunious younger brother of a marquess for his eldest daughter, rather than trying for a title.

****

After supper, Adelaide remained for a musical entertainment featuring Charity and Sophia singing while their mother played the harpsichord. Adelaide clapped with some enthusiasm; Leonora played well and with feeling, the best thing Adelaide knew of her. Did she wish she had been accompanying someone with a better voice than either of her daughters?

After the mandatory compliments to her nieces, Adelaide was moved to add, "Brava, Leonora. I wish you would play more often. I envy your talent."

Her sister-in-law, startled, actually stammered her thanks. Chagrin followed. She had not missed the implication to be drawn from Adelaide's praise, though Leonora did not deceive herself as to the girls' musical ability. Adelaide had often heard her admonish them for their mistakes both in playing and singing.

Her nieces failed to notice. Sophia whispered to her sister, "Music has charms to soothe the savage beast," and Charity snickered. Had Sophia misquoted out of ignorance or out of reluctance to utter the word "breast"? Almost certainly the former. Leonora turned pink and rarity of rarities, aimed a Medusa-like glare at them. Edward, addressing some remark to Ducane, had not noticed. Ducane glanced surreptitiously at Lady Adelaide, who detected the satirical glimmer in his eye while maintaining a politely attentive face. The tea tray appeared, and soon they were freed.

The sun had come out at the end of the afternoon, drying the grass enough for a walk. Adelaide followed the others upstairs, but once in her room, changed her gown for an old petticoat and jacket and her shoes for a sturdy pair meant for walking outdoors and sat down with Pope's translation of the *Iliad*.

At eleven, she extinguished her candle. When her eyes were dark-adapted, she murmured to Tabby, "I won't stay out late." Locking the door behind her, she flitted along the hall to the end of the wing, pausing before the first step down to touch the ornately carved newel post. She had come this way so often she knew by instinct where she was. No sound carried to her ears except the creaks, taps, and rattles to be expected in any old house.

Had she been housed near the family instead of at the end of the oldest, least-used wing, she would never have been free to ramble in the orchard and park at night. A footman was not always on duty in the old wing even during the day. How convenient that she was near the end of her wing, where the door into the grounds was secured only by a sliding bolt. No one would notice her slipping out.

The bolt was not in place. In theory, her half brother went around before retiring and made sure every door and window was locked. Certainly he had done so in London when she was there. Here in the country he might feel it unnecessary, or else both he and the butler had forgotten. And why was it unbolted? She was the only one who used it, so far as she knew, and she always threw the bolt on her return.

She loved to walk in the park at night. Several days full of events and change had left her both invigorated and unsettled. A stroll before bed would be soothing. Tonight the moon would still be almost as bright as day, although she cared nothing for that. Roaming the park often both early and late, she believed she could find her way blindfolded, and besides, her night vision was excellent.

After pulling the door shut quietly, she stood breathing the soft air. It carried different scents from those the sun forced from aromatics like roses and lavender and rosemary. At night, she could smell the grass. With the feeling that all was right in the world, she followed the path to the grove where the parkland began. Unlike the orchard, it was dense with trees and shade-loving plants.

In its center was a clearing where nothing grew but grasses and a few wildflowers. At its edge was a block of masonry, a convenient seat. Had there been some building here once? If of wood, it might have rotted to nothing, perhaps, but that would not explain the failure of trees to take over the open space. If the building had been stone, its blocks might have been carried off for use elsewhere, but its stone-flagged floor left behind. That would account for the open space. She would like to dig into the turf and find out. Applethwaite would lend her a tool. Would she have to work in the daylight? She spent the greater part of the day indoors, reading, writing in her commonplace book, exploring the vast attics used for storage or the little-used rooms in her part of the house. Outside, she might meet with Sophia and Charity with their companion, who had been their governess. But they almost never left the parterre and the flower garden. Leonora, like a glasshouse plant, only thrived indoors.

Mistress Stoddard was a stern-faced woman about ten years older than Adelaide, and from certain things overheard, well educated. Wasted on her nieces, alas! Adelaide would have liked to talk with the woman, but the times they had met, her guarded expression told her the girls and her sister-in-law had warned the chaperon against her.

Still, she might do some digging early one morning and be inside before the girls left their beds. The little meadow had fascinated her for years. She could even probe the sod in various places tonight to feel if there seemed to be a hard surface beneath it.

Ahead, the deep darkness under the trees ended at the clearing. She had almost reached it when she detected aqua mellis and a hint of brandy. She froze. Someone, *some man*, was nearby, and she sensed he was moving around. She turned slowly and retraced her steps, holding her petticoat close to make her passage silent and keep it from catching on the brush on either side. She heard nothing behind her. Silence was her friend.

The intruder had been Gervase Ducane, she was sure of it. No servant would smell of scent and brandy. She would know Edward by the snuff he used. Whatever was Ducane doing out so late? He had been, the night she rescued Tabby, but sometimes men in their cups sought fresh air to clear their heads. Inebriation would explain why he hadn't heard her approach with Applethwaite, or indeed her ascent of the ladder. Tonight he had taken little wine at supper and unless he had imbibed much port afterward or sat drinking brandy in his chamber until coming out, he could not be very drunk. Did he make a habit of roaming the night as she did? How vexing, if true. Would he be dangerous if inebriated? She could defend herself, but the situation would be fraught with peril for both of them. For tonight, her wandering was at an end. She really could not bear to lose her nights' exercise for the weeks he would be at Lamburne. It would serve him right if she bolted the side door, locking him out. But the recollection of his courtesy and wit tempered her annoyance.

Chapter 9

Preparations for the first house party in three years were in hand. The death of Leonora's father and then of Edward's mother had made entertaining at Lamburne Chase impossible (though mourning had not kept Edward and Leonora from going to London) in those years. Previously, Adelaide had kept out of sight without regret; she chose to avoid exposing herself to the contempt of her half brother's guests.

The household was a-hum with activity as chimneys were swept in the guest chambers, more leaves were added to the table, and various unused rooms in the main part of the house were given a thorough cleaning. The chandeliers and sconces in the ballroom and music room were polished. The meals were simpler than they would ordinarily be, with the kitchen busy making dishes that could be kept until needed for the party: Portugal cakes, Savoy and Naples biscuits, potted meats, pickled pigeons. Adelaide and Tabby were unaffected; their meals had almost always been either plain or stolen from the pantry.

Adelaide was happy not to be involved; her sister-in-law was nearly frantic however well she concealed it from Sophia's suitor. The orgy of cleaning did not affect the old part of the house. There would have to be many more guests before it was necessary to put some in Adelaide's wing.

The first guests began to arrive, which did not mean serenity reigned. Beds had to be arranged for the visiting servants (the butler and housekeeper had a list showing to whom each guest room was allotted) and the trunks, valises, portmanteaux, and other luggage hauled upstairs.

"A great deal of extra work for all of you," Adelaide commented when Jenny brought her chocolate. A packet from her trustee was on the tray. She was not due to receive his half-yearly letter, and why was this so thick? She would read it later. For now, she wanted to talk with the maid. The girl had not yet succumbed to the servants' contempt for her.

"Ay, but they say there's vails, too, which makes up for it, and it's exciting. I never saw so many fine folk. And there's never been a masked ball here, Cook says, and that'll be something to see."

"A masked ball? Really?" She had known of the ball, but no one had mentioned it would be a masquerade. She had hardly seen Leonora or the girls, however, or she might have heard. Or mayhap not.

"Oh, yes. Wonderful costumes, I hear from some o' the visiting maids and valets. They won't describe 'em, as no one's supposed to know who's who until the unmasking before the supper."

Jenny kept up a gentle flow of anecdotes about the oddities of the guests and their servants, the ladies' gowns, and the fine gentlemen, but Adelaide did not come out of her brown study until she heard the maid's judgement on wigs.

"...nor I can't think a man looks good without his own hair."

"I hope that does not mean you have seen a man

without his wig." Which would mean when he was in a state of undress.

"Can't help it sometimes, my lady. Late in the evening, some will take off their wigs if they're too warm or itchy and their heads is just stubbly like a cut field or else naked. And o' course in the morning if I bring in their chocolate, sometimes they've shed their nightcaps."

"I had no idea." What a lot of things Adelaide had missed by avoiding company, though perhaps a lady would only see a shaven head if she were married.

"Well, you wouldn't, ma'am. They'd not do it with a lady present…I don't think."

After considering naked male heads and stubbly ones, an objection occurred to her. "But I'm sure I've seen men wear wigs sometimes and not others, and they still had their own hair."

"Those gentlemen use bobbing pins to hold their hair close to their heads and put the wig on over, when they need one for a formal occasion. That's what Mr. Jenkins, Lord Gervase's manservant says."

"Hmmm." She would miss the girl's unguarded remarks when the rest of the staff turned her against Adelaide. If Jenny continued to hold out, the others would find ways of making her life a misery. Pleasant as it was to have one partisan among the indoor servants, she really could not allow the child to become an outcast among her fellows. They would find a way to get her dismissed. "Jenny, you must have realized the others dislike me."

She twisted a corner of her apron in her square little hands. "It's not right for them to talk about you the way they do."

"I'm used to it. They take their lead from my family. I hope you haven't tried to defend me."

Jenny blinked and sniffed. Holding back tears? "I've wanted to, often and often. But I daren't. I haven't been here a month, and when you're new, it's best to do your work and keep quiet."

"Very good. What I think you should do is to begin to agree with them about me. Today you might mention how angry I was that my chocolate was late again. If you seem to come around to their way of thinking, you'll get along better."

"It would be lying, my lady."

"But it would keep you safe, and if you hear anything interesting, you could still pass it on to me." She smiled. "Until there's someone newer than you, I think Cook will continue to have you wait on me. Think carefully about it, Jenny."

The future, both near and more distant, occupied Adelaide for some minutes after Jenny whisked out to return to her duties in the kitchen. The news about the ball made her wonder: did Lamburne expect to announce the betrothal of Lady Sophia to Ducane then?

She poured another cup of chocolate and contemplated the packet. She might as well deal with it now, whatever it was, before she dressed.

My dear Lady Adelaide,

I trust you are in good health and spirits, and your family the same.

I must impart to you some sad news. Your godmother, Lady Creighton (the former Lady Beverley), is no more. You may not recall her, her attorney having informed me she removed to Northumberland on marrying her second husband in 1710 when you were three or four.

Now the good news. Lady Creighton was her husband's only heir, neither his first wife nor she having produced a living child. His estate was not entailed. It consists of a house, eight tenancies, and a large flock of sheep. They are left to you, together with a pleasing fortune and investments in the Funds.

While I recall you expressed an interest in living apart from your brother, it seems unlikely you will wish to remove all the way to Northumberland. However, if you do choose to leave Lamburne, you would be able to maintain a house of moderate size in London or Bath, afford the servants to care for it, and pay a companion to lend you respectability. I do not recommend it, but you have the ability to do so, as Lady Creighton's will leaves everything to you, except a few bequests to faithful servants, with no conditions whatsoever, though she expresses the wish that if you marry, you will make sure the settlements secure your rights to the property so that your hypothetical husband cannot sell it or gamble it away. I would give you the same advice.

The servants will be retained on board wages until you have decided what to do with the house and land, whether to live there yourself, lease it out, or sell it.

I enclose a letter she wrote shortly before her death, which was to be given to you with a copy of her will, also enclosed. I have appended a list of annual rents the estate receives, amounts invested, and their annual returns.

Your servant,
Thaddeus Tate

Her chocolate grew cold while she read the letter a second time, and then broke the seal on a fine sheet of paper. The spidery hand covered less than the whole page. Its burden was an apology for failing to perform her duties as godmother but hoped she was now making some amends.

Not long after I moved to Northumberland, my health failed, or I would have visited you whenever I traveled to London or to your part of the country. I did maintain a correspondence with your papa until his death and wrote your half brother a letter of condolence and ten or twelve other letters to which I received the briefest of replies. I did have my attorney investigate to assure myself you were being cared for, but I have never been quite happy about your situation. All he could report was that you were alive, had a governess, and were well-dressed. There seemed to be nothing I could do when Edward, whom I remember as a priggish little boy, would not write more fully than to state you were well. After your season in London—a ridiculously short time in which to find a husband; it took me three years to get the first—all I could learn was that you were residing at Lamburne Chase and were seldom seen, though it was said you were ailing or shy.

Either Lady Creighton's informants had misreported the gossip they heard, or Godmama had softened it.

I am sorry I failed you. I hope my will, which is like to be soon executed, will make some amends.

Louise, Lady Creighton, formerly Beverley

She stared at the letters for several long minutes, wondering if she were sickening with an ague, given her rapid breathing and heartbeat and a sensation of heat. Forcing herself to sip the chocolate remaining in her cup to calm herself, she thought, *This changes everything*. She was free. Tate would hardly fail to mention anything that would affect her possession of a home and fortune. Lady Creighton had solved all her problems…unless Edward bowed to Leonora's often-voiced opinion. Nevertheless, Adelaide would leave nothing to chance.

The notion came to her all at once, the offspring of the collision of several ideas. Ducane thought her unremarkable, even after speaking with her at some length. Leonora (and presumably Edward and the girls) wanted her out of sight during the house party. Adelaide would read the will later. At the moment, she needed to dress.

Chapter 10

The Haymarket masquerades Ducane had attended, open to anyone with the admission price, had been notable for less-than-genteel conduct. Presumably those attending the Lamburnes' ball would behave better. On the other hand, anonymity provided a certain release from restraint. The event might be delightful…or it might result in a forced marriage or two, if the younger guests were inadequately chaperoned. At least he need not worry about what to wear, as the Bautta costume he acquired for the Venetian carnival had dignity and was more than slightly sinister with no buffoonery about it. Fortunately, Lamburne had warned him of the masked ball in a letter, saying he supposed Ducane would not like to be surprised.

An hour into the event, he concluded the affair would be humdrum. Most of the men wore a domino and simple half-face mask. The highest ranking guest was an elderly, rakish viscount who had come in a monk's robe. Many of the women had made an attempt at more elaborate costume—a lady in supposed Turkish costume, a shepherdess, a medieval queen. The rest of those in attendance consisted of a baron, several baronets, a knight, and a number of country gentlemen and their ladies and sons and daughters, of course. He chatted with the men and danced with some of the ladies.

He had forgotten that the anonymity of a mask did not necessarily make the wearer more interesting. The young ladies still giggled. Their mamas asked probing questions about his family and his circumstances in the hope of discovering his identity and eligibility. He parried these.

The presence of a lively widow or two, and one or more rakehells might have made an amusing evening. There was not even a card room, though a salon had been provided for those who needed to sit down away from the crowd and noise. Alas, he was destined for boredom.

Ducane leaned against a pillar and admired Lady Lamburne's attempt at decorating. Exotic trees and shrubs in pots had been brought in from the glasshouse, to the gardener's anguish, he supposed. Out on the parterre, arbors of willow work twined with vines had been added over the benches. The vines were not real although the bunches of grapes hanging from them were.

His gaze wandered over the ballroom and back again. He had not seen Lady Sophia yet, or else not recognized her if she had been near. He would have known her high, breathy voice. An advantage of his costume's mask was that it changed the sound of the wearer's voice. She would not recognize him if she heard him speak.

The musicians were refreshing themselves between sets at the moment. They must need it badly, as warm as the night was—for England. Their place on the minstrels' gallery would be worse than the floor, given the propensity of heat to rise. Probably the mixed odors of burning beeswax, perfume, sweat, scented hair powder, and the gods only knew what else, also rose.

Only half the candles in the chandelier were lit, though there were candles in some sconces as well, leaving the long chamber shrouded in a mysterious twilight. It might all have been conducive to dalliance, had there been anyone to dally with. One thing was certain: if some charmer attempted to lure him into an empty room or curtained window embrasure, he would not go.

Across the room almost directly opposite him, was a lady with a void where her face should be. The sight gave him a long moment's qualm, until he realized the featureless expanse must be a vizard, a black velvet mask covering a lady's face to protect her identity, like those worn by ladies during the Venetian carnival. He remembered his grandmother describing a similar one her own grandmother had worn to shield her skin from the sun.

He found himself striding toward the masked lady without any conscious decision to do so, as if under a spell. He did not believe in witches or fairies and was not at all sure he believed in angels or devils, either, but whatever drew him, she would not be boring.

When he approached, he laughed, a sinister sound under his mask. The lady's jacket embroidered with gillyflowers and vines and the green petticoat were very like those in his great-grandmother's portrait at Blacklaw Hall. The dowager marchioness would know all of her names and those of her immediate family and probably the year of the painting, mayhap 1620 or thereabouts. Not long before Charles I ascended the throne, anyway. His mother took an interest in their lineage. Gervase's indifference annoyed her. "How can you not think it important?" she had demanded once.

"They're all dead. They have no effect on us, and we have none on them." The thing he chiefly recalled about that long-dead lady was that the design on her jacket was of field poppies and her petticoat had been red to match.

Now he was before the Fair Unknown, making a reverent bow. "My lady."

The opening notes of the next set almost drowned out her "My lord," as she curtsied. They were standing almost under the gallery.

"Will you dance?"

"Yes."

The minuet's elegant formality, not unlike the rites of genteel courtship, appealed to Ducane. What a pity he was supposed to be here to offer for Lady Sophia. No, nothing was settled. He was only a potential suitor. If he chose to become an aspirant for her hand, his next action would be to speak to her father. He was not, thank God, obligated to do so. With any luck, his mother would suggest several other young ladies or one of his many acquaintances would. Robert did not give a straw who he married. Gervase could please himself; his sole requirements were that she have an adequate dowry and be tolerably likeable.

He performed the figures of the dance without thought. All the other dancers knew the steps, though some of the men must be more at home on horseback than on the dance floor and some of the young ladies could not manage to keep their faces composed. One chit giggled at her partner repeatedly. The gillyflower lady executed the movements with grace and precision, as composed as a tomb effigy, as far as he could judge when her face was covered from brow to chin. What was she thinking?

The set ended too soon. Or perhaps they need not part at once. In any ordinary ball, she would have been with her chaperon or friends with whom she had attended and he would have returned her to them. Here she had been standing all alone. At the usual sort of ball, he could not have asked her to dance without an introduction. Perhaps she would grant him her company until the next set formed.

"Madam, would you care to stroll on the parterre?"

"I would, sir."

Few had braved the night air, so much cooler than the rooms, perhaps because of the hint of dampness. Many of the ladies wore silk gowns that left much of the neck, bosom, and lower arm exposed. This lady's long-sleeved jacket covered her almost to the collarbone. A midsummer evening would not chill her. He was sweating in his shirt, neckcloth, waistcoat, and full-skirted coat under his silk cape.

What did she look like, under the mask? A close-fitting coif, embroidered like her jacket, concealed her hair. The candlelight inside had been too dim for him to see her eye color. The sum of his knowledge was that she was a little shorter than he, slender in her close-fitting jacket, had a pleasant voice, and was graceful. They circled around several of the plantings, none of them tall, toward the most distant rustic shelters, the better to have privacy to talk. Most young ladies would have demurred.

"May I compliment you on choosing so original a costume? Milkmaids and queens are here in excess, I feel. Should I be able to guess who you represent?"

"I am no one, really. The garments belonged to one of my ancestresses. And you?"

"Mine is merely a carnival costume. As this is a masquerade, I cannot ask your name, madam, but is there some appellation by which I might address you?"

She tilted her head, studying him. "You may call me Queen Mab."

Queen of the Fairies? Oddly appropriate in some indefinable way.

"And your nom de guerre, sir?"

The magic of darkness, seclusion, moonlight, and the scent of roses, seized him. He spoke without thinking. "Tam Lin." His use of the name of a man captured by the Queen of Fairies in a Scottish song once heard seemed inevitable. "Do you live nearby, Queen Mab?"

"Quite near. Do you live far away?"

"I have rooms in London. My family's home is in the north." They reached one of the farthest of the benches. "Shall we sit?"

She did so, remarking, "These little rustic kiosks were an inspired idea of Lady Lamburne's."

What should have been a compliment sounded faintly ironic. She might not be an admirer of his hostess.

"Have you traveled in the Italian states, then, Tam Lin, to possess a carnival costume?"

"I did during my Grand Tour, though in my case 'twas more of a Little Tour, as I had duties at home. Italy was delightful—full of antiquities and gaiety and sun. Sometimes too much sun and heat." As she appeared to wait expectantly, he went on. "In spite of my tutor, I gave the German principalities short shrift.

The Germans are so lacking in fashion sense…" He shrugged.

She laughed a little. "And gaiety is not a noted characteristic, either, I believe. Please tell me more about your travels. As a mere female, I lead a sadly circumscribed life."

He added a few more details and an anecdote or two. At her encouragement, the history of his peregrinations flowed out. He had never recounted them before. His brother had had his own tour, and their father, probably having heard Robert's stories, had no interest in Gervase's account. Ducane lost himself in memories of that happy period, prompted at any pause by some question or perceptive comment from Queen Mab.

He was describing the appallingly unsatisfactory Portuguese inn at which he had spent two days because of a trifling mishap when he saw Queen Mab's attention was distracted. Her eyes followed several other couples who were proceeding toward the house.

"Can it be time for supper already? And the unmasking, I suppose." They kept early hours in the country. By midnight, those not staying overnight would be on their way home by the light of the moon. "Let us go in, my lady." He regretted the necessity of ending their tête-à-tête but looked forward to seeing her face.

"Oh, only see that bench to our left. Someone has left a cape or domino. Pray fetch it so it may be returned to its owner."

He rose and peered at the little arbor and bench. There did seem to be something dark which might be a cloak, though the contrast of moonlight and deep shade made it difficult to be sure what it was. The lady's gown rustled as she also stood up.

When he reached it, there was no cape nor anything else on the bench except a shadow. When he turned back to tell Queen Mab, she was gone. The paving stones between the benches and the french doors into the ball room lay pale under the moon. She could not have covered the distance between their seat at the end of the parterre and the house in the time his back had been turned.

He strode past the wicker arbors along the way, glancing between them, in case she had stepped aside to sniff one of the roses. Then he checked the other sides of the parterre. She had vanished.

Except for the pair of glazed doors, there was no way to escape—escape? He meant only, leave—as the paved area was surrounded by a low wall, the rustic shelters built up against it.

"My lady? Queen Mab? Where are you?" He sounded like an idiot, a fate he always strove to avoid. But he could not assume she was safe and go into the house. He called again. No answer. He was near where the wall met the corner of the house when he noticed that the last of the arbors was not against the wall but a little farther from it than the rose bushes were. He edged between a damask rose and the wickerwork and made his way along the narrow alley behind bushes and bowers. A slender lady wearing an old-fashioned petticoat without panniers would have no more trouble than he did.

He came to the corner where the side wall met the one parallel to the house. Halfway along he came to the shelter where they had sat. Directly behind it was an opening in the wall separating the parterre from the parkland. Queen Mab need only have slipped behind the trellis-work and crossed a swathe of grass and shrubs to be among trees. She could be anywhere.

Queen Mab was an appropriate name. But why had she chosen to disappear rather than taking her leave in a more mundane way once they entered the ballroom?

Ducane searched around the bushes outside the wall, calling softly, "Queen Mab." Was it likely she had gone farther? Probably not, as she would have to return to the house eventually. What the devil had happened to his peaceful, rational existence? His visit to Lamburne had possessed a fairy tale quality from the beginning. At last he had no choice but to admit he had lost her and return to the house.

The ballroom was emptying as couples, now unmasked, moved toward the adjoining saloon where supper had been set out. Removing his own mask, he followed them in, looking for an embroidered jacket and coif. At such a festivity in town, there would be too many guests to make finding one easy. At a mere country ball with everyone assembled to sup, it should have been no challenge, especially when the lady was distinctively clad. As he lingered near the door, Lady Sophia, now recognizable in pink silk, spangles, and little filmy butterfly wings, appeared and put her hand upon his arm in an unbecomingly familiar way. She had been looking for him as he had been searching the crowd for Queen Mab, the Lady of the Gillyflowers.

"Were you trying to find me, Lord Gervase? Our table is over here by the windows."

He let her lead him to it because what else could he do? Courtesy required it. He filled plates for her and for himself, paid scrupulously equal attention to her sister, her mother, and some female cousin or other, and bantered with the men.

"I wonder you did not discover me before the unmasking," Sophia murmured during a lull in the conversations.

I did not look for you would be an impossible reply. *I do not know you well enough to recognize you masked* was as bad and would lead to an invitation to remedy the circumstance. He believed he would know Queen Mab if he saw her again in any guise. "In a rose garden, picking out one rose would be a challenge worthy of Hercules." Granted, most of the hero's labors had involved beasts in some way. One must hope the ladies did not have the benefit of a classical education. Apparently not, for they all smiled or giggled or beamed at him.

He needed an income. The possibilities were terrifyingly few, mostly because of his own poor choices. Or not entirely that. If he had taken to some profession after school he would not be in this position. His father had still been vigorous even in his older years, and he had had an adequate bailiff. But Gervase could not have refused his father's request to help with the management of Blacklaw and the other properties. Robert, eight years his senior, was living in London, acquiring the polish of a man about town and sowing his wild oats. More important to the family, he was making useful friendships and connections at court. Gervase did not mind acting as his father's assistant, as the marquess had previously devoted most of his attention to his heir. Now perhaps Gervase could become better acquainted with him. Then once Robert married and came home, Gervase would be free to pursue some profession. No doubt their father could help him to some well-paid sinecure like Assistant Inspector of the Royal Table Linen. But too many years had gone by before Robert returned to Blacklaw.

When Robert issued his ultimatum, Ducane cut back on his expenses. He gave up his comfortable chambers and moved to Blacklaw House. He made do with his own hair and powder to save the cost of re-dressing his wig. Now he was coming to believe himself willing to consider a cit's daughter if only she were sensible and possessed good taste and manners.

Queen Mab of the Gillyflowers would do well, if she had a dowry, and if he could find her. She had been invited, so Lady Lamburne would know who she was. He almost asked her, before realizing it would be tactless, when she hoped he would offer for Sophia. Also, they had spent an hour or more together, out of sight of others, which would be ruinous to the lady's reputation if it came out. His valet might be able to discover her identity and whether she had left the ball early. For some reason, Ducane felt reluctant to reveal his personal interest in the lady even to his servant. However, with Jenkins's interest in fashion, he might not think an inquiry about so memorable a costume unusual. Perhaps he and the other servants had discussed the guests and their costumes.

Jenkins shook his head in response to Ducane's casual inquiry. He and most of the others had peeked at the ballroom; Jenkins had taken particular interest, in case he should see something his master might adapt for a future occasion. He had noted many of the ladies but none dressed as his lordship described. He was sure he would have remembered. The close-fitting embroidered cap covering all her hair would have been noticeable.

A ridiculous idea took possession of his brain: was the Lady of the Gillyflowers the one who had bent over him and wiped the blood from his brow? They were both mysterious and both encounters affected him as somehow magical. Queen Mab fell into the same category as that hallucination in the park: a mystery.

Chapter 11

She woke in the morning to memories of the ball and stretched luxuriously, as Tabby did. Her governess had made sure she knew the common dances, but performing them with a man to music rather than with Mistress Henderson to her hummed accompaniment was a revelation.

She had entered through the concealed servants' door, intending only to observe from the shadow of a pillar. The spectacle enthralled her until that sinister white mask turned toward her. Adelaide suffered a moment of alarm, convinced its wearer was staring at her. Or was it excitement? Then he stalked toward her, black silk cloak billowing around his black suit. She almost fled. Yet when he spoke, she had been unable to resist dancing with him. After that, she let him lead her out to the garden as if bewitched. But she was not so lost in the night's enchantment that she failed to steer them to the opening to the lawn and park.

She met few men and knew none well except her brother, if she discounted her father who had died when she was a child, and Tate, whom she knew only through his letters. Tam Lin fascinated her as if he were a being from some jingling country ballad. *The Devil came to court a maid/And she was called Mad Adelaide…* It would end badly for the woman. Not that her brother or even Leonora called her insane as the slightest hint of madness damaged a family far more than suspect parentage.

She had been charmed by their conversation, after a rather stiff start. Tam Lin had spoken to her as if she were a lady he would like to know, an indescribable feeling. Lord Gervase talked to her, too, although with her brother and sister-in-law and nieces present, their speech had been limited and formal. What did he think of the countryside here? What was Northumberland like? No, she had never been outside Wiltshire except for her one visit to London. No real meeting of minds occurred so their exchanges could not match the thrill of dancing and speaking with the masked stranger. To discover two men in a week who saw her as merely an ordinary lady or better still, a somewhat interesting one, seemed a miracle.

Lord Gervase and Tam Lin might prove her old governess's assertion that she was not hateful and awkward. She had never quite believed it in her heart. Was it possible that those who had not been primed to think her bizarre would find nothing odd about her?

Girls escaped unhappy homes by marrying, a means of getting away barred to her unless she met a man with no preconceptions about her. He would have to be outside their social circle and willing to marry a lady of four-and-thirty. She might be a desirable bride, given her inheritance, even if Tate kept control of her money as he was able to do. How particular would he be about her husband's rank and fortune, taking into account Adelaide's spinsterhood and the scandal? Thaddeus Tate was both honest and practical, she judged. A laborer or groom would be out of the question, not that she would consider one. A half-pay officer or genteel merchant might be acceptable. A dissolute gentleman or wastrel would be unlikely to win Tate's approval. To meet a suitable man posed a challenge, but now she had encountered two.

During her one London season, Leonora had tried to teach her how to show discreet interest in a man, without success. Those lessons contradicted years of admonitions: not to stare at men, not to put herself forward, or flirt her fan, or laugh too freely (as if she ever did!). Nor was the countess's heart in the effort. As much as she might have preferred to have her unwanted sister-in-law out of the house, her fear of Adelaide embarrassing her made Leonora more critical than usual and rendered Adelaide more shy and clumsy rather than less.

Had she not been so timid and lacking in conversation, she might be married now with a home and children of her own. Or she might be a widow, free to please herself. If Mistress Henderson had still been at Lamburne and come with her to London, she might have had some confidence. If she had played with other children when she was a child, she might have become accustomed to conversation. Other young ladies had been almost as shy and tongue-tied as she and had received offers.

But their parents or guardians praised their beauty, gentle nature, and accomplishments; her brother and sister-in-law had been silent when they did not let slip some disparaging remark. Still, someone might have courted her because she was an earl's daughter, if either Leonora or Edward had made any push to help. The best Edward had managed was a discreet word here and there about the jewelry she had inherited. Those who were not put off by uncertainty about her portion and her lack of response to their overtures were given their *congé* to withdraw by Edward. He had no intention of making a fool of himself by sending a gazetted fortune hunter to Tate. She understood his reluctance. A fortune hunter might treat her as badly as her family did, or worse. Still, between her fearfulness and her brother and sister-in-law's lack of enthusiasm, her season had been wasted.

They should have been happy to be rid of her. Looking back, she guessed they had not pursued a match for her more aggressively because they feared the talk about her mother and birth would be revived. The following year, they left her at Lamburne Chase.

Maybe they could not help themselves. Edward had been thirteen or fourteen when she was born, the only one of her half siblings still at home. From a chance word or two, she guessed Edward had spoken of it bitterly at Eton. No doubt the other boys made cruel sport of his father's shocking second marriage and its reason. Edward's humiliation must have wounded him deeply. By the age of six, she knew he detested her and her mother. After Papa's death, she heard a servant say her father had caned him for his loose talk at school. The late Lord Lamburne recognized what Edward, at fourteen, did not; such talk would rebound on their family.

When he married, his bride fell in with his views. Adelaide herself had believed in her unworthiness even after her brain knew she was not at fault.

She lay in bed and discovered the absence of shame. Her manners and behavior were no worse than those of the ladies and girls she had met in London. She was more intelligent than many, and she never spread gossip. Granted, while she had turned the other cheek to her family's insults, she could not take credit for doing so, as she submitted to them out of fear. But what was unreasonable about asking that her wash water be brought up hot? The girls or Leonora or Edward would all have complained loudly if their water was lukewarm.

O brave new world, that has such people in it! How appropriate the quotation from *The Tempest* was, when the people were Lord Gervase Ducane and Tam Lin. The memory of her scandalously long tête-à-tête with Tam Lin warmed her. She wondered about his face. All she knew was that he was of average height or a little more, and not fat. She would not care if he were ill-favored; he could be as ugly as Caliban for all she cared. She had seen Italy through his eyes.

Ducane, too, had been more than courteous to her. He was not precisely handsome, with his aquiline nose and narrow, heavy-lidded eyes, but he was intended for Sophia, poor man. Might he be happy with a lovely, well-dowered goosecap? Not if his conversation with Adelaide was any indication. And if beauty and a dowry were all he required in a bride, he deserved Sophia. He would discover too late she was not tractable and bad-tempered with it.

Adelaide was still wrapped in pleasant memories when Jenny brought in her chocolate. The maid whispered, as if anyone could overhear, "I complained about you yesterday, my lady."

"Well done. You should not linger with me too long. They'll expect you to hurry through your work for me." She would have liked to confide some of her experiences at the ball to someone, and Jenny was the only person to whom she might do it. But the servants would wonder if she did not return as soon as she could. Tabby would listen to her. Or mayhap she should not speak of them lest somehow their charm vanish like fairy gold.

But she did tell Tabby, and the enchantment did not fade. She continued to feel the surge of joy on remembering the masquerade ball. She would hug the memory to her all the rest of her life. She was still smiling when Jenny delivered her hot water and her breakfast together.

"We're terrible busy today," she said apologetically, "there being more folk for dinner than just the house guests. What will you wear this morning so I can lay it out?"

"My habit."

She and Tabby washed and breakfasted, and Adelaide dressed. Downstairs she meant to tell one of the least-senior footmen to have her horse saddled. If she had instructed one of the upper footmen to send a message to the stable, she would have waited an hour or more. As it was she could sit in the morning room or back parlor, whichever was empty, for a few minutes. Tabby was safely locked in her room.

Approaching the back parlor, she heard Leonora's shrill, "But we can't have unequal numbers at table! Ducane would be disgusted. How could Lady Fairchild let me down at the last minute?"

"We've had more females than men at dinner and supper before. Families do."

"Dining *en famille* with one guest is one thing, Lamburne, I agree. This is a dinner party, which is very different."

"Invite the parson's sister. She'll be grateful enough not to feel insulted to be asked on short notice."

"She's too young and quite pretty. We don't want Ducane distracted."

"By a chit with no dowry? Hardly."

Really, if one wanted to have a private conversation, one should close the door completely. Tiptoeing as well as she could in riding boots, she retreated some distance along the passage before turning back and clumping noisily.

She paused at the parlor door, glanced in, and said, "Oh, Leonora and Edward, good morning."

"Good morning, Addie. If you are riding, be sure to take a groom." Leonora had once encountered her on horseback with no groom—the only one available was a man she disliked—and never failed to caution her now.

Her half brother was frowning slightly. "Before you go, let me ask, would you be willing to dine with us today?"

"Why, of course, if I am invited." She smiled at him, sunnily, she hoped.

"Addie, you do not need an invitation. You are one of my family."

The assurance came a little late; she had disconcerted him. Adelaide did not choose to discuss why she felt unwelcome when the family gathered, nor did she wish to admit she was willing to expose herself to their obvious scorn on this occasion because she wanted to see and talk with Ducane again.

Leonora's agreement came even later. "Do come to dinner. You would be the answer to my prayer, Lady Fairchild having sent a note saying she has sprained her foot and cannot come."

"Then I will be glad to take her place. If you will excuse me, I'll have my exercise. There's plenty of time to change before dinner, if only I can get one of the maids to help me."

Her sister-in-law appeared to have bitten down on something sour. A lemon, perhaps. "I will make sure one is sent to you an hour before, if that will do?"

"Certainly, Leonora. Thank you." She nodded pleasantly and slipped out. Leonora was willing to have her attend because an old maid like Adelaide would be a safe choice to make up the party. As she hesitated momentarily, deciding to go direct to the stable block, which would be faster than sending a message, she heard Leonora say, "But what if she disgraces us?" and her half brother's reply, "She behaved rationally when she dined with us the other day. You insisted on another lady. If you would not have the parson's sister, who else was there to ask?"

The countess's fear of mortification produced results. The laundry maid, who yearned to be a lady's dresser, arrived promptly to assist Adelaide. Bess's sidelong glances proved she knew Adelaide's fascinating reputation and was hoarding details to pass on in the servants' hall.

"Do you know what gown you wish to wear, my lady?" She posed the question timidly. The girl's world was the laundry and the servants' hall; her path and Adelaide's had never crossed. Of course she would fear Adelaide's wardrobe held nothing better than the sacque-back gown she had thrown on after removing her habit.

"I think the moss green robe à la française."

Adelaide opened the door to her dressing room where her newest clothing was kept. Though fewer in number than for her own season because one did not need so many in the country, she seldom wore them out. Previous years' garments, except her particular favorites, were stored in the attic with the family's trunks and valises and such things as were not needed at the moment.

She pulled open the bottom drawer of one of the two chests of drawers. The laundry maid's eyes widened, and she breathed out an "Oooh" before lifting it out reverently and stroking the brocade.

Adelaide had yet to wear the gown—had not even tried it on, because it required a maid's assistance with the corset, panniers, and stomacher. The golden-yellow petticoat and stomacher would be visible between the front edges of the gown. Mme. Bernard never loaded Adelaide's gowns with bows and lace. She had told Leonora rather brusquely that Adelaide would shine most brightly in simple clothing. Her sister-in-law left the matter to the mantua maker's discretion thereafter. What a pity she had insisted her daughters be garlanded in whatever embellishments were in vogue.

Laced, hooked, pinned, and tied into the various parts of her clothing, Adelaide sat at her dressing table while Bess put up her hair in a more elaborate style than Adelaide ever achieved. Bess stared at Adelaide's reflection in the mirror when she finished and chewed her lip. She was wondering how to ask if Adelaide possessed any jewelry.

Adelaide saved her from her predicament. She opened the inlaid box on the table and took out the parure of delicate topaz blossoms and green enamel leaves. "The necklace, earbobs, and bracelets will do. I think the brooch would be too much. Oh, and these rings." By happy coincidence, the citrine and peridot rings echoed colors in the stomacher's embroidered design. The jewelry was not very valuable, but it had been her mother's.

"Most ladies would wear diamonds or emeralds," the girl offered after a brief hesitation. More cheerfully she added, "But those are just right for the gown and this is the country, anyway."

Bess was more skilled than Jenny and had done a fine job. *Only think how she might advance if Mad Adelaide looked like a fashionable lady!* Adelaide was grateful for her help and could not blame the chit for believing what the upper servants believed. Before Adelaide dismissed her, she gave her one of her simpler gowns from last year, a golden-brown not too ornate to serve as the girl's Sunday best, striking her too overwhelmed to do more than stammer "T-thank you, my lady!"

Chapter 12

The neighbors invited to dinner were known to Adelaide from encounters on Sundays in the churchyard. The guests she had never met were clearly puzzled to meet their host's unknown half sister. Had she been living elsewhere? Why had he never mentioned her? Had they seen her at the unmasking? They could not voice their questions without rudeness though one lady appeared tempted.

Ducane was seated between Sophia and the middle-aged wife of the elderly viscount. His technique with both was admirable. Sophia was pouting; the viscountess was captivated by his conversation. Adelaide had a young man recently down from Oxford on one side and a Mr. Franklin on the other. She drew out the first with questions about Oxford and his studies. He blossomed once he realized she had read some of the same books. Then she was able to relax and listen to Franklin talk about his horses and dogs. She would not want to spend much time in his company, but talking about horses for the space of a dinner was tolerable as she herself was an enthusiastic rider. Neither of the men showed any sign of having heard the various rumors Edward feared.

The scandal was more than thirty years old. Perhaps it was dead and Edward was haunted by its ghost. When Leonora signaled the ladies to rise,

Adelaide went along to the drawing room with no qualms. A woman of about Leonora's age seated herself in the chair nearest Adelaide and confessed with a wry smile that she had heard her talking about horses.

"I wondered if you enjoy riding as much as I do? Sir Archibald and I are very fond of the exercise."

Her complexion was unfashionably brown and somewhat weathered; her movements were energetic. One might have guessed Lady Smythe spent a great deal of time out of doors. Her face reflected every thought. Adelaide liked her immediately.

At their introduction, Sir Archibald and Lady Smythe's recent purchase of a manor a few miles away had been mentioned. "I do ride as much as I can." Though in deference to Leonora's concern for propriety, she could do so only when the stable could spare a groom. "You are only some twelve miles distant, I think?"

"About that. None of the other ladies I have met in the neighborhood admit to being enthusiasts for the sport. I have been hoping to get up a party to ride to Avebury. May I hope you would join it?"

"I would be delighted, Lady Smythe."

"Please call me Helen. I do not stand on ceremony."

Helen Smythe mentioned the excursion when the men joined them, with the result that a date was agreed upon. Lady Smythe did not mention the idea originated in talking with Adelaide; why should she, after all? If she had, Leonora might have balked. Instead, relieved of the need to find amusement for her guests, she encouraged the expedition. Charity was concealing reluctance. She was not fond of riding. Sophia was pleased, having been told (usually by admirers) that she had a pretty seat on her horse.

At breakfast the morning of the riding party, Leonora was scarcely able to conceal her annoyance at Adelaide's presence. The guests greeted her in their various ways. Sophia and Charity ignored her. Only Leonora and her daughters appeared to think it strange she would come to breakfast.

Her sister-in-law inquired sweetly, "Addie, are you quite sure you wish to ride today?" She patently did not want her to join the party.

Once Adelaide would have taken the hint. This time she would keep to her new policy. "Why, yes, Leonora. I have always wanted to see Avebury, but it is too far for a lady accompanied only by a groom, and no one made up a party to view it before."

The little crescent lines at the corners of Leonora's mouth showed what she thought of Adelaide's inclusion, but there was nothing she could do to prevent Adelaide from joining the group.

The day was perfect for a meandering ride. Adelaide wore her newest habit, garnet with a modest amount of silver braid, and a neat little black tricorne edged with the same. Madame Bernard knew her preferences almost better than she herself did. Few things gave one more confidence than flattering clothes. Leonora also deserved some credit, the second virtue Adelaide could allow her: pride which did not permit her to insist her resented sister-in-law wear shabby clothing. While in charity with her sister-in-law at the moment, Adelaide did not regret her absence from the riding party.

Sophia wore a silvery blue a shade darker than her

eyes, a fact of which she was all too well aware. A good deal of lace edged her neckcloth and wrist frills: rather fussy but not quite so much as to be vulgar. Charity's was a deep rose and much simpler. Together they presented a charming appearance. If only her younger niece did not end the ride prematurely by falling off her horse, Adelaide expected to enjoy herself.

In addition to Edward and Lord Gervase Ducane, among the older men were Sir Peter Weston and Mr. Sidney Franklin. Sir Peter was a magistrate and a particular friend of Edward's. He was also a widower, which for the purposes of the ride was more to the point, as an extra man or two was always welcome except perhaps at formal dinners.

The cavalcade set out more or less on time, to Adelaide's surprise. Charity had made heroic efforts to be only a quarter hour late. Sophia was in high good humor, having maneuvered to place herself beside Ducane. She may have believed he was fascinated by her prattle. Adelaide thought his bland expression no more than good manners.

Leonora had remained behind with those who did not care to ride. Edward's presence should be adequate protection for his daughters, but she should have been present to chaperon the other young guests. They were as high-spirited and silly as puppies or kittens and as difficult to tell apart except by sex, hair color, and degree of shyness or forwardness. Adelaide had scarcely spoken with most of them, as the girls and youths clung together in one group, the older guests in another: two separate house parties rather than one.

Lady Smythe took it upon herself to deliver a scold here or there to the more hoydenish girls, and Edward spoke to the boys as necessary. Sir Peter also kept an eye on them. Adelaide rode with her recent dinner partner, Mr. Catlin, too serious for the other young people and too shy to approach the older guests. He recommended a recent book she might find interesting, a study of Stonehenge by an antiquarian. They discussed that for some time. After a couple of miles, he smiled apologetically. "I beg your pardon for rattling on, ma'am. I fear I'm bookish."

"So am I, Mr. Catlin."

The ride to Avebury was no more than ten miles, not much of a challenge even to Charity. They trotted or cantered part of the way; a few of the more adventurous riders, including two of the girls, broke into a gallop. Sir Peter followed them, after a meaningful exchange of glances with Edward. Charity remained with the main group. Adelaide guessed Sophia stayed behind because Ducane did. Her tiresome niece did not appear as put out as she ordinarily would be to miss a run: one cannot converse or flutter one's eyelashes at the gallop.

She herself enjoyed the ride and the company very much. Gigantic stone blocks scattered the fields around—and in—Avebury like giant sheep. Catlin opined they were originally a circle, or several circles like the one at Stonehenge, though older, as the stones were rough, not worked. He supposed, as the antiquarian William Stukeley thought, they had been placed by Druids. Avebury lacked anything more of interest, and they soon proceeded on a little way south.

Servants had been sent ahead with refreshments as the party would not return to Lamburne in time for dinner. They ate a simple al fresco meal by a brook where the horses could be watered. Catlin and several other gentlemen debated whether the manmade hill nearby had been built by the Druids, the Romans, or the Danes, without reaching any conclusion.

Sitting in the shade with people who did not ignore or berate her was delightful. Conrad Catlin hovered near where she sat with Lady Smythe and her husband and two of the more mature guests. One of them, finding that Catlin had been enrolled at Magdalen College, his own alma mater, engaged him in reminiscences of academic life and pranks.

Lady Smythe asked if Adelaide hunted.

"I could not like to see a fox killed, even if they are vermin and raid the poultry yard."

"Oh, neither could I. Where we used to live, I would either go home before the end or retreat to wherever the servants had set up the food and drink. But I love a good gallop."

"I wonder you did not take part this morning."

She lowered her voice. "I felt my highest duty was to act as a chaperon, though of course you were present, too, and could have quelled any fooling." Adelaide did not miss the amusement in her voice. "Sir Peter could ensure that group did nothing indiscreet." She placed a slight emphasis on "that."

"I am not sure the girls would pay heed to any admonition from me."

"You underrate yourself, Lady Adelaide. You lack only confidence, not authority."

If only life at Lamburne could be like this.

The day was unalloyed pleasure until they started back. No doubt Sophia intended to keep Ducane to herself again. After helping her mount, he moved away to assist Adelaide into the saddle. Somehow, his horse ended up beside hers.

Uneasily aware Sophia was sitting her horse slack-jawed with shock, Adelaide murmured, "But Lady Sophia…"

"Will ride with someone else. 'Tis only polite to make oneself agreeable to all the company in so small a group. Come, let us ride."

A discreet glance back once all were mounted showed that Mr. Franklin was now Sophia's escort. Oh, dear. She would be in a fury or a fit of the sullens once they reached the house; but let Leonora deal with it. Most of the riders had switched partners two or three times, as Adelaide and Catlin had and so should Sophia have done. No matter what Lady Smythe claimed, Adelaide suggesting to Sophia that she should not devote all her time to Ducane would not have gone well. Apparently no one else had tried to interrupt the tête-à-tête either; possibly they knew or suspected that he was courting her and were allowing them time to become acquainted. Edward should certainly have done so, however, no matter how much he wished for the marriage. Adelaide was beginning to doubt Gervase Ducane did mean to offer for her.

"How pleasant to hear the birds and the breeze among the leaves," he observed innocently.

Sophia had been chitter-chattering whenever Adelaide observed Ducane and her niece. He seemed to say little in reply. Perhaps she had given him no chance. Adelaide stole a look at him and met his satiric gaze.

"Quite so, Lord Gervase."

He remarked on the traces left by earlier inhabitants, whoever they were, and she mentioned Mr.

Catlin's views on the subject. When that was exhausted, Lord Gervase observed, "I believe it is time for you to suggest a topic, my lady."

"Do you have an opinion of cats, sir?"

"Excellent animals. They keep down the mice and rats and are graceful and elegant." He paused and cast glances hither and yon. "You won't tell anyone I praised them, will you, Lady Adelaide? An Englishman who prefers cats to dogs is considered no kind of man at all. Not that I dislike dogs—it's just that so many of them are not well trained. My brother's favorite setter reared up and planted his muddy paws on my knees. Alas for my new silk breeches. The absence for the most part of such unmannerly beasts is one of London's chief advantages."

The sound of Mr. Franklin's voice, lauding some lady of his acquaintance who was an intrepid horsewoman, warned Adelaide that he and her niece were now close behind them in the lane.

"She'd jump any fence, hedge, wall, anything," Franklin was saying. "She'd have jumped the moon if her horse was willing." He brayed a laugh.

The grassy stretch to their left ended at a stone wall marking the boundary of the next property. A rather dilapidated cottage was visible beyond it.

"Oh, look," Sophia trilled and spurred her mare into the field and toward the wall.

"Sophia!" Edward shouted and galloped after her. "Damnation," he muttered as he passed Adelaide.

Tiresome of Sophia to make a foolish spectacle of herself. No rider with any experience would be impressed by a jump over a wall no more than four feet high. She would probably destroy part of the cottage's vegetable garden, for which Edward would pay generously.

Ducane's soft "No…" alerted her. The jump itself was well executed. But the horse came down off-balance on the other side. Mare and rider fell, vanishing. A horse screamed.

Edward pulled up hard, threw himself off his mount, and vaulted the wall.

"There's a gate farther on," Sir Peter yelled, and spurred for it, Ducane and Adelaide right behind him. A young man pelted past them, reaching the gate right after the magistrate. Sir Peter snapped at the boy to hold his horse.

The gate hung crooked on its hinges. The cottage was derelict, with no garden to be trodden down. Ducane dismounted, passing his reins to the young man as well. Over his shoulder, he said, "You should wait here, Lady Adelaide."

"Nonsense." She slid off her own hack and hurried after him.

Sophia's Princess was down, struggling to stand.

"Thank God she wasn't pinned under her horse." Sophia had thrown herself off to the left while the mare fell to the right, though her foot was still tangled in the stirrup. Ducane went to the mare's head to try to keep her from thrashing while Edward attempted to disengage Sophia's boot. Sophia whimpered.

Ends of bone jutted through the skin of Princess's right foreleg. Sickened, Adelaide joined Ducane, murmuring to Princess and stroking her sweating neck and shoulder. A human might die from such an injury. A horse certainly would. Ducane put a hand on her arm to draw her away. "Best to stay back." Adelaide ignored the suggestion.

Edward finally got Sophia's foot free, with difficulty because she kept moaning and crying that it hurt too much.

Some of the other men in the party had come over the wall, others by the gate. Sir Peter raised his voice. "Who has a pistol?"

Edward having pulled Sophia some distance away was fully occupied as she clung to his hand.

"My ankle hurts, Papa. I think it's broken."

No one spoke. The magistrate tutted.

"Someone will have to ride to the house." He looked around for a trustworthy messenger and settled on the young man who had been holding the reins of several horses. "You're a spanking rider. Back to the house with you to fetch a pistol and ask for a carriage to be sent. Catlin, take charge of the horses, if you will." Catlin, still mounted and outside the wall, sensibly had not thrust himself into the confusion, choosing instead to discourage others from crowding into the cottage garden.

Adelaide continued petting the mare with her left hand and crooning to her. The horse had given up trying to stand. Adelaide felt in her right pocket and drew out a sheathed knife. She paused her gentle stroking long enough to free the six-inch long blade and dropped the sheath. "Here, now," she whispered. "Only a moment…"

"I'll do it," Ducane said, to her surprise. Before she could reply, Sir Peter stepped closer and held out his hand.

"I've had to do it before. Lord Lamburne, you should move Lady Sophia farther away."

Adelaide gave him the knife, hilt first. He tested the blade on his thumb and nodded.

"Franklin," Lamburne called, "can you help me lift my daughter so I can support her ankle? There's a bench in the shade in front of the cottage where she can rest until the coach comes. Ready? Lift."

Sophia began to weep noisily. Sir Peter waited until they'd turned away from the horse. "Lady Adelaide, you should move back."

"I will stay. I think it soothes her to be stroked and spoken to."

"As you wish," Sir Peter grunted and edged behind her to stoop by the horse's head. Adelaide turned her head away as he slashed both arteries in Princess's neck. Shuddering in sympathy, she remained kneeling, hand on the mare's neck. When she began to rise shakily, Ducane steadied her with an arm around her waist. She leaned into it. That blissful support conjured memories of the protection of her old nurse's arms.

Sir Peter wiped the knife off, first with a handful of grass, then with his handkerchief, before sheathing it and offering it to her. "Lucky you had it today."

How he would stare to know she always carried it.

Chapter 13

Part of the group was sent back to the house with Sir Peter. Ducane, Lady Smythe, Edward, Adelaide, and some of the others remained either to make themselves useful or because they hoped for more excitement. Lady Sophia was happy to oblige with her impression of a young lady tragically dying, Ducane noted cynically. One of the young men contrived to draw up a bucket of water from the cottage's well, dampened his handkerchief with it, and offered it to Sophia to cool her forehead, for which she thanked him prettily in a fading voice.

The blacksmith was sent for, and he and his sons arrived with a wagon to remove the mare's carcass. The earl had removed the saddle and bridle, although Sophia cried out that she could never, ever bear to use either again: there was blood on the latter. When she broke into hysterical sobs, Lady Smythe took charge, holding a vial of sal volatile under her nose. Shocked out of the threatened bout of vapors, Sophia reverted to her die-away airs. The Dowager Lady Blacklaw would likely have given her a slap and a reminder to conduct herself like a lady.

The Lamburnes' carriage arrived, and Lady Sophia was placed in it with the greatest care, accompanied by Lady Smythe and the rather plain young lady who was Sophia's best friend. Helen Smythe raised her eyebrows at Adelaide Setbury, evidently expecting she would also go in the carriage. Ducane heard her murmur, "Best not, I think." He could not tell whether Sir Archibald's wife understood her meaning or not, but she did not press the issue.

Predictably, the house was in an uproar when they arrived. The countess had sent for the bonesetter, and the kitchen was busy making barley water and caudles and Lady Sophia's favorite dishes. Such an upset presented social challenges. What was one to do when one's hostess was distracted with anxiety for her daughter and the servants were run off their legs fetching and carrying for the invalid?

After changing out of their riding clothes, some of the party clustered in the drawing room to describe the accident to those who had not been present. Ducane retreated to the library with Franklin, Sir Peter, Sir Archibald, and Catlin to avoid the most tiresome younger men. The latter had congregated in the morning room where it was now pleasantly cool and shady, to talk about feats of horsemanship, falls they or their friends had taken, and fatal riding accidents, over tankards of ale.

No one said much in the library until Franklin began. "I, er, suppose much of Lady Sophia's distress was for her poor horse. Being in pain with her ankle broken, she could not be expected to, ah, be in control of herself."

Sir Peter passed out tumblers of their host's brandy. He did not comment. Neither did Ducane.

Young Mr. Catlin remarked hesitantly, "Some females possess more fortitude than others, I believe. My little sister fell out of the hayloft and broke her arm.

Never cried, that I saw, just got up, walked into the kitchen, and asked the kitchen maid to help her up to her room and let our mother know she might need to have the bone set. It must have been painful for Lady Sophia when her foot had to be moved to free it from the stirrup."

"It's the horse I pity," Sir Archibald said bluntly. "A fine animal destroyed by carelessness."

Sir Peter, frowning, did not make a remark. Ducane wondered if he was also thinking Sophia had displayed no sense and no self-control.

Lamburne entered the library and closed the door. He glanced around the room, and said, "I think you were all present in the aftermath of the accident?"

They all nodded or mumbled, "Ay."

"I have heard a disturbing rumor and wish to confirm its truth. If it is true," he added perfunctorily. "Someone has informed me that my half sister was armed with a knife and cut the horse's throat."

"Thank God she had a knife, or the poor beast might have suffered for an hour before a pistol could be fetched. However, I dispatched the animal."

"I see, Sir Peter. Still, I cannot like that she was armed. Why would she have a knife with her? Or possess one at all?"

"I cannot speculate about Lady Adelaide's reason. I am merely grateful she had it. I doubt any of the men present had anything bigger than a penknife, which would not have been adequate."

No one else was going to speak. "Lord Lamburne, when a lady feels she must be armed, it suggests she senses she is not safe from serious insult."

Lamburne stared at Ducane. "What do you mean?

Why would she suppose she was in any danger?"

Ducane consigned both tact and gentlemanly reticence to the devil. "Lady Adelaide is sometimes treated with less than courtesy." He would not say by whom. "I would not be surprised if some man had attempted worse."

"She has not mentioned any lack of respect to me."

Lambourne should not have asked his question in a group. Better to have questioned Sir Peter in private. Ducane found the family's contempt for Lady Adelaide more annoying by the day. Damned if the earl did not deserve a brutal snub, which should dispel any illusions the man might cherish about securing Ducane for Lady Sophia. "Perhaps she felt no notice would be taken of a complaint, Lamburne. Servants generally ape their masters. I will be frank, sir. I have observed that your family, including Lady Adelaide's nieces, often speak slightingly to the lady."

His lordship opened his mouth to reply but thought better of it. He flushed and visibly groped for words. "In a family, formal manners—" The other men stood silent. Franklin took out his snuff box and fiddled with it while Catlin studied the billiard table, and the magistrate stared at Lamburne and Ducane as if listening to testimony.

Ducane interrupted. "If my brother ever spoke to my sister as I have heard Lady Adelaide addressed, I would thrash him, marquess or no."

"My half sister is often difficult and has been since she was a child."

"Jolly right, too, if she's treated badly," Catlin muttered to Franklin. His voice carried.

Sir Peter said smoothly, "While I have not

observed this myself, I have not spent much time in Lady Adelaide's presence. However, from what I have seen of her, she seems a lady of uncommon good sense. This reminds me, did you notice the hole which caused Lady Sophia's horse to fall?"

"Hole?"

"Ay, a depression some six or eight inches deep. Mayhap someone dug up a plant and did not fill the hole."

Franklin, staring at the floor, mumbled, "I fear my telling Lady Sophia about my sister's exploits encouraged her to emulate them."

No one responded to his confession because it changed nothing. Sophia had been wrong to jump a wall without knowing what was on the other side, she had been wrong to jump into a cottage garden, she had been courting attention, and her lack of concern for her injured mount laid her open to criticism from anyone who valued his animals.

"I will be speaking with my daughter about her actions when the laudanum has worn off. Thank you for your account of the event. If you will excuse me?"

When he was gone, Archibald Smythe remarked, "An unpleasant scene."

"But necessary." The magistrate flicked open his own snuff box. "I have never known a lady to keep a knife about her person. Certainly not a large one. It needed explaining. And if she does not feel secure, Lamburne should do something about it."

Ducane said, "I hope we have not made matters worse for Lady Adelaide. She seems not to have the support of her family."

"Lord Gervase," Catlin began, "I do not at all

understand why Lady Adelaide would be treated badly. Even if she is a poor relation, who are often not valued, and how can she be, when she is Lord Lamburne's sister? I didn't notice until you remarked upon it, but I heard Lady Charity speak to her rudely, and Lady Lamburne seems to ignore her as if she isn't there."

"I have no idea, Catlin."

Sir Peter sneezed prodigiously, shoved his handkerchief into his coat pocket, and scowled. "I have seldom seen or spoken with Lady Adelaide, except occasionally at church, and assumed her to be in poor health, though I also heard she is somewhat of a recluse. I do recall remarks by Lamburne and Lady Lamburne which led me to think she might be somewhat simple-minded. Until now, the few times I have seen her with her family, she was almost silent and very timid. Clearly this is not the sum of the lady's character."

"Whatever her faults, the servants should not be permitted to show her disrespect. Certainly her family should not do so."

"I agree with you, Ducane, and will talk to Lamburne about it later. Servants are expected to obey their masters. If they cannot or will not, they must be turned off or else give their notice. May I trust no one here will repeat what I have to say?"

Nods and murmurs of agreement all around.

"You, Catlin? You won't make a story of this to your university friends or family?"

The boy blushed. "Sir, I have the greatest respect for Lady Adelaide, and I would not blacken any lady's name."

"Well, then. Lamburne and I were at Eton when his

father married Lady Adelaide's mother. Possibly a boy of that age would resent any stepmother. That the late Lord Lamburne married an actress must have added to his bitterness. 'Twas no surprise her new stepson loathed her. No doubt he could not feel warmly toward his half sister." He refilled their glasses.

Sir Archibald nodded his thanks. "That he could not love her may be understandable. But damme, he has a duty to be civil to a female relative who is also a dependent."

The baronet might not object to a little incivility to a non-dependent female. Ducane had some sympathy with the distinction, having known one or two irritating females himself.

"Again, I agree. Lamburne is a friend, and yet I knew nothing of his treatment of Lady Adelaide. Perhaps I should have thought of questioning the gossip for I recall she was taken to London for a season years ago, which Lamburne would not have allowed if she were unmarriageable. Today I saw nothing strange about her conduct, and like you, Catlin, I find her a well-behaved lady of at least normal intelligence."

Later, meeting Franklin alone on the way to supper, Ducane said, "I know one thing about ladies. Even the most rational may take offense when a fellow praises another female."

"But 'twas only my sister I spoke of. I never meant Lady Sophia should attempt to emulate her."

Ducane took pity on his bewilderment. "Nevertheless, admiration of another is seen as disparagement of the one you address. As you were speaking of jumping and she was mounted, she took it as a challenge of sorts."

Franklin objected, "That doesn't make any sense. No rider would be impressed by a jump over so low a wall. Her seat's not that good, either."

"The lady may consider herself an accomplished horsewoman."

Then they reached the drawing room, ending the conversation.

Chapter 14

To everyone's relief, Sophia's ankle was sprained rather than broken, though she lamented as if she were to lose the foot to the surgeon's saw. She insisted on being carried downstairs to recline on a divan in one of the parlors. There she held court, though with fewer devoted courtiers than she might have expected.

Adelaide stopped in at least once a day to ask if there were anything the sufferer needed. Sophia always replied to Adelaide with a negative and a sickly-sweet smile, while her eyes would have drawn blood.

Taken up with the house party, Lady Lamburne had little time to spare for her and not much sympathy now she knew Sophia was not seriously injured. "A sprain? Pooh," she dismissed it brusquely. She was not a doting mother at the best of times. Charity popped in briefly but claimed to be needed to help entertain the guests. While everyone came to greet Sophia, few of them lingered long. The younger people soon went off to entertain themselves, the older ones found her airs and complaints tedious, and she was out of favor with those who valued their horses. Even those who did not hold her responsible were shocked to hear her blame Princess. Almost her only frequent companions were a spotty youth and Sophia's bosom-friend, Diana. The latter probably kept her informed of the activities Sophia was missing, but Adelaide also overheard her confiding that Charity was taking the opportunity to play the coquette with the younger male guests.

Adelaide rather hoped Sophia would continue to be invalidish, though she did not expect it. Meanwhile, she was savoring the rare sensation of enjoying herself. She could always find someone with whom to converse and had made several friends, if only they did not hear about her scandalous background. Quite often she and Ducane spoke. While his bored manner and exceeding fine dress suggested he was a fop, no one could accuse him of extremes of fashion. He always looked elegant. His care in dressing should not be surprising, if as she understood, he was the only man present who had a connection to court circles. Despite his languid air, he was capable of a rapier wit, though she had not seen him exercise it at anyone's expense. And he had been willing to give Princess the coup de grâce and had comforted Adelaide afterward.

"He is a gentleman to his fingertips," she told Tabby. "Kind, and with an almost feminine perception. Unfortunately for Sophia." If only he also possessed Tam Lin's air of strength and danger. Though he was physically strong: his arm had easily supported her when her knees had turned to custard after the mare's death.

She nuzzled the top of Tabby's head and whispered, "You may amuse yourself with the mice while I go out. I know there are some behind the paneling."

Tonight she started for the little ornamental tower built by an earlier Setbury. In daylight, the eight windows on the top floor gave fine views of the lake, the village, the house, and a vast expanse of trees. It had been her favorite place to play and to hide when she escaped the house as a child. On reaching it, she would turn right and walk in the orchard and from there—she froze at the sight of something tall moving on the path ahead of her. Under the trees, night had fallen. Perhaps she gasped, for whoever it was turned on his heel.

"Ma'am?"

Her heart gave a skip. She trusted Ducane. Another man might be courteous in company but behave badly on finding a woman alone. She would defend herself at need, creating another scandal. The man would not be blamed. Edward and Leonora would be furious and say she had brought it on herself by going out at night alone. She would have to apologize, plead the need for fresh air, promise untruthfully never to do it again, and hope there were no further repercussions for her. With Ducane, she could take pleasure at the prospect of his company.

"Lord Gervase."

He had no ear for voices. "Lady Sophia?" he inquired warily.

She laughed, a sound quite unlike Sophia's titter. "Lady Adelaide, sir."

"Lady Adelaide? What are you doing out all alone?"

"I came out to contemplate the stars."

"Because it is the stars govern our conditions?" he inquired lightly.

"If we are to believe astrologers, Lord Gervase. In another play, Shakespeare tells us the fault is not in the stars but in ourselves."

He failed to suppress a sigh. "Now, that is painfully true."

Her sigh echoed his own. "Yet I can also argue the other side, that sometimes we have no control over our circumstances."

"Or does it only seem we have none, Lady Adelaide? I too can promote the opposite view."

She laughed softly. "Mayhap sometimes one is true, and sometimes the other."

He offered his arm, reflecting on the truth of that statement. Her situation was somewhat like his own: the only way she could escape her unhappy dependence upon her brother was by marriage. The difference was that he was penniless but marriageable while she, being a penniless old maid, was not. "Shall we continue walking?"

She did not speak immediately, although she hooked her arm through his. "You are troubled, I think?"

He turned to stare at her. He had learned to wear a mask during his years in London; those of a frank, open countenance were figures of fun, like bumpkins. Lady Adelaide was contemplating the stars, her face as composed as if she had not just asked an extremely personal question. Did she not know how intrusive the casual inquiry was? He did not wish to snub her; he enjoyed her company. He would have confided in a friend. Here was a lady he liked and respected, in the darkness that made it possible to speak of things which could not be said in daylight.

"I suppose my remark about the stars led you to that conclusion."

"Being familiar with such ruminations myself, the idea did leap to mind."

How could he answer? Did she know how he came

to be at Lamburne Chase? While he pondered, she spoke.

"Lord Gervase, did you become acquainted with my family in town?"

Evidently she believed in the surgeon's approach to amputation: do it quickly. Her question gave him a place to start. "I met Lord Lamburne once or twice, I believe, perhaps at a coffee or chocolate house." He could not think of anyplace else he might have encountered the earl. Ducane's presence at his home must seem odd, given how slight their acquaintance was. After a longish pause during which he began to feel some explanation was called for, he added, "My mother met Lady Lamburne's mother in town, and they became friends. They are both prodigious correspondents, so…"

"She sent you here to court my niece?"

"The Dowager Lady Blacklaw has no power over me." Or not much.

By her silence, he knew she had detected the evasion and not-quite-lie in his tone. His brother, like the centurion in the Bible, could say to him "Go," and he would have to do it. As indeed he had.

"And yet here you are. I do not know you well, sir, but I do not think you are enjoying your stay. While it appears to me you possess a great deal of address, I have not seen you exercising it upon Sophia. You cannot be said to be courting her actively, but why else would you be here?"

One never found—or almost never—such appalling frankness in polite society. He was forced to admire it. "Nothing was agreed upon except that I would meet your niece. When my mother arranged for me to visit Lamburne Chase, I made clear that I was coming only to, er…"

"View the livestock."

He endeavored to keep his lips a flat line and not laugh. The phrase exactly summed it up. "No gentleman would put it that way."

"Not in a lady's hearing. If your visit was arranged by your mother and my sister-in-law's mother, are you quite sure that all was made plain to Lady Lamburne and my brother? Could it be like rumors, which change as they pass from one person to the next? A word here, an altered emphasis there, a touch of envy or ill will, and the original statement becomes unrecognizable."

"I had not thought of that," he admitted. "However, I do not consider myself bound by another's misunderstanding."

"Good. I'm tolerably sure you are reluctant to bring the matter to a head."

He winced at her outrageous plain-speaking. Adelaide Setbury was certainly an original in more ways than one. He had been wishing for someone with whom to discuss his dilemma. He had assumed it would be a man he knew well and trusted, except there was no one who met those criteria. Several of the gentlemen he had met at Lamburne might become friends, but it was too early to regard any of them as confidants. Lady Adelaide was compassionate enough to be willing to cut a suffering horse's throat and was not likely to share anything he told her with her family. Here in the dark, telling her his trouble seemed possible.

"I have begun to understand the feelings of young ladies forced to marry men willy-nilly, like them or not." Since childhood had he ever had a conversation stripped of all polite circumlocutions, an exchange of such naked honesty that there could be no misunderstanding?

"You are not in that position, fortunately. A girl who is underage and intimidated by her father, or who has been compromised—I mean raped, not merely kissed in a dark corner—has no choice at all."

"I concede the point. My own situation is less dire." No parent or guardian was forcing him to marry, after all. 'Twas only circumstances, which were compelling enough.

They were now by the little lake (contrived to make use of a previously boggy spot, Ducane suspected). He smelled dampness and reeds and heard the distinctive "too-wit, too-woo" of a tawny owl. A bench gave a view of Lamburne Hall's façade.

"Yet you were potentially willing to subject yourself to an arranged marriage rather than find a bride yourself."

"My brother did not marry until he was near my present age. That is not uncommon in our family. My father was turned forty before he wed." He smiled wryly. "I don't think our mother expected my brother's bride would not give birth to the heir apparent for another ten years."

A flicker of movement over the lake: a bat hunting its supper, he guessed.

"So you should marry to secure the succession, in case your brother has no other son? That is reasonable. Unless there is cause to suppose Lord Blacklaw or his son is in poor health, I confess I do not see any need to marry at once. You have time to find a lady more to your taste."

"The ladies I meet in London are too young and have no conversation."

"And silly? I believe that often goes with youth."

"Alas, yes. I do not enjoy being bored. Some of the widows are lively, but…"

"But?"

"Some are butterflies now that they are free of their husbands and choose not to settle in a new marriage. Others want a marriage of convenience, preferably with wealth or a title, without the inconvenience of giving up their freedom." The ones who might do well enough for him were impoverished and dependent upon their families' charity. "I asked my mother's advice. She was optimistic about my chances with Lady Sophia, but I am not sure she is the correct choice. She is very young."

"And as foolish as the girls you met in London. She is also rather spoiled and not likely to be a, mmmm…conformable wife."

"However, if I do not offer for Lady Sophia, I must look elsewhere. There were two other possibilities. One had not yet replied to the letter sounding out the girl's mama, and the other is in the wilds of Cornwall. I may have to go there as if on my way somewhere else and stop in to present my mother's compliments." The expense of traveling would cut sharply into his funds. "I should have married long since. I did not notice how the years were slipping away."

"That happens too easily. One sometimes does not know what to do, and so does nothing." She sighed.

"I suppose that is the nub of it." Occasionally he had thought of wedding. Marriage marked the end of irresponsible youth and the beginning of stability. "I could have looked around me for a wife, although a second son without independent means is no great bargain for a well-dowered lady. A cit's daughter who possessed a lady's graces can hold out for a title. Besides, most wish to spend months each year in town. I could not envision our staying at Blacklaw House as my brother's guests. Every lady wants a home of her own, where she can command the servants and impose her taste."

She laughed. "May I offer some advice?"

"My lady, I will take any counsel I can get."

"Do not offer for my niece, neither Sophia nor Charity. If there is any chance at all of meeting a lady you would prefer, take it. Go to London when everyone else goes. If you cannot find a better bride there, offer for Sophia then."

"If I leave here without raising expectations, she and your brother cannot be expected to accept my offer in several months."

They sat in silence for a few minutes, gazing at the house where a few lights still burned. He had been out longer than intended. "I hope we will not find ourselves locked out, Lady Adelaide."

She smiled at him, or he thought she did. Hard to tell in the dark. "We won't be. The door in the end of the old wing won't be bolted. I assure you, Sophia will not turn you down out of pique."

A fox yapped. Did Lady Adelaide mean to avenge herself for years of slights by wrecking her niece's chance to marry?

"Do you want to prevent Lady Sophia's marriage?" he asked. Brutal, but his future was at stake, and she was not reluctant to speak plainly.

"Good God, no. The sooner my nieces are married and gone, the better. They are far more annoying than Edward and Leonora. Sophia in particular is…vexing. She plays tricks on me, and I suspect her of inciting—"

He waited, wondering why she had broken off the sentence.

"Of inciting some of the servants to ignore my instructions."

He heard no falsehood in the words, but they were less than truth. Beside him, she stirred, almost the first sign of discomfiture Adelaide Setbury had shown in his presence.

She said, "I don't think you like her, and she would make you unhappy."

"But if you want her out of the house, why interfere?"

"I don't meddle, as a rule. But that day we met, when I was present at dinner, you treated me as if I were no different from anyone else. You have done the same ever since. I owe you a good turn."

"The merest good manners, my lady."

"You have no idea how rare that is, sir. You have noticed I don't always receive them from my family. Edward is decent to me in the material sense."

He had been lucky in his own family. He had never doubted his father and mother cared about him in their distracted way. Once or twice as a boy he had spent school holidays with the family of another student and envied their warmth and the way they understood each other's interests and foibles. "He doesn't know you, does he?"

"I suppose not. He never wanted to when I was a child. Even if he had not resented my existence, we would not have been close as he is so much older. By the time we might have become better acquainted, his distaste was set in stone. I am not without blame. I am held to be difficult. At times I am prickly. They prefer it when I keep to my chambers and flee from any unkind word."

"Lady Adelaide, is there no one with whom you could live who would be kinder to you?"

"No one in Lamburne's family. I don't know what people my mother had. I assume she was either an orphan or her connections cast her off. Why else would a gently bred lady resort to acting upon the stage? My old governess was kind and I think even liked me, but she left to marry. We correspond, but she and her husband have several children. I could hardly ask them to take me in, even if they had the room."

He wanted to ask if her father had not provided for her. Such a question was far too personal. If she had inherited anything, surely it would be available to her at her age.

"I'm sorry. You are correct; your choices are more limited than mine." The poor woman did not even have the option of marrying now.

" 'Tis the way of the world. Now we had best go in. It is becoming a trifle chilly."

Chapter 15

Conversation, real conversation, was as delicious as hot, fresh bread and butter or syllabub, neither of which often came her way. He liked to walk in the park at night, as she did, and now he knew he could go out by the door at the end of the old wing.

She could not resist watching from her parlor window the following nights, hoping to see him emerge from the door almost beneath her bedchamber. She would not follow him…exactly. She would merely take her own walk in the same direction. Should they chance to meet, she would be pleased, but she would not force a meeting. Ducane probably escaped the house to find some solitude; courtesy demanded she not intrude intentionally, though she did pray to meet him again some night before he left Lamburne.

Every night she thought, perhaps tonight? When he left Lamburne, she would mourn losing a friend, based on that one midnight exchange of confidences. They spoke during the day, but in company, it was impossible to share anything meaningful. They were merely a lady and a gentleman who were slightly acquainted.

Her casements stood open to admit the night air. It was balmy, perfect for walking in the dark and admiring the stars, listening for the other creatures that roamed at night. Everyone but the footmen on duty in the front hall and family wing was in bed, if not asleep.

She was a little later than usual in going out. No, she would be honest. She had been waiting to see if Ducane went out. If he did, she might encounter him, and they could enjoy the night air together. Foolishness! But as she turned from the window, she heard the sound she had been waiting for—a faint creak.

"I'll be back," she told Tabby. Locking her chambers and slipping down the stair to the side door took only moments. She averted her gaze from the candle he had left burning on the side table to avoid being dazzled by its light.

She heard him before she saw him and followed, her own passage through the shrubbery silent. On that one enchanted evening, he had mentioned that the lake was his favorite view. She could recall everything he said that night, and indeed, any other time they had spoken together. Easy enough, given how seldom she conversed with anyone. How she would miss their chats. Once he was gone, would she sink back into invisibility and fear? All too likely, unless she could maintain her spiderweb-thin acquaintance with Lady Smythe and one or two others of the neighboring gentry. Now that he knew her, Sir Peter might stand her friend. As both Edward's friend and a magistrate, his good opinion mattered.

Ducane was approaching the ancient oak to the right of the path ahead. She had wished to climb it as a child and hide in its branches like Charles II fleeing the Roundheads. She was close behind him when a shadow separated from the trunk and threw its arms around him. A girlish voice trilled, "Oh, you have come!"

His recoil and demand, "What? Who's that?" confirmed her suspicion the meeting was an ambuscade, rather than a tryst. Ducane did not want to marry Sophia, not even for her dowry, yet he was in danger of being forced to wed the chit. He could do nothing to save himself unless he simply refused, which might sink his chances of marrying someone else. Fury swept over her like a burning tide, near as hot as when Thomas abducted Tabby.

Running the last few steps to catch up, she rapped out the words before she considered them. "How dare you throw yourself at my betrothed?"

Sophia gasped and shrank back. "A-A-Addie?"

"Indeed. Go to your chamber and consider your disgraceful behavior."

She could feel Ducane's gaze on her face. Once the scheming little baggage was gone, she would apologize and assure him she would break their supposed betrothal as soon as he wished. If he decided he actually wanted to marry the girl, Edward would certainly agree. Sophia breathed noisily, the prelude to hysterics.

"If you indulge in a fit of the vapors, Sophia, I will slap you until you stop. Further, you risk rousing the house. The gossip would destroy your reputation."

Ducane drawled, "You should heed your aunt's very sensible warning."

"I-I-I…"

From farther ahead, footsteps thudded and a male voice called, "What's this, then?"

Sophia had provided herself with a witness. Adelaide did not need to see him to know who was approaching. She recognized Thomas's voice. Bad enough he smirked, hid her embroidery and books and pretended she had forgotten where she put them, and worst of all, stolen Tabby, now he was helping Sophia to force Ducane into an unwanted marriage. Sophia and Thomas deserved whatever retribution Adelaide could inflict.

Ducane might be as shallow as Sophia, but he was kind and did not deserve to be made unhappy.

"Why are you prowling out here, Thomas?" she inquired silkily.

The man stopped short, realizing for the first time he had come upon three people rather than the two he expected.

"Why…Lady Adelaide…'tis warm in the attics. I was taking a breath of fresh air before going to bed."

"Or sneaking out to meet Lady Sophia, more like. Sophia, are you so lost to every decent feeling that you would slip out to meet a servant? Your papa will not be pleased to hear how you have behaved."

Sophia gasped. "You can't speak to me that way. You're nothing in our family."

"I am your aunt. If you wish ever to marry, I suggest you mend your ways. Your father should cane you into better behavior."

"If a footman attempted a flirtation with a lady of my house, I'd thrash him soundly before turning him off. If he debauched one, I might not wish it known he had seduced a lady, which would ruin her. An accusation of theft, on the other hand, is easy to make and difficult for the miscreant to disprove," Ducane remarked helpfully. "Once made, whatever the fellow said would be taken as a lie."

"Or perhaps we should wake my brother now, for how are we to be sure what mischief Thomas may be about if left alone. Lamburne can confine him until he decides what to do."

"I agree, my dear Lady Adelaide."

"I haven't done a thing wrong," Thomas protested. "I was only out walking."

Her rage reborn chilled her voice like frozen iron. "Yes, you have. 'Tis time to pay the piper."

"Come along, man, or it will be the worse for you."

Adelaide shuddered internally at the thought of effete Gervase Ducane trying to overpower the strapping footman. "Lord Gervase," she murmured, "now I think on it, if we waken my brother, we may also wake some of the guests. That would lead to gossip spreading over half of England."

"Eh, I suppose it would. Embarrassing for your family and ruin for Lady Sophia. Well, if you prefer, we can leave it until morning and have a private word with him then."

"I think it best. Go in, Thomas. No, don't argue. Do it now." She marveled that her voice cracked like a whip. When the footman hurried away, she said, "Sophia, Lord Gervase and I will escort you to your room. You are not to leave it again tonight."

Sophia complained (but in a whisper) all the way back to the house, merely an attempt to shift attention away from her conduct. No one would approve of the girl being outside alone at night, making an obvious attempt to be found in a compromising situation with Ducane, and using a servant as a conspirator. No matter how much her brother and Leonora might wish her to marry the marquess's brother, Adelaide did not believe Edward at least would condone his daughter's actions tonight. After all, they might cause talk.

After leaving Sophia at her bedchamber—which would not guarantee she would stay there, but what more could they do?—Ducane said, "I'll escort you to your chamber, Lady Adelaide."

"Very well. We must talk."

"Ay, but we can't do it tonight. Tomorrow morning."

And so they left the matter there, though she would have liked to put his mind at rest about the claimed betrothal. Her last words to him as she unlocked her door were "I suggest you lock your own door tonight, Lord Gervase. Sophia has never been denied anything she wanted and will not take rejection well."

He did lock himself in. What an appalling evening. He hoped he would not have to jilt Adelaide Setbury. She had never shown him any particular favor or led him to think she was interested in marriage. He inclined to believe she had spoken without guile, merely to save him from Sophia's clutches, as the look she had given him had been reassuring rather than lover-like. If so, he was grateful.

After a disturbed night's sleep, he was downstairs early, though no earlier than he had previously found Adelaide in the dining room. With luck, they could have that conversation about last night. She was not present. Catlin was, and one of the other young men. They intended to go out for a good gallop. Franklin came in and made conversation with Ducane about life in the country as opposed to town. Franklin had little use for London, whereas Ducane enjoyed the theater, book shops, coffee houses, and newspapers available the day they were printed, while missing clean country air, the scent of wood smoke rather than coal smoke, and the signs of the changing seasons.

Where was Adelaide? Was she avoiding him? For that matter, where was the earl? He took breakfast early as a rule. Franklin went off to visit a man who bred spaniels, and several ladies fluttered in. He remained long enough to greet them and ask how they did before excusing himself. In the passage, the footman murmured deferentially that his lordship requested Lord Gervase join him in his study. The man eyed him speculatively.

Ducane's hackles rose. Was last night's affair already known to the servants? Ducane nodded curtly and turned on his heel.

To his tap on the door, the earl called, "Come." Lamburne's tight-lipped face signaled a stormy interview to come. "Ducane, pray sit. I feel certain you know why I asked for your presence this morning."

"Perhaps you would tell me, my lord?" He took a moment to give the skirts of his coat a flick so they would hang gracefully.

"I wonder you should ask, as you are a gentleman."

Ah. Someone had been foolish and seriously miscalculated. Well, he was no sheep to be sheared. "I trust you will explain that remark, sir."

"Lady Lamburne informed me this morning that Sophia is prostrate with shock and humiliation at the liberties you took with her last night. While they might—I say, *might*—not be inappropriate for a betrothed couple, she did not expect them or give you leave to take them." His lips compressed. "She should not have accompanied you out to the garden, of course, but she is young and sometimes heedless."

"I perceive you have had an account of the events

last night which strays far from the facts."

"Are you claiming my daughter lied?"

"As she must have realized that I would be reporting to you the situation I discovered in the garden last night, I conclude she thought she would strike first."

If the earl were a bull, he would be pawing the ground. He controlled himself. Barely. "Then perhaps you will give me your account of what occurred."

"I went out, as I often do before retiring. As I passed the oak tree by the path leading to the lake, Lady Sophia flung herself into my arms. There is no other way to describe it."

"Sophia is a lady. I cannot believe she would do something so lacking in decorum."

"Not even if she hoped to trap me into offering for her?"

Lamburne's face, which had been rather pale, flushed. He did not speak at once, as good as an admission that she might indeed try such a stratagem.

Should he leave it at that to spare the man's paternal feelings? No, Sophia's papa should know the worst, no matter how uncomfortable for all concerned. Ducane had often wondered at men who would sacrifice both happiness and good sense to allow themselves to be maneuvered into an undesirable marriage.

"There is another possibility which I wish I could keep from you, Lord Lamburne. In the long run, doing so would be no kindness. Lady Sophia did not address me by name. She cried out, 'You have come,' or words to that effect."

"Are you saying she intended to meet someone

else? Why the devil would she when you came here to court her?"

"I came to visit your home so that I might meet your daughter and decide whether we would suit."

"She has no reluctance to receive an offer from you. I would not marry any daughter of mine to a man she disliked."

"Be that as it may, last night your footman, Thomas, arrived moments after she accosted me. I can only suppose that either she intended to force me to offer for her and had your footman standing by to act as a witness or that she had come out to meet him." To offer a challenge to a guest would be as unthinkable as a guest challenging his host. Every feeling would be offended. He did not want to wound Lamburne, but if it came to a meeting, he would do so.

"She did not mention his presence." A brief hesitation, then, "It is your word against hers."

"I take it she did not mention Lady Adelaide's presence."

"Addie? My sister was there?"

"She was."

The Earl of Lamburne sat staring. "What was she doing there?"

Ducane cleared his throat. "Perhaps you should ask her, sir."

"Addie." He flapped a dismissive hand. "She would say anything to be disobliging."

"Do you dismiss unheard her testimony as a witness? Summon her, and ask her what she saw."

Lamburne strode to the door and shouted for the footman to send for Lady Adelaide. Then he took his seat behind his desk again, saying sourly, "I don't know why you would not wish to marry Sophia. You are without any significant income, and her dowry would be a prize for any man."

"I must marry for money, but I am not willing to make a marriage without any fondness or respect for my bride. While Lady Sophia may not have been at her best a few days ago, many ladies would have exercised some restraint and shown concern for the horse. As for her behavior last night..."

Sophia's papa compressed his lips but could not in honesty deny she had behaved badly when he himself had said he would speak to her about her conduct at the riding party. They sat in silence until a knock at the door was followed by its opening. Lady Adelaide stood for a moment to survey them before entering without hurry. Ducane rose. Her brother did not.

"Good day, Edward. Good day, Lord Gervase." Her greeting to him was accompanied by a slight smile. "I apologize for my appearance, but the maid was slow to bring wash water."

"Who's your maid? I'll have the housekeeper speak to her if she's slacking her duties."

"I have no permanent maid. This morning it was the under-housemaid, I think. The scullery maid has been attending me for the last week or two, and she has been very diligent. I suppose she was busy this morning."

Her uninflected revelation before a guest that the earl's sister had no maid of her own threw him off his stride. "Ah...I'll see to it." He took a deep breath. "Now, the reason I sent for you is to ask what you did after you retired to your chamber last night."

"I went out for a walk when I discovered I was not

yet tired enough to sleep."

"Can anyone confirm you did so?"

"As if we were in court? Yes. I met Lord Gervase, Sophia, and the footman, Thomas. Had I not been delayed in dressing this morning, I meant to speak to you about Sophia being out at almost midnight without a chaperon. 'Tis one thing for an old maid such as myself, but for a young girl to wander at night is unwise." She pursed her lips in a spinsterish way, and went on, "I know it is difficult to get good servants, but I cannot like that smirking fellow."

From her brother's frozen face, Ducane concluded he had begun to regret opening this Pandora's box. Perhaps he was now sorting what he had been told into a different order. At last, he inquired, "When did you come upon them, Addie?"

"I was a short distance behind Lord Gervase when I saw Sophie rush at him and throw her arms around him." From her tone, one would conclude she was reluctant to make the admission.

"Did she speak?"

"She said, 'Here you are,' or something of the sort. I was so surprised, I took less notice of her words than of her behavior."

"Could you tell if she recognized him?"

Adelaide frowned a little, meditatively. "I would say she thought she knew who she was embracing. But it was dark, and then Thomas appeared. He and Lord Gervase are much of a size."

"I see. Thank you, Addie. I have no more questions. You may go."

"Thank you, Edward. I trust you will speak to Sophia, and to Thomas, as well. Talk would do her reputation no good." The door closed softly behind her.

"On your honor, Ducane, did you and my half sister come up with that story between you?"

"I make allowance for your paternal feelings, Lamburne, or I might overcome my reluctance to meet my host over smallswords. No, Lady Adelaide and I did not concoct a Banbury story to blacken your daughter's name. When would we have had an opportunity, even if Lady Adelaide or I had a reason? Did we conspire in advance? How would we have made sure she was out in the garden at that place in the middle of the night, and the footman as well? May I also ask how this farrago of nonsense came to your attention?"

The earl sat back in his chair. "I beg your pardon. I was taken aback to learn of the—the occurrence. My wife came to me this morning before I left my chamber and informed me."

"And when did she learn of it?"

"Early this morning Sophia came to her and poured out her distress."

"Have you questioned her?"

A long pause. "I leave management of the girls to my wife. Nor did I wish to cause Sophia more humiliation."

"I advise you to question Thomas, as Lady Adelaide suggested, and your daughter also."

"I shall certainly do so."

The meeting was at an end, to Ducane's relief. Now to seek out Adelaide. What an unalloyed piece of luck she had happened to be taking the night air in time to save him.

Chapter 16

She had almost finished her breakfast when Ducane found her. A few others were still present, including Lady Charity and Sophia's plain friend, Diana, but not Lady Lamburne or Sophia.

"Lady Adelaide, I wondered if you would care to walk with me in the grounds and show me some of the pleasing views."

She patted her lips with her napkin and rose. "I would."

The men present were too deep in a discussion of horses to take notice. Charity and the other girl stared at them disbelievingly. "I'm sure Sophia will be down soon, Lord Gervase," Charity said.

"Will she. Shall we go, Lady Adelaide?"

"We shall, Lord Gervase." She smiled kindly at the girls and accepted his arm.

When they were out of the house, Ducane asked, "Do they know?"

"I don't believe so. Both girls were ignoring me and discussing the ball gowns they hoped their mamas would let them order. If they had been aware of last night's little performance, I don't believe they could have avoided knowing glances, smirks, and veiled references. Diana is my niece's lap dog, but neither Sophia nor Charity would trust her with a secret like that, I think. Did Edward say anything?"

"About our betrothal? No. He accused me of luring Sophia into the garden and compromising her and was surprised when I mentioned you and Thomas were also present. He agreed he must question Thomas and Sophia. He was relying only on what Lady Lamburne told him Sophia had claimed."

"I want to reassure you, in case you had any doubt, that I spoke only to protect you from Sophia's wiles."

"I assumed as much, and thank you for rescuing me. If anything is said, I think we should not disavow the betrothal too quickly."

"Because my family may not have given up hope yet?"

"Indeed."

"I wish I could say that shame would prevent a continued pursuit. And perhaps Edward would not press the matter, but Leonora is determined to get Sophia a husband. Her recent season must not have prospered. When they came home after Easter, Sophia boasted of all the men who courted her, but if a gentleman she met there had shown any interest, he would have been invited here. That is why I told you your suit would likely be accepted even if you did not offer until later."

"I must marry, but I won't be marrying Sophia, come what may, Lady Adelaide. When I leave, I'll take your advice and find a lady in London."

"I do wonder why no one has mentioned anything about my claim," Adelaide commented. "I have not seen Sophia since last night, but surely she must have told her mother. Or if she didn't, I can't imagine Thomas keeping it secret."

"But if Lady Sophia mentioned our betrothal, it would end any possibility of my requesting her hand."

Adelaide's cynical smile suggested otherwise. "My lord, you overestimate both Sophia's sense and her scruples." She went on more seriously, "If she succeeded in compromising you, I have no doubt that both Edward and Leonora would expect me to cede my supposed claim on you in favor of Sophia."

His heart ached at her calm acceptance of such behavior by her family. "Lady Adelaide, if your horrid niece picks the lock and creeps into my bed, I beg you will not disavow me, at least until I have managed to get myself hanged."

This startled a laugh from her. "I promise." Her laugh was wholehearted.

****

Her alleged betrothal to Ducane was not mentioned, but during the course of the day she heard other bothersome mutters. The servants were usually careful not to let on that they knew as much as the family did. This time the tidbit was too juicy, possibly because neither Sophia nor Thomas was popular. Sophia was demanding, unreasonable, and sometimes threw things at her maid. Thomas was sly and tattled about other servants' mild transgressions.

She heard them because she moved silently, making herself invisible, an ability which saved her much difficulty with her family and was useful in raiding the pantry when necessary. Sooner or later, however, one of the upper servants would hear, and then Edward's valet would murmur to him, "I hardly like to mention it to your lordship…" or Leonora's maid would whisper as she dressed milady's hair, "There's such talk about Lady Adelaide being out that night…"

Even Tabby's purr and her gentle nips did not help. Adelaide was frightened to her soul.

****

Ducane spent an evening listening to Sophia's inanities and attempts to claim his attention. She showed no consciousness of wrongdoing over her thwarted attempt, a remarkable absence of embarrassment. Did she lack any semblance of a conscience? Charity warbled a few of the less demanding popular songs, accompanied on the harpsichord by the girls' seldom seen governess/companion. Sophia had decided to ignore the betrothal or perhaps simply chose not to believe it.

Lady Adelaide put in an appearance at supper but slipped away before the men joined the ladies in the drawing room. Mayhap it was wise of her to be out of her family's sight and out of mind.

Before he could start upstairs, however, Lamburne asked him to come to his study. Ducane feared the worst, just as he had begun to relax.

The earl waved him to a chair and poured two glasses of brandy.

"Ducane, I must apologize to you for my daughter. Sophia confessed she had hoped for a clandestine meeting with you, like something in some overheated novel she had read. All an innocent girl's foolishness and no harm done, thank God." His tight-lipped face led Ducane to believe he would as soon have all his teeth drawn as make the admission.

As an apology, he found it unconvincing. If not for Adelaide, Lamburne would have expected him to marry Sophia and been pleased about it. "I trust Lady Sophia now understands how dangerous to a lady's reputation it can be to go out at night unaccompanied…when servants are free to roam the grounds."

"I have given orders to prevent any future reoccurrence," the earl grated. "I hope you can forgive my daughter her mistake."

He could, had it been an innocent error. "We all make an occasional faux pas, young or old. How fortunate Lady Adelaide was present."

Lamburne grunted. "My sister should not be out at night either."

They exchanged a few more words before Lord Lamburne excused himself to see to his duties as host. Was it possible neither Sophia nor Thomas had spoken of Adelaide's false betrothal? Ducane betook himself to his bedchamber, alternately congratulating himself on his escape and puzzled by it.

Jenkins came in as Ducane was unbuttoning his waistcoat. He went straight to the bed rather than moving to assist him.

"What's this, sir?" He held up a folded, grimy sheet of paper by one corner.

"I've no idea. It was on the bed?"

"Ay. Addressed to you."

Ducane took it. His manservant dusted his fingertips fastidiously on his breeches. The paper was cheap, the hand badly formed with a quill that needed trimming.

"An infatuated kitchen maid, no doubt."

Jenkins sniffed. "Hardly, sir. Kitchen maids cannot read or write."

My lord,
My conshence troubles me fierce that I have not

told his lordship his half sister says you are promised to her. Knowing as you would not wish to marry Lady Adalade, a payement of 50 pounds will keep me mum. I will speak to you later.

Ducane frowned at Jenkins. He had not told the man about his encounter with Sophia and Adelaide and that smirking footman, though the valet might have heard some version of the event. Apparently no one but those present knew of their supposed betrothal. He hesitated to confide in anyone when Lamburne was unaware of Lady Adelaide's claim. But Jenkins had been with him for years, and while finicky, he was trustworthy and his only ally here if one discounted Adelaide herself. "I assume there has been some talk today about an incident late last night."

"I heard a few whispers, sir, but no one talked around me…if they knew I was about. There seem to be half a dozen competing stories, and no two of the servants agree which is most likely."

Ducane raised his eyebrows interrogatively.

"Probably the witches' Sabbath is mere nonsense. The footman Thomas sneaking out to meet some female is one suggestion. The scullery maid slipping out to meet some village lad is another. A gang of housebreakers has also been rumored, as has Lady Adelaide prowling the grounds in search of prey. My apologies for the term; 'tis the one Lady Charity's maid used. I fear she reads novels. Lady Sophia is said to be keeping her chamber with either a megrim or a tantrum." Jenkins studied Ducane surreptitiously while folding the waistcoat.

His valet was a useful intelligencer about the

household. Ducane needed all the help he could get. "As it happens, I walked in the garden last night. Lady Sophia was lying in wait for me, with a footman to act as witness to my compromising of her, ah, virtue. Luckily for me, Lady Adelaide arrived and saw Sophia fling herself at me."

Jenkins tutted. "Such doings."

"Now someone is threatening to tell Lamburne that Lady Adelaide announced we are betrothed unless I pay him fifty pounds. At a guess, it's the footman."

Jenkins pursed his thin lips and ignored the latter statement. "Did she, sir?"

"Ay. She was trying to prevent my having to marry Lady Sophia. Not that I would do so now in any event. She assured me later she would disavow it as soon as I was away from Lamburne Chase."

"How could the scurvy fellow think to extort money from you to keep silent, Lord Gervase? Lady Sophia being present, she must have heard. Even if she used the footman as a witness, she wouldn't conspire with him to blackmail you, I don't think."

"I wouldn't have thought so. But Lamburne did not know of the alleged betrothal during our interview this morning when he accused me of compromising his tiresome girl. He was surprised when I informed him of the presence of witnesses and suggested he question them and his daughter. The earl had all day to question his daughter and that plaguey footman and still made no mention this evening of the 'betrothal.' He did apologize for Lady Sophia's behavior."

Jenkins scrutinized the limp, crumpled neckcloth for stains or damage to the lace. "Very odd, my lord. But of course if his lordship knew of it, Thomas could not blackmail you." He added, "That fellow is a bad piece of work."

"Quite so."

"At the servants' supper, Lady Sophia's maid let slip that her mistress was in a right taking after his lordship sent for her. I don't know if Lord Lamburne sent for Thomas. But he looked uncommon smug."

"One must conclude neither Thomas nor Lady Sophia has divulged Lady Adelaide's revelation."

Jenkins puttered over the dressing table, aligning comb and hairbrush and returning the box holding Ducane's jewelry to the bedside stand's drawer. "She might not want to admit you preferred her aunt, sir. Or she might have thought if she told her mother and father, they'd accept it and stop her trying to snare you. Or mayhap she didn't believe it?—thinking you couldn't choose Lady Adelaide over her, I'd guess, because why would you? Lord Lamburne's daughter is young, beautiful, and has a dowry. With all due respect to her, does Lady Adelaide?"

"If she did, why would she live here like a barely tolerated poor relation?"

"A point, sir. Still, Thomas revealing your betrothal to Lady Adelaide might end your chance of securing Lady Sophia."

"I have no intention of marrying her in any case, Jenkins."

"The family don't know that, nor Thomas neither, which makes him think the threat will work. And begging your pardon, sir, if his lordship was to hear, he might insist you marry his sister, mightn't he?"

Which would be a disaster, when Ducane needed to marry money. Not a great deal, perhaps, but enough to live comfortably. For Lamburne's purposes, it might hardly matter whether Ducane married his daughter or Adelaide. The Lamburne family would be connected to a marquessate if only by the earl's half sister. Another consideration occurred to him. Would the earl retaliate against Adelaide for her claim if he knew of it?

Given the family's treatment of her, Gervase could not risk her humiliation, or worse, for trying to aid him. Worse? What more could Lamburne do? No matter. Ducane owed her protection. "I think I had best not ignore the demand. I'll tell him I can pay him something, but I don't have fifty pounds with me. I wonder if he would take an IOU?"

"Probably not, sir. Besides, why bind yourself to pay more than you need to? Especially since once you're away from here, there's no need to pay him at all. He might take that set of rock crystal sleeve links. They're worth a bit, though nowhere near what he's asking, and it's not as if they're any use to you."

"No, I admit you were right, they were a mistake. They are vulgarly ostentatious."

"I would not call them vulgar, merely not in keeping with your usual taste in apparel."

Which was to say, Jenkins's taste, as Ducane had dressed like any country gentleman until he moved to town. The buttons had been an early, ill-advised purchase before Moses Black, the Blacklaw House butler, found Jenkins for him. A good manservant would know where he should order "town wear," as Black tactfully phrased it, and be able to keep it in good condition. Jenkins had been the perfect choice and taught him everything he knew about fashion and fashionable manners.

"They may appeal to him."

"I am sure they will," Jenkins said.

Chapter 17

As well they had discussed the matter, for Ducane woke to dawn light and the sound of movement in his chamber—not the girl come in to light the fire or Jenkins. Ducane sat bolt upright and threw back the bed curtains on the side nearest the door.

The footman, Thomas, bowed respectfully. "A word with you, if you please, sir."

"Ah, the author of that hopeful note. I fear you will be disappointed."

"Oh, I do trust not, sir. Fifty pounds is a trifling amount, set against Lady Sophia's fifteen thousand."

"Any dowry is in the future—"

"But it's as sure as eggs is eggs." With a familiarity Ducane found almost more offensive than the blackmail, Thomas went on, "I don't know why the young lady didn't take in London. She's pretty, and then there's the money, which 'ud make her more than acceptable to most. Must be something she does or don't do in company with eligible gentlemen."

Ducane chose to ignore the latter remarks. "Unfortunately for you, I haven't fifty pounds to spare, even if I were willing to let myself be blackmailed."

"What I hear is, you've no choice but to find a bride who comes with gelt. Your people are set on you marrying so you're not a drain on them, and I can't see you being happy to take a post as some lord's secretary or the like, as gentlemen without a penny do. Lady Sophia's your best and easiest chance. His lordship wouldn't look so low as an untitled gentleman for his daughter as a general rule, but your brother's a marquess, so you'll do."

How he would like to throw this scoundrel out of his room and preferably down the stairs.

"Now, if 'twas known you was betrothed to Lady Adelaide, who's naught but a poor relation when all's said and done, and half mad, too, that would end your chances with Lady Sophia. I reckon his lordship would be glad to rid himself of Addie."

The effrontery of the fellow, referring to a lady by a nickname. If 'twere not for the need to placate the rogue at the moment, Ducane would toss him out. "It's true I need to marry for money. The point is, I haven't got fifty pounds to give you. I tell you frankly, my situation is worse than you know"—if not as bad as he was claiming. "I will give you an IOU for fifty, payable once I'm back in London."

"I need something on account. And if you think to get away with not paying what you owe once you're in town, I'll not hold my tongue about you and Adelaide. Lord Lamburne would break your engagement to Sophia, and even if he didn't force you to marry his sister, the scandal would sink your chances with other ladies."

"I've only enough to get back to town and a few shillings more. It puzzles me how I am to find anything to pay you at once."

"Go longer between changes of horses," the footman said dismissively. "And you'll add interest into the IOU."

With an air of having stumbled upon a solution, Ducane said, "I do have a set of sleeve links with me. They are too ornate for country wear." When Jenkins saw them on his second day as Ducane's manservant, he'd loathed them on sight. Ducane himself came to agree soon after. The setting was gilt, and the clear center stone had been said to be rock crystal, surrounded by topaz stones. "Glass," Jenkins had pronounced, and put them away.

Thomas's forehead creased. "Let me see them."

Ducane retrieved the box and opened it, careful not to let the footman see its contents. Thomas took the offered sleeve links gingerly. Ducane saw his eyes widen slightly before he turned and carried them over to the window.

After a long scrutiny, he said, "I'll take them as an advance payment."

Ducane said, "Their value is eight pounds, so I'll owe you forty-two."

"Not when I sell them."

"I paid eight."

"I won't get above three. I'll take three off the fifty."

"Mayhap you'd like my silver-embroidered pink waistcoat instead." He liked the waistcoat, which was exceeding handsome with his fawn-colored suit, but it was several years old, after all.

Thomas was frowning at the links. *He's lusting for those buttons.* "Let me see the waistcoat."

Ducane rose languidly and found the waistcoat. It had been well cared for and worn seldom enough to suffer few signs of wear. The silver thread buttons in the death's head design made a brave showing. *Why call it a death's head when it's a geometrical pattern?* One of those little mysteries, he supposed. He had encountered a number of puzzles since coming to Lamburne and he did not like it…or did he? A chill ran down his spine, not accounted for by the temperature of the room: a phantasmal face half seen by moonlight and a masked lady who vanished.

The footman gave a brisk nod and said, "I'll allow you four pounds for the waistcoat and buttons, and I want a pound in addition. You can change horses less often if you go slow. Write out the IOU now, and be sure you put in that you gave me them things as part of the payment."

Let the scoundrel think he had the upper hand, much as it went against the grain to do so. Ducane scribbled out the avowal of his supposed debt and sanded it. Annoying to submit to blackmail and worse yet to deplete his already slender means, but he would not expose Adelaide to her family's wrath when she had risked it to save him from Sophia's claws.

As he was now wide awake, he washed in the water left over from last night. The weather had been warm enough that it was no penance, and he could not loll in bed until Jenkins arrived. By the time his manservant brought his chocolate, he was fully dressed.

"Sir, if I had known you meant to rise early, I would have—"

Ducane waved him to silence, recounting Thomas's visit between sips.

"Hmmm. Well, the buttons are no loss." His valet fell silent, perhaps meditating on what color waistcoat to pair with the fawn suit. Orange might be interesting. When he spoke, he said, "Once you are away from here and back in London, I think you can safely disavow this 'debt.' 'Twas was pure extortion, not a debt of honor, after all. Report the crime to the magistrate, and the next time he comes to town with the family, you can charge him."

"He would not hold his tongue, Jenkins."

"What would it matter, Lord Gervase? By the time he knew you did not mean to pay, you might be betrothed to some other lady. And what of it? Lady Adelaide making the claim would present a problem, but you say she didn't mean it. If she sticks to that, it's only a footman's word against hers and yours."

"And perhaps against Lady Sophia's. You are correct that it would not affect me much. Probably I could find some cit's girl to marry quickly and talk would not matter to her papa or her. But someone else stands to be harmed by disclosure."

"Lady Adelaide, you mean, sir? She'll deny it, won't she?" Jenkins paused, lips pursed. "But if Lady Sophia supports Thomas's claim, ay, you might be in the muck then. On the other hand, they all know Lady Adelaide's not right, so it wouldn't matter to Lamburne."

He said more sharply than he intended, "I don't believe the lady is as freakish as her relatives think. I have seen no sign of it."

"No, sir, no more do I from what I've seen of Lady Adelaide. But it's what they believe as counts, isn't it?"

True enough. But what could he do to protect her? And should he tell her about Thomas's extortion?

He saw the servants had not finished setting out the dishes on the sideboard when he went down to breakfast. They were not tardy; he was inconveniently early. Rather than disconcert them with his presence, Ducane passed by the door without hesitation. A stroll in the fresh air might help him decide whether to inform Lady Adelaide or not.

The door to the garden at the back of the house opened as he approached it, and he beheld the lady in question. She wore a gown six or eight years out of date and somewhat faded and clutched a large black cat to her bosom. If he meant to tell her at all, the time was now, given the difficulty of speaking privately with her when others were about.

"Lady Adelaide, would you care to keep me company in the garden until the servants have set out breakfast?"

She nodded and led him out, past the roses and formal garden, stopping only when they reached the informal garden. The carnations—gillyflowers— were in their glory, but the beds teemed with other flowers as well.

"You have an excellent gardener, I see."

"Yes. He was here as an under-gardener when my mother was alive. She preferred the spicy scent of these to the roses." She pointed out the African marigolds, Virginia spiderwort, and some other exotic species introduced from foreign parts. Hollyhocks, daylilies, hellebore, and poppies were familiar to him from other gardens. Native species like lady's mantle, primrose, and mallow grew at Blacklaw; his mother had little interest in gardening unless the plants were useful, like tansy.

They did not have time to linger. He told her briefly of the note and Thomas's early morning visit and was sorry to see her pale. The cat, still in her arms, patted her cheek with one paw and Ducane heard its rough purr.

"What do you mean to do?"

"I am not sure. How would you be affected if I could not pay him the full amount quickly enough to satisfy him? If he spoke out?" He could not tell her he had considered taking Jenkins's advice and reneging on his promise to pay the scoundrel the balance.

Instead of replying, she asked, "How would it affect you, Lord Gervase?"

That she avoided his question confirmed his worst fears. Humiliation and concern for her feelings tempted him to lie. The idea was repugnant; instead he told the truth. "A rumor I had jilted a lady or even raised expectations and failed to carry through might damage my chances of marrying suitably."

"Possibly, though even a second son of a nobleman may be considered a catch by families with lesser titles or by those of good lineage who are not titled. Not a few are wealthy."

"If he does not allow me leisure to find someone I can respect, I will have to take some wealthy tradesman's daughter."

"You really *must* marry so soon, sir?"

In his encounters with the lady, he had found her a good listener. He was not in the habit of sharing his thoughts, but now he needed to talk to someone, even if he appeared to be weak or a fool. "Ay, as I did not go into the military, the church, or the law or pursue some other genteel profession."

"Why did you not?"

"Marry? Or—?"

"I believe many men do put off marrying as long as

they can, as your father and brother did. I meant, why did you not take up some career?"

"My brother lived in London until he was wed. Our father had his responsibilities in Parliament and oversaw the properties the rest of the year. I assisted him to the best of my ability. When my brother did return after his marriage, he told me 'twas time I had my chance to represent the family in London and sample its fleshpots." It had been a knock-down blow for Ducane. "My father did not demand that my brother or I wed early, as he himself had not. With only two sons, he preferred I remain at our seat and assist him with the property. Robert was rather wild, as our father had been, and if he had died, I would be the heir. As the heir presumptive, I received an allowance. Robert sowed his wild oats and did not take up management of the estates until he married. His first three children were girls. I continued to receive the heir's income."

"I see," was her only comment.

"A year ago, the marchioness gave birth to a boy." They came abreast of a bench. "Would you care to sit?"

She agreed. Lamburne's old maid sister was undemanding company, unlike some ladies he could name. A scent of honeysuckle drifted on the warming air.

"Two months ago, Robert informed me that now he has an heir of his body, he will discontinue the allowance. 'Tis not unfair. He has daughters and a son to provide for. I am relieved he is being sensible, and I was a fool not to foresee my current situation. When he married and returned to Blacklaw, I should have gone into some government office, the sort where one draws a satisfactory salary and pays some genteel purse-pinched fellow to do the work. Unfortunately, we Ducanes tend to be frivolous in our youth." Robert certainly had been true to that pattern. "Though for all my father had a reputation for gambling, wenching, and dueling as a young man, by the time I was old enough to know him, he was a painstaking landlord and father. Now Robert has followed that example."

"A compelling reason for marriage, I agree, Lord Gervase, and yet I do not see why you must rush into the parson's mousetrap." She produced the bit of cant with amusement in her voice. Then she was serious again. "You really have no better prospect than Sophia? Some young lady or widowed lady living near Blacklaw? Or someone in town?"

He sighed. "None I can think of. My choices are limited."

Some of his mother's and father's remarks had led him to believe class distinctions had been far more rigid thirty or forty years ago. The boundaries were less clearly marked now, but while he might secure a post managing properties for some wealthy landowner, working for another in a menial position would be almost as bad as going into trade. Serving as an army officer or in some government post was respectable. Little disgrace attached to marrying money.

"I have five months, or mayhap six or seven if I can make my funds stretch and sell some trinkets." And if Thomas did not continue to blackmail him. Exposure might not affect Ducane much, but if Adelaide feared revelation of her announcement, he owed it to her to continue to pay. "Four months takes me to November, when the season begins with the Parliamentary term. With a number of prospective brides to choose from, I might be able to find one quickly, but I could hardly expect to woo her and wed her before January, if then."

"There is no hope your brother would give you a little longer?"

"I will not ask it of him, when he has already been generous." Robert would let him live on the estate, would probably buy him a new suit when his clothing became too threadbare. All the same, he would be a poor relation. His pride would not permit him to dwindle into a hanger-on, what he had heard a plain Northumbrian merchant term a "ne'er-do-well." Robert would not let him starve if he could not find a bride with a dowry immediately. But Gervase would be a dependent, and even if his brother gave him an allowance, he did not suppose he would be able to afford to pay the forty-five pounds. One mustn't forget the interest, either.

"If you can continue to live at Blacklaw or Blacklaw's London house, I don't understand why you cannot take a little more time to find a bride. I spent only one season in London, but I doubt a rumor or two would damage your value as a connection to a marquess. Unless you have significant, pressing debts?"

"No."

"Then why—?" She answered for herself the question she had begun. "Are you concerned that what Thomas can reveal would harm me?"

She was too perceptive. "That did occur to me."

A long pause ensued while she stared at her hands clasped demurely in her lap. The cat, near her feet, batted at a passing butterfly but did not pursue it.

"I dislike to ask this, Lord Gervase, but how much do you need as a dowry?"

"Not a great deal. I lost interest in town life years ago. I do not play deep, as my mother's father lost much of their family's fortune and lands by games of chance. Long after his death, she still bitterly resents his carelessness." He did not blame her. Although she had already been married to his father, her younger sister had had to settle for marriage to a squire.

"Pray, let me put it another way. What would content you?"

Who but Lady Adelaide would ask such a question? "A manor with sufficient income that I could educate and settle my children, if any, comfortably."

"I would not have guessed. You seem such a complete man about town."

"I have been. But there's nothing new in a continual round of balls, the theater, parties, entertainments at Vauxhall, and all the rest, and no challenge. One does the same things over and over with the same acquaintances. One drinks too much, makes foolish wagers, talks about the same topics, enlivened only by some new bit of gossip perhaps. One cannot escape town life even when riding, as every other gentleman is riding in the same park." The words were on his lips before his brain considered them. "Lady Adelaide, if I did not need to marry at least that well, I would suggest we make our betrothal real."

He had discomposed her. She sat searching his face until he began to be uncomfortable. What on earth possessed him? He never spoke without thinking, and in London, he seldom spoke seriously to casual acquaintances. True, she was an interesting woman, poised, intelligent, and not in the common way, either.

She was memorable rather than young or pretty. Easy to talk with, almost like a friend.

Chapter 18

The idea was so unexpected, she could do nothing but stare at him. He must be jesting. "Are you serious, sir?"

"I am. We have much in common. Alas, we must both marry money."

She was silent while a blackbird sang in a nearby tree. He was a fortune hunter, of course, a class of suitors usually best avoided. But he admitted it frankly, which was in his favor, and given what he had told her, his situation was understandable. Marriages were made every day to secure wealth for a son or a titled husband for a daughter. Ducane had been courteous, had paid attention to her when he thought her dependent upon her brother's charity. He had had no reason to try to impress her when he had come to court her niece. He could not know of her recent inheritance or of her other resources, when even Edward was ignorant of them.

He was idle and a fop, but he was also intelligent, pleasant, and not physically repellent. Was he a gambler or libertine? She saw no evidence of these faults, and neither would bother her much. He would not be able to gamble away her money, and the other did not matter. Men had mistresses, that went without saying. She did not expect devotion.

If she married him, Ducane would be saved from penury and from Sophia. His was the only offer she was likely to receive. She would be free of Edward and Leonora, and safe—as much as any woman ever was, at least. From what she had seen of him, she did not believe Ducane would have her confined as a madwoman, whereas Edward might. She could not bear to think of what might become of Tabby if she were not free to protect her.

Frowning slightly—in spite of oft-repeated advice to ladies that doing so would cause wrinkles—she asked, "Are you sure, Lord Gervase?"

"I know I must. Wouldn't you leave your brother's home for one of your own if you were able?"

She ignored the question as rhetorical. "If I had a manor and perhaps even a small dowry, *would* you be willing to marry me?"

"I've said so. Believe me, ma'am, I'm not fool enough to say such a thing if I didn't mean it."

She looked down at her hands clenched white-knuckled in her lap. "What made you think me a poor relation?" Admittedly, she was treated like one by her family.

"Why, the fact you are unmarried."

If Ducane was willing to put up with her age, lack of beauty, and reputation in exchange for a country gentleman's home and income, both she and Ducane would get what they needed from the marriage. Having never expected to marry for love, she would not miss its absence. They could have a comfortable life together, even if he were not as exciting as Tam Lin. Her fascinating cavalier of the dark garden would never have married her, no matter how well they had got on, because only a man who was desperate for a wife with money would court her.

"As it happens, Lord Gervase, I recently heard from my man of business that I have been left a manor in Northumberland. I have read the will, and the property produces enough income to live on quietly in the country. I also have a small dowry, though not enough to make me a desirable bride to most." Would her next admission disappoint him, perhaps make him retract his offer? "And that only if Mr. Tate approves my suitor. My father trusted him not to turn it over to a man who would squander it."

"We would be near my family, then, if not yours."

"The distance from my brother and his wife would not be a consideration for me." She stole a glance at him, which he met.

"If we married, it would solve your problem and my own," he said slowly. "You understand, I would want children."

That thought was worrisome. But she would try to cherish a child if she had one. At worst, children left to nurses, governesses, and tutors did thrive, making it a minor concern. "I have no objection to children."

She paused. His willingness to live like a country gentleman did not mean he knew anything of agricultural matters. However, he need not, as Tate said the land was competently managed by the bailiff. At a pinch, Adelaide knew a good deal about the subject. She had paid attention to what her brother and his bailiff did at Lamburne Chase, only partly from boredom. *Nam et ipsa scientia potestas est.* Knowledge is power, according to Sir Francis Bacon's dictum. Her nephews' tutor had set them to writing the quotation out in a fair hand a hundred times for the crime of not taking their studies seriously.

"You wouldn't have to trouble yourself over the tenants and lands. A bailiff has overseen it for many years, even before Lady Creighton's husband died, I'm told. Living in London and not brought up to…" She had spoken unwarily. How was she to end the sentence?

"Not brought up to be the heir? Whatever my reputation as a man about town, I do know something about managing a country property. Marriage might serve us both well."

Her smile felt tremulous. "You should consider carefully. My dowry is only two thousand pounds. My father did not want me to attract fortune hunters, and the property and investments must be secured to me in the settlement documents. Your family is unlikely to approve. I speak too freely, am reclusive, odd, and far past my youth. Your friends will regard it as a mésalliance. My family will be furious, because of Sophia. I will understand if you don't wish to pursue this, this…"

"Negotiation? I would be happy to marry you. I've never cared much for the opinions of the ill-informed. Or even the well-informed." He quirked an eyebrow. "Those of our class marry for advantage of one sort or another. I think we enjoy each other's company. At least, I enjoy yours."

"You are the first person with whom I have been completely at ease since my old governess left."

"Would you be willing to accept my hand in marriage, Lady Adelaide?" Even if he had not liked her, how could he fail to pity anyone who made such an admission?

"I would, if you can accept me with all my disadvantages. I will lend you the will and Tate's letter.

He is my trustee and man of business. Naturally, you will want to verify the financial arrangements before committing yourself. Then I will write to Tate, giving him permission to discuss them with you."

He regarded her gravely. The day, his whole future, suddenly looked brighter. She must recognize as he did that their lives would alter dramatically if they married. Where they lived, how they spent their days—and nights—things they had never thought of. They would have a home. Children, God willing.

She was biting her lip. Was she having second thoughts? He was not; the idea of wedding Adelaide Setbury seemed increasingly desirable and not only for her property. There was something slightly untame about her. *Feral.* The thought was oddly attractive.

"Adelaide? May I call you Adelaide? What troubles you?"

"If you are certain you wish to marry me, please do not tell anyone of our betrothal or of my inheritance, either. Sophia must have dismissed my earlier claim as a mere stratagem because why would you tie yourself to a penniless old maid when you could have her? But if she hears we really are promised…"

"By George, no. It doesn't bear thinking of." He could easily imagine fits of screaming hysterics.

She went on, "Which means no one at all can hear of it. You will wish to write to your family, but please do not do so yet lest it get back to Leonora and Edward." She continued inexorably, "You need not regard our agreement as final until you have assured yourself I am worth marrying."

"My dear Lady Adelaide," he protested. Had she been the sort to try to trap him into marriage, she could have married years ago.

"Now we should go back before we are missed."

As she stood, her cat uncoiled itself from its place by her feet and looked up in a hopeful manner as its pink tongue flicked out. With a glance at her pet, Lady Adelaide said, "Yes, Tabby, breakfast next. Shall we shake hands on our agreement?" She offered her hand to Ducane.

A handshake was likely to be more acceptable to Lady Adelaide than a kiss, though he trusted they would arrive at kissing if they did marry. As they walked back toward the house, he could not resist asking, "Are tabby cats not usually striped?"

She laughed. "They are. But my Tabby is named for my old governess, whose given name was Tabitha. She was always kind to me."

No one was in the dining room yet when they entered, except one footman standing ready to assist the guests. His eyes followed Adelaide as she entered, cat at her heels. Ducane watched with interest as she added portions of several meats, a roll, some fruit, and a dish of cream to a plate, then hurried out, Tabby in close pursuit.

Later, he caught sight of her strolling around the lake with several of the older ladies. He did not see her again until supper. Ducane controlled his curiosity, waiting for the evening's amusements to break up. By unspoken agreement, he and Adelaide kept their distance, apart from common civilities. He spent the time playing piquet with Sir Archibald to avoid Sophia, who still cherished hopes. He would continue to lock his door. Young Catlin sat beside Adelaide for half an hour at a distance from the other groups, talking with her in a low voice. Probably pouring out his heart to a sympathetic older woman. If he were asking for advice, Adelaide might give good counsel.

He did wonder how she would contrive to get the documents to him unseen. Then one of the men who had gone outdoors to smoke a pipe re-entered to announce, "There's a fine display of the aurora borealis, if anyone cares to see it." Three-quarters of the guests made an immediate exodus from the drawing room, leaving behind the more staid or the more elderly. Adelaide allowed herself to be caught up in it; Ducane followed, one eye on Adelaide and one on Sophia, to keep out of her way.

Some of the group took the opportunity to move apart in pairs so those who had come out of doors to admire the celestial display were somewhat dispersed. His betrothed halted at the back of the migration, making it easy for him to stop beside her. While everyone's attention was on the rippling curtains of pale green light, she passed him the letter and the will. Once they were safe in his coat's pocket, he spoke close to her ear. "May I escort you back to the house?"

"I will stay out for a little while, but you should make your escape while I guard your flank against my niece."

He retrieved the papers from his coat as Jenkins helped him out of it. Ducane had reached his chamber unmolested, having gone upstairs with several others.

"You'll not be offering for Lady Sophia, sir?" The valet set aside the coat for brushing while Ducane began unbuttoning his waistcoat. The third button from the top had frayed slightly. Annoying, if Jenkins did not have a replacement.

"What makes you ask?" Ducane inquired cautiously. Could there already be talk about him and Adelaide?

"You will recall I said the servants don't criticize the family, sir? The dam broke. The grooms as came with the guests were talking at the servants' table about the young lady killing her horse. Lady Sophia, I mean. They'd already passed the story on to their masters if they didn't know and down in the public house in the village, I wouldn't wonder. Once they'd let it out, the mischief was done. The Lamburne stable hands were right put about over it anyway and don't reckon as it's disloyal to repeat what was being talked of by everyone else."

"I'm surprised it took this long to come out."

Jenkins lingered after he was in his shirt and banyan. "Is it true the Lady Adelaide was carrying a great long knife, sir?"

"She did have a knife, yes. You need not talk about it to others."

"I don't need to say a word. It's been whispered about. Our Robbie"—Ducane's groom—"says she's a right'un, and the head groom here wouldn't say no. Not much sympathy for Lady Sophia."

"You may go, Jenkins. I mean to sit up a while."

"Very good, sir."

He glanced over Tate's letter, then went on to Lady Creighton's last will and testament. If anything, Tate's summary understated Lady Adelaide's inheritance. From the attached inventory, apart from the manor, there were herds of sheep and cattle, a good deal of jewelry, and a pair of small properties, one in Surrey and the other in Kent, both leased out. When she gave him the letter, Adelaide had murmured they would talk if he agreed after reading the will.

In spite of having sat up late, Ducane did not sleep at once. How would Robert and their mother respond to the news? Adelaide might seem an unusual choice, especially if they had heard about her mother. On the other side of the coin (and how appropriate that metaphor was), her inheritance of a manor made her a better choice than Sophia. Besides, his mother would have no patience with Sophia's tantrums and silliness.

He did not doubt Adelaide was correct about her family opposing their match. They would be furious at Sophia losing her chance, certainly. They might well be angry that Adelaide intended to marry just when she had received a substantial inheritance. An old maid's connections might feel that they had a right to be her heirs.

When his mind finally stopped churning, he waked half a dozen times from troubling dreams: waiting at the altar for Adelaide, who never came, or marrying her to discover the will was a forgery. He knew them for what they were—suppressed worry revealed when his waking mind was absent. One dream was different. He and Adelaide were standing before the parson. When Ducane turned his head to look at his plain, peculiar bride, the woman beside him turned into the mysterious being who bent over him as he lay on the dewy grass and then into Queen Mab. Both encounters now seemed more enchanting than enchantment. But the first had been the product of drink and a blow to the head. Hadn't she? If she had been real, she would have turned out to be an impossible choice—a well-spoken milkmaid or wandering madwoman, with no dowry at all. The second remained a tantalizing mystery.

Chapter 19

Lady Adelaide was engaged in conversation with Sir Peter and young Catlin when Ducane came down to breakfast. She smiled and asked if he knew what pleasures were in store. The first thing that came to mind was not one he could mention in mixed company and in any case must be postponed until marriage. His prospective bride-to-be might be plain of face, but she had a trim figure, neither too thin nor plump.

"I have not heard."

"Some of the gentlemen mean to get up a cricket match, and some of the ladies will take part in archery. A few plan to ride to the village, as the church possesses some interesting features."

"And which do you and Sir Peter and Catlin plan to do?" He suspected Adelaide would be going to the village, where it would be easy for them to discuss matters with some privacy.

"I intend to go to the village. Lady Lamburne will remain here with those who prefer more sedentary amusements. Lady Sophia will join the archers, and Lady Charity wants to watch the cricket match."

Sir Peter took a last swallow of his ale. "I'm off to ride home for the day to meet with my bailiff. I'll take my leave of you now until supper. Lady Adelaide, gentlemen, 'servant."

"I am torn between church and cricket." Catlin's

rueful grin at Lady Adelaide hinted that in a few years, he would attract young ladies by the score. "But I cannot resist a chance to play cricket."

"Lady Adelaide, I would enjoy seeing the church."

"Very good, Lord Gervase. We will leave at eleven and take our dinner at the inn. I am told that sitting on benches to eat simple fare is not to be missed."

The party was oddly assorted. Most of the younger men preferred the cricket match. A few chose to cheer on the ladies' archery contest and a few, with some of the older men, meant to get up an informal horse race. The village expedition was limited to the more sedate, most of them above thirty, married, and fond of walking. One of these was Lady Smythe. An older gentleman was interested in ruins, having found a few relics in a mound on his property. The youngest lady was Miss Diana Jelliffe, Sophia's bosom-bow, he thought. When Sophia was not exercising her wiles on foolish young men (and himself), she and Diana often had their heads together.

Fortunately, the group broke into parts on arriving at the village. Adelaide whispered to him, "Say you wish to see the water mill." In the absence of other members of the Setbury family, wandering away from the others with Adelaide proved not to be difficult.

Obligingly, he voiced an interest in the mill. The others scattered to the church and the remains of the old chapel, to the village shops, to the smithy, to a scenic prospect. As he and Adelaide drifted away, Diana's head swiveled to follow them. With some sprightly remark, Lady Smythe linked arms with the girl and strolled off with her toward the shops.

As they rambled down the lane, Ducane said, "I

read the document last night. It is as Tate represented it."

"The income from the manor is not a great amount," she pointed out. "You have been accustomed to much more, I'm sure."

" 'Tis more than I received as Blacklaw's heir. Granted, it would not support a couple in the style expected in London's beau monde. Is that the life you wish, my lady?"

"I would not, but would you be willing to give it up, Lord Gervase?"

"Despite my reputation, I would prefer to live in the country. We might stay in London for a month every year or every other year, perhaps." He quirked an eyebrow. "You would need new gowns and a new riding habit and boots occasionally. So would I. Boots, I mean. I do not think a habit would become me."

Her choke of laughter was cut off quickly. "Are you sure you would wish to be seen with me?"

Lady Adelaide had endured years of scornful treatment. "Whose opinion will you trust? Your brother's, when you are aware he resented you because of your mother, which has nothing to do with you? Or that of Sir Peter, Catlin, Lady Smythe, and myself, among others? Including my groom, incidentally? Have any of the guests been discourteous? Leave me out of the reckoning, if you will, because I have a selfish reason to court you. The others accept you for yourself, and your people know that now."

"Do you think so? I believe their opinion of me is set and will never change." She stared at the mill pond.

He smiled at her wryly. "Then let us marry and live our own lives. Now, shall we walk a little farther down this lane to give the others time to tire of the church and walking and go to the inn?"

As they continued along the road, he asked, "As you do not wish your family to find out at once, when shall we announce our decision?"

Her hand trembled on his arm. "We must not tell them during the house party. Will you not wish to see Tate before committing yourself?"

"His letter and the will speak for themselves. What did you intend to do if we had not agreed to marry?"

"I would have written Tate to order the house be made ready for me at once, and then I would have packed, arranged for a hired coach, and announced my departure the morning I left. If you are sure you need not see Tate, my letter to him will include news of my betrothal and give instructions about the house."

He rested his hand on hers where it clung to his arm. The tension was still there. "Would you have been able to keep your preparations to move to your manor secret?"

"No one pays much attention to my doings, unless I am vexing them in some way. The scullery maid likes me, and together she and I could bring down the trunks I would need, the older ones no one cares about, and I could pack them. If anyone did ask, I would have said I meant to store some of my older gowns. Apart from clothing, I would take my cat's basket and a few small things which would fit in a trunk: my sewing box, a few trifles from my childhood, some books, and my mother's portrait. I need nothing more. The house is furnished."

Ducane studied the half of her face he could see. She was looking down pensively at the path.

"Could we elope?" she asked.

Elopement was a shocking thing: a scandal, an embarrassment to both families, and it might affect their children, if any. He would have argued against it, if her hold on his arm did not suggest a drowning woman clutching at rescue.

"Are you afraid that if I leave, I won't return?"

"No! Not that." As the day was warm, she had not worn a cape or mantle. Her rapid breathing made her bosom heave enticingly.

"My dear Lady Adelaide..." He was searching for words to reassure her, when everything he had seen and heard at Lamburne came together. "You fear to let them know lest they try to stop you."

"One would think they would be glad to be rid of me." She turned to face him, her eyes blinking. He had seen something similar before a lady burst into tears.

"Here, we will step into this spinney for a moment." He led her off the lane, fortunately not much used, and into the grove to give her time to compose herself. "Do you fear they might avenge their wounded pride by taking it out on you?" Stupid question; of course they would.

"Or Tabby."

She gave a little choke, the kind presaging a sob rather than suppressed laughter, and he did the only thing a courteous man could do. He took her in his arms and held her. He could not recall ever having to comfort someone before and did not know what to say. She leaned into him, her cheek against his shoulder. Her hair smelled like rosemary and tickled his nose.

She did not feel soft under his hands: what corseted lady could? The sensation was quite different from holding one of his mistresses. She would be at least half undressed and any contact between them would be no more than a prelude to his bedding the woman. This was different. He liked and respected Lady Adelaide in spite of her peculiarities. Mayhap because of them: she was witty, sharp-tongued, vulnerable without being weak, and a puzzle to him. Marrying Lady Adelaide would be no sacrifice. He took a deep breath, dropped his arms, and stepped back. She sniffed and composed her expression.

"Then we must prevent your family from retaliating until you are mine to protect. If you wish to marry the way you would have gone to your manor, with no advance notice, we would need a license. If you are willing to marry in the village church, it needn't be a special license. I could obtain one after leaving, return to call upon you, and we could go to the church and be married."

"Would you have to leave to get a license?"

"My knowledge of marriage licenses is limited. Someone would have to make the application and post the bond."

"I could ask Tate."

"The mail is slow. If he could obtain one, my stay here might have come to an end before it arrived."

"No, please. If you must go, take me with you. If you decide you don't wish to marry me, at least take me to Tate."

"Adelaide, what is it you fear? I understand your concern that your brother might try to dissuade you from marrying me, and that your sister-in-law and nieces might be unkind, but is that anything you have not suffered before?"

She made a small sound in her throat, like an animal caught in a trap, rending his heart. "They have told our neighbors and people in the village again and again that I am odd and unnatural."

"Your neighbors have seen that you are no such thing."

"If my brother sent me to a madhouse, would they intervene?"

At first he could scarce believe he had heard correctly. Then he feared he could not conceal his anger in spite of years of masking both boredom and impatience. Somehow he must have done, as she seemed not to notice his reaction. "Has he threatened to do so?"

"Not he. Leonora did, once. And between your refusing to marry Sophia and I having imposed my presence on them—which I have seldom done before—I fear she might insist and he would agree."

"Then write to Tate requesting he get the license. Would he send it by messenger if you asked?"

"I think he would come himself as we have never met. Lord Gervase, even if he sent the license by courier, is there enough time before you must leave?"

"I would not care to trust to the mail. I received a letter from an acquaintance a day or two since, asking if I cared to go to Bath with him on my return to London, Bath being cooler and less dirty than town. I will write to him to decline and send it by my groom, letting it be supposed to be a matter of some urgency. If you write to Tate, I will have my fellow deliver that as well and wait for Tate's reply and the license, if we are lucky." He saw her face cloud suddenly with some frightening or worrisome thought.

"What troubles you, Lady Adelaide?"

She swallowed. "I must be honest with you so you are not taken unawares when you hear of the scandal. You may not wish to marry me once you know of it."

"Scandal?" He had not heard from his mother in reply to his letter. Of course Lamburne would not mention anything discreditable in the family.

"It's an old one, mayhap forgotten by most, but Edward and his wife are all too well aware of it. They have been worried about finding husbands for the girls, and for my nephews, too. Were you given a tour of the portrait gallery?"

He had hardly set foot on solid ground since arriving. Like the old tales his nurse had told him, things simply happened without explanation and with no clear connections between them. A rational man was lost.

"I was. You have a long line of distinguished forebears. The age of some of the paintings is impressive. One looked like a Hans Holbein."

"You need not be overwhelmed, Lord Gervase. All the earlier ones, from Queen Elizabeth's reign and before, are modern. Forgeries, if you will. My Lamburne grandmother commissioned them from a young artist. He studied paintings of that age for details of clothing and the like, and produced portraits of our earlier ancestors. A ridiculous vanity but harmless. Do you recall a painting of my mother?"

There had been so many. He remembered Lord Lamburne's portrait, showing him as a young man, and his and Lady Lamburne's portrait with their children, the marchioness's expression as smug as a cat's that has found the cream pitcher. His visual memory was reliable as a rule. Adelaide was the child of the late lord's second marriage, so a painting of the second Lady Lamburne should have come before the one showing Edward Lamburne on his accession to the title. "My lamentable memory has failed me, I fear. Was it a picture of both your parents together?"

"No. You need not wrack your brain. My mother's likeness does not hang there now. Edward took it down on returning from Papa's funeral. He let me have it, which was kind of him. I feared he would burn it."

Ducane waited. He could not think of a response that would not be graceless at best. When he did not probe, she continued. "My mother was an actress. Her mother was French, her father Scottish. I need not tell you, I suppose, how actresses and Scots are viewed by society. I can't think how the family greeted news of the marriage. I understand Edward smashed an oxblood-red Chinese vase on learning of it. Augusta, my oldest half sister, has never forgiven him, for she particularly admired that piece. The last time she visited, she was still complaining that my father should have caned him. More than thirty years ago!"

"Poor child."

"Yes, I know it made Edward's school days torture. A caning would be nothing to it. When I think of how he could have treated me once our father was gone, I am amazed at his forbearance and half sick with relief and guilt."

"I meant you, Lady Adelaide."

She had not been looking at him. She might feel that facing him would be too intimate. "I? My brother is generous. When I outgrew my pony, he bought me a horse. I am provided with pin money and more clothing than I need."

This time he heard dry humor. "Little enough care, I think."

"When I was grown, he could have given me in marriage to some horrid old man or—or a poxy roué, and I would have had no choice but to submit or run away, unless Tate heard of it and was able to intervene to prevent it."

"I do not think I could be as forgiving of the earl's and his lady's unkind behavior and remarks, if they were addressed to me."

"You are a man. You have freedom."

Not in his circumstances. However, as she had pointed out, women led more circumscribed lives. They were generally unable to earn or manage their money and needed protection. Except for females like Bertha Foote, owner of the coaching inn near Blacklaw, who ruled her business like Queen Elizabeth, though he could not quite envision Elizabeth felling an insolent stable hand with one blow of her fist. Strange that women of the lower classes often had a degree of freedom seldom possible for ladies.

"I have heard that confession is good for the soul. Now that you have shared your secret, do you not feel better?" She need not know he had already heard about her mother.

"I do. You need not feel bound to marry me now you know my discreditable origin."

His mother and brother might care about an ancient *on-dit*. He himself did not give a rap. Adelaide was an earl's daughter. She was an heiress. Equally important, her company would be easily endurable. "Lady Adelaide, I know men and women of the most impeccable breeding who are petty, dishonest, stupid, and a disgrace to their families. No number of worthy or even saintly ancestors can make up for bad character. Conversely, to blame you for your mother's background is unfair and I will not do it. Please do me the honor of marrying me."

The relief and gratitude dawning in her face made him feel like an impostor.

"Pray, do not mistake me for Sir Lancelot or any other of King Arthur's knights. Our marriage will benefit us both. I do think you might call me by my given name rather than my courtesy title."

"Sensible is preferable to gallantry, I believe. Though if the license does not come, I hope you will carry me off over your saddle bow, Gervase."

Since he met her, she had smiled politely, wryly, and ironically. This mischievous curving of her lips displayed the points of her eyeteeth.

"We would be more comfortable in my coach. My brother's coach, which I borrowed," he amended. "May I kiss you, Adelaide? To seal our bargain?"

"Yes."

He tilted up her face with one index finger under her chin and touched his lips to hers. His first kiss had been with a dairy maid, and she had initiated it. He could still recall its thrill: revelatory, terrifying, and fraught with possibility. Adelaide's lack of response disappointed him until he remembered that she might never have been kissed. From a combination of his own shyness and lack of opportunity, then from awareness of the danger of compromising a young lady, he had never bestowed a girl's first kiss.

He kept the kiss gentle. Ladies did not enjoy

having their lips mashed against their teeth, according to one of his early mistresses. "Or slobbering," she added, "at least until later in the proceedings."

He wanted her to enjoy her maiden experience of a kiss as he had done with that rustic seductress. Pulling her into a close embrace now might panic her as his earlier chaste hug had not. Instead he ran one hand down her back to her waist. She arched slightly, like a cat, though the smooth fabric of her gown over her rigidly boned stays was less rewarding than contact with fur over flesh. Her lips parted under his, and the tips of her eyeteeth grazed his lip. His well-tailored breeches were suddenly too tight in one salient area; if he did not release her, his enjoyment of their embrace might soon be entirely too evident.

Adelaide pulled away slowly, possibly in surprise. Neither fright nor offense, anyway. She gazed at him owlishly. "Oh, my stars. That was interesting."

"I hope you also found it pleasurable. I certainly did."

She laughed suddenly and blushed like a young girl.

Chapter 20

What an odd experience! She hardly knew how to think about it: the entire walk with Ducane, not merely the kiss. He could gentle a horse with those hands she had felt even through layers of clothing and her stays. Marriage to Lord Gervase might be a source of pleasures other than freedom from her family and being mistress in her own home. Whilst the world might consider him frivolous and effete, she felt safe with him. Under the foppish clothing, the man was kind and something else she could not name.

They met the others at the inn where food had been set out for them in a private parlor. She and Gervase did not sit together. He had Diana on one side and the amateur antiquarian on the other. She herself sat by Lady Smythe and a rather deaf lady who had come to sketch the church.

On returning to Lamburne, some of the men decided to have a game of billiards. She cherished Ducane's pained expression at mention of the billiards table in the library, wondering whether its cause was the thought of books displaced or distaste for such a modern innovation. He excused himself to write a letter he must send the next day.

The ladies wanted to rest and change before supper and the evening's activities, and Adelaide needed to write a letter of her own. Together, she and Lord

Gervase could escape: she from her family and he from his circumstances. All that would make the prospect of marriage more satisfactory was if her affianced husband were her Tam Lin instead.

Mr. Tate,

I am writing to make known to you that I intend to marry Lord Gervase Ducane, brother of the Marquess of Blacklaw. As you know, I have not been happy living with my half brother (nor he with me) but have been denied the ability to live in my own establishment. Lord Gervase and I will wed, whether you agree to release my dowry or not.

Do not be misled by the opinion I understand is commonly held in town that he is no more than a coxcomb. After all, my own family has always maintained that I am stupid and unreasonable. You know this from Lamburne's own communication to you shortly before I came of age, proposing that he should take over management of the funds left to me, as your guardianship would terminate at my birthday. I know my father's instructions to you were not to inform my half brother of my finances. I hope I need not add that you must not tell him of my betrothal either.

Please advise the housekeeper and butler at Dale Tower to make all ready for us, as we mean to move there in the near future.

Now, I have two more requests to make of you which are a little outside your usual services. I wish you to procure a special license for my marriage to Lord Gervase Everleigh Ducane if it is possible to do so (neither Lord Gervase nor I know if it is necessary for one of the parties to apply). In response to the question you are surely asking, no, I dare not let Lamburne or the others know of my plans.

Second, will you come to Lamburne? Lord Gervase's man will wait to bring the license back if you can get it, or your reply if you cannot or will not, but I should like you to come with it, if you can do so immediately, as the gathering will soon break up.

Your most obliged,

Lady Adelaide Elspeth Setbury

From a window overlooking the stable yard early in the morning, she saw Ducane send his groom off on his mission with both letters. Afterward, Harris, the head groom, approached and spoke briefly to him. He would not need to assure Ducane his horse would be cared for while his own man was away. Was the exchange meant to show she was held in some regard in the stable? Harris had always been kind to Adelaide for her father's sake. He had given her riding lessons on her first pony and remembered her from before her father's death, before anyone thought her strange. Since the riding party, the stable hands were quick to saddle her horse. They smiled, commented on the weather, and wished her a good ride…as long as none of the family were present.

Ducane intended to ride. She would go out to meet him after she ate a quick breakfast. Edward was already at the table. The other guests were either still asleep or else breakfasting in their bedchambers. Her half brother waited while the footman poured her chocolate and filled her plate. When it was before her, Edward gestured impatiently for the man to leave. "Addie, I've been informed that you spent a good deal of time alone with Ducane yesterday."

She raised her eyebrows. "He was the only one who wished to look at the watermill. He had a curiosity to see if the one at Blacklaw could be improved. I felt it my duty to escort him. The rest of the party split into several groups according to their interests." Diana Jelliffe was the likely informant: Diana to Sophia to Leonora to Edward.

"An unmarried lady cannot go off with a man without causing talk. Even you know that much. What if he had offered you insult?"

With a bland, meaningless smile, she said, "Edward, I am an ape leader, too old and too ugly to attract the sort of attention I assume you mean. If you mean some other form of insult, I have been subject to that sort for years, both from my family and from the servants." Adelaide could not believe she had uttered that last statement. Her appetite abruptly deserted her.

He reddened but did not contest the statement. There were limits to his hypocrisy. "You should have taken one of the grooms with you."

"I have ridden and walked to the village without a maid or groom in attendance often without your protesting. Or Leonora's, either."

"This time is different. I suppose you know Ducane must marry for a dowry and came to court Sophia. If he compromised you, he could not marry you to make it right, which would damage his reputation."

And what of my reputation? That would not weigh heavily with Edward as long as it could be hushed up. She dismissed his lack of concern for her. His assumption that Ducane could not marry her confirmed what she had long suspected: her brother did not know the truth.

She had never questioned the size of her dowry until she was taken to London and heard of young ladies with dowries of five or ten thousand pounds or more, compared to which a mere two thousand was a pittance. She had believed, indeed, knew, her papa had loved her. She could not be mistaken in that. Had he been in financial difficulties? She could not write to her trustee without Edward or Leonora questioning her about her reason for writing, and going to his office was equally out of the question.

When she was one and twenty, Tate began to write her with information about her finances. The late Lord Lamburne had indeed dowered her poorly, but he had also left a trust fund with substantial investments which produced an excellent income, part of which was banked and part invested. Tate explained it thus: "The amount of your dowry could not be concealed from his heir, nor could the smaller trust monies which pay for your maintenance. Your father did not care to leave you dependent upon your brother. The greater fund, outside the assets of the earldom and not left by will, is unknown to the present Lord Lamburne."

She was an heiress. The knowledge had not made a great difference in her life until now. Between the insignificance of her known dowry and her lack of social ease, she had had no prospect of marrying. She could have lived alone happily, but Tate refused to release any money to her so she could set up her own residence. She did wonder if the funds set aside for her maintenance would revert to the earldom if she died unmarried, which might explain Edward's failure to find her a husband. She could not bear to ask Tate.

"Whyever would he do so, Edward? Do you think he is utterly without discrimination about females when he is finicking in all other matters? Too, I am already an embarrassment and a scandal because of my supposed reclusiveness and difficult nature and my mother. I dare say being compromised would not add much fuel to the fire."

"I am only trying to protect you, Addie."

With a herculean effort, she suppressed any trace of cynical amusement. "When I returned from London unmarried and with no affianced husband, one of the stable hands attempted to molest me. Harris stopped him before any real harm was done, beat him, and threatened worse if he dared move before Harris informed you."

"Why did I not hear of this?" Her half brother's brows drew together.

"Harris escorted me back to the house, knowing the groom would flee. You would have turned the man off. You would not have sent for the magistrate because of the potential scandal. Harris punished him and made sure he would leave the neighborhood as fast as he could hobble."

"Harris should have informed me."

"I begged him not to tell you. If I learned anything in London, it was that when a man takes liberties with a female, 'tis always thought to be her fault."

He harrumphed, and his face turned as red as a chicken's comb because he could not deny it.

"You would have been angry and worried and what more could you have done, Edward? Harris provided me the knife I have carried ever since and instruction in how to use it and some other ways of dealing with an importunate man, too. Far more effective in securing my safety from physical insult than your shouting and insisting I always be accompanied by a footman or groom who might himself have been a danger."

"I can't believe any of our servants would risk their livelihood by imposing on a lady." Edward exhaled sharply.

"Believe it," she said dryly. She was actually arguing with Edward. Her newly discovered courage came from knowing she could escape.

He opened and closed his mouth, resembling a fish as much as a man could who had such a pronounced nose and chin. Wisely, Edward abandoned the topic.

Her half brother had not heard the thread of rumor which had made its way back from wherever the groom had died of the bite she had inflicted on his hand before Harris came to her rescue. Not in the nearest village; he would not have stopped there for fear of Edward and the magistrate. He had gone farther to recover from the beating and expired there, a fact she had overheard only by accident a year or more later.

She had gone to the stable to ask for her horse to be saddled. In a stall, a young groom newly hired had been babbling to Harris about a prodigious strange happening only a few miles away. "And to a groom, same as me! Died, he did, his hand rotted off, from a witch's bite."

Adelaide had paused; they had not heard her approach.

Harris had snorted. "Did you see the fellow yourself?"

"No, but I heard about it from a peddler who'd been there."

"Did he see it? What would a peddler be doing with a man on his sickbed?"

The groom scratched his head. "I don't know as he said he'd seen it with his own eyes. He said it was all they talked of in the ale house."

"Hmmpf. Where was the groom employed?"

"I never rightly heard. He died at the ale house, seemin'ly, where he was took bad with the hand when he was passing through the place."

"Out o' work, then, likely turned off for being clumsy or useless. If he was bit, I warrant 'twas a horse done it. Loose, foolish talk if it b'aint a pack of lies. Witches and goblins! I'll have no such nonsense talked here, scaring the maids and children."

And that was the last mention she heard of it, though somewhere farther afield, the poisonous bite of a witch had passed into legend.

Edward moved on to a different concern. "Addie, please at least spend less time in Ducane's company. Leonora still has hopes of getting him for Sophia. Her conduct on the ride offended him, understandably so in my opinion, but his situation is urgent. Sophia would make a suitable bride for him and has the approval of his family."

"Was anything agreed before his arrival?"

"Leonora's mother and the dowager marchioness of Blacklaw were sure they would suit." He shoved his plate away.

"Evidently he does not think so."

"Then why hasn't he left? Remaining suggests he still has an interest here."

How powerful self-deception can be. Little as she knew of the beau monde, she was not ignorant enough

185

to think Ducane could leave early without giving offense.

"I am not a man, Brother, but if I were, I think her little stratagem would give me a disgust for her."

"You know nothing of how men think, Addie. He understands she's young, heedless, and a little spoiled. She only meant to give him some encouragement to declare himself."

"With a footman as a witness?"

"Thomas has sworn on the Bible that he came upon them only by chance. He should not have been out, of course, but neither should you and Sophia. Please allow her the chance to change Ducane's opinion of her."

"As you wish." Adelaide smiled blandly to reassure him. "If you will excuse me?"

"If you go riding, take a groom."

"Very well." She could agree cheerfully, knowing Harris would assign a trustworthy man who would not report back to Edward.

She did not have to offend Edward by fixing a plate for Tabby, having already secreted adequate food for her breakfast in a handkerchief in her lap. She bunched it up and took her leave.

Chapter 21

Adelaide had been avoiding him; if she had not managed to whisper, "I am ordered to keep my distance from you," he would have been worried. Four days remained until the guests would begin leaving. Lady Adelaide's composure was unflawed, except for moments when her questioning eyes sought Ducane's. No one else noticed. He gave her a smile or a slight nod, hoping she understood the message. *I will not leave without you.*

The afternoon was far advanced, and the day hot. Many guests had gone to their chambers to rest or change their clothing after riding or walking in the park. The earl and countess and a handful of others were sitting in the shade on the parterre, the ladies with lemonade, the gentlemen with ale. Conversation was desultory. Both Sophia and Charity were in their chambers, repairing any damage done to their appearance by heat and sun. He rather thought Charity at least had a touch of sunburn. The absence of coy chatter made it possible to relax and think.

Queen Mab, the Lady of the Gillyflowers, lingered in his memory like the scent of roses in the air. Where had she gone? Ah, well, that strange interlude was all of a piece with his accident early in his visit. If he had stumbled into fairyland somehow, he had emerged into the real world again and the safe if unromantic prospect of marriage to Lady Adelaide. No one needed romance in a marriage.

"Do tell us what makes you smile, Lord Gervase," Lady Lamburne invited.

"Why, only a faux pas I observed some time ago, my lady." He dredged up a mildly scandalous and very funny anecdote from his years in London, omitting names to protect the hapless. The men present laughed heartily, the countess tittered but exclaimed, "La! I should have died of embarrassment."

Sir Peter Weston voiced the opinion of the gentlemen, snorting, "Bottle-headed young pup! The girl would be better without him." The sentiment, "How romantic! What a pity it ended in low comedy," prevailed among the ladies. Adelaide's lips twitched, and her eyes twinkled at him.

The butler approached Lamburne and waited to be acknowledged.

"What is it, Lowe?"

"My lord, a Mr. Thaddeus Tate is requesting to speak with Lady Adelaide. He is in the reception room."

"Tate? I wonder what he can want. I'll attend to him. Your pardon, ladies, gentlemen. I will not be long."

Adelaide rose. "He is my trustee and man of business, Edward, and asked for me. I will see him."

"It would not be proper for you to be closeted with him alone. As your brother, I should be present."

"You may accompany me to the reception room, if you wish. Then Mr. Tate and I will discuss whatever he has to say on the lawn in plain sight, if you care to have someone observe us from the house."

"Very well." Lamburne strode ahead, without offering his arm to his sister.

One or two of the gentlemen had watched this exchange with surprise, not because Lamburne's suggestion that he be present was remarkable but because of his display of ill humor.

Tate had come. Did that mean he had brought the license? Or did he mean to counsel Adelaide against the marriage? He might yet have to elope with his bride-to-be. Ducane's social veneer concealed his uneasy thoughts.

Lamburne's reappearance a few minutes later did not end the suspense. Lady Lamburne asked, "Whatever did he want?"

"To speak with my half sister." The curt reply was followed by a question to Sir Archibald Smythe about one of his hunters.

To excuse himself and find a place from which he could view the lawn was tempting. Some servant was bound to take note of it, however, and tell the earl or his countess. He would control his impatience until he could see Adelaide at supper. Her expression might give him a hint of the state of their affairs.

Meeting her privately would be a challenge. There was now a lock on the door they had used for their nighttime walks. The earl's sudden decision to install one bore out Adelaide's fear that he held her to blame for Ducane's failure to offer for Lady Sophia. Foolish of them, when he had shown no partiality for the little jill-flirt. If he had considered marrying her, the ambush in the garden would have put an end to it. Better to wed some cit's girl, so long as she was well-behaved, but Lady Adelaide spared him that fate. Whatever Tate's decision, they would manage somehow.

****

Tate was present at supper. Part of Lamburne's annoyance must arise from having to invite the man to accept his hospitality, as the trustee claimed he had several matters of business to discuss with Lady Adelaide and she would need time to review some documents. From Adelaide's placid expression, Ducane could not determine whether the news was good or not. She was as skilled at masking her feelings as he was.

As the men left the dining room to join the ladies, Tate addressed him. "Lord Gervase, I am slightly acquainted with your cousin, Everleigh. When he heard I was to come here, he asked me to present his compliments and request you visit him the next time you are in London."

As Everleigh was an invalid in his seventh decade, and he and Ducane had met no more than half a dozen times, this must be a pretext for a conversation.

"I will. It's been too long since I saw him last. Come, tell me how he does. He's no sort of correspondent." Linking his arm through Tate's, he almost dragged the man of business to the morning room. Unused at this time of day, there was no footman posted nearby and the long summer evening made it unnecessary to light candles. With the door closed, they could talk with no fear of being overheard.

Ducane gestured him to a chair. Unwontedly nervous, he rested an elbow on the mantle and awaited judgment.

"Lady Adelaide informs me that you have requested her hand in marriage. As her trustee, it's my duty to interview you, the late earl having given me authority over her dowry and her investments and their income. Do you understand that you may have to make do on the income from her manor if I find you to be a fortune hunter?"

"Mr. Tate, by anyone's reckoning, I am a fortune hunter. My income as Blacklaw's heir ends in several months. I was never trained for a profession. I helped my father manage Blacklaw and the other properties until my brother took them over after his marriage. The alternatives available to me are finding a post as a bailiff, which would humiliate my family, marriage to an heiress, buying a commission, or asking my brother to help me obtain a government post. I have the greatest admiration for Lady Adelaide. I have already told her I would marry her if all she had was a manor, having lost my taste for town life some time ago. I miss the country." This was no occasion for gentlemanly reticence.

Tate listened impassively until Ducane's bald summation ended. "I investigated you before setting out for Lamburne. That is why I am later than perhaps you expected. You have a reputation as a *chevalier des dames* rather than a rake. No one calls you a drunkard or spendthrift or gambler, and a number claimed you were all but a pattern of rectitude. Compared to many men of the beau monde, I assume."

"That is not precisely a compliment, sir."

"A rakeshame would not think so, but in my opinion, a man of some principles with no serious vices is not a bad choice for a husband. You are not pompous, sanctimonious, or stupid." He paused. "Until today, my only knowledge of Lady Adelaide came through the letters she wrote me. I believe she would not suffer a fool gladly. You should do well enough, as her brother has singularly failed to arrange a marriage for her."

Tate's easy acceptance was so unexpected that Ducane was momentarily at a loss for words beyond, "Thank you, sir."

"There is one thing about your proposed marriage I dislike and to which I cannot agree, as it is damaging to Lady Adelaide's reputation and that of her family. To be marrying on the last day of Lamburne's house party and immediately leaving will cause disagreeable talk. The betrothal can be announced after a decent interval, as even I, a stranger in these parts, heard talk at the inn about Lady Sophia's anticipated marriage to a marquess's brother."

"There was never an understanding, even an unspoken one." Ducane heard a note of defensiveness in his own voice.

"Nevertheless, gossip is harmful. After another interval, you may marry with as much or as little ceremony as you wish. On the instructions in Lady Adelaide's letter, I thought it best to apply for a special license rather than the common license which in theory requires the marriage to take place in the parish in which one of you resides." He frowned. "It occurred to me that as Lady Adelaide clearly anticipated her brother's opposition, marrying in the local church might be difficult, as the incumbent must keep Lord Lamburne's favor."

"A problem neither Lady Adelaide nor I had thought of," Ducane admitted. He at least should have considered that the living would be at the earl's gift. Reverting to Tate's earlier objection, he asked, "Did

Lady Adelaide not explain the reason she wanted an immediate wedding with no announcement being made?"

"She said she wished to remove from her brother's house with all speed. I know she has not been happy here. Having now met her people, I understand her feelings. However, she has lived with them since she was a child. A few more weeks can make no difference."

"She fears it will. Ask her if Lady Lamburne once spoke of having her committed to a madhouse."

"A madhouse? Lady Adelaide? She is sharp as a pin. I wish all my clients were as sensible."

"I have repeatedly heard her brother and sister-in-law and her nieces speak of her in terms that might lead the hearer to suppose she was mentally or morally deficient. I have no difficulty imagining her brother consigning her to an institution for the deranged or feeble-minded, or confining her to some locked room here."

"That is extremely distressing. I have not heard them do so, although I did think there was something strange in the conversation I had with his lordship."

"You have been here a matter of hours, sir. May I ask what would happen to her property if she died unmarried or was judged to be incompetent?"

The question disconcerted Tate. "A very good question, Lord Gervase. Lady Adelaide has never asked. If she were found incompetent, nothing would change. I would continue to control the trust. If she died before marrying or without issue, her dowry and her investments would be disbursed to various charities the late earl specified. I don't know if she mentioned to you that she inherited her mother's jewelry, which consists of a number of fine pieces of considerable value."

"I've seen an emerald necklace and earrings and one of topaz and peridot."

"There are others, as well as rings, bracelets, brooches, and the like, all of which her father gave her mother. None of them are Lamburne heirlooms. I had them delivered into her hands by messenger when she came of age, concealed in a pretty sewing box. They also would not go to Lamburne. If we could get them back," he qualified. "Which is not to say I necessarily distrust Lamburne." He twisted the carnelian signet ring on his finger. "I made the last earl's will and set up the trust. I was young, however, and had only recently taken over acting for him on my father's death. Looking back, I should have questioned him about the arrangements. One would ordinarily expect that the amount in trust would go to the nearest family member or as governed by the laws of inheritance. The trust was rather cleverly set up to protect Lady Adelaide, I assumed from a fortune hunter. Now I wonder if the late Lord Lamburne was equally concerned about his son."

"Does the current Lord Lamburne know about the provisions of the trust?"

"Lady Adelaide's father explicitly instructed me not to discuss it or her financial status with anyone, including her brother. I have followed those instructions, except that once she was of age, it was proper to communicate with her, and now, by her instruction, with you. As Edward, Lord Lamburne was neither Adelaide's legal guardian nor her trustee, it was no business of his anyway. I have paid into his account quarterly sums sufficient to support her based on her age and her residence at Lamburne and of course, paid for the costs of her season. To his credit, Lamburne has never requested an increase or additional sums. But he does not know the funds would go to charity after her death if she does not marry. Well! We need not worry about that now."

"I think we must worry until Lady Adelaide and I are married, Tate, unless you can somehow let slip to the earl that he would not benefit by his sister's incapacity or death without issue. Indeed, he would lose whatever you've been paying him for her maintenance."

"It would have to be done slyly," the man of business remarked after a thoughtful pause. "I confess I do not know how it could be accomplished without sounding as if I were suspicious of him."

"If you think it impossible to do discreetly, the best guarantee of Lady Adelaide's safety is to keep our betrothal secret until we are married. Under no circumstances would I let him know she has inherited her godmother's property. If I understand you correctly, while the trust monies would not go to him, her recent inheritance probably would."

"Ay." After a moment, Tate commented with a trace of surprise, "A good point; you think like a lawyer."

Ducane supposed it was a compliment.

"While I do not like deceit, I begin to agree that there is no choice." Tate smiled grimly. "Did you know Lady Adelaide has asked me to take her back to London with me?"

"No, but it's a very good idea and relieves me of

one concern. She made me promise that if you refused to procure a license or it did not arrive before my departure, I would take her to you in London."

"Good God. Why did she not reveal her concerns to me?"

"She has perfected an appearance of composure which I envy, but she was fighting back tears when she told me why she feared to let her relations know she meant to marry. She would not want you to think her a vaporish female."

"She warned me in her letter not to mention her inheritance or the money her father settled on her," he admitted. "Naturally I would not consider doing so, given her father's orders. Even after meeting her family, I can hardly believe her brother would be guilty of the sort of action we have been discussing."

"Yet despite all our fine talk about protecting females, they are at the mercy of men. You must know how easily an inconvenient woman can be sent to a madhouse, Mr. Tate."

"Previously I have given it little thought, but you are correct. I am sorry to say that from Lamburne and his lady's response to my arrival, now the issue is raised, I cannot completely discount it." He scowled ferociously, his brows almost meeting over the bridge of his nose.

"Once I am her husband, her brother will have no power over her."

"But such a scrambling marriage can only lend support to an allegation of Lady Adelaide's incompetence, as well as being scandalous."

"More so than if she simply departs with me?"

"Well…no. How are we to resolve this curst

tangle?"

"Your approval of the match once 'tis done will surely take away much of the impropriety. I assumed you would either agree to our immediate marriage, as Lady Adelaide mentioned you knew about her unhappy situation here, or else would oppose any marriage to me on the ground I am a fortune hunter. There may be a way to protect her and allow a decent period to elapse between the announcement of our betrothal and our wedding."

"Pray tell me what it is, Lord Gervase. I must have led a simple, innocent life for I cannot think of one."

"Can you not do as she requested and insist she return to town with you to deal with some complicated business matter? No doubt the documents are too bulky to be brought here, and one would hardly risk losing them during the common mishaps of travel. Let it be thought she will be absent no more than a fortnight or a month. I will remain here, defending myself from Lady Sophia's wiles as best I can for the last few days of my visit. Once I leave Lamburne, permit us to be married secretly, then after a suitable interval, announce our betrothal, with our wedding to follow when the settlement documents and her bride clothes are ready. If his lordship storms up to town on hearing of the betrothal and attempts to break the betrothal or have his sister declared incompetent, he will have no power to do so because she will already be my wife."

"While I cannot like it, that is a very clever solution. I'll let it be known only that she has received a small inheritance from her godmama, making it necessary for Adelaide to come to town to review documents, execute the sale documents if she wishes to sell the property, and decide how she would like to invest it. Sir, you have the makings of either a Machiavelli or a rogue."

"Thank you. Will you see if Adelaide agrees? No one will think it strange if you meet with her privately, whereas I must try not to pay too much attention to her lest I bring down her family's wrath on her head."

"I will confer with her in the morning. I have already let Lord Lamburne know my business with Adelaide might require more than one day." Tate smiled sourly. "He disliked inviting me to stay but could think of no way to refuse."

Chapter 22

The next two days would live in Adelaide's memory forever among the worst of her life. On the one hand, with both Tate and Ducane in the house, she felt safer than she had since her father's death. On the other, she was terrified something would go wrong. Lord Gervase would take a dislike to her or decide his family would never accept her and disavow their betrothal. Tate would receive a message that a later will had been discovered, and she had been left nothing that would tempt Ducane. Edward would find some excuse to confine her, or Tabby or Tate or Ducane would die. Her fears were ridiculous, but in the middle of the night she could not convince herself. Believing her situation had changed was almost impossible.

Tomorrow she would leave with Tate. Neither Edward nor Leonora had made any objection, indeed, seemed relieved. Of course, they would be pleased to have her out of the way, leaving Ducane to Sophia. And what if her niece succeeded in compromising him? There would be no marriage for Adelaide, a thought she found surprisingly melancholy, though she would not need to marry once away from Lamburne. As an heiress established at Dale Tower, she would be safe. Or would she? No man could claim her as property if she were not married and was of age. But could her half brother assert some right over her as her nearest relation? If he tried to commit her to a lunatic asylum, would Tate be able to prevent it? Perhaps when she was so far out of the way, she would be safe from Edward and his family. She would exert herself to make friends among the local gentry, and especially the magistrate. The guests at the house party accepted her; why should her new neighbors (who knew nothing of Lamburne and her family's history) suspect her of anything?

Somehow she managed to maintain her composure. Leonora, after consulting the cook, was willing to let Jenny go to London as her maid. There was always a girl on one of the tenant farms or in the village who was glad of temporary work. She need not be skilled to perform a scullery maid's duties.

Jenny was ecstatic. Adelaide let her believe the visit would only be temporary. If the girl did not want to continue as her maid, she could be sent back to the estate. That was one worry Adelaide did not suffer: Jenny was an orphan with no kin and would certainly rather be her lady's maid.

Before her second trunk was corded, and while Jenny was out of the room, she packed her mother's portrait. There was room for it, as she had instructed Jenny to make sure enough space remained for any last minute item. She did not leave her chamber until the footman came to cord and carry it downstairs. She followed him down to see it loaded onto the coach as soon as it should be brought around to the door. She drank a cup of chocolate and ate a slice of toast, all she could manage in her state of excitement and foreboding.

"Are you sure you have had enough breakfast?" Tate asked. He had dispatched a plate of cold beef and two buns.

On her nod, he rose, bowed to Edward and the others who had come down early, and said, "Thank you for your hospitality, Lord Lamburne. Please make my compliments to Lady Lamburne and Ladies Sophia and Charity. We must be on our way. 'Servant, ladies, gentlemen. Lady Adelaide, if you are ready?"

She had taken her leave of the guests the previous evening, apologizing for the circumstances which required her to deal with some little matter of her godmama's bequest. The guests had expressed their pleasure at having met her and wished her an easy journey and a pleasant stay in London. After she was safe, she hoped to carry on a correspondence with Lady Smythe, whom she liked exceedingly. Lord Gervase's farewell was no more effusive than theirs. Even now they must not be seen on terms of too much intimacy.

"Yes. Goodbye, Lamburne."

Jenny was in the hall with Tabby, who spoke sharply from her covered basket when she heard Adelaide's voice. She did not care to be confined, a sentiment Adelaide understood well. "I know, I know," she whispered. "As soon as we're in the coach, you can come out."

Tate maintained the grave expression appropriate to a staid professional man, but his eyes twinkled.

As they turned onto the road to Marlborough, Adelaide's heart lightened. On her lap, Tabby rolled onto her back and purred audibly.

****

They changed horses at Marlborough on the London road. She had forgotten the peculiar conical hill known as the Marlborough Mount, thought by some to be the remains of a Roman fort and by the locals to be Merlin's burial mound. Jenny goggled at the wide High Street. Twenty miles from Lamburne at the second change of horses, the maid broke her awestruck silence to say, "Who'd 'a thought I'd ever go so far! Are we in another county, sir?"

"If we aren't yet, we will soon be in Berkshire," said Tate.

Jenny sighed with pleasure.

Tabby napped, full of minced chicken and kipper. How could life hold anything better?

Tate and Ducane and her godmother had freed her. With a faint tingle of unease, she conceded she would not feel really safe until she married. Ducane might not be a mighty defender, but as her husband, he would be able to protect her from Lamburne. Still, she could count her blessings: Lord Gervase was a good bargain, if not as thrilling as Tam Lin of the masquerade.

****

The earl's family seemed to breathe a sigh of relief after Tate's carriage rolled away. Possibly Ducane was the only one to notice.

"What a pity Lady Adelaide's visit to town takes place at the worst time of year to enjoy it," Lady Smythe remarked. "Hot, dusty, and lacking in company."

Charity's smirk suggested she found it a pleasing thought; Sophia's smug face and arch attempts to claim his attention gave Ducane pause. If she thought she still had a chance to snare him, she was doomed to disappointment. In the evenings, he remained in the company of the billiard contingent and the card players and made a habit of not going upstairs alone.

Lady Smythe's pursed lips and gimlet-eyed study of Sophia told him she had noticed her behavior. Even so, the girl might have been able to pounce had he not found himself often in Lady Smythe or Sir Archibald's company, and when neither was present, two or three men and one old lady Ducane knew were friends of the Smythes happened to be nearby when Sophia sought him out. They were impervious to hints. Had he wanted to court Sophia, this would have been annoying. Instead, the chaperonage was more than welcome. He needed only to evade Lady Sophia's clutches for one more day and night. He had already informed his brother's coachman that he intended to leave the day after tomorrow.

Ducane and most of the others were on the grass at the front of the house watching a lawn bowls match when a dust-covered groom from Blacklaw rode in on a tired horse, bearing a letter from the dowager marchioness.

"I hope it is not unhappy news," Lady Lamburne said.

Most likely 'twas a reply to his own letter to his mother. Ducane's first thought was to read it in private. His second, seeing Sophia watch him like a hawk ready to stoop on its prey, was to read it right there in broad daylight with twelve or sixteen people at hand. He withdrew from the sidelines just far enough that no one could look over his shoulder.

Gervase,
I was troubled to hear you had taken a dislike to Lady Sophia. She is so appropriate in every way. I shall renew my efforts.

As to the family, there was a good deal of talk about them some years ago. Hard upon the death of his first wife, the previous earl married an actress who had been his mistress. That would have been bad enough, but the wench was with child, which she must have got deliberately in the hope he would marry her. The earl accepted it as his own, but I know little about her. I do recall the daughter of that union had a season in town and I truly pitied Leonora, Lady Lamburne, as the girl was ill-favored, almost silent, and awkward when one tried to engage her in conversation. I have not seen her since, and no loss, in my opinion.

Now, we must consider the second Thorne girl. She has not received as much attention as her older sister who was the nonpareil of the year she left the schoolroom, but she is well worth pursuing. There are several others who might do though not of the highest level of society...

His mother's description of Adelaide in her first season might have been applied to many girls newly introduced to society and to many callow young men. He had spent almost no time in London until his brother took over Blacklaw's management and sent him to town to represent their family. The prospect of living in London had been appealing but not wholly comfortable to him when he had lived the life of a country gentleman for so long. By London standards, he had been a bumpkin in spite of possessing a gentleman's education. He sympathized with Adelaide in her first season. At least he had had Moses, the Blacklaw House butler, to hint him into fashion.

He was folding the sheet when Lady Lamburne

glided toward him.

"Not bad news, I hope, Lord Gervase?"

His usual mask of indifference must have failed him when he read his mother's comments on Adelaide. Now his hostess was determined to pry. "No, my lady. My mother merely wondered where I would be going after I take my leave of your family tomorrow."

"I suppose you mean to visit other friends? That is the usual summer activity of unattached gentlemen, isn't it?"

As Lady Lamburne well knew. She was fishing to find out what family he would visit next in his bride search. "A friend invited me to join him at his cousin's house." Ducane had already declined by the letter that provided the pretext for sending Robbie to London with Adelaide's letter to Tate. He did not like to lie, but the hard-pressed fox must be allowed to use whatever wiles he possesses to escape the hounds.

"Oh, a bachelor household. Hardly a good place to find a wife," was her peevish remark.

Instead of saying, "That would be its attraction," he murmured, "Alas, no. Perhaps I should buy a commission. So much easier," and enjoyed her discomfiture.

Chapter 23

He climbed into his brother's traveling coach the next morning with a sigh of relief. In Newbury, market day proved a stroke of luck, as otherwise he would have had to plead some indisposition to account for stopping early. Though the other house guests had mostly not got off as promptly as they had intended because of last-minute packing or prolonged leavetaking, Ducane's tardiness had been planned to get him to Newbury in the afternoon. He had idled in his chamber, taken a leisurely breakfast while engaging the others in unnecessary conversation, found he had misplaced his pocket watch and sent Jenkins to search for it, and did not make his departure until midmorning.

Ducane instructed his brother's coachman he wanted to stop and enjoy the market day throng. "We may as well put up for the night. Not at a coaching inn, however," he said, "as they all appear to edge the market. They will be crowded and busy and perhaps noisy tonight. Then you and Robbie are at liberty for the rest of the afternoon and evening."

They might also visit the market and then spend the evening eating, drinking, and gossiping. Little could be kept from one's servants. They probably had been wagering on the results of his courtship. Let them speculate as much as they liked. The question of his marriage would soon be settled.

The marketplace boiled with activity. He wended his way through it to an inn not too far from the one at which they would sleep. Tate and Lady Adelaide were waiting in their inn's only private parlor; it would have been awkward if Tate had found no room available at the inn. Ducane said as much.

"There wasn't a chamber to be had. I paid two men to give up their places to us, and they were happy to leave."

Ducane's surprise must have showed. Tate said, "You cannot have thought, Lord Gervase. I've lodged here before because it is quieter than a coaching inn or the others close by the market. Those who stay at this inn are respectable but not gentry. I imagine I could have secured as many chambers as necessary."

He went on, "I am sorry the wedding must be done in such a hugger-mugger way, but as Lady Adelaide pointed out, it would be difficult once she is in London. I have spoken with the vicar, explaining that family opposition makes secrecy necessary for the moment. He will perform the ceremony as soon as you wish."

Ducane raised his eyebrows inquiringly at his betrothed. She had greeted him warmly and now said, "I think it too late today to impose on the Reverend Mr. Samuelson. The morning is soon enough. If you agree, Lord Gervase?"

"I do. Most particularly as I am rumpled from travel and would like a bath and a meal."

"I've prepared the settlements for you to review tonight. They are as we discussed. You will remember that the greater part of Lady Adelaide's inheritance is secured to her and her children. Is that still acceptable?"

"It is, sir. How shall we go about meeting the

vicar?"

"I think inviting Mr. Samuelson to take breakfast with us before we continue our travels would be preferable to holding the ceremony in the church or at his residence. I will mention to a servant that I am interested in the boys' charity school here, as education of the poor is an interest of mine."

"Is it?"

"Not until now, except in the most general way. I heard of the school soon after our arrival and thought it would make a good excuse for talking to Mr. Samuelson." His lips quirked. "I'll send my footman with a note to him requesting he break his fast with us tomorrow at nine and perform the ceremony afterward. Not the dignified celebration of marriage you are entitled to, Lady Adelaide, but it must do for the time being."

Ducane took his leave and ate a simple supper before ordering his bath and retiring to his room to read Tate's documents. There were no surprises. Later, while he soaked in the tub, he informed Jenkins of his imminent marriage. After considerable debate, they agreed on his cerulean blue suit of good wool broadcloth. John Coachman and Robbie would wonder if he wore clothing suited to a wedding when he went out for a walk before spending the day traveling. Jenkins unpacked and brushed the suit and laid out a fresh shirt, stockings, and neckcloth to be ready in the morning.

He would be married. His life would change forever. The idea was as terrifying as when he had left home for his first term at school and as exhilarating as the day his father had asked him to help with the properties. His pointless existence would be at an end, and he would have a home. If his bride was not as mysterious and alluring as the Lady of the Gillyflowers, Adelaide was not only suitable but excellent company. No doubt his mother would come around eventually. If she did not, no great harm would be done. Robert wouldn't care, although his lady might. Adelaide and he would seldom travel to London, and he did not suppose his connections would visit Dale Tower often or for long. He drank one glass of brandy before going to bed and sank into a sound sleep, musing on the many advantages of marriage.

****

They ate a substantial breakfast while chatting about charity schools in general and the local one in particular and had the table cleared of its remains. The door closed on the last of the inn's servants, and the Reverend Gregory Samuelson said, "I would hate to believe Lady Adelaide is correct that her brother would try to prevent her marriage, but I cannot discount it as Mr. Tate is of the same opinion. It is also a saddening fact that the love of money does sometimes lead to bad behavior even by those who should most have one's interests at heart." He was a round little fellow with a good-humored face. In a monk's robe, he might have been taken for Friar Tuck. At the moment, his expression was grave. "Lady Adelaide, Lord Gervase, are you both still of a mind to wed?"

The answer being in the affirmative, Tate produced the special license, Samuelson took an octavo-sized Book of Common Prayer from his pocket, and Jenkins and Jenny were summoned.

In discussing the need for witnesses, Adelaide had

requested that Jenny be one of them.

"Would my footman be a better choice than the girl?" Tate had asked. "When she returns to Lamburne, will she hold her tongue? And if she does not betray the secret, when your family is informed of your marriage, will they not turn her off for not telling them we met Ducane here?"

"She will stay on as my maid."

"We are becoming a household already," Ducane remarked.

His soon-to-be bride beamed a smile at him that made her almost beautiful. Good God. Why had he thought her plain?

The maid, entering behind Jenkins, stopped short at seeing them all standing in the parlor, looking toward the door.

"Come, Jenny. I have a task for you."

She bobbed a series of unpracticed curtsies. "My lady?"

"You will be a witness at my wedding."

"Stand over here by me," Jenkins whispered, and the vicar opened the book.

****

Adelaide—his wife!—proceeded to London with Tate, while Ducane made his own way to town. His life had changed as thoroughly as if he had bought a commission, though he did not actually feel married yet. Once they moved to Adelaide's manor, they would settle into married life.

In the immediate future, he had purchases to make, though one less than expected. For their wedding, he had slipped onto her finger a ring that had been a gift from his grandmother on his eighteenth birthday. He would have used his signet ring if the other had not been more suitable in two ways: the size was small, to be worn on a man's little finger, and the table-cut hexagonal stone was an emerald. He associated emeralds with Adelaide—her eyes, her cat's eyes, her emerald necklace—making it a fine substitute for purposes of the ceremony. After the wedding, he promised Adelaide he would buy a ring for her. She had run a finger over the band with its delicate engraving.

"No, don't, Gervase. I like this one—oh, unless you prefer to keep it? As a gift from your grandmother, it must hold fond memories for you."

"It does not. It was my grandfather's, but I never knew him. If you like it, 'tis yours." The old lady was long dead, and he believed she would prefer her gift to be used as a wedding ring rather than what he originally planned. He had brought it on his journey to Lamburne in case he needed to pawn or sell it for extra funds.

Adelaide would take it off as soon as they went their separate ways, as she could not very well wear a ring before their second, public, wedding. Meanwhile, he would spend his time in London ordering boots and clothing more suited to the country than to town and find Adelaide a wedding gift.

He returned to Blacklaw House, both glad to be away from Lamburne and impatient to get on with the next chapter of his life. Marriage seemed a most desirable state. Was it the prospect of Adelaide or the manor? He didn't know and wasn't sure it mattered. He liked the idea of living quietly in the country with her.

Chapter 24

When she had rejoiced at being free of her family, Adelaide had overlooked the fact she would be staying at the family house in London. She stepped into the chill, formal hall past the rigidly correct butler and footman and realized it would be as uncomfortable as Lamburne Chase. No, not quite. Neither her family nor Thomas were here. Fortunately, Jenny was overcome with awe at the splendor. She herself had forgotten how impressive Lamburne House was, being newer and more fashionable than the estate.

As soon as they reached the safety of her bedchamber, she whispered, "Jenny, please let the others think you are to be my maid only for this visit. Anything you confide to them will be reported to Lamburne. You may talk as you like about the wonders of London, but let them believe you are no more than a scullery maid assigned to the earl's despised sister for the journey because she had to have some female to accompany her."

"Like as it was at Lamburne?"

"Exactly. 'Twill make it easier for you with the servants here. Mind you do not mention my nuptials or Lord Gervase. That too is a secret, remember."

"I won't, my lady."

Adelaide had been under its roof less than a full day when she knew by subtle signs that her precaution had been wise. Her brother must have sent instructions by the footman or one of the outriders that she was to be watched. She did not suspect the coachman. Like the grooms and stable boys, he was now friendly when he could be. He had given her a smile or a wink at times when the others could not observe it.

She was to meet with Tate the next day to support the fiction that she had come to town to review documents. The earl's coach stood at the door, a footman waiting to assist her to step up into it. She tip-tapped briskly across the hall, conscious of looking her best. The butler opened the door for her as she approached, Jenny hurrying after her.

She came to a halt so quickly Jenny squeaked. "Briggs, you have not had the doorknocker put up."

"No, Lady Adelaide. His lordship sent word that as you were come to town on a matter of business"—his tone made clear his opinion that ladies should not have "business" of any sort—"you would not wish to be bothered by callers."

"I see." She forced herself to add, "How thoughtful of him. I do expect much of my time to be taken up with my trustee."

In the coach, she sat silent. The pretense that no Setbury was in residence was welcome in one way, as she did not wish to waste time listening to a gibble-gabble of gossip. On the other hand, she was sure Edward had intended to avoid the possibility she would embarrass him before the Lamburnes' friends. Her situation was actually no worse than she experienced at Lamburne, and much the better for the absence of Leonora, Sophia, and Charity. The servants could not keep her from meeting with Tate, her reason for coming to town.

Jenny said timidly, "You'll miss seeing your friends if the knocker's off. 'Less you write them to visit."

"I don't have any friends in London, except Tate."

"And Lord Gervase, milady?"

"Yes." The thought of a husband being a friend was new to her, but then, so was the idea of being married.

The maid frowned a little, choosing her words. "But if the knocker b'aint on the door…Mr. Tate knows as you're here, but Lord Gervase wouldn't. I mean, he knows you're in town, but he's not supposed to, is he? So with nobody home, like, he wouldn't be able to call."

The former scullery maid might not be as clever at dressing hair or caring for clothes as a lady's maid should be, and yet she saw the problem.

Lord Gervase had planned to call upon her, and then they would encounter each other at entertainments and eventually announce their betrothal. With the knocker off, it would be assumed none of the family were in London or at least, if someone was, that person was not receiving company. No one would call, there would be no invitations, and therefore no opportunities for her to meet Lord Gervase to become acquainted sufficiently for the betrothal to be credible.

In Tate's office, she raised this difficulty, giving the blushing Jenny full credit for pointing it out.

"Let me give it some thought," he said. "Now, I have the inventory of the furnishings at Dale Tower. I have only glanced over it, but even I notice that the bed linens are described as worn and darned and some of the bed curtains have suffered greatly from the moth. Very likely there are other needs you will see. You will wish to review the list to decide what must be replaced."

"It will be difficult to visit warehouses," she said. "The coachman or footman may report to the butler, who would wonder why I would shop for furnishings."

"You sent your coach away with instructions not to return until four, did you not?"

"Yes, I could hardly keep the horses standing when our appointment was supposed to take some time."

"Then the next time you come to my office, I can have a hackney summoned and send you to suitable merchants accompanied by one of my clerks. On other days when you come here, you could pay calls...hmmm, no, perhaps not. Lady Lamburne's friends might write her, mentioning they'd seen you."

"They are no friends of mine anyway."

"Well, I'll think of something. Your papa was some years older than I, but he once paid me the compliment of saying I was a wily fellow. That was when he consulted me about settling money upon you."

"You and he did an excellent piece of work. Thank you, Tate. Is there a place I can look over the inventory without being in your way?"

The most junior clerk showed her to a small office and invited her to inform him if she needed or wanted anything, anything at all: tea? Lemonade? Ratafia or sherry? Another branch of candles? Assured she needed nothing more at the moment, he bowed and departed.

Adelaide glanced over the multiple pages. "Jenny, would you know what is needed in the scullery or kitchen?"

"I know some, I reckon, but I can't read."

"I'll read the inventory to you, and if anything is missing or seems too worn to be useful, tell me, and I will make a list."

"Ay, my lady. I can do that."

They passed an agreeable several hours and partook of a meal brought in from a cook shop, at which Tate joined them. When the Lamburne coach came back, he accompanied them to it, saying, "I will call upon you the day after tomorrow to discuss matters with you in greater detail. I need a little time to catch up at my office, and by then we should have received a reply to my letter regarding your questions." She had no doubt the coachman and footman heard him, which was the point, of course.

Tate presented himself at Lamburne House as promised to request a series of meetings at his place of business, ostensibly to review more documents. Early the following day as soon as she and Jenny arrived, Tate shouted, "Bailey! Fetch a hackney, quick as you can." He addressed Adelaide in a normal voice. "You should finish your shopping and be back by three so as to be here when your carriage arrives."

The hackney bore them to a warehouse to choose sheets, pillowcases, and blankets, accompanied by Bailey, a strapping young man who did not look at all like a clerk. Adelaide and Jenny spent two enjoyable hours over the task. She ordered linen sheets of good quality because if Ducane's people came to stay, she did not wish to be shamed by the bedding. Consulting her list, she said, "Ten of the best quality Witney blankets as they are the softer and fleecier. That should be enough for now."

"I fear we do not have that many of any one color, Lady Adelaide. There might be a little delay in getting enough. And do you want them whipped or bound? That is, whipped with a strip of thin fabric over the edges or bound with blanket stitch? Whipped is less expensive."

"Bound for the ten blankets meant for the family and guest bedchambers. The color matters little, as they'll be covered by quilts, with coverlets over the top, but I'll order those when I see the rooms and decide what color the curtains and coverlets should be. Next we will need blankets for the servants. I fear theirs are in worse condition."

He led her to a pile of thin gray blankets, coarse and scratchy.

"Jenny, are these what are used at the Chase? Or at Lamburne House?"

"Very like, ma'am."

"Are they warm enough?" She feared she already knew the answer; the servants' attic rooms were not heated.

"Not really, on a cold night," Jenny muttered apologetically. "But there's usually a quilt or some such thing as well."

"We will not take the cheapest, then…" She almost said, "for it will be colder in the north." She would be wary and not mention her destination to anyone. "What do you have that is suitable?"

"There are the cabin blankets, meant for ships, my lady. They are somewhat more expensive than the others, but they are warm. They only come whipped, and as you see, in the natural wool color or dark green or gray."

"They will do. Fifteen of those, for now, five of each color or whatever you have to make up that number." The old blankets and quilts could supplement the new ones. "I will need swatches of suitable fabric for curtains, bed covers, and upholstery." She would consult Ducane as to his preferences.

The next day, they remedied the deficiencies Jenny had found in the scullery and kitchen goods. Jenny endorsed the salesman's suggestion she purchase a clockwork device to turn the spit. "Them turnspit dogs make a mort o' work, and they b'aint even friendly," her maid said.

Another day, Tate brought an elderly friend, Mistress Nugent, to call on Adelaide, claiming she was a friend of Adelaide's late godmother.

"When I heard from Tate you were come to town, I thought, I must visit dear Louise's goddaughter and offer my condolences on my friend's death. I regret I had not seen her for many years for health kept her in the north and me in London. Now she is literally buried in the country," she caroled as they were ushered into the drawing room. The old lady was afflicted with rheumatism and found it difficult to go about but was as full of mischief as a monkey. For its amusement value, Tate explained softly when they were private, she was happy to create opportunities to further Adelaide's and Ducane's acquaintance so the acquaintance appeared to lead to the betrothal.

He had other matters well in hand. Ducane would contrive by arrangement made through Tate to meet her walking in St. James's Park, frequented by the world and its wife. Adelaide would be accompanied by a footman as well as Jenny, but a seemingly chance encounter would provide an excuse for him to call upon her.

The maid and footman brought in an assortment of cake and biscuits and the laden tea tray. The housekeeper preceded them, bearing the key to the tea chest, as Adelaide had not been entrusted with one.

Mistress Nugent, as brilliantly clad as a parrot, prattled about her girlhood friendship with Lady Creighton until the servants departed. "I haven't enjoyed myself so much in years," she remarked brightly. "I never knew Lady Creighton, indeed, never heard of her, but Tate is the nephew of a friend of mine and almost like a nephew to me. Do I understand I am helping to promote a match in the face of your family's objection?"

"Their anticipated disapproval, at the least. They had hoped he would offer for my half brother's daughter."

"Very well. I'm happy to assist. Tate vouches for your gentleman, and I have met him. He is not easy to know, for while he converses readily, I found it impossible to get any real sense of his character. All was on the surface, and no one is that shallow. His manners and dress are exquisite, however, and I never heard anything bad of him, except that he is 'devilish correct,' which I would consider a good thing. He should make a serviceable husband."

How perceptive Mistress Nugent was, to realize after such short acquaintance how little Ducane revealed of himself. Adelaide had noticed his reticence. Perhaps he would be more forthcoming when they knew each other better. Tam Lin's lack of reserve had charmed her. In that one assignation in a dark garden, she felt she had come to know more about him than she had discovered of Ducane during his entire stay at Lamburne. But perhaps she had been deluded by the almost enchanted circumstances of the masquerade into imagining she understood Tam Lin well. She knew a handful of facts about Ducane, his situation, and his family, but those only skimmed the surface. They had discussed little of substance beyond their own circumstances. She knew Tam Lin's humor, his interest in everything he had experienced on his travels, and his enjoyment of life, including its less comfortable bits, like his stay in the Portuguese inn.

He had even seemed interested in her family and home; she had evaded his questions. At a masquerade, one concealed one's identity, of course—that was part of the pleasure. Yet surely she could have told him something of her own life without risking her anonymity, that she liked riding and books and music, if nothing else.

She and Ducane had spoken frankly of their families over several meetings, perhaps because they were matters of immediate concern. If she had met Tam Lin on several occasions, they both might have revealed more of themselves. Most couples probably did not really know each other when they wed, as money and family connections took precedence, with small consideration given to anything else, including the lady's preferences. At least she and Ducane liked each other. Besides, Tate and Mistress Nugent approved of him.

Mistress Nugent's visit led to her own call upon the old lady, followed by an invitation to a card party, then to calls upon and invitations from several of Elvira

Nugent's friends. Many were older ladies, but they had adult children and Adelaide met some of them also. They were on the outer fringes of the beau monde, and the only person she encountered who belonged to her brother and sister-in-law's circle was Ducane. She need not fear word of her expanding social life reaching Lamburne. A pack of elderly folk, untitled and connected to a mere man of business, were of no importance. Their names were unknown to Briggs and outside the charmed circle the Setburys inhabited. While he might report their calls on Adelaide, even her half brother was unlikely to worry about a few connections and friends of her godmother. By agreement, Gervase Ducane did not come to Lamburne House, which would certainly alarm her family when they heard of it.

On her return from walking in the park (and meeting surreptitiously with Ducane) some two weeks after her arrival, she found a letter from Lamburne, inquiring when she meant to return. Adelaide wrote that same day, explaining that Tate's research into what to do with Lady Creighton's bequest was taking longer than expected. This was an easy, credible excuse. At Lamburne, Tate had managed to be so vague in his description of the issues on which he needed her approval that Edward could only have concluded the question was complicated, might take some time, and somehow involved a part interest in a tobacco or sugar plantation in the colonies or mayhap investment in the slave trade.

She wrote, "The concern is said to yield good profits, but I cannot like the idea of slaves being used. Tate is investigating sale of my shares so the money may be put into some business here, perhaps in a mill using the flying shuttle to produce wider fabric, making it unnecessary to sew two widths together to make sheets, which seems to me a very good idea. Or rental property here in town is said to be always a good source of income. I hope we will have enough information to decide within another two or three weeks." She closed with the hope that he and Leonora and their children were well, though she did not add, as perhaps she should, that she looked forward to seeing them. She doubted she could make such a lie sound convincing. Then she attended a musical evening with Tate and his son and daughter-in-law and Ducane.

The days passed in the blink of an eye. She did not hear anything more from Lamburne, to her relief. She had amusing friends as Mistress Nugent had little patience for the dull or querulous, and plans for her new home occupied much of her time.

She put Lamburne Chase and her family from her mind and did not think of them again for a fortnight. She forgot to be afraid.

Jenny brought her morning chocolate. "I heard something in the kitchen this morning, my lady. The other servants don't pay any mind to me 'cept to tell me what I need to know as I'm naught but a raw country girl, a jumped-up scullery maid. But I hear them talking, and they're as bad as the ones at the Chase."

"What did they say?"

"The under-footman said, 'That Thomas is a prime favorite with his lordship, ain't he? Sending him to town to idle about.' And the butler says, right sharpish, 'None of your business, saucebox. He's doing as he's been bid, and that's all you need to know.' "

"Thomas?"

"Ay. Will you take your breakfast here or go down?"

"It is ridiculous to sit by myself in the dining room." She dined and supped downstairs in an attempt to appear normal but breakfasted in her chamber, as many ladies did. The presence of a footman standing by to fill her plate or pour more chocolate was uncomfortable. Also it was easier to share her breakfast with Tabby than to send Jenny down to request food for her cat. She had tried that once. The kitchen had supplied only the nastiest trimmings of fish and meat. She chose not to make an issue of it, in case Briggs reported to her brother that she was being difficult.

By the time Jenny returned with a tray holding eggs, bacon, some ham, and a currant bun, she was great with news. "I went down to the laundry and asked if your shifts was dry. They wasn't, but I chatted with the laundry maid for a few minutes while your eggs was cooking. She's from the country, like me, so she's not uppish. Thomas has been sleeping here, and the scullery maid has to take his breakfast up to his room. She complained about serving 'a footman as isn't even in livery like a guest.' Mostly he comes and goes without a word about where he's going or what he's doing and takes his dinner out. And he meets the butler in private. Bess took an interest in Thomas at first because he's handsome, but handsome is as handsome does, Bess says."

Disquieting news. "I would have thought Lamburne would hesitate to trust him, sly as he is." She had not told Jenny about his presence when Sophia tried to trap Ducane, but all the staff at Lamburne knew

Thomas for a sneak and telltale. "I wonder what he's doing here. Whatever it is, it can't be good."

"Shall I try to find out more?"

"No. The chances are only Briggs knows, and I don't want anyone to suspect you of nosing for information. As long as I don't have to see him…" Was Thomas spying on her for Lamburne? If he was, what had he seen or deduced? Briggs, a few years older than Adelaide, seemed to have dismissed her visits to Mistress Nugent and her elderly friends as harmless. She doubted the footman would waste time on them. He might follow her to Tate's office, however. Edward must be curious about her business dealings. Not a comforting reflection, although if Thomas was following her, would he not assume he need not remain once the coach left her at Tate's with instructions to come for her at such and such a time? Thomas would consider that license to amuse himself in the interim. Had he seen her come out of Tate's after a short time and leave in a hackney as she had done when she ordered the bedding and kitchen goods? She explained the problem the next time she met with Tate.

"That is troubling," he allowed. "However, there is an alley behind us that leads to a stableyard. In the future, I will send to fetch a hackney to the alley, and you should return the same way."

Chapter 25

The weeks passed quietly. Ducane had not sought out entertainments or allowed the knocker to be replaced on the door. The last thing he wanted was callers. He explained this to Moses Black as wishing to avoid questions about his stay at Lamburne. Somehow everyone would know he had gone with an eye to courting an heiress. If he did not show himself, all would assume his supposed courtship had failed and he was licking his wounds. If he did encounter them, they would not ask.

Ducane returned from a bookseller's where he acquired copies of two books he had found helpful at Blacklaw and a new book on modern agricultural methods. He had not shed hat and gloves before Moses Black approached him. The man had served the family since before Robert was born, indeed, had served their mother before she married. He had come to her as a page boy of seven or eight, a gift from an admirer who thought the boy's coffee-bean-dark skin made a fine contrast to her creamy complexion. The family story claimed his mother had laughed gaily after the suitor departed, because after all, what use was a page boy of any color?

A Black page was a fashionable accessory, but when he was too old for a page, he made himself indispensable by undertaking any task the other servants did not want to do. In a few more years he became a footman. When the London butler retired, Black was promoted, having proven his ability over and over.

Black was bearing disquieting news of some sort. At a gesture from the butler, the footman on duty took Ducane's hat, gloves, and parcel of books.

"Bad news?"

"That would be for you to decide, sir. A person brought a letter for you." His use of the term "person" suggested disapproval. The fact he had concealed the letter in the hall table's drawer was also a clue. And no wonder. Delivered by hand, Ducane's name was written in pencil in an execrable fist which he recognized as Thomas's.

"How odd."

The soft noise did not qualify as throat-clearing or even a suppressed "hmmm," but it heralded Moses's next words. "If there should be anything with which I can assist you, Lord Gervase…?"

Uttered in Black's faint French accent, a remnant of his childhood in Martinique, the question suggested absolute discretion, no matter how clandestine the unsavory affair in which Lord Gervase found himself.

To be considered by their butler no better than a buffle-head who might fall into any sort of mischance was humiliating but perhaps not surprising. All Black knew of him was the little he had observed since Ducane came to live in town. His frivolous existence in London might support that opinion.

"If there is something, I will certainly rely upon your help." He had no doubt at all that the Dowager Lady Blacklaw's trusted butler could deal with anything. The least part of Black's genius kept the house free of the problems common to gentlemen's houses in London: pilferage, cheats with the household accounts, misbehavior by the footmen, tantrums by the cook, and other domestic disruptions. Either in spite of this or because of it, the servants were cheerful and willing.

Dealing with a little blackmail would be no challenge at all to Black. The trouble was, his first allegiance was to Ducane's mother and then to the marquess, making it impossible to reveal Thomas's crime to the one man who could advise him. "Oh, there is one thing. Can you discover who delivered this peculiar message?"

"I questioned William, who took it in, about that very matter. He described the messenger as a sleek fellow, dressed as a footman but in very poor livery and what he called a 'queer flash,' which I understand to be an old, badly kept wig. If he is a footman, which I take leave to doubt, sir, it can only be in a shabby household."

"I see. Well, I'll know more when I read the note." Thomas must have rigged himself out in borrowed or secondhand clothing and wig. Lamburne's livery might have been recognized. Ducane slid the letter into his pocket to read in privacy.

"Very good, sir."

What the devil was that curst Thomas doing in London? And what was to be done with him?

The footman's message was brief and infuriating.

I await payement as promised. Meet me with the gelt at the John Bean Coffee House, John Street by

Oxford Market between two and five of the clock the next three days. Fail and you will find yourself married to an old maid with a piddling portion.

Ducane frowned over this insolence. Nevertheless, he could not risk the footman's revelation just now. In another week or two, he and Adelaide could announce their betrothal, rendering Thomas's threat toothless. He yearned to give the fellow the beating he deserved, but he had given him his IOU. Some might feel that the man having extorted his agreement to pay relieved Ducane of the obligation, whereas they would hold that if tricked into compromising a lady, one would have to marry her. He took exactly the opposite view. Odd of him, but there it was.

While he winced at the thought of paying Thomas, he could see no help for it. As the man was aware of Ducane's circumstances, he would probably not demand more than forty-five pounds and the interest immediately, and this would be the last money Thomas got from him. He had time to visit his banker, but unless Thomas lingered in the coffee house long past five, Ducane would have to deliver the money tomorrow. Curse the fellow, he could wait a day.

****

Ducane was enjoying a morning ride over rolling moorland when a sound never heard under Northumberland's wide skies jarred him awake: the pounding of a fist on a door. His bedchamber was at the front of the house, and his windows were open a crack in the hope of a little cool air even if it was scented with coal smoke. Who the devil would come calling so early? A faint murmur of voices carried up to his ears as he stretched, followed by the sound of the door closing. He was falling back into slumber when he heard Jenkins's brisk footfalls, more audible than usual. Coming with his chocolate, he hoped, rather than a problem.

His manservant entered, bearing a letter on a salver. "I beg your pardon, sir, but Mr. Black says this came by a messenger who impressed upon the footman on duty it is a matter of extreme urgency."

Ducane recognized Tate's fist and tore the sheet open. Its three lines caused him to fling off the bedcovers and demand, "Wash water, now!" before re-reading the last line over Tate's signature: *Lady Adelaide is more afraid than she will admit.* "No, never mind, there's still some in the jug from last night. Lay out a suit. I'm going to Tate's office." By then Gervase was splashing cold water on his face.

"Very good, sir. Will you have chocolate first?"

"There's no time. Once you've shaved me, send for a hackney."

He found Adelaide and her man of business in Tate's private office. Both started up as he thrust his way past Tate's clerk.

Adelaide cut across Tate's greeting. "I have received a letter from Lady Smythe. Her groom delivered it yesterday evening. She learned that my brother is on his way to town to take me back to Lamburne. One of her maids is walking out with a Lamburne groom."

Tate added, "Apparently someone in Lamburne's townhouse wrote him to report on Lady Adelaide's activities. Though what there could have been in them to alarm him baffles me. I do not understand his objection to your attending a few sedate entertainments with people who are not members of his set. Why should your brother object to that? Your conduct at the house party was that of a well-bred lady."

"I doubt that is the cause of his coming. The footman, Thomas, is staying at the house, I suppose to spy on me." Neither Adelaide nor Tate noticed Ducane's start. "I am sure Lamburne gave the butler instructions to send him reports. If someone followed us to the warehouses when I shopped for Dale Tower, he might learn I'd placed a large, inexplicable order. My shopping for household goods would worry Edward, as I could have no reason to do so. I am fortunate Lady Smythe gave me a little warning. She also imparted something I never knew or thought of." She passed Ducane the sheet. "The section is about one-third of the way down the page. It somehow makes me feel…oh, I can't explain it. But I'm glad she mentioned that I am not alone in being despised by my family."

He skimmed over the first, conventional, lines to read

I hope you are enjoying a delightful time in London, as you have not often gone to town, as I understand it. My husband tells me my tendency to be helpful sometimes leads me to be meddlesome, and perhaps this is one of those times. It seemed to me at the house party that you and your brother's family were not as close as one would expect of family. I do not wish to give offense, but in some families, one person is designated by unspoken agreement to be the butt of everyone's ill humor. This was the case with one of my cousins, so I am familiar with the signs. No matter what poor William did or achieved, he could never change his parents' and siblings' belief that he was stupid. He came to believe it himself.

"Lady Smythe is percipient. However, Lamburne has no power over you now, Lady Adelaide. We are wed, and it is for me to protect you."

"Still, we must decide how to proceed, and the sooner, the better," Tate said grimly. "Lady Smythe did not know whether Lamburne had already started out. When he arrives…" Tate, excellent man of business that he was, had arranged their marriage efficiently, but clearly the prospect of opposing an earl in person worried him.

Adelaide's face revealed nothing, but her body was taut with anxiety. She said, "Ducane," voice shaking.

She was afraid. That she did not trust him to shield her from her brother's bluster and threats was painful. Then he thought, *She has been at his mercy near all of her life. She has known me a matter of less than two months.*

He sighed deeply. "Adelaide, while I deplore scrambling haste in anything, I think we must set out immediately, even without luggage. Tate, send an announcement of our marriage to the newspapers in, ah, two days," he murmured.

"But where can we go? And I cannot go without Tabby and my mother's portrait and jewels."

"How big is the portrait?"

She indicated a rectangle of about two feet by two and one-half feet.

"Have you recently purchased any garment you might take back for some little alteration?"

"Why…umm, no?" She turned pink.

Ah, had she bought pretty night rails? He did not even try to conceal his smile. "Then any dress will do. Have your maid wrap it up with the picture inside as if it is being returned to your mantua maker. Better yet, have an entire change of clothing wrapped around the painting, if it is not too bulky."

"But Tabby—"

"Does Lamburne House have a garden?"

"No. It faces the square, but I do not take her there because of the dogs that bark and run loose. I take her into the passage from the kitchen to the street."

"I thought Tabby might be taken out by the back gate, if any. Might you take her to visit some friend, perhaps?"

She leveled a satirical look at him. "I am thought peculiar by my family and many others, but even I do not take Tabby calling with me. She wouldn't enjoy it."

Tate uttered a thoughtful "Hmmpf."

"What is it, Tate?"

"If a little girl, my son's child, for example, were confined to bed with a head cold and was anxious to meet your cat about whom she has heard so much, would you bring Tabby to visit?"

Adelaide's blink and slow smile called to mind a contented feline. "I would be pleased to do so."

"We must act quickly, Tate." He would not let his bride know he was not certain they were secure yet, with the marriage unconsummated. If Lamburne persuaded a doctor that Adelaide had been of unsound mind when they wed, would he be able to have the marriage set aside? They needed a legal opinion but had no time to get one. "Lady Adelaide, as soon as you can have your maid wrap up the clothing and picture, we will leave. How soon is your carriage to pick you up here?"

"I was not sure how long I would be, so I sent it back to Lamburne House and told the coachman Tate could escort me home when I was done." She gave a wry twist to the word "home."

"Then go to Lamburne House in a hackney with Tate and have it wait, because you will go out again at once to leave a gown at your mantua maker's, and then you will take your cat to amuse Tate's granddaughter. If anyone inquires, Tate will bring you home after supper with his family. You do not think it necessary to have Lamburne's horses hitched up again to stand waiting. I will engage a traveling coach and wait at the Red Lyon, Holborn, within two hours." He frowned as an objection occurred to him. "Two coaches. 'Twould be an uncomfortable journey with four people and a cat packed into one."

Tate had been busily writing the announcement. "Very good, sir. I'll provide funds enough for your journey to…where will you go?"

Ducane glanced at Adelaide and raised one eyebrow. "To Dale Tower, do you think, Lady Adelaide?"

"It is mine, and it may be far enough. I am not sure my brother knows where it is or what it is called," she said doubtfully.

"He thought you inherited a few shares of something in the West Indies and a cottage on the Welsh border, not a property called Dale Tower. He never inquired as to where it was, and I never told him." Tate pursed his lips. Clearly he had not liked what he had seen of Lord Lamburne. "A long journey."

"Ay, but once there, Lamburne can do nothing to break our marriage. In Northumberland, my brother, the marquess, will carry more weight than a mere Southron earl. We will not take the Great North Road, in case Lamburne should pursue us."

Adelaide said, "I think the servants at Lamburne House will do nothing without instructions from Lamburne or Lady Lamburne, so until my brother arrives in London, or until the butler receives written instructions, there should be no pursuit."

"They would not become alarmed until nine or ten tonight, I suppose."

Adelaide bit her lip at Ducane's statement, revealing the points of those tantalizing eyeteeth. "They might. 'Tis not late by town standards, but they do watch me. I cannot swear Briggs would not send the carriage for me before then, to 'save Mr. Tate the trouble' of bringing me back."

"My dear, you should write a note saying Tate and his daughter and son-in-law have invited you to go to Vauxhall Gardens, and you will stay with them overnight. Add they can expect you back by noon. Tate, can you arrange to have a note from Lady Adelaide delivered this evening?"

"I can, indeed. Lord Gervase, had you been in command at the Battle of Malplaquet, it might have been a genuine victory for us, rather than a pyrrhic victory."

Ducane bowed ironically, acknowledging the compliment.

Chapter 26

Her escape was so efficiently accomplished that she had no time to worry. She returned to Lamburne House by hackney, escorted by Tate and Jenny. On entering, Adelaide told the footman the hackney would wait as she would be going out again in a few minutes.

Briggs appeared in the hall as she was giving the order. "His lordship's carriage can easily be harnessed up, Lady Adelaide. No need to make the hack wait. Where shall I tell the coachman you will be going?"

The lie about taking her cat to amuse Tate's granddaughter tripped off her lips easily. "I should not want my brother's coach horses to stand, and to send them home only to have them return later makes no sense. I will also be making a stop at Mme. Bernard's to leave one of my gowns for alteration." She could only pray the man did not find her plans suspicious, though if he did, he still could not prevent her from going. "I have been invited to dinner on Sunday by my late godmother's friend, and I wish to wear that mantua, but it does not fit quite comfortably in the sleeve."

Jenny had already gone up to make a package of the portrait and a change of clothing for Adelaide and herself. They would be travel-worn after the first day or two, but she did not care. Adelaide would pack all her jewelry into the pockets under her skirt.

Ducane was a stroke of luck. She had known his

235

good points, but his decisiveness came as a revelation. Despite the soft, drawling voice which made him sound almost too lethargic to sit up, he had devised their escape and issued his instructions as briskly as a general. Yes, their marriage should do very well.

He handed her into the coach less than three hours after their meeting in Tate's office.

"I hope you do not mind that your maid will be in the other coach."

"You were correct that with four and Tabby it would be crowded. Tabby will prefer to have her own seat rather than riding on my lap all the time."

"We will also have an opportunity to become better acquainted."

That he wanted to know her better was perhaps the best compliment she had ever received. She studied him from under lowered eyelids as he pored over a book showing their route in several vertical sections per sheet.

"I've never traveled north except by the Great North Road. I hope to reach Stony Stratford tonight and lie there." He pronounced the word "lie" rather tentatively. " 'Tis about forty miles, so we will be late in reaching it."

Despite his stated intention that they come to know each other better, he was taken up with studying the map strips to form an idea of where they would stop for the next several nights. She did not feel cheated of his company. They needed to outrun any pursuit; she could not help fearing that somehow her brother would catch them. Tabby's contented buzz was welcome reassurance.

Before her father died, he promised her she would

be introduced to society when she was older and marry a man who loved her. Adelaide remembered the occasion clearly because she had few opportunities to receive her papa's undivided attention, and because he had been quite fierce about it.

She had cherished some hope his promise would come true, until it died a lingering death during that season in town. She knew then there would be no joyful wedding, no marriage at all, for one as unattractive and tainted as she. On her return to Lamburne, all she could hope for was that she would be able to escape someday.

Huzzah! She had not married for love, but she was escaping, and that was enough.

They reached the coaching inn in Stony Stratford midway through the evening. Adelaide drooped with fatigue, and Tabby had been grumbling at intervals for some time. Lord Gervase remained imperturbable. He secured a bedchamber and private parlor, lodging for Jenny and Jenkins, and ordered their supper, not forgetting to ask for a dish for Tabby after consulting Adelaide as to her pet's preferences.

They drank a glass of wine while waiting. Ducane said, "We will try to reach Litchfield tomorrow if we can, though I would like to make a stop at Coventry to purchase a few necessities for you."

"Very well. Changes of underclothing at least, I hope."

"At the very least." His eyes glinted over the rim of his glass.

His calm was as soothing as her dear friend's. She smiled down at the emerald ring she had slipped onto her finger as soon as she had entered the coach at the Red Lyon.

Tabby finished her bits of meat and fish left over from other diners' meals and sat washing her face. By the time their own food was served, she had curled up on the hearth. The waiter departed, and her husband cleared his throat.

"Our circumstances are unusual. If we had been able to carry out our original plan of becoming betrothed and then marrying, the matter would not be so awkward. I am sure you are correct that your brother cannot yet be aware you have left your family's protection." He hesitated.

"The protection of my family, who either ignored or berated me, and whose servants were insolent or played tricks on me." Best, perhaps, to get the embarrassment past, if that was what made him falter. "You refer, I apprehend, to our postponed wedding night."

"Ah…yes. I think it would be wise to, er, consummate our marriage. In case…"

"I agree. It is an expected part of marriage, after all. I think we want children?"

After a long moment when he searched her face, he said, "I would. And you will want an heir for your separate property, as it might otherwise pass to your brother or your nieces and nephews, which I am convinced you would dislike excessively," he added dryly.

She laughed. "I have felt more lighthearted since we rolled out of London than I can remember since before I lost my father. I may not be the bride you wanted, but we may do very well together."

He raised his glass. "To our marriage."

She raised her own, and they drank.

"Do you know, Adelaide, before now, it never occurred to me that someday I would be eloping with a lady. I have a reputation for tediously correct behavior and general uselessness."

"I never expected to marry. I thought I would run away to live by myself with Tabby. And a few servants, of course, but at least without my half brother, sister-in-law, and their offspring. However, neither of us is underage, so we've a perfect right to elope if we wish, as I most certainly do."

"Do you suppose it is elopement when we're already married?"

They finished their wine, and Gervase ordered a second bottle, shedding his coat while they drank it and speculated about Adelaide's manor. She knew little more about it than he did, which was to say, they knew there were both sheep and cattle, and she knew of the deficiencies of its furnishings. There should be a home farm if there was not one already.

"It's an opportunity to try new crops and methods in the hope tenants will adopt them if they thrive," he said. As he was refilling their glasses, Adelaide went to the door connecting with their bedchamber and opened it.

"Jenny, if you've fetched up the washing water, you may leave it on the hearth and go to bed." She glanced over her shoulder. "I suppose we will be up early?"

"I think we had better leave by nine of the clock, or earlier if possible. We'll go fifty miles tomorrow if we can. Jenkins knows already."

"Jenny, order our breakfast delivered to us in our parlor when first you go down to have yours, and be ready to leave soon after."

"Ay, Lady Adelaide. Lady Gervase, I mean."

"I think, as both are only courtesy titles, we will find it less confusing if I continue to be Lady Adelaide. If you do not object, Lord Gervase?"

"I vastly prefer your name, my dear."

As she reseated herself, her husband—and what a strange, lovely sound that phrase was—asked, "You won't need help in, er, disrobing?"

"I am wearing jumps, so I will require only as much assistance as you care to offer." Seeing his arrested look, she feared he might think her forward. "When one is never certain a maid will be available to lace one's corset and hook up one's gown, 'tis best to dress simply. I have not yet quite grown accustomed to having Jenny's services whenever I need them."

"Perhaps I may act as your maid some night when you do need unlacing." He raised his glass, and she solemnly touched the rim of hers to it in salute: a promising start to their journey and marriage.

"To our adventure." Adelaide had seldom taken more than one or two glasses of wine. She bubbled with the unaccustomed drink, and it made her bold. "And it is, isn't it? There is everything to learn: whether the property is in good heart, whether the house is well maintained, what the countryside is like, how to keep household."

"I don't think I've had an adventure since I left Eton, and those boyhood undertakings were brief and no real challenge. I am ripe for one."

She emptied her glass. "What if it's dreadful?"

Lord Gervase Ducane, man about town, idler, and beau, *her husband*, smiled at her. "Then we'll improve it."

"But I've never managed a house! No one taught me anything about overseeing a household. What if I don't give the servants the right orders? Or they won't obey me? Or—" *the thousand other things that could go wrong*?

"The chances are the housekeeper will be a fount of information. You've only to explain you've never had a house to manage, and she will probably be glad to give advice. Any servants who fail to do as you tell them or are insolent will be turned off the same day."

"Oh." She stared at him, fascinated. He had changed in an instant from town beau to the stony-eyed son of a Northumbrian marquess. Was the granite under his fashionable veneer really so surprising? The old raiding days in the Borders had bred hard men, she supposed. He had planned her rescue in half an hour, his voice soft and uninflected. Ducane could protect her. For a moment, she experienced the same thrill of excitement and danger she had felt when she saw Tam Lin across the ballroom.

"Jenkins will aid you in dealing with the servants if you need advice. He's very capable." His tone was light and almost humorous again. He drank the last of his wine. "Now, if we cannot dally in bed all morning, we should embark on the next stage of our adventure."

Adelaide was not reluctant to follow this suggestion.

When he had put on his nightshirt in their private parlor, because one should not offend one's bride's modesty on her wedding night, he slipped into the bedchamber. Adelaide was sitting up in bed, petting her cat, a lit candle on the stand. Expecting to find her up to her neck under the bedclothes and with her eyes shut, the sight took him aback. She did not appear to find a man in nothing more than a shirt either startling or offensive. Her smile was neither nervous nor seductive. A practical woman, an endearing trait which promised a comfortable partnership. He smiled back. The only disconcerting thing was that he felt he was smiling at her cat as well as Adelaide, as the beast's gaze was on him, strangely like his wife's. He did not believe it was smiling, however.

"May I join you?"

"I hope you will, Gervase."

His candle took its place beside hers on the bed stand before he drew back the sheet and coverlet.

With the first sign of embarrassment he had seen, Adelaide said, "I wanted to buy a prettier night rail, but my brother's servants might have found out and wondered. Perhaps I need not have been so timid, but I am accustomed to being criticized for all manner of things."

"Adelaide, 'tis not the wrapping but the gift inside." He eased into bed.

Adelaide turned pink with pleasure at such a little reassurance. When they had agreed to marry, he had anticipated no more than that they would be contented. Now he hoped he could make her happy—no, that they could make each other happy.

The cat did not move. Tabby's green eyes were upon him.

"Mmmm, Adelaide, this may be a trifle difficult with three in the bed. Er, Tabby is rather large for a cat."

"Oh, of course." She uttered a soft sound, and her

pet ("familiar" was the word that came to mind) gave him a last look and sauntered down the bed and onto the bench at its foot, where it sat and proceeded to groom itself.

He told himself that a cat trained to obey a command was really no stranger than a dog, which would sit or stay at its master's word. Was it?

Chapter 27

Dim morning light creeping around the curtains' edges woke him. Lying on his side, he breathed in the rosemary scent of his bride's hair. It was almost in his nose as she was lying with her back to him. They need not rise quite yet, but if he woke her now…No. She was deeply asleep. He would like to take the credit, but most likely yesterday's travel and perhaps nervous exhaustion accounted for it. He could look forward to tonight and the following night and a string of others. He would indulge himself by putting his arm around her. He reached over her side in search of her warm, soft …fur?

His eyes popped open to meet round green eyes in a black-furred face. He and Tabby regarded each other across Adelaide's slumbering form. The cat uttered an irritable word.

"I beg your pardon." *Am I apologizing to a cat for taking a liberty with her?* Ducane supposed he was.

She exhaled irritably and, after staring at him a moment longer, turned her back and jumped off the bed.

Ducane estimated twelve or fourteen days would take them to Dale Tower. Even on the heavily traveled Great North Road, the journey might take that long in bad weather. As their own party was going by a less traveled route, they might take longer yet. It mattered little; they were in no particular hurry now. Good heavens! This was their bridal journey.

In the late morning of the second day, Ducane remarked, "By now your servants are wondering at your not having returned from Tate's son's home yet. Do you wish to write to your brother?"

"Not until we reach Dale Tower, or at least the town nearest it with a receiving office." While she trusted Ducane to protect her, she could not quite rid herself of the fear her brother would pursue them. Rationally she knew he was more likely to breathe a sigh of relief to have her off his hands. He did not know she was an heiress, a detail that might give him a reason to keep control of her. Impossible now she was married, but still, he might make trouble.

Her father had been very sensible to let his son know only that she would have only several hundred pounds a year for her maintenance and a small dowry. Lamburne would learn of Dale Tower when she wrote to request he send her possessions, of course, but there was no reason for him to suspect she had inherited a substantial fortune as well.

In Coventry, they stopped for two hours to shop for clothing for Adelaide and Jenny. Ducane pointed out that they could not be certain of finding anything to buy in the smaller towns on their way. Adelaide worried about the delay.

"In case your brother or his servants suspect a connection between us, I had Jenkins complain to the butler at Blacklaw House he needed to pack a trunk for me all in a flash, as I'd taken a sudden notion to join a friend who was leaving that very day for his estate in Cornwall. If they suspect we have eloped—"

"For my little inheritance from my godmama?" she inquired sardonically.

"No, for your own pleasing self. Better that they should either assume you did not go off with me or if you did, we are on our way to Cornwall."

He was correct about the wisdom of laying a false trail. And she cherished the compliment. Even if it were no more than flattery, she appreciated the effort. Now they were married, he did not need to court her.

As it happened, the stop proved a good idea. A seamstress had two gowns made up for a lady who died before collecting them. The fit was a little loose for Adelaide and they were not fashionable, but at least she need not wear the same clothing all the way to Northumberland. The woman recommended a shop that had some ready-made garb for laborers and lower servants. She had no gowns, but Adelaide purchased four plain, rather coarse shifts and under-petticoats, allegedly for her maid, explaining that the girl's little chest of clothing had somehow been left behind. The garments were a bit long for Jenny, but she could easily take two of them up. The other two, for Adelaide, were somewhat short but would do. Ducane bought a traveling chess set, two packs of cards, and several books. Then they resumed their exodus, armed with amusements to while away the miles.

A market day was in progress at Nuneaton, so they stopped early. There they found a woman selling used clothing and were able to buy Jenny two dresses, one wool and one cotton in a cheerful pink. At another stall, they found a mantle for Jenny, and Ducane purchased one for Adelaide in a shop.

On the following morning, after her husband had

been silent for a time, Adelaide asked hesitantly if something troubled him.

"I have been thinking about something you said earlier, about Lamburne's servants being insolent and playing tricks. Your half brother did not turn them off?"

"I learned early that if I complained, he would say either that I was thin-skinned or I had brought it on myself by being difficult. I tried to be silent and invisible so as not to annoy them, but it never worked. They still despised me."

"Your brother has much to answer for."

"If my father had not died when I was eight, my life might have been quite different. Papa hired my governess, Mistress Henderson, when I was six. While I was in the nursery or schoolroom, Edward ignored me. When I was twelve, he married and I came under Leonora's scrutiny in those places and everywhere else. I became speechless when she upbraided me and fled in tears to hide as soon as she dismissed me. I suppose I seemed to my brother to be everything my sister-in-law said of me."

"Lamburne and his shrew of a wife deserve to be whipped at the cart's tail. I cannot think how you grew so strong." He slid his arm around her shoulders. Adelaide leaned against him; how comfortable to have his support.

"I owe a great deal to my governess." Mistress Henderson had not possessed an affectionate nature, but she was painstaking. Her dispassionate cultivation of Adelaide's mind and character had served her well, while kindness from even one person might have broken her. When she left to be married, Adelaide had missed her but was able to console herself with books filched from the library when Edward was occupied elsewhere. Leonora never opened any book except the Book of Common Prayer and the Bible on Sunday. "I noticed Mistress Henderson's ramrod posture and cool composure in all circumstances, whether berated by Lady Lamburne or slighted by guests. I tried to comport myself as she did and pretend to be unaffected though I still fled or became mute at any criticism."

"Or because you had been made to feel you deserved their mistreatment."

The idea was so unexpected, it stole her breath. Had she come to believe the worst of herself? She had known she was not stupid because she learned her lessons easily, earning her governess's praise. She embroidered better than either of her nieces or Leonora. She had grown less clumsy as she learned to keep her composure when her sister-in-law castigated her. Yet she had also accepted Edward and Leonora's judgement of her as odd and difficult.

"Another part of me did not believe it. Though I am somewhat eccentric," she admitted, because it was true.

"Perhaps you are what they made you. For some years, I frittered my life away in London, although I did not begin by being aimless and pleasure-loving."

She meant to ask him to explain, but the coach pulled up at a coaching inn then for a change of horses and the moment was lost.

They came to Uttoxeter on the fifth day. They were fortunate to have reached such a substantial stopping place, as the next day was Sunday. It would not be quite decent to travel on the Sabbath, and by then, neither of them truly feared pursuit. The notice of their marriage would have appeared two days after they left London, which should have discouraged the Earl of Lamburne from pursuing them.

"I expect he was glad to be quit of me," Adelaide said.

They rose late and attended the parish church of St. Mary's. As they strolled around the town afterward before returning to the coaching inn for dinner, the sight of a footman hurrying on some errand surprised a laugh from Ducane.

"Gervase?"

"I have only just recalled an incident which occurred the day before I received Tate's summons."

"It must be prodigious amusing. Come, tell me what it was."

"The afternoon before our flight, I received a note from Thomas demanding I pay the rest of the money I promised him—" He stopped in mid-sentence when his bride froze in place on the footpath.

"You promised that scoundrel money?"

He could only be grateful no one was close enough to hear or even to see his wife's face. She was white with rage. If she had been a cat as he had sometimes thought of her, her back would be arched, her tail would be fluffed out, and she would be hissing, and he didn't even know why.

"As I mentioned at Lamburne Chase, he tried to extort money from me to conceal his knowledge of our supposed betrothal."

"Tried? He must have succeeded, for I distinctly heard you say 'the rest of the money.' "

"He got a pound, a set of shirt links, and an old waistcoat from me. I told him I had little more than enough to get back to London and no way of getting more until I was in town."

"How much more did he want?" his inquisitor asked. At least she no longer looked as if she were about to swipe at him with claws out.

"The total was fifty pounds. I gave him an IOU for forty-five to keep him quiet, Adelaide. What else could I have done? Your family might not have taken the news well."

She gave a gasp of laughter. "How delicately you put it. I am vexed that blackguard cost you five pounds. I had more than fifty in pin money on hand. There was no need for an IOU, which I trust you have no intention of paying."

"My dear, I could not have allowed you to pay him, quite aside from the fact I wanted to spare you worry. Besides, it would only have encouraged him to ask for more."

"But fifty pounds! I can scarce bear the thought of his squeezing you for hush-money in addition to whatever Sophia gave him for his part in her scheme. I am tolerably sure she paid him to witness you 'compromising' her."

"I would have liked to beat him soundly, but that would not have kept him quiet and would have created another problem. Be at ease, my little pineapple—"

"Pineapple?"

"You are prickly but sweet, hence a pineapple. I do not understand how the French term *petit chou* can be considered an endearment. 'Little cabbage'? Anyway, he sent a letter to Blacklaw House instructing me to meet him at a coffee house to pay him the balance. I intended to go the next day, as it was too late when I received the message. Then in the morning, I heard from Tate, and by the time I would have met Thomas, we were on our way and I forgot to make arrangements to pay him."

"How could you have paid him when it was vital we leave London quickly?"

"I could have had the Blacklaw House butler deliver the money." As he said it, he realized doing so would have led to another complication.

His mother would sooner give up her lady's maid than Black, who ran the London house to perfection. The late marquess had once remarked that it was too bad the man couldn't be put in charge of organizing the House of Lords. Ducane would have trusted him to deal with Thomas. The man was utterly loyal to the family and in particular to the dowager marchioness. Therein lay the difficulty. Moses would have delivered the money to Thomas without fail and made sure to get the IOU. As he clearly believed Ducane had got himself into trouble, he would also discreetly report the matter to Blacklaw, probably by messenger.

Adelaide frowned.

"Damme, I'll have to find a way to get the money to him somehow. I suppose he is in London because your brother has turned him off? At least it doesn't matter that I failed to meet him, as he has no secret now to divulge."

"You need not worry about poor Thomas needing your money to survive. He was sent to London to spy on me." Adelaide glared at him. "Why would you even consider paying him?"

"I gave him my IOU."

"Which he extorted from you."

"Some gentlemen regard gambling losses as debts of honor which must be paid and ignore what they owe merchants and tradesmen. My friends consider me eccentric for paying all my debts promptly and in full. I promised to pay Thomas, so…"

She took a breath and softened her tone. "Gervase, money owed to your tailor is a legitimate debt, and I understand your reason for giving Thomas something to keep him quiet until we could get away from Lamburne. To submit to his blackmail now when there is no need would be ridiculous."

"I know he is no pattern card of virtue, but servants must often compromise their own principles or risk losing their employment. If he had refused to be a witness to Lady Sophia's scheme, would she not have complained of him to her father and lost him his position?"

"That devil abducted Tabby, put her in a bag, and hung it from a branch in the park. I searched for her for the greater part of the night. Bad enough that the sneaking wretch was insolent to me and encouraged the other servants to ignore me or give me saucy answers, but when he endangered Tabby—" She was biting her lip and blinking rapidly.

He wanted to gather her into his arms and hold her, not a possibility in public. The impropriety of weeping in the street must have occurred to her as well. He watched her struggle to suppress her tears. That ability must have served her well in the past.

"I'm sorry, Adelaide. I didn't know."

Her voice under control once more, she said, "You couldn't know. He is clever and sly, and Edward and Leonora think him the very model of a good footman.

No doubt he will be their butler one day, unless he hangs first." From her tone, he guessed she would not waste a moment grieving if Thomas ended dangling from a rope at Tyburn.

Compromise should be part of marriage. "While an IOU for a gambling loss or debt is binding, I concede I am not at all certain the same is true for blackmail."

"I should think not!"

"Strike me dead if he sees a penny more from me, then." He let a moment pass. "Have we just had our first quarrel?" he asked plaintively. "And over a rascally footman, at that?"

Her chuckle reassured him. "Yes, I think we have. Shall we return to the inn and play a hand or two of piquet before dinner?"

All the way back to the inn, something Adelaide had told him niggled at the back of his mind. At the time he had taken no notice. What was it? He had an uncomfortable suspicion that it was something important.

Chapter 28

Before noon on the eighth day, they reached Preston in Lancashire. Adelaide exclaimed at its size, good streets, and brick houses, which gave it an air of prosperity. They had arrived on a market day, one of three each week, but not, alas, on Saturday, when the busiest market was held. All four chose to walk around the square to stretch their legs, though Adelaide's cat preferred to remain in their rooms at the inn. Or so Adelaide said, explaining that Tabby did not care for much walking, crowds, or dogs. Ducane suspected he would not be keeping dogs in the house.

Making their way through jostling locals shopping for necessities soon palled. Adelaide timidly expressed a wish for a bath; Ducane was pleased to return with her to the inn so she might gratify it. He studied the map while she scrubbed herself and washed her hair. He poured fresh water over her and helped her wrap herself in a bath sheet when she emerged, rosy and otter-sleek. Or cat-sleek, but you would never find a cat taking a bath. He would have liked—but Jenny and Jenkins would be returning, and then it would be time for supper. He did make use of his wife's bath water before summoning the inn servants to empty the tub and remove it.

Adelaide sat on the settle by the hearth, combing her damp hair, Tabby curled up against her. "Gervase, about children…"

She could not be certain they were expecting one already, could she? Surely it was too soon to know? "Ay?"

"I am a little afraid of having a child."

Here was a delicate topic. "Because you are not in your first youth? Or did your mother—?" The second Lady Lamburne had died when Adelaide was five or six, he thought. Childbirth was hazardous for women.

"No. I have heard of women giving birth who were older than I am, and my mother died of smallpox, not in childbed. But I do not know if I would be a good mother."

"I suppose a woman cannot help but love her baby—" Was that true? He knew ladies who spent little or no time with their offspring and showed no interest in them. Some spent more time pampering their lapdogs. His own mother had not paid much attention to him, as long as he did not embarrass her. He had striven to make her proud but seldom succeeded, so far as he could tell. Adelaide's expression was politely skeptical.

She would not value anything but truth. "I beg your pardon. I'm accustomed to society's commonplaces, but I don't usually utter them. What can you tell me of your mother?"

"She died when I was six. I recall little except that she hugged me and laughed and could sing and play the harpsichord. There must be more to being a mother than that."

"If you play with your—our—child and sing or tell him or her stories, I believe you will excel most mothers of our class. My nurse did those things, and I was very fond of her. My mother accompanied my father to town and was active in court circles. On my father's annual visits to the other properties, I was left at home with my mother. In his absence, she oversaw the estate and the marquessate's other business as he would have done. I can't blame her for having little time for me.

"My father was very much what the French call a *grand seigneur*: conscious of his rank and dignity and the importance of Blacklaw. He spent a good deal of time with Robert and took him along when he visited the other properties. I did not have much to do with him until my brother took up residence in London and I returned from my tour of Italy. When or if I am a father, I intend to do nearly everything the opposite of my own father. No doubt we would contrive to be at least as good as most parents and better than some. After all, you have the benefit of your mother's example, and I have my parents' failings to avoid." He was rewarded by seeing some of her worry fade away.

But after a moment, she asked, "Failings? I have been envying you your family. Your brother giving you time to establish yourself, your mother helping you find a wife, the stories you have told me about your life at Blacklaw, all sounds so pleasant."

"Compared to what you suffered at your family's hands, I suppose it was."

He thought she would say no more, having fallen into a brown study. Instead she surprised him. "I think you once said you had not started out to be an aimless man about town."

Amazing she remembered his unconsidered remark, which he had regretted making. "I was a responsible boy, although not because of any inborn virtue. My parents were busy with the properties, with court, and with training my brother. I hoped to impress them by good behavior, doing well in my studies, and never being tardy or untidy. Robert was always in mischief, neglected any subject he didn't enjoy, and frequently was late, rumpled, and sometimes bruised or bloodied." *I would have done better to behave badly. At least they would have taken the time to correct my conduct.*

"I suppose they thought I didn't need their attention, while Robert in his wildness did. But perhaps they did notice me, as my father asked me to assist him with the properties." This was the most interest he had ever received from the marquess. He had been flattered. Even that might have been only from necessity because his lordship expected Robert to live the life of a man about town for years to come, as he himself had done. "I enjoyed those years learning the estate, the other properties, and the investments. Eventually he left it all in my hands, and I traveled to the other estates to deal with any problems and inspect the ledgers. In his later years, he only journeyed to London for Parliament and court, activities of greater importance to him than dealing with tenants, leases, and account books."

"Your family was fortunate to have you."

"I enjoyed it and believe I did well. However, when Robert took over, I moved to London to represent Blacklaw's interests there, so I was still of some use to the family." Although not immediately. Before Gervase finished packing to leave, the marquess asked him to remain to refresh his memory about sundry matters. Robert had not been directly involved since being dispatched to London after Oxford. Escorting him around to the tenant farms to re-introduce him to their holders, explaining the changes in methods and how they had increased profits, and reviewing the account books took almost a year.

He could not replace his brother at court—only a second son!—but Ducane had found it easy to cultivate Frederick, the Prince of Wales, who had his own circle. Ducane's way with a bon mot gained him a place among the fashionable set. His reputation as something of a stickler for correct conduct did him no harm among the more sedate. He graced the usual entertainments and visited the country homes of friends in the summer when everyone who could left London. He usually spent part of the summer at Blacklaw. The years had passed comfortably enough though without much challenge.

"I became an idle, pleasure-seeking fellow rather than be an embarrassment to my family." At her questioning look, he said, "When you were in London, did you not notice that earnest, virtuous fellows were considered laughingstocks?"

"As a source of humiliation to my own family, I confess I did not notice others who may have been in similar straits."

"We have escaped our circumstances, Adelaide. You will be respected for yourself, for being Lady Creighton's heir, and as mistress of your own house, and I will be a country gentleman. But I promise not to turn into an uncouth country gentleman, letting my hunting dogs loose indoors to create havoc."

The cat raised her head, sighed blissfully, and stretched.

Clean and dressed, they awaited Jenny and Jenkins

and their evening meal. They would retire early tonight in order to push on as far as possible the next day. They could not hope to reach Carlisle, near seventy miles, in one day.

****

A journey that should have taken only two days brought them to Carlisle in four days, as they had at last suffered some of the expected hazards. First a broken wheel delayed them, then the driver of the second carriage reported the coach box on which he sat was loose, necessitating a stop for repair lest it separate from the body of the coach. They spent two nights in villages where the inn was hardly better than an alehouse. Adelaide ate tough mutton without complaint. She smiled sympathetically at Ducane's ill concealed distaste.

They reached Carlisle on Saturday afternoon. The city appeared to Adelaide to have been busier and more prosperous formerly than it was at present, but the inn was comfortable and Adelaide had high expectations of the bed. After a good supper, Ducane spent part of the evening in the inn's common room, inquiring about the road to Corbridge. Adelaide passed the time by having a bath. At Lamburne, some difficulty had always attended her request for a tub. Even when it came promptly, hot water was so slow in coming that she seldom got a really warm bath.

She was already tucked into that bed in her night rail with Tabby beside her when Ducane returned.

"Wise woman! We should retire early. It's forty miles or more to Corbridge. I could get no definite report as to the condition of the road, but it was built by the Romans and still connects Carlisle and Newcastle, so I suppose it will be in reasonable condition. I wish we could build as well as those fellows did. If we cannot reach Corbridge in a day, there are several villages where we might stay overnight, though the accommodations may be primitive." He was shedding his clothing as he spoke, coat, waistcoat, and neckcloth draped over a straight chair. He had already sent Jenkins to his night's rest, as Adelaide had dismissed Jenny.

She had not expected to be so much at ease with her husband. In the days on the road, which would be trying for the most even-tempered traveler, she had never once regretted their marriage. Somehow that made it worse that she had held one secret back.

"I have a confession to make, Gervase. I hope it does not change things between us."

He paused in unbuttoning his breeches. "This sounds serious, yet we are so well suited that I can hardly imagine anything you could reveal that would disconcert me."

She swallowed to relieve the lump in her throat. "I am sorry I did not tell you before you committed yourself. My only excuse is that I was afraid."

Shoes, breeches, and stockings went the way of the other garments. He sat on the edge of the bed in his shirt, half turned toward her. Tabby stood up, stretched, and ambled to the foot to jump down, then made her way to the chair. She leapt up onto it, turned around, kneaded his discarded clothing briefly and settled down for the night. They watched this performance, Adelaide nervously, her husband quizzically.

"I believe I am flattered," he commented before turning back to Adelaide.

"I told you about my mother," she said. "But Edward doesn't despise me only because she was an actress and what he called a mongrel, being half-Scottish and half-French. That would be bad enough for most people." She was sitting bolt upright in bed. Now she gave the impression of straightening even more, drawing her shoulders back and raising her chin. "She was my father's mistress for several years before his first wife died. Then a few months after the first Lady Lamburne's death, my mother learned she was enceinte. Of course everyone thought she had deliberately let herself get with child, perhaps by some other man. I don't know whether either is true, but it seems strange to me she would have thought he would marry his mistress. What nobleman would?"

"Your papa, evidently. He must have loved her. I can understand there being talk, however."

"From what I have heard, 'nine days' wonder' does not begin to describe the beau monde's reaction to their marriage." Arid humor tinged her voice as she went on, "I'm glad I wasn't there to see it. I should have told you I might be some other man's bastard, rather than the previous Lord Lamburne's legitimate daughter."

Set against the fact she was an heiress and his genuine liking and respect, the question of her birth would have carried no weight in his decision to marry her. Telling her so would be no consolation to her. She would assume her fortune outweighed rumors about her birth. Adelaide's left hand rested on the bed, clutching the coverlet. He placed his own over it.

"Adelaide, you were born within their marriage. You are legitimate in the eyes of the law, and your mother's husband acknowledged you. He need not have provided for you if he did not consider you his daughter. And whatever your parentage, I value you for yourself."

She stared at him. "I expected you to be horrified or at least surprised."

"I already knew about the rumor your mother was his mistress."

"You did?"

"Mmmm." No need to mention he learned of it only after asking her to marry him. It would have made no difference anyway.

Her smile was like the sun rising: glorious. "Oh, thank you for not caring. I have worried and worried for weeks because I had not told you. I was so ashamed both of the secret and of not giving you the chance to change your mind. You are the best of husbands."

He raised her hand to his lips. "I aspire to be. Do you think we might now snuff the candle?"

And they did.

Chapter 29

A little more than a fortnight after leaving London, they paused at the top of a gentle rise for their first sight of Dale Tower. Its name suggested something vaguely like a castle, but Tate had called it a manor. Adelaide had been unable to imagine how the two might combine. She had seen gentlemen's homes near Lamburne, and none of them had towers.

Dale Tower bore no resemblance to Lamburne's utterly symmetrical façade. If one could slice her brother's house in half, the left and right would be reversed images. This house appeared to have been built in three different periods. The first addition had been grafted on to the long side of the rectangular tower; the farthest section jutted out farther in back than the rest. The house sat at an angle to the road, revealing that the old tower was twice as deep as wide. The difference between the sections was easy to see: the first possessed four stories, and was severely plain, with small windows and an exterior stone stair leading up to the first floor. The rest was two stories with a gabled attic and slate roof. The pale buff sandstone did not quite match from one section to the next. Probably building stone was like yarn or fabric. One could not expect one lot to be exactly like the next. Weathering would account for some difference, too. The newer parts had quoins and window and door surrounds of a purplish pink stone, an odd but rather cheerful touch. Beyond the house lay a collection of outbuildings and beyond those, fields. The lane to the house ran through a band of trees perhaps intended to shield it from the wind.

"The tower is medieval," Ducane said. "Built when this land was disputed. I've seen something similar before. What do you think of the house?"

"It's ours, which makes it perfect. If the chimneys don't draw and the roof leaks, we can make repairs." Half an hour dragged by until the coach rattled to a halt at the door. Adelaide could hardly wait to get into her new home.

Instead of offering his hand to assist her, Ducane put his hands on her waist and lifted her down, surprising her with his strength. They both stood gazing at the façade for a moment before he set her hand on his arm and led her up the shallow steps. Before he could rap on the door, it was opened by an elderly butler.

"Lady Adelaide and Lord Gervase Ducane? Welcome. I'm Greer." He held the door wide and bowed them into the hall. "I apologize for not having the staff waiting to greet you, but we had not heard when you might arrive." A smiling middle-aged woman appeared slightly behind the butler.

"We were not quite sure ourselves."

"Perhaps you could assemble them by the time we have tidied ourselves? In an hour, perhaps?"

Ducane heard the hesitation in his bride's voice.

"Certainly, Lady Adelaide, Lord Gervase. Mistress Hopkins, the housekeeper, will show you to your chambers."

They had adjoining bedrooms, and each had a

dressing room. Adelaide also had a parlor. As they did not mean to change, and in Adelaide's case had nothing better to wear, they did no more than wash their hands and faces after hot water was brought to them. They went downstairs before an hour was out.

Greer had the servants waiting. All looked pleased to see the new owners, boding well for Adelaide's relationship with them. Greer, the butler, explained the small staff—only two footmen and two maids—as the result of Lady Creighton's years of poor health.

"Her ladyship did not entertain the last ten years."

"I suppose once we meet the other families in the neighborhood, and of course when your family comes to visit, Gervase, we'll need more servants." Momentarily it occurred to her that she should have addressed him by his title. Then she thought, No, calling him by the name she used when they were private felt right. They were far from the beau monde here.

"There are people in the village who would be glad of work." Greer murmured apologetically, "There are some repairs to be made in the house, as well."

"Is there a list of what's necessary? We will review it and have the work done in order of importance."

"Certainly, sir." The butler paused. "Ah…I should mention a letter has arrived for you. Will you have it now?"

She and Ducane exchanged glances. "Perhaps in the drawing room before supper? Or after," he suggested.

"Before, I think." Otherwise she would wonder and worry and lose her appetite.

The letter from Tate had made its way north faster

than Adelaide and Ducane had traveled, the post having gone by the Great North Road as far as Newcastle. Her man of business wrote that the day following their departure, the Lamburne House butler sent a coach to his nephew's home. His nephew, stout fellow, had merely informed the footman that the lady and her maid had gone, perhaps implying she had set out for home. Tate had received no inquiry as to whether he knew where Adelaide was, though it was only a matter of time before he did, if Lamburne was expected in London. He would write as soon as he had more news.

"There's nothing Edward can do now," Adelaide observed. Life was good.

They sat down to supper with excellent appetites, having eaten only a perfunctory midday meal at an inn. They had been anxious to reach Dale Tower. The cook sent her apologies through Greer that the supper would be simple and plain, though she would add syllabub and biscuits and preserved fruit for the second course. After days of inn fare, they both found the meal more than acceptable, and Tabby enjoyed her serving of mutton stew and a bit of cheese.

"I would like to inspect the house this evening," Adelaide said as she nibbled a coriander seed biscuit. "Not a thorough inspection, which will take days, only a quick look."

"We can certainly do so. It's too early to retire, and I don't feel like sitting, do you?"

"Not after days in the coach. Although in truth, I simply can't wait to see the house."

The kitchen and pantry were in the ground floor of the tower. The reception room, drawing room, a less-formal parlor, dining room, and library made up the rest of that floor in the new house. There were ten bedrooms besides their own suite on the first floor and several more, as well as the nursery and schoolroom, on the second. The servants' quarters were in the attic.

"I see nothing to dislike in the furniture, unless you object to it, Gervase."

"It suits the house and appears adequate. Though we will have to test the beds tonight."

"I like it, don't you? I will see about replacing some of the curtains and upholstery. The new sheets and blankets and other things I ordered in town will be coming." She hoped he was not disappointed. He had not seemed dissatisfied, but he would mask his feelings if he were. His family's home must be much larger, as was Lamburne Chase.

"It has a charm Blacklaw lacks. The only part of that house that felt like home was the nursery suite," he said. "This is a country gentleman's residence, and I like it very well. There's only one thing…"

She waited his judgment with some anxiety.

"The nursery will need work. I cannot think it has been changed in the last half century or more."

"I suppose it has not. My godmother never had children, and if Lord Creighton did, they did not survive childhood. We need not worry about improving the nursery suite yet, however."

"Then when we need it, we will furnish it."

"I suppose we will find the nursery things put away in the attic. I think the upper floors of the tower are used for storage."

Later they sat in the parlor as the sky dimmed.

"While you conduct your inspection with Mistress Hopkins tomorrow, I mean to look at the stable and outbuildings. We must see about a horse for you, as I don't suppose the old lady had ridden for many years. I'll speak with the bailiff, too, and ask him to present his accounts in two or three days. We should both ride around the manor with him."

Having an estate to manage appealed to her husband. Before, she had not quite believed he would enjoy country life.

Sipping ratafia as he drank brandy, she thought to ask, "Have you written your brother?"

"Well…no. We left London so quickly, and it was not convenient to do so while we were traveling. Anyway, I thought to wait until we were here. I suppose I must do so."

"Lord Blacklaw and your mother should certainly be informed."

"I'll do it…though they may have seen the notice in the papers. Do you mean to write Lamburne?"

"I must." She sighed. It need not be a long letter, after all.

Dear Lamburne, you have no doubt seen the announcement of my marriage. My husband and I are residing at Dale Tower, Northumberland, not far from Otterburn, which I recently inherited from my late godmother, Lady Creighton. Tate will arrange to ship my clothing and other possessions from Lamburne Chase and Lamburne House and will provide a maid and footman to pack them to spare your servants the effort. I trust you and your family are all well. You are welcome to visit us, if you have no objection to a simple country gentleman's house.

She hoped they wouldn't visit, and why should they? They did not care for her, and she certainly did not miss them. "I'll write Tate, as well, to let him know we arrived safely."

Had she ever been happier? Her first six years had seemed carefree as she looked back on what she remembered of them, but snatches of happy memories do not amount to an entirety. Then she lost her mother, although she did not remember much about her death and its aftermath. Her father had loved her, she believed. His death began the long, long years of being first ignored and then made miserable, once Edward married Leonora.

Her life was now as delightful as anyone could wish. Each morning she woke to a new day in which no one was unkind to her and she had interesting things to do. She had her own home, the friendship of Gervase Ducane, and certain other benefits she could never have imagined. Mayhap she would have children. Could heaven be better?

Chapter 30

They had been in residence for several days when she thought to discuss needed improvements to the kitchen with Mistress Jones. Adelaide had not been sure Cook would embrace the spit jack, a relatively modern invention, in place of the spit dogs. Adelaide's friend accompanied her, as she had not yet seen the kitchen. When one of the nasty little brutes snarled at Tabby, Adelaide scooped her up while Cook grabbed the offending dog and returned him to his pen in the scullery, nudging the second one before her with one foot.

"I keep them confined as a rule except when one is turning the spit, but when it's chilly like today and there's no fire in the scullery, I let them into the kitchen. They can go right back out now. Horrid things, *if* you ask me, your ladyship, which you haven't."

Her concern about how Tabby would be received proved unnecessary. The cook, who was fond of cats, had had worries of her own about a new mistress. Ladies favored lap dogs as pets.

"Our Tom keeps the pantry and kitchen cleared of mice and rats. I hope your dear little cat won't mind not catching her dinner, my lady?"

"Not at all. Chopped meat or poultry or fish with perhaps a bit of vegetable or cheese hashed up with it will do very well, served in the dining room." "Dear little cat" was not quite how she herself would describe Tabby. Not since kittenhood, anyway.

"Very easily done, ma'am. There is just one more thing?"

"Yes?"

"Tom has his own little door out into the kitchen garden. Jed as does whatever bits of work needs doing took out a pane in one of the scullery windows so Tom can come and go."

"It is not safe for a cat to go out," Adelaide said. In Tabby's case, danger hadn't always been confined to marauding foxes or dogs, either.

"Oh, he can't get out of the kitchen garden. It's walled to protect the plants from the wind, which can blow something fierce." She added, eyes twinkling, "I had him from a kitling. He doesn't know there's anything more than the kitchen, scullery, pantry, and the kitchen garden."

Tabby would enjoy going out on her own. "Tabby and I will see, Mistress Jones, if Tom has no objection to sharing his domain."

"Not he, Lady Adelaide. Very placid he is, excepting with vermin or when the spit dogs bother him. He sorts them out quick enough."

So Cook was pleased with the idea of a clockwork device and said she would see the dogs depart to another home with pleasure when the spit jack arrived.

Adelaide introduced the idea of the new "stew stove," a sort of brick enclosure in which to make a fire, with openings on the top where pots could be set to cook. Her new familiarity with kitchen work showed that hanging cauldrons over the fire or putting small pots or frying pans on trivets over the coals was far more arduous than she had known. She and Cook agreed they would wait to decide about the stew stove until she had spoken with someone who possessed such a thing.

Cook had hesitantly inquired about purchasing certain other items. Several of them were things Adelaide had already ordered in London, like the spit jack; they were on their way north by country carrier. She approved the others, which could be easily obtained nearby. Only after they had reached accord on all these matters did she realize that the cook was working at a time when there should have been nothing for her to do. They had eaten their dinner, and she would not have to begin preparations for their simple supper for hours. Instead something was baking, and a tin sheet covered with sugared almonds lay on the work table. Before Adelaide could ask what the preparations were for, Mistress Jones said, "I thought to be ready for your visitors, my lady. They'll be coming to pay their respects as soon you've had time to settle. Dale Tower is an important house hereabouts. There's already potted meat and fruit put up in syrup." She took a crock from a shelf and began to transfer the almonds to it. "I mean to make almond Portugal cakes, too. That sort keep well."

Visitors! With a qualm of foreboding, Adelaide asked, "How soon should we expect them?"

"Within the week, I'd say. Likely Vicar and his lady will come first. There's Sir Humphrey and Lady Collins, Lady Agatha—she's elderly and was a great friend of Lady Creighton—and her son and daughter-in-law, and the Loudons. They b'aint titled but own a great property and the family is old. Those four's the nearest. The rest will come in time."

Adelaide made shift to thank Cook and compliment her on her preparations, all the while thinking, "What will I wear?"

She had been too busy inspecting the house and learning all she could about its management to think much about her wardrobe. She wore the gown and petticoat and casaquin she had brought from London when she escaped and several other garments either bought on the journey or stitched by the best seamstress among the maids. Even the good gown was old and out of fashion. The jacket and skirt, though newer and well-made, were too informal. There had seemed no hurry about acquiring anything else. If Edward never sent her clothing, eventually she would have to visit the nearest town with a skilled mantua maker. Would there be one in Otterburn or Rothbury, or would she have to travel all the way to Newcastle? The idea of more travel did not appeal to her, and anyway, Gervase was busy learning about the property. Now she must face her new neighbors appearing to be a country dowdy. Nothing she had was suitable for receiving calls.

"What am I to do?" Adelaide uttered, more to herself than Jenny. Jenkins might have a suggestion, but even he could not conjure a wardrobe in mere days.

"Mistress Webb!"

Jenny's exclamation conveyed nothing to Adelaide. Her maid, seeing it, said, "The old ladyship's maid. She's still here, in a little room near the kitchen."

There had been a number of bequests to servants in Lady Creighton's will. While Adelaide had paid scant attention to them, she had seen some mention of her godmother's maid. "She'd been with Lady Creighton a long time, I remember that much."

"Fifty year, Mr. Greer told me."

"She received a pension," Adelaide said slowly, "and something more? Bed and board here for life, was it?"

"Ay. They say her old ladyship wanted to be sure she was cared for, which she mightn't be, if she'd been given a cottage as she hadn't no family left."

"A grace and favor apartment, in other words."

Jenny looked blank. "She's been showing me how to go on as a lady's dresser. She still does some of the finer sewing. T'other day when I stopped in to see her, she was mending the lace on one of her old mistress's gowns. Beautiful, it was."

She thought Jenny's skills had improved in the last few days but put that thought aside in order to satisfy curiosity. "Why?" Lady Creighton no longer had any need of a mantua or of a lady's maid.

"She takes care of Lady Creighton's wardrobe. Always has and always will, she says. My lady, mayhap we should see her."

"Are you thinking she would lend me something of my godmother's to wear? If she were willing, how likely is it any of her clothing would fit me? And I suppose most of it would be out of fashion."

"Won't know 'less we ask, my lady."

Adelaide had assumed the door between the stillroom and the kitchen led to a storeroom. Instead it opened to reveal a snug chamber.

"I'm pleased to see my lady's goddaughter," Hester Webb said when she welcomed them. Lady Creighton had made sure her former maid had a window on the kitchen garden and a fireplace. "You're the image of your mother."

"You knew my mother?"

"Ay, I served my lady since I was a girl, and before her ladyship married the second time and we came here, her ladyship called upon your mother, Lady Lamburne as was, many a time. Lady Lamburne didn't care a groat that society looked down on my lady's papa, and my mistress didn't care your mama had been on the stage. Sharp wits and good nature was what Lady Creighton valued. Lord, I wish you could have heard them laughing like girls at society's nonsense, in spite of my lady being considerable older than Lady Lamburne."

"I should have come to see you sooner, but there has been so much to learn about Dale Tower and the household…"

"And you a new bride, too. And glad I was to hear it, as my lady often wondered how you did. She wrote to Lord Lamburne a dozen times or more when you were younger. Received mighty short replies." She clucked.

Adelaide gathered her courage. "Jenny thought you might advise me. My trunks can't be expected to come for some time yet, and Cook says we will begin to receive visits soon. Would it be possible to furbish up what I have here enough to make it acceptable?" she asked hollowly.

"My lady, you arrived without even one trunk, and I have spied you in the garden. You have one sensible gown that might be freshened with new ribbons and lace, but the others I have seen are fit only for visiting the dairy or making cordials or other housewifely tasks."

"I feared as much."

Jenny was biting her lip.

"But you'll not be shamed by dressing like a country wife, though you'll not have many gowns," the old woman said. "No one will wonder that the greater part of your clothing has not arrived yet. Lord! When my lady was young and traveled, we needed a second coach for her trunks. Lady Creighton's things are stored on the fourth floor. We will see which gowns and accessories will do."

Mistress Webb was a thin old woman but not feeble, and clearly still had all her wits about her. She led them briskly into the kitchen. The cook and kitchen maids began to curtsy before they saw Adelaide. Apparently their late lady's maid kept her place in the hierarchy. Adelaide and Jenny followed her up the stairs.

The chamber on the highest floor was a treasure trove. Even in the last years of Lady Creighton's life she had dressed in the current fashion and insisted on the highest quality. Jenny gawked at the clothes presses, chests of drawers, hatboxes, bandboxes, and trunks. Adelaide stood out of the way as Hester Webb examined the carefully stored garments and muttered to herself.

"This color will do Lady Adelaide no favor. Ah, the crimson *contouche*. My lady loved that one, and it will be easy to alter." She lifted it out reverently and held it up. "The length is right. I thought my lady was of a height with you, Lady Adelaide. In her later years, at least; she shrank somewhat in her old age, as I have myself." She chuckled. "But Lady Creighton was a fine, tall girl when I first served her." Hester draped it over a work table she must use when caring for her mistress's clothes.

"Now, let me see…the painted silk *robe battante* will do well and need no fitting. The peacock blue is pretty, though perhaps not your best color. We'll take the bronze damask sacque gown. This yellow is too bright."

She pulled out half a dozen more: wool for chilly days, and two or three linen gowns meant for informal wear. Before releasing Adelaide, she took measurements. "The less-fitted ones should do well enough as they are. I've noticed that even when a gown is not perfect, 'tis the whole effect that strikes the eye, not the details. Not too much to be taken in on the robes à l'anglaise, thank the Lord, but I'll need Susan to help. And Jenny can search through the other things for petticoats, kerchiefs, a cape, mantle, fan, gloves, hmmm, and all else as I am sure you have none. Oh, and a pair of stays, for I'll swear you brought none with you. Wellaway, there's no riding habit. My poor lady had to give up riding many years ago, and we gave them to the daughters of a friend of my lady's who was terrible purse-pinched. The girls were at their best on horseback, and all three married well because of it. One's the wife of a general." She sighed reminiscently. "Now, have you enough jewelry? You must not be wearing pretty gowns without a necklet and earbobs, and a few other trifles, though much of my lady's jewelry is a trifle old-fashioned or too elaborate for a country toilette, as perhaps you've seen."

Adelaide assured her that she had her mother's jewelry and—goodness! She had forgot Lady Creighton's jewels as well and had not looked at them yet. Tate had told her they were secured in the strongroom.

"Tomorrow if you can spare the time, we will see which of your pieces should be paired with each garment." The old lady's maid agreed Lady Creighton's collection would not be necessary for the moment. "Near all was bought in her first marriage or before. Some should be reset in the modern manner. Still, at home in the country, simple will be best. Your girl and I will pack the things to be carried to your chamber. Welcome to Dale Tower, Lady Adelaide. Her ladyship would be pleased to have you here."

Taking it as dismissal, Adelaide made her way downstairs, as weary as if she had been running or had ridden for hours, but with the conviction she would not disgrace herself before the local gentry. Not by her clothing, at least. She left Jenny to look through the old lady's accessories to choose the ones she thought her mistress should borrow and have them approved by Hester Webb.

Chapter 31

A letter from her half brother arrived. It was addressed to Ducane, a slight which she could not regret although she was curious. Her husband stopped a moment after beginning to read the missive. His brow furrowed but he said merely, "Your brother has learned of our marriage."

"I suspect this is your diplomatic translation, Gervase. What does he really write?"

"Are you sure you want to know?" At her nod, he sighed. "Shall I read it to you or summarize it?"

"Nothing Edward can say is likely to offend me. Remember, I've lived with him."

"Here it is, then. He begins, 'On arriving in town I learned almost simultaneously that my half sister had left Lamburne House two days before and failed to return, of your marriage to her, and of your rumored secret betrothal to Addie during the house party.' Damme! That curst footman must have spread that around when I failed to meet him. He cannot have seen the notice of our marriage. I suppose it must have been printed the day after our last day to meet."

" 'Tis what I would expect of Thomas."

"An arch-scoundrel. To continue: 'The latter mystifies me as much as it appalls me for your betrayal of our hospitality. To turn down the opportunity to gain my daughter for a little manor and a pittance and my

279

spinster half sister and her crotchets shows you to be as totty-headed as she. I suppose I must be grateful you married the…' I wonder what he meant to write? There's a great ink blot."

"An indication of his state of mind as his hand is quite precise as a rule."

"Wait, I have it. '…grateful that you married the jade.'" He looked up, thin brows arching in disapproval. "Pretty language to use of one's kin. Where was I? He continues, 'You and Addie between you have harmed my daughters' chances of making good marriages by this double scandal—'"

"I take it he does not mention the scandal of my niece trying to force you into marriage." In her lap, Tabby looked up at her and blinked before curling into a ball, one wrist and forearm over her face.

"Ah, but that is not a scandal because no one outside the family knows of it."

"A point, Gervase. Except Thomas, of course. I suppose he is too cowardly to try to extort money from Edward. What a pity I am too well-behaved to reveal it to some friend."

"Lamburne goes on, 'The pair of you have made my family a laughingstock and I wash my hands of my ungrateful half sister who has put her own selfish interests before the good of her family. I urge you to avoid whatever society is to be found near your new home to conceal Lady Adelaide's peculiarities, and I hope your family will not regret your hasty, ill-sorted match.' He signs himself 'Lamburne' with no closing. Well! Fine talk from a man who should have treated you well for your father's sake if he could not cherish you for yourself."

The accusations did not pierce her, being either untrue or unfair or simply things he and Leonora had said often. "That last part sounds like Leonora. She must have been haranguing him while he wrote. She would be furious about my selfishness in stealing you from Sophia. They must still be unaware of the size of the trust from my father or how much I inherited from Lady Creighton. They would both have been enraged if they knew and would have railed about that, too."

Ducane put the letter aside and picked up his recently purchased copy of *The New Horse Hoeing Husbandry*. "Just as well they don't, then." He tapped his book. "Let us put them out of our minds. I talked with a gentleman in Rothbury last week. He thinks well of many of Tull's ideas, though he admits some of them are controversial. Jackson, your bailiff, disagrees with his theory that manuring the soil is of no use, for instance. He does think hoeing between the rows of plants is worthwhile and says Tull's seed drill has merit. I mean to talk to others about the drill and try the hoeing method on our home farm. Tull invented a new sort of plow that seems promising. He died earlier this year, unfortunately. I would have liked to correspond with him."

How delightful they could sit together and discuss anything, including manure and crops. She would never have guessed the elegant Gervase Ducane would be an enthusiast for farming methods. But then, she could not have envisioned learning to preserve fruit and make cordials and other remedies. Cook was pleased by her interest in the work. Mrs. Jones had gone so far as to say Lady Creighton would have approved and had complained that ladies nowadays learned nothing more practical than dancing and coquetting. With the assistance of an old book titled *Delightes for Ladies*, Adelaide was making good the deficiencies in her education: the making of mead and other wines (though she could not help but feel Gervase would prefer claret to elderberry wine) and how to make cheese. Adelaide meant to study the dairy maid's work, for as detailed as the written directions were, the procedure would surely be more easily understood in person.

****

Ducane had begun with the stable, finding it well managed though somewhat deficient in cattle. There were several carriage horses for the coach, two hacks, one nearly of retirement age, which the bailiff and grooms rode when they needed to ride, and a plough horse. For the time being, he himself could use one of the hacks. Neither was trained to sidesaddle, so Adelaide would need a mount. Jackson would know if anyone had suitable horses to sell.

This morning Ducane meant to ride the bounds of the estate with Jackson. Before he could get out his chamber door, Jenkins said, "Stop a moment, sir. There's a smudge on your left boot, though I polished it yesterday evening. I'll just give it a quick rub."

"Jenkins, I'll be riding. By the time I return, my boots will be all over dust and so will I."

"Lord Gervase, I cannot have you leaving your chamber looking like a shag-bag. A moment, please."

Ducane gave a martyred sigh and put his foot up on the stool by the hearth. Amusing to think that in London, he would have shared his manservant's horror. There was indeed a slight mark on the side of the boot. Having observed similar smears on some of the windows, he recognized it as the sign of a cat's damp nose pressed against the glass. Or the boot, in this case.

Jenkins emerged from the dressing room with a little white rag. "It shouldn't need more than a wipe, sir."

As he bent, the piece of fabric looked less like a scrap and more like a lady's handkerchief. What was there—?

"Wait, Jenkins. Let me see that."

He took the square of fine linen. It must have been employed as a polishing cloth previously and not been laundered, as it bore a brownish stain. It felt familiar in his hand. His mouth went dry. In one corner, a cat leapt, finely executed in white silk thread.

He was blinking up at...a cat? One of Mme. d'Aulnoy's fairies? A female? The moonlight illuminated half of a triangular face, wide at the brow, with high, sharp cheekbones and a pointed chin. She was bending over him, a woman like a cat. Not really, of course not, and yet in some way she made him think of one. He heard the emphatic purring of a cat who is delighted rather than merely comfortable. She wiped blood from his temple with this little square of linen, murmuring, "There, there, now, we will go back to our chamber and breakfast. I'll insist on bacon or a kipper or something good, and then we will sleep." The opalescent light glinted on a fang.

The vivid memory of half-light, a fairie lady or possibly a cat bending over him, murmuring while she dabbed at his forehead, washed over him. He'd dismissed the strange encounter as a dream resulting from drink and a blow to the head. How had he not realized it was based in truth, however fancifully embroidered by his stunned brain, when he had picked up the handkerchief?

The answer was easy. He'd been dizzy and fuddled. By the time Jenkins inquired about the lady's handkerchief, Ducane had dismissed the incident as a dream and moreover, one that was uncomfortable to recall. Rationally considered, the lady and the sense of a cat's presence had not been frightening. Very few dreams were, in his experience. Even that one had seemed merely strange. Mayhap his disquiet afterwards arose from the existence of the little square of linen, the unacknowledged proof that the event had actually occurred. He had forgotten or put it out of his mind as something impossible to reconcile with reality.

He'd met an East India Company man who claimed the natives in both India and China believed a sorcerer could change into another creature, like a tiger or fox. Nonsense in the rational world, of course. But now the truth of his memories had been forced upon him, he was sure there had been a cat. There must have been a woman also, as here was her handkerchief. Unless it belonged to the cat? No. There had to be some explanation that would make sense. Otherwise, the world would be a terrifyingly uncertain place. Or—? Hadn't Adelaide said something during their journey?

Ducane strode across the room to the door to his wife's bedchamber, with Jenkins calling after him, "My lord?"

Jenny was pinning a little oval cap over Adelaide's hair when he burst in. She squeaked.

"Gervase? Is something amiss?"

"Jenny, I need to speak with Lady Adelaide, if you are finished here."

"You may go, Jenny," Adelaide said.

Her voice sounded thin in his ears. Although she did not actually shrink away, he had frightened her. And her cat, who had been lounging on the bed, sat up and looked at him.

"I beg your pardon. I did not mean to startle you. Does that cap consist of nothing but a few bits of lace and ribbon? 'Tis very becoming." In fact, she was striking, if not beautiful, in a deep red jacket and petticoat: a country lady attired for a busy day.

She turned on the bench before the dressing table. "I feared you had received bad news."

"No, my dear, not that." He offered her the crumpled handkerchief. "Is this yours?"

"Oh!" She paled. "Yes, it is. I wondered where it had gone." She swallowed.

Damme, she is still so easily discomposed. He had hoped escape from her curst family had freed her from her fears.

After a moment she said, "When I discovered it was missing, I supposed one of the servants had filched it. They did sometimes take things or hide them. Small things only," she continued hurriedly, "nothing I could be sure I hadn't misplaced myself."

"I picked it up soon after I arrived at Lamburne Chase. I went walking one night and came to my senses in the dawn, lying beside a fallen tree branch. Jenkins put it aside until I should determine whose it was and return it discreetly. But I forgot all about it until Jenkins tried to wipe a cat nose print off my boot with it. 'Tis yours, I think?"

"Oh! Yes. Thank you for not asking the family about it. I tried not to come to their attention for any reason."

"Years in the beau monde taught me discretion, so I'm due no credit. Do you suppose Jenkins or Jenny can get the blood out?" He rather hoped not.

"No, don't. I prefer not to be reminded of my life before you rescued me. I'm sorry Tabby left a smutch on your boot. I'll ask her not to do it again, but…" She shrugged. "She is a cat."

"So I had noticed."

If his wife did not wish to keep it, he would put it away as a memento of his strange adventures at Lamburne Chase.

Chapter 32

Ducane talked to her about everything: the property, what the bailiff thought, and his own thoughts, and asked her opinions, which only heightened her guilt over his injury at her hands. She should have confessed, but somehow she could not. Maybe some day when they were both old and could laugh over it.

"The methods used both on the home farm and by the tenants could be improved. Jackson admits it and mentioned some modern innovations he would try, with permission. The Tull seed drill would be a good way to start," he said. "I've seen it used, and it produces a better yield and sows three rows at once, too. In fact, it was in use on two of Blacklaw's properties. I don't know whether my brother introduced its use on any of the others. We would begin by using it on the home farm. Jackson tells me her ladyship saw no need for change and without her support, he couldn't do anything. 'We've stubborn folk in Northumberland,' he says."

"So I've heard." Some inexplicable association of ideas prompted her to inquire, "Have you heard from your brother? Or your mother?" She did not believe a letter had come, although she gathered he was on good if not precisely warm terms with both.

He hemmed and eyed her guiltily. "Ah…as it

happens, I have not yet written. I wanted to get a better notion of the property first. With one thing and another, I've put it off."

"I feared they were angered and turned against you." She would ache for him if he had been cast off by his people. Estrangement from her own relatives was cause for something like rejoicing, but he seemed to like his, or respect them, anyway. "Perhaps you should write, however. They must wonder why you have not, when they may have seen the notice." *If the London newssheets ever make their way so far north.*

But they had both been busy. Gervase had taken her to a farm near Otterburn to look at horses, and they had returned home with a bay mare for her and a big roan gelding for him. On the days her husband did not go out to see tenants or inspect some part of the property, they planned improvements to the estate and house, with the property taking priority. They agreed to change nothing in the house immediately except what was essential to their physical comfort. However, they both conceded that painting the walls and replacing the upholstery in the entrance hall, reception room, and drawing room were necessary to their social comfort.

The housekeeper had a list of the sizes and amounts of fabric needed for the curtains and upholstery, making that project easier. Adelaide made her own notes about what would best suit each room. Her husband voiced no opinions as to what colors he liked for the drawing room or his chamber or any other room.

"Whatever you think suitable," was his reply, followed a moment later by, "I know you have excellent taste."

When she asked Jenkins, he was more forthcoming. "Lord Gervase dislikes gray, both for paint and furnishings." He paused. "Lady Blacklaw favors it for the formal rooms. He is not fond of pale blue for walls or upholstery. If I may suggest, as Northumberland has long, dark winters, a light color on the walls might be more cheerful than darker tones."

Based on his taste in suits and waistcoats, a rich, creamy color, lighter than his fawn velvet suit, was chosen for the walls, with color provided by upholstery and hangings in yellow, mossy green, and rose, according to the room. She wasted no time in sending to Newcastle for paint.

Jenkins appeared to approve of her, and Jenny no longer behaved as if she expected a scold for the slightest mistake. The girl was learning to read, she discovered. The valet had been in the habit of reading to Jenny in the evenings on the way north.

"When I said I wished I could read, Mr. Jenkins began teaching me, my lady."

Adelaide knew he had explained the care of clothing and the other duties of a trained maid during each day's travel. Jenkins had confessed to so demeaning himself when Ducane asked about his progress in reading one of the books provided for the valet's entertainment. As trying to focus on print while in a moving coach gave Jenkins a headache, he had made use of the time by teaching Jenny her work and taught her card games for amusement. He had done well; if she was still unpolished in manner, she was proving skillful at her duties, and Hester Webb's tutelage filled in the gaps in Jenkins's instruction.

"They don't teach them much in the almshouse,

seemingly, Lady Adelaide," he commented privately to Adelaide and Ducane.

"Lady Adelaide does not need a dresser as we will live in the country, merely someone who can keep her gowns in order, lace her up, and arrange her hair."

"Which the girl will do well enough, and she's needle-witted. She'll be a decent maid for a country lady, and loyal to the bone." That last counted for a good deal in Adelaide's opinion.

Adelaide hoped to begin accompanying Gervase on his visits to their tenants once her new habit, ordered from Newcastle, came. Any who were ill or had a new baby should be given whatever assistance they needed. That was what a country lady did. Not that Leonora had troubled much over such things. Adelaide doubted Sophia and Charity even knew the tenants' names.

Jackson had dealt with Lady Creighton's tenants when she could no longer call upon them, but he had not delivered soup and custard for the ill or gifts of clothing or simply sat and talked with them. Adelaide looked forward to making their acquaintance, as she had no fear of being greeted coldly or with suspicion here. She and Tabby basked in the pleasure of having a home.

She was alone in the dining room, drinking a final cup of tea with the last of her toast. Gervase had gone out with Jackson to ride to some of the more distant tenant holdings. If only she could go with him. Then Greer brought in a letter on a salver. The direction was in Tate's hand.

Her first thought was, *bad news*, followed by the old instinct to hide. Ridiculous because she was no longer dependent on her brother or at the mercy of his household. What if she had somehow lost all her money? As long as she had the manor, she would not particularly care, but her husband might. However, her dowry was safely deposited, and her own and her godmother's jewelry were in the strongroom with the estate's legal documents and records. To worry about all of it disappearing was as unbalanced as Leonora claimed she was.

She stared at the letter, wanting not to read it or even open it, as if doing so would release evil into her little Eden. She wanted to escape to yesterday when she had been happy and busy, talking to the gardener about the flower garden.

A warm, soft mass landed in her lap. Tabby rested her forepaws against Adelaide's chest and butted her furry head against her chin. "It's all right, Tabby," she whispered, cuddling her friend, as if the cat were the one needing reassurance. After a few minutes, her companion settled into a ball on her lap, and Adelaide's hands were free to pry up the seal and unfold the sheet.

The missive was short compared to Tate's usual letters. The opening sentence, *I write to advise you that the Earl of Lamburne has written to me...* made her heart thump. Hearing Tabby purr, she continued reading.

...irate that I did not tell him your godmother bequeathed much more to you than I implied. He discovered this when a clerk at the bedding warehouse mistakenly delivered your bed linens and blankets to Lamburne House. The head clerk discovered the error, and one of the partners called upon Lamburne to apologize and arrange to take them away. When the

earl demanded to know if he was expected to pay for goods he had not ordered, the partner assured him you had already paid. He also revealed you asked for recommendations for the purchase of other goods. The earl spoke with those companies as well. I am sorry to say two or three thought there could be no objection to providing him with the nature and amounts of your purchases as he is your brother (and an earl). I have written stern letters to admonish these mercantile houses.

As we let him think Lady Creighton left you only a few shares of an investment and a cottage, he was curious enough to search through his father's records from the several years preceding his death and found the monies used to fund the trust. He railed at me for not informing him of the amount invested. I replied I had been named your guardian and trustee and was now your man of business and had no obligation (nor indeed, the right) to discuss your affairs with him or anyone else. The old earl appointed me to ensure the handling of your interests would be entirely separate from those of the earldom. There was some vague bluster about his seeking counsel, in response to which I informed him that the late earl had taken legal advice from a member of the Court of Chancery, and his lordship the present earl was welcome to do the same. He would be informed that he had no case, and any attorney who told him otherwise would merely be milking him for fees for the years it would take such a case to be decided.

He also accused me of aiding you in your flight. Perfectly true, of course. I did not apologize for doing so and informed him he had his and his lady's mistreatment of you to blame.

I pointed out that you were of age and almost unknown to the beau monde, making any reflection on his family unlikely. Further, any talk would be the result of his and his household's complaining of your marriage. His best course is to appear to accept it.

I believe he will do so, for I mentioned that if he chose to hazard the Court of Chancery (or "Court of Chancy," as one of my colleagues refers to it), I would require an accounting of all monies he expended on your behalf. He will think twice before letting it be known that he received far more from your trust than he can have spent on you. I have long suspected it and after visiting Lamburne, I have no doubt I am correct.

Tate ended by hoping she was enjoying Northumberland and married life, which latter he had found very pleasant. Adelaide took a deep breath, letting relief wash over her. In her nephews' terms, Tate was a trusty Trojan.

She picked up Tabby and kissed the top of her head. Freedom was sweet.

Chapter 33

She and Tabby were in the drawing room, alternately reading about cheese-making and admiring the warm, creamy walls and the yellow curtains and upholstery (she had paid extra to have the work done quickly) when the sound of coach wheels startled her out of her reverie. They had received visits from neighbors of the gentry class, but she could not call to mind anyone nearby who had not yet come to call. This was late in the day for visitors anyway.

Greer entered. From the rigidity of his posture, he was offended. "Lady Adelaide, his lordship, the Marquess of Blacklaw, and her ladyship, the Dowager Marchioness of Blacklaw, are here."

"Did you put them in the reception room?" Fiddlesticks! It had not been redecorated yet.

"No, madam. They are waiting in their coach. A groom came to the door."

"Have them come in. Have Hopkins prepare bedchambers for them, and send for refreshments at once." Cook would know just what to provide. The bedchambers were at least clean, recently aired, and there were the new bed linens and blankets. If Gervase's family had given them some notice—no, there still would not have been time, most likely, to refurbish the rooms.

"The groom asked for Lord Gervase," the butler

said.

"Send for him, too. He's in the stables."

"Ay, madam."

She encouraged Tabby to remove to a footstool and attempted to brush cat fur from her petticoat. She gave up the task and rose as the door opened.

"The most honorable the Marquess of Blacklaw," Greer intoned, "and the most honorable, Alison, the Dowager Marchioness of Blacklaw." He stood aside and bowed them into the room.

Adelaide curtsied. This would not go well, to judge by their impassive faces. What would she do if his family was like her own? She had begun to get over being intimidated by them before she married, but these people terrified her.

"Lady Gervase?" Blacklaw inquired. His tone implied some doubt. Small wonder when she was wearing a gown suited to her earlier visit to observe the dairy maid's work.

"I use my own courtesy title, Lord Blacklaw. My husband will be in shortly. Please, be seated." Adelaide could feel the dowager marchioness's eyes on her. Cat fur still clung to her clothing, particularly visible since she was wearing a pale rose color.

They sat side by side on one of the settees, like a jury of two.

"I trust my son will not be long," the dowager marchioness remarked.

"He was in the stables and has been sent for." Adelaide hoped he had not decided to ride out. If he had not, would he take time to change his clothing or not, and which would be worse?

"Did you have an easy journey, Lady Blacklaw?"

Coach travel was never without its inconveniences and delays; no floods, mud, or broken wheels or axles were the best one could expect.

"The roads were no worse than usual. Even on bad roads, thirty or forty miles is endurable."

She must confess her ignorance. "I regret to say I did not know Lord Blacklaw's seat is so near."

"Blacklaw is a few miles west of Rothbury, on the River Coquet." Lady Blacklaw's cool tone told Adelaide she was on trial. The dowager marchioness had been in favor of Gervase marrying Sophia. Adelaide felt herself shriveling as she so often had in her own family's presence.

"I'm sure Ducane will be here soon." Her voice sounded insubstantial in her own ears. Suddenly, Tabby appeared in her lap. She must have slunk off her stool to lurk under Adelaide's chair, where voluminous petticoats hid her from the visitors' sight. Tabby had always been clever about staying out of view, which had no doubt saved her from many kicks and blows from brooms.

Tabby stood up, paws on her mistress's stomacher, to lick her chin and give it soft nips. Grateful for the support, she stroked her pet. "Thank you, my sweet," she murmured. Too late it occurred to her that the freedom of speech she enjoyed at Dale Tower might be startling to guests.

Ducane reached the door a few strides before the maid and footman bringing the tea service and bottles and glasses. He opened the door for them and gestured them to precede him. His first sight as he followed them in was of his mother's and brother's rigid faces. Adelaide was sitting composedly, her cat nursing on her chin. The first words he heard were his wife's, evidently addressed to the animal.

His brother rose from the settee. "Gervase."

Ducane made a leg to him. "Blacklaw. Welcome to our home." He bowed to his mother also before he approached and kissed her cheek. "Thank you for coming to meet my wife."

"We could hardly ignore your marriage." She inspected him from head—hair tied back but still somewhat windblown—to foot—scuffed, unpolished boots, though he had scraped the stableyard off them before entering the house.

Thank God for the servants. The tea tray was placed on the table beside Adelaide, who had already unlocked the caddy and spooned tea leaves into the pot. Wisely, Tabby vacated her lap to sit pressed against her petticoat. The tray of decanters and glasses were on a side table. The footman and maid retreated, no doubt to describe the meeting to their fellows in the servants' hall.

"Milk and sugar, Lady Blacklaw?"

"Both, thank you."

"Brandy or claret, Blacklaw?"

"Claret."

Ducane had never found himself in so confounded awkward a situation. His mother was already prejudiced against Adelaide because she was not Lady Sophia. Now Adelaide had not made a good first impression: not that it was her fault, as his family had arrived unexpectedly.

He poured garnet-red wine into a glass with an elegant twisted stem. "Is Magdalen, Lady Blacklaw, not with you?" he inquired, passing the glass to his brother.

"She is in delicate health at the moment."

Which was to say, breeding again. Difficult to know how to respond, given the phrasing. One could neither offer congratulations nor express a hope she would soon be better.

"Ah. We will look forward to seeing her on some future visit."

"So you have married," his mother said.

"I have."

The tea was brewed. He took the prepared cup from Adelaide and presented it to his mother. The little table beside her end of the settee was old and a bit rustic but well-polished, and the room's fresh paint and newly upholstered furniture should meet with his mother's approval.

"We were surprised."

He contemplated Alison, Lady Blacklaw, as he thought of her in her present mood. Robert was wearing his marquess face, but that would be because the unexpected marriage had upset their mother. Blacklaw himself would not care who Gervase had wed, he hoped.

"I am surprised you recommended Lady Sophia as an appropriate bride, although I suppose you had never met her."

His mother stiffened, difficult when she already had a spine like a ramrod. "Her lineage is impeccable, and she has an excellent dowry."

The marquess said, "This is really not—"

His mother and his father, too, had always been somewhat arrogant. The nobility were, in general. He had never given their privilege and attitudes much thought until now, when he could not overlook discourtesy to his wife.

"Those advantages do not compensate for several disadvantages. She is too young, has been too much indulged, and has not a thought of anything but getting her own way. No wonder she did not find a husband in her two seasons in town."

"I believe it's quite the fashion nowadays for girls to conceal their intelligence lest it make them appear less than womanly," Lady Blacklaw began.

"The last straw was her attempt to compromise herself with me, aided and abetted by her favorite footman, who then attempted to blackmail me."

He had never expected to see his mother struck speechless. Robert's jaw almost dropped before he recalled his dignity.

"Gervase, she cannot have done so! You must have misunderstood," she protested when she was able to speak.

Before he could recount the whole unsavory history, his bride said, "Unfortunately, 'tis true. I witnessed my niece throwing herself into Ducane's arms and the footman's arrival in the garden, well after all in the house should have been abed except those of us who enjoy the cool air and peace of late evening."

"I find it difficult to believe such conduct in my old friend's granddaughter. Lady Lamburne's mother is a notable stickler."

"My niece is very beautiful and is accustomed to getting whatever she wants. Lamburne and her mama have spoilt her, I fear."

"Madam, I believe Lady Sophia correctly concluded I would not offer for her and thought to force the issue. Write to Lamburne, by all means. He knows the truth, as on questioning the girl, she confessed it to him."

Out of the corner of his eye, Ducane watched Adelaide pour a little milk into the spare saucer provided for Tabby's use and casually set it down by the side of her chair. He hoped his family's attention was on him. Alack, he saw the marquess's attention had shifted from him to Adelaide. She sipped her tea as if unconcerned by his scrutiny.

His mother took a deep breath and conceded defeat. "Then you have had a lucky escape."

Blacklaw relaxed slightly and hauled the conversation in another direction. "This appears to be a tidy manor. Er, do you plan to spend much time here?"

"We will live here for the most part. We may visit London for a month or two each year."

"I see. Who did you have review the settlements?"

The marquessate's man of business would have informed Blacklaw if he had seen them, hence the question.

"I reviewed them. They were not complicated. As our father's and your steward, I often dealt with more challenging documents."

Robert sat blank-faced for several moments, until he finally harrumphed. Perhaps it was occasioned by the thought Ducane had married a female with no more than a small manor.

Tabby was no longer visible. The creature had the way of all cats in being able to come and go unseen. Rather like his bride, who sometimes arrived at his side as if conjured up from thin air.

Adelaide set down her tea bowl and entered the conversation.

"Lord Blacklaw, Dale Tower is a recent inheritance from my godmother. When my father knew his health was failing, he appointed a guardian for me as I suppose he felt my half brother was too young to be burdened with the responsibility."

His wife was either charitable or did not care to reveal how badly her brother had treated her.

"Although he set aside only a small dowry for me, he also made some investments to provide funds to support me. They have always exceeded the generous amount allotted to Lamburne for my expenses except for my one short season in London. The income has accumulated and will continue to do so as my former guardian, who is also my man of business, invested some of the amounts in excess of what was needed for my maintenance, and that has also increased."

How like Adelaide, and how much better her forthright explanation had served than avoidance would have done. When he and Robert were private, he'd disclose the other details of Adelaide's inheritance from her godmother. He himself had not comprehended how rich Adelaide was until after they married.

"I see." Ducane's brother looked more cheerful. His mother was still troubled.

"Gervase, how did you and Lady Adelaide decide to marry?"

They exchanged looks. They would definitely not be telling Lady Blacklaw how it had really come about. "I discovered I wanted a lady who was intelligent and preferred country life, as I do. And there she was, at Lamburne. I must thank you for suggesting Lady Sophia for otherwise I would never have met Adelaide."

"You like country life?" The marquess stared at him. "I thought you preferred London. You could scarce wait to leave when I came home to take over the estate."

"Once you did, there was nothing for me to do." He almost said, "I was *de trop.*" That would have hurt his brother. "I thought I would see how I liked life in London." Years wasted in the endless pursuit of something to do, all of it ultimately pointless.

"Adelaide—I trust I may call you by your name as you are now my daughter-in-law—do you find enough to occupy you here? Do you not pine for town?"

"I never liked London when I was there, Lady Blacklaw. The theater and opera and concerts were delightful, but I do not miss the rest in the least. Here I can see to the tenants' and laborers' welfare and plan the redecoration of the rooms. I am making a small batch of mead and learning to make cheese. I watch the garden being brought back to order, and I have found wild flowers to transplant to one section. I have never been happier or busier, and I owe it all to your son." The sincerity in her glowing face made his heart skip a beat.

His mother was at a loss for words, and it served her right for trying to discompose his wife. "I suppose you are well matched, then." It was an oddly hesitant remark for his mother. Afterward, talk flowed more easily.

Chapter 34

Ducane's mother succeeded in cornering him the next day. Her concern had not been laid to rest.

"You must not have received my letter," she said.

"I did. But by that time, I had formed my own opinion based on observation. Lady Lamburne undermined whatever confidence Adelaide may have had in London. Not that most girls have much self-assurance on first entering society."

Alison Blacklaw's moue expressed her opinion. "Her mother's…trade…made her an unsuitable wife for a gentleman, and impossible for an earl."

"The late Lord Lamburne obviously disagreed. And under no circumstances would I have agreed to marry Lady Sophia. Apart from her attempt on my, ah, virtue, her careless riding led to her horse having to be put down. 'Tis a wonder she did not break her neck rather than the horse's leg." He proceeded to recount her behavior at the riding party, at which his mother looked uncomfortable.

"Not all ladies are skilled in the saddle," she protested.

"She thinks herself an accomplished rider and wanted to be the center of attention. She sprained her ankle and came the tragedy queen while the horse was suffering, and spared it not a thought."

"That was not well done." His mother was a

notable horsewoman who doted on her own horse. "Hardly the sort of behavior one wishes in a wife," she admitted. "Still, when we are young, we sometimes make mistakes or behave badly. Most of us outgrow such faults. Was it really necessary to marry Lady Adelaide? Setting aside the matter of her dubious birth, she is old for a bride. I hope she can give you children. She is also rather odd. Some ignorant person would have thought that cat was suckling on her chin as witches are said to nurse their familiars, not that I have ever believed in such nonsense. And she talks to it."

"How fortunate that none of us are rustics and thus do not believe in nonsense." How to explain all the components that had affected his decision? He would not tell his mother he feared the Lamburnes would punish Adelaide for thwarting Sophia. Best to avoid why it had been necessary to marry secretly and then to spirit his bride away. He certainly could not explain that he found Adelaide strangely fascinating, and "strangely" was definitely the correct word. "I admired her wit and wits and her composure even in trying circumstances, such as when Lady Sophia's horse was crippled," and her fortitude in a house where she was treated less kindly than a poor relation. "Adelaide and I enjoy the same things: the country, riding, books, good conversation."

Alison Blacklaw sighed. "Well, 'tis not as bad as it might be. The pearl necklace and the ruby ring last night were not trumpery, nor what one would expect an actress like her mother to possess. And that Chinese silk became her well."

He suppressed his own sigh. He had no notion where the sacque gown had come from or the jewelry either: yet another mystery. He had sat up late with his brother and had not wanted to disturb Adelaide when he finally went up to bed. His own chamber had been lonely and uninviting.

"I suppose 'tis well enough, Gervase, if you are content with a manor and a little income. I do wish you had not married in such indecent haste, which is bound to cause talk."

"As you and the Lamburnes would have opposed the match, there would have been gossip anyway."

"Why would they—no, never mind. Of course they would have done, if they expected you to marry Lady Sophia. I would have come around if I had known you would be happy ruralizing. But a betrothal and a wedding at Lamburne Chase or at Blacklaw would have prevented gossip."

"They expected I would marry Sophia. And why was that, Mother? I believed we had a clear understanding that I was at Lamburne Chase only to meet her so we might decide if we would suit."

Lady Blacklaw compressed her lips. "I'm sure I never gave the impression we considered it a settled matter, and I don't think Agnes Portland thought so. She did call Sophia a 'lively miss' which sounded as if you might take to her, in light of your apparent fondness for town life and entertainments. There was no mention of Lady Adelaide at all. Of course, given her advanced age, we would have supposed you would not be interested in her."

"Well-informed and witty appealed to me far more than youth, silliness, and petulance. Adelaide proved popular with the guests who met her at the house party. They found her sensible and pleasant, which agreed with my own judgement."

His mother's startled expression alerted him to his slip. "Had they not met her before?"

Lady Adelaide had been meeting many of them for the first time. How could that be explained when she had lived all her life at Lamburne? He had not been aware of her existence until two or three days after his arrival. Fortunately, something Adelaide had told him supplied an answer to his mother's question.

"One does not introduce girls from the schoolroom into adult company." Which would not explain why she knew no one her own age in the neighborhood although even if she had, they would likely all have married and moved away. "When they took her to London, by her admission and your own letter, she was shy and awkward. Her sister-in-law's carping made her season such a misery that once home, I imagine Adelaide chose to avoid entertainments." There! That accounted for it, and likely mostly true, as well.

Lady Blacklaw contemplated this and finally remarked, "It is true that many young girls are 'sair hadden doon' by their mothers, as my old Scotch nurse used to say. At seventeen, even I was made rather timid by all the rules my mother said I must observe or forever be scorned as a hoyden or minx or wanton. She was not an unkind or unusually strict parent." She meditated. "Lady Adelaide has shown no sign of eccentricity since we arrived…apart from talking to her cat and serving the beast milk in the drawing room."

"Mother, you talk to your horse."

She laughed suddenly. "And so I do, and Robert sometimes feeds his dogs tidbits from the table. Well, then. Given there is some money and you are happy, 'tis not a disaster. As you are past your youth and not a fool, I do not suppose this is a mere infatuation. You must expect some talk, the marriage having been sudden and to a lady who is almost unknown...except some will remember her mother and the gossip about her marriage. I never heard a word against Lady Sophia, although I am glad you did not offer for her, if she is given to freakish tantrums. One could not expect her mother to speak of her faults, because what mother would, with a daughter to marry off? But I would have expected Lady Agnes to mention the girl is still a little childish, a bit spoiled, and would need to be gently schooled by her husband." The pique in her voice hinted at her annoyance. "But I suppose she might not have known Lady Sophia was sometimes badly behaved. She would be on her best behavior in her grandmama's presence, and my old friend lives at such a distance from town and from Lamburne Chase, she may seldom have seen her." His mother gave a brisk nod, dismissing the subject. "Your bride will do, I think, though it might be best if you do not go to London for a year or two. By then your marriage will no longer be a current topic."

"I believe so, too." And that closed the matter, he trusted.

He was mistaken. The next morning after breakfast his brother begged a few words with him. Mayhap "begged" was not the right term; "issued an elder-brotherly command" came nearer the mark. Ducane suggested the marquess accompany him on a ride to one of the farther holdings.

Robert studied the outbuildings and fields, evaluating their state of repair. He had already remarked on how well the stable was maintained. Gervase said, "The old lady had an honest, competent bailiff. We continue to employ him. He could do nothing about the house except for repairs to the roof and chimney stacks and the like. According to her housekeeper, in her latter years, Lady Creighton did not care to 'have the house overrun by workmen with all their noise and dust and disruption.' "

His brother barked out a laugh. "I know all about that! We had work done to the nursery parlor. Magdalen thought the oak paneling made it too dark. I never noticed it when we were children. Did you find it conducive to melancholy?"

"No. I remember it as warm and snug."

"I would not permit the panels to be sold for scrap or burned. Would you care to have them? We have not yet chosen your wedding gift as we were taken by surprise. I'll send them off to you with whatever my lady decides we will purchase once I've reported to her."

"Thank you, Blacklaw. We would appreciate the panels. I can think of a room which would benefit from them." Linenfold paneling might be thought old-fashioned, but it would improve the rather stark Dale Tower nursery.

They were passing the home farm cowman's cottage. His wife was bent over a row in their little vegetable patch, a basket holding a few carrots and turnips at her feet. She stood up on hearing their horses and curtsied on seeing Ducane.

"Good day, mistress. Is little Will recovered from his fall?"

"Ay, sir, and thank'ee for asking." She beamed at

him, stealing a glance at Blacklaw.

"Blacklaw, Mistress Whyte is my cowman's wife." He enjoyed his brother's brief, incredulous stare.

Her eyes widened, and she dropped another, deeper, curtsy. All of the servants and most of the tenants were aware Ducane was the Marquess of Blacklaw's younger brother. The Blacklaw seat was near enough to be known to them, giving the relationship an added luster.

Robert inclined his head. "Mistress Whyte."

When they'd ridden on, the marquess turned his head to stare at Ducane. "Did you just introduce me to your cowman's wife?"

"Hardly. That was not a proper introduction; I merely told you who she was. Though if you should cross paths again, I believe you could give her a nod without inviting her to encroach upon you. Not that she would."

"Are you on terms of such familiarity with all your laborers' kin?"

"Not all of them, not yet. Adelaide and I are coming to know them."

"It seems unlike you."

"Why? Because I'm a frivolous fellow?"

"You were such a creature of the beau monde. Finicking in your dress..." He eyed Ducane's brown wool coat and waistcoat and biscuit-colored leather riding breeches. "Here I find you dressed like county gentry and consorting with your tenants."

"I am a country gentleman, thanks to my wife."

" 'Tis your sudden transformation from beau to squire..." Blacklaw shrugged.

"We do not know each other well. We did not play

together as children because I was so much younger. You were away at school and in the summer you visited the other properties with Father. Then you toured the Continent. After that, you were in London, and I was at Blacklaw."

"I'm sorry you were left to rusticate, Gervase."

"No, don't apologize. I had never spent much time with Father and was glad to have the opportunity. His asking me to help him with the properties was the best compliment I ever received."

"You helped him?"

"Ay."

"I thought he relied upon our steward."

"The man saw to the minor matters. You keep a firm grip on estate business as our father did. After all, the family has more at stake than an employee."

"I know. He did drum that lesson into me, and I learned it well. But I assumed old Crenshaw was his assistant."

"With so many properties, there was more than enough to keep one man busy, even with competent bailiffs on them. I was his aide-de-camp at first."

"How did I not know this?" his brother asked.

"When you were at university, then on your Grand Tour, and finally in London, he gave me the same training he'd given you. In the summers, you often stayed with friends and came home only for a short time. Why would you have noticed?"

Blacklaw rode on without speaking, evidently sunk in thought. Had he taken offense? Ducane searched for something to say to breach the silence. Before he could do so, his brother spoke.

"I do remember Father saying how clever you were

at dealing with estate matters."

The late marquess had never expressed approval of Gervase as de facto steward of the properties. Years later, hearing at secondhand he had been pleased with Ducane's efforts was bittersweet.

Blacklaw continued, "I suppose I thought he meant passing on instructions to Crenshaw. I should have wondered why Crenshaw told me you would go over the accounts with me. You knew every farm and holding and all the tenants. It never occurred to me to wonder how you knew, though Crenshaw was doddering by then and past being able to do much." His brow furrowed, Blacklaw continued, "My tenants and workers still mention you: what you decided in some dispute of theirs, what a good notion this or that suggestion of yours proved to be. They seemed to like you."

"As a younger son, I need not be high in my manner."

"But you were. You were tedious correct in your behavior and dress."

"Only in London or when you or our parents were at home. You were careless, so I had to be precise. Otherwise I would have been a pale shadow of you. When Father needed someone to help him with the properties, I was glad to do it."

"And I neither realized nor thanked you for it. After you left, I did wonder how the properties had fared so well when Crenshaw was near useless. That's when I grew into being the marquess rather than only playing at it. I pensioned him and hired a new man a few months later."

"I think Crenshaw was able enough earlier, though

311

in his old age he would not do as steward for an inattentive or absentee owner," Ducane said. "He was painstaking about keeping ledgers and was exceeding honest about expenses and rents. By the time I began assisting Father, the man had grown hesitant about bringing problems to our father's attention, perhaps because he felt unable to cope with them. I hope your new steward is more useful."

"He is. And thank you for your efforts for the marquessate and in training me to take charge. I'm glad you have your own place to manage."

"It was my pleasure to do what I could."

"Did you feel displaced when I married?"

At the top of a rise overlooking the house, Ducane reined in and blew out a breath. "You were the heir, and I was the younger son. I never lost sight of those facts. Once you came home to take over, I had no purpose at Blacklaw and could not remain."

"I all but threw you out, I fear, thinking you would be glad to spend time in London. Doesn't every young man?"

"Probably I would have been, when I was younger. My short stays in town did not prepare me for the beau monde."

"But you became accustomed."

Ducane found himself grinning at the memory of moving into Blacklaw House. "Thanks to Moses Black. He found me a valet. I knew how to interview a prospective tenant farmer or stable hand. I had no experience with hiring a manservant. I asked Jenkins a few questions and decided he'd do, as Moses had approved him. Between them, they settled on my tailor. Black told me everything I needed to know about anyone I was likely to meet and which gaming houses and bordellos to avoid and a deal of other helpful stuff as well."

"Good old Black. There's not much he doesn't know."

They'd almost completed a circuit of the northeast section of the property when Ducane thought to ask, "How did you know Adelaide and I were here? I'm sure Tate's notice to the papers did not mention it." They had not wanted Lamburne to learn too quickly where they had gone.

"Not from you, at any rate. Mother was quite put about to learn you'd absconded without a word to us. You've had time to write."

"I meant to, but—"

"You were in your honeymoon and establishing yourself here as well. Found it awkward to explain how you came to be married to a different lady than you set out to court, did you?"

"Ay."

"Moses wrote to me. The day after you left town, a rapscallion came to Blacklaw House claiming he had an urgent message for you. When the footman mentioned it to Black, he realized the man had left a message for you before. You hadn't told Black where you were going, just a vague, 'traveling with a friend in Cornwall.' He concluded you were in some difficulty and went to the livery stable our family has used occasionally, in case you'd hired a coach. They provided your destination."

"I had some notion of being gone from London before the notice of our marriage appeared in the paper. We did not wish to be inundated with callers, and we were also anxious to see Dale Tower." Those were as good reasons as any. No need to explain that if Moses Black had known where he was going, he would have informed Blacklaw, as indeed he had when he smelled a rat at Thomas's second appearance.

His brother tactfully did not question his reason for wishing to slip out of town, leaving behind a false destination.

"Who was the fellow with the urgent message?"

Blacklaw hit upon the very point Ducane had hoped he would overlook. He sighed; there was nothing for it but to tell his brother the truth.

Robert gave him a hard look. "So then Lady Adelaide was able to force you into marriage."

"No. She made it clear as soon as we were alone that she had spoken only as a stratagem to discourage her niece and would disavow the betrothal as soon as I was able to get away from Lamburne Chase."

"Yet you married her." Blacklaw conceded, "Which was not a bad choice if you knew of her fortune."

"I didn't learn of it until later. Sophia reported to her mother I had taken liberties and her papa called me to account. Neither she nor the footman had revealed that Lady Adelaide was present. When she told Lamburne what she had seen, she did not tell him about our supposed betrothal as it seemed that Sophia had not spoken of it. Adelaide and I were thrown together by the need to discuss the chit's silence on the matter. We found we had much in common. By then, all that kept me from offering for her was her apparent poverty. She finally told me of her recent inheritance, which made it possible for us to marry, but we did not wish to humiliate Lamburne or his daughter by announcing our engagement." Substantially true. "The footman thought to extort money from me to prevent his making known my betrothal to Adelaide. He supposed I still needed to marry Lady Sophia for her dowry."

"But if you intended to marry Lady Adelaide anyway, how could he hope to blackmail you?"

"The matter was a little awkward. The Lamburnes were unaware of my decision."

"You were keeping the betrothal a secret even after you and Lady Adelaide decided to wed?"

"I did not wish to offend by announcing I had courted Adelaide, when I had gone there to meet Sophia."

"Embarrassing, but if they were determined on a connection to our family, Lady Adelaide would have done as well, surely?"

"Well, no. Not Lady Lamburne's daughter, you see. My courtship of Lady Charity might have been annoying but acceptable, though her older sister was nearly on the shelf. My choice of Lady Adelaide, merely a spinster half sister, with Lamburne resenting her because of her late mother, would have been a signal humiliation."

His brother contemplated this, brow creased. "A devilish tangle, which you somehow got clear of. Fast work, to leave Lamburne and marry only a month later. But how did it come about? Black's message said nothing about your marriage."

Worse and worse. "He didn't know. Adelaide and I had meant to allow a little more time to elapse before announcing our news. We left London the day after the extortioner delivered his first message."

"But if you meant to marry anyway, why not tell him to go to the devil?"

"There were reasons we felt it best."

"Strike me blind if I can see what they could be. I'd—" There was a discernible pause. Blacklaw gave him a look before saying, "You left London together without being wed? When did your marriage take place?"

"We'd already married."

"I see. A Fleet wedding?"

"No, a respectable marriage by special license with Tate in attendance."

"I don't think I care to know why you married secretly. The playhouses have nothing to match this. The only possible improvement would be the addition of a highwayman or some comic *banditti*."

"Ha! Those were the only complications we did not suffer." Perhaps Blacklaw would now let the subject die. "I trust you will not recount this to Mother."

"Not a chance. She would not be amused." His brother cleared his throat. "I wish all could have been accomplished in a less irregular way. However, what's done is done. About Lady Adelaide…Mother is willing to accept your marriage."

"Gracious of her."

His brother frowned. "You cannot deny Lady Adelaide was not the perfect choice. The talk about her—"

"Most of it started and passed on by those who are either evil-minded or have never met Adelaide."

"She is unusual, you must admit."

"She is, indeed. She's not feather-brained and doesn't have megrims or whims. Have you seen any sign of eccentricity?"

"N-o-o-o." Decidedly a grudging admission.

As the marquess had not mentioned it, but must be thinking of it, Ducane pointed out, "Talking to a cat is no odder than talking to one's horse or dog."

His brother guffawed. His mother was guilty of the one and he of the other. "I confess I have seen ladies feeding their lap dogs treats in the drawing room. A saucer of milk is not much different."

"Blacklaw, I could name you half a dozen ladies—including a duchess and a countess—who are far fuller of whims and fantastickal notions and fits of vapors than Adelaide."

"I have met ladies whose talk and behavior caused me to doubt their rationality. Well, well, you might have done worse. It's too bad about her background, but her father's mésalliance is well in the past and if you mean to live here for the most part…"

"Living here with Adelaide will be a pleasure."

"So much the better. Still, there must have been a girl you could tolerate who would have a substantial dowry."

His brother and mother could not help thinking that way. Most noble families would prefer a son or sibling to marry money and would deplore the choice of a poorly dowered bride. Thinking Adelaide such was so ludicrous he laughed. Robert turned his head in surprise.

"Robert, I would have liked you and our mother to accept my wife on her own merits, so I did not mention that Adelaide is an heiress."

"I do not suppose it amounts to the kind of dowry you might have expected. Creighton had little more than Dale Tower and enough income from it to live decently. Even with a little more income from investments, your lady cannot be considered a great heiress. She might have been a good choice for someone of the gentry."

"Adelaide's godmother had an adequate dowry and inherited more."

"She was originally Lady Beverley before she became Lady Creighton, Mother says. The Beverleys never had much though they're an old family. No vices, however, that I ever heard of."

"Before she was Lady Beverley, she was Louise Andres."

"Andres? The banking family?"

"The daughter of Simon Andres, who founded the bank."

"Even I have heard of him." A long, thoughtful silence ensued. "She was well-dowered, then?"

"Ay. And inherited his private fortune on his death. His nephew was left the bank."

"There's no more to be said, then."

"Good, because Adelaide is my wife and I am a fond and protective husband." Ducane was startled to hear the frost in his own voice.

"Ah. Should I drop a hint to our mother?"

"Perhaps your visit will be more comfortable for Adelaide if you do."

His brother nodded, then turned the conversation to the Cheviot sheep on the hillside, asking how large the flock was, and if the manor had no other breeds. They spoke of sheep and cattle and crops for the rest of their ride.

Chapter 35

She had been braced for the worst when Gervase's mother and brother arrived. She had not been the Dowager Lady Blacklaw's choice, and both were at least skeptical about her, if not actually hostile. Once she would have been reduced to hiding in her chamber. Now she had the support of all the residents of Dale Tower. Her godmother must have been a wonderful woman, to inspire a devotion in her servants that they accorded to her heiress as well.

The day after the Blacklaws' arrival, Adelaide overheard her mother-in-law comment to the housekeeper on some pieces in the dining room.

"That pewter plate is very battered. Such odd markings, too. A memento of foreign travel might best be displayed elsewhere. And is it necessary to have a third candle branch that does not match the other pair?"

Mistress Hopkins's reply, "Those pieces have sat on the sideboard ever since Lady Creighton came here with his lordship after their marriage. They belonged to her mother. They'll be changed when Lady Adelaide chooses to change them, your ladyship."

Adelaide resolved not to move them.

Chapter 36

On the fourth day of his mother and brother's visit, a freight wagon arrived from London with his and Adelaide's clothing. No difficulty had been encountered in collecting Lady Adelaide's possessions from Lamburne House, Moses Black reported in the letter accompanying the wagon, though Black had been obliged to purchase trunks to transport them. He had arranged the carrier's wagon, driver, and outriders for its protection. Lord Lamburne had sent word to Lamburne Chase that Lady Adelaide's belongings were to be packed and dispatched to Dale Tower. Black trusted the wagon bearing those would not be much delayed.

He read his mother's expression when she saw the trunks and boxes being conveyed to Adelaide's chamber. When they were private, the Dowager Lady Blacklaw murmured, "I see she has an adequate wardrobe if they are all of the quality she has worn so far. Except for the day of our arrival when we found her in her housewifely attire."

"She does, indeed. Her brother was generous in that, anyway. I suppose he felt honor bound, as I am told he received a generous allowance for her expenses."

He had startled her. "The head of the family is expected to provide for dependent female relatives. Of course, if the family has few resources, 'tis understandable if a dependent is not clothed lavishly, but Lamburne was surely well able to support her without payment from her trustee, which might have depleted the funds available for a dowry." She made an irritable sound. "Robert told me Adelaide inherited more than we knew both from her father and from her godmother, but that does not excuse her brother from his obligation to her. I am thoroughly disgusted with that family."

She must have seen his surprise. "My eyes were opened by certain things Adelaide mentioned. She did not know how revealing they were to a discerning person, which I believe I am. I quite pity her—though she is now well settled."

"I think we both are, Mother."

"Good. I'm happy for you."

This brisk, unsentimental statement struck Gervase as both revealing and laughable. A doting mother would have uttered it with warmth and a fond smile. Alison, Lady Blacklaw's was the same she accorded a tradesman who had served her satisfactorily: slight, brief, and disinterested. Gervase would hoard the exchange to recount to Adelaide, who would find it amusing.

A little later when they gathered before dinner, the marchioness casually inquired of Adelaide if everything had been unpacked. Adelaide admitted that two of the trunks were still corded.

"There is not much chance to wear fine gowns here. I will sort through them and find some unused chamber where I can store the ones for which I have no immediate need."

Ducane suppressed a smile. Until his family's arrival his wife had spent the week in the dowdy garments bought on the way north. They were not likely to be damaged by walks in the garden or by a cat's affectionate kneading. She wore her one decent gown for church on Sunday. She would have little use for finery here for some time.

Evidently feeling she should explain further—Lady Blacklaw affected most people that way—Adelaide added, "They were only the things I had taken to London. I have not yet received my belongings from Lamburne Chase, where most of my wardrobe is."

"Then it would require no great effort to come to Blacklaw. This chicken à la daube is quite good."

Adelaide's face froze at the first remark. He feared his own had done the same, though he should have expected his mother or brother to suggest a visit.

"But we have been here at Dale Tower so short a time, Mother. We are still growing accustomed, and Adelaide has in hand a number of schemes for refurbishing the house."

"Pooh! This is the perfect occasion to make your wedding visit to your family home—"

"The manor is in good heart, and your bailiff is excellent," Robert Blacklaw interjected as his mother was drawing breath. " 'Tis not far and the roads are good now."

"More important, your courtship and wedding were carried out in secrecy and unseemly haste. While I understand your reasons," his mother added, just late enough that he knew she did not understand them, "the sooner Blacklaw is seen to approve the connection, the better. If we were in London, we could hold a ball to celebrate the marriage and everyone who matters would know at once."

He suspected Adelaide shuddered inwardly at the thought.

"As everyone we would invite is in the country now, we must do the best we can. A few of our guests will come some distance and can stay for a week or two, and I will write my friends who live at a greater distance to inform them of our pleasure at Gervase's marriage. And when you come to London, we will have a series of entertainments and see to it Adelaide is presented at court." The dowager marchioness frowned ever so slightly. "I don't think I recall your being presented during your season, Adelaide."

The statement was not quite a question. "Preparations were made for my presentation, ma'am, but I did not stay in London for the entire season."

The dowager marchioness regarded her with delicately arched eyebrows raised. She expected an explanation. Adelaide supposed she was owed one.

"I was eighteen, but I had attended few entertainments in the country." None, in fact. "The strain of mingling with strangers rendered me even more silent and awkward than usual." Leonora's continual hissed admonitions to smile, to talk with whatever man she danced with, to stand straight, and not to fidget all did their part. "Then someone remarked to Lamburne that I was the image of my mother. As I am sure you know, Lady Blacklaw, she was an actress and a scandal. My brother and my sister-in-law weighed the potential for disaster against the advantage of perhaps finding me a husband. They decided the nine years since my father's death were not enough for the talk about his second marriage to be forgotten. I was sent home to recover from a minor ailment in the country's more wholesome air."

"I see. However, you have gained confidence since then, and we will have no difficulty in introducing you. Another reason for your coming to Blacklaw now is that by the time we leave for London, you may be enceinte, making the journey uncomfortable or inadvisable. If you must miss the season for that reason, at least you will have been welcomed by your new family and our friends in this county, and in town I will express my pleasure that you will be providing the marquess's children with a cousin."

"I believe our mother's idea is a good one," Robert stated. "Do you possess a coach, Gervase?"

"We do. It is rather elderly but has been maintained. It will serve to transport us and our baggage to Blacklaw."

If her husband was willing to fall in with his mother and brother's plans, Adelaide had no great objection. She would rather stay home, but Gervase's family had accepted her with more grace than she expected. "There is one thing," she began.

"I am sure we can deal with it, whatever it is."

The Dowager Lady Blacklaw appeared capable of dealing with anything, for which Adelaide envied her. But how unwary of her mother-in-law. "My cat must come with me. We have never been parted, and I would not trust her to servants."

"Your cat," Lady Blacklaw repeated. Perhaps she envisioned Tabby joining her other guests for a saucer of milk in the drawing room.

"Yes." As a child she had learned there was no

point in trying to explain anything to Leonora, as she always sounded first defensive, then incoherent.

"She will not roam free, I hope? While the dogs are kept in their kennel for the most part, one or two are permitted in the house and might trouble her."

"Tabby will stay in my chamber unless she is with me. Of course, she can remain in my chamber at all times if you object to her presence in the public rooms. I do take her out for walks each day."

"Oh, quite. I'm sure she will be no trouble at all." Lady Blacklaw recovered her poise, adding, "I take it we are all agreed. We can leave early the day after tomorrow. Our horses will be well rested by then. With the road dry, we should be at Blacklaw before full dark."

Her brother-in-law's eyes glinted with amusement. Gervase wore the slightly bored mask she had often seen at Lamburne. How did he feel about this proposed expedition? "Gervase?"

"I had hoped to be here for the haying, but I apprehend our bailiff has overseen the harvest for years. If you have no objections, I must agree with my mother that a wedding visit to the family seat would quell gossip."

And it was decided. Lady Blacklaw's maid and Lord Blacklaw's manservant were given orders to begin packing their clothing. Adelaide excused herself, ostensibly to give Jenny more detailed instructions but instead to decide what to take to Blacklaw. She was now supplied with more elaborate gowns than she needed but had few simple garments appropriate for informal country wear. Would Hester Webb have time to alter something of Lady Creighton's?

But late the following day, a pair of wagons arrived from Lamburne Chase with all her clothing, books, knickknacks, everything she had left on her dressing table, and the pretty sewing box Tate had given her for her twenty-first birthday. Her sister-in-law had wasted no time in purging Adelaide's unwanted presence from her home.

The wagons and drivers had been hired, but the outriders were Lamburne footmen and grooms. Leonora would not want to risk Adelaide claiming anything had been pilfered on the way. She had provided a list of everything sent and which wagon it was in. Every trunk and box had a pasteboard tag indicating its contents. How thorough of Leonora or whoever had done the packing, to make unpacking so easy. Adelaide glanced at each as it was carried in and exclaimed at the sight of "Riding habit, red," "Riding habit, green," "boots &c" at the top of one card.

"Put this one aside for the trip to Blacklaw," she told Greer.

Seeing the Lamburne servants' eyes widen as they brought in the chests and boxes was satisfying, too, as was the remark of a groom unaware she was just out of sight around a corner.

"Who'd ha' thought Mad Adelaide'd done so well for herself?"

"Jenny that was only a scullery maid near stripped Rafe's hide off for calling her mistress so, and the valet had a few choice words to add," the second voice said. "That's why Rafe's shifting the goods from the wagon to the ground."

The men moved off then, but a warm core of satisfaction lingered in Adelaide. The Lamburne servants would go home bearing tales: of the prosperous manor, the handsomely furnished rooms (how fortunate the entrance hall had been completed), the presence of Ducane's marquess brother and his terrifying mother. They would hear that Adelaide and her husband were to visit the marquess's estate. And Leonora and Edward would hear the servants' gossip.

With Jenny assisting her, Hester Webb chose the clothing, hats, and other accessories that would accompany her to her husband's family home. Lady Creighton's maid knew to a nicety what clothing was suitable. Adelaide found the box containing most of her shoes and unpacked those she would need. What a relief! She had been wearing her plain, sensible shoes with all her dresses, Lady Creighton having had smaller feet than she. Until the Blacklaws' arrival, acquiring more elegant footwear had not seemed urgent. Of the ones she had taken to London, only one pair had been for formal occasions, as she had supposedly gone to consult with Tate, not to take part in society. Now that all her clothing had come, she would not embarrass her husband or his family.

Jenny had already assisted her in putting on a favorite robe à l'anglaise, cream silk embroidered with primroses. Gervase had changed from riding clothes to an oyster-colored moiré suit. Seeing she was dressed but for her earbobs and a necklace, he dismissed Jenny.

"I hope you do not mind too much, Adelaide."

"Not at all. I am sure you can tie my necklace."

"I meant about visiting Blacklaw." He picked up the topaz and peridot ornament, lifted it over her head and tied the silk ribbons in a neat bow at the nape of her neck. She put on the matching eardrops and bracelet.

"I don't mind that. Your mother is correct that it is necessary to establish our position. Though I cannot claim I look forward to a London season."

"By that time, you will be comfortable in your new role. Or mayhap pressing family matters will keep us here."

"Family matters—?"

"We have been working toward that end, have we not?"

"Oh. You mean your mother's suggestion…" The warmth in his hooded eyes made her face heat. He was not Tam Lin, but he was the perfect husband in all other ways. As she smiled back at him, she discovered that his once elegantly pale face was now biscuit-colored from hours spent riding over the property. He moved (and sometimes spoke) briskly. She had somehow failed to notice Ducane had shed the languor of the man about town as if it had been a cloak. As perhaps it was, given that he had arranged their flight from London with such speed and efficiency.

"Just so, my dear."

For a heartbeat, she thought he had answered her thought rather than her own last comment. She used not to woolgather, being always on guard for anything that might affect her or Tabby. How much their lives had changed in less than three months. Ducane had turned into a hard-working landlord and country gentleman. And she woke every morning looking forward to the day instead of dreading it. She was never bored or frightened.

The members of the local gentry accepted her without question. Either they had never heard the rumors about her mother and her own birth or else her godmother's status in the community carried more weight than an old scandal in London. Her husband's close connection to a marquess must help, also. She found herself looking forward to their departure in the morning.

Chapter 37

They set out early, a cavalcade of two coaches and outriders. Gervase and his brother chose to ride, leaving Adelaide, Tabby, and Lady Blacklaw to occupy the Blacklaw coach while both maids and valets rode in the old Dale Tower coach. During a pause for refreshments and to rest the horses, Alison Blacklaw said, "Blacklaw, I have an idea: we will make the ball we give to celebrate the marriage a masquerade."

"Will it not require a great deal of preparation and effort? With Lady Adelaide and Gervase with us for only a month and Magdalen in a delicate condition, might it not be better to add a dinner and dancing to the usual harvest festival? Besides, I don't recall anyone in our area hosting a masquerade. In London, certainly, but in the country?"

"Pish! That no one else has done it will make the event memorable. I vow 'twill be spoken of for years. Magdalen will likely be past the uncomfortable stage and not yet so far advanced as to make it impossible for her to take part. Nor will I let the arrangements fall upon her. She can help with the invitations, which we will send out as soon as we can write them, and I can easily manage the rest. We will hold the event a few days before Gervase and Adelaide depart. There, have I answered all your objections? Adelaide, what do you think?"

"If it is not too much work for you, I would enjoy a masquerade very much. I never attended one during my London season." Nothing would delight her more; that enchanted masked ball at Lamburne Chase was among the best memories of her life, most of them from this summer.

Ducane's brother said, "Some of the guests would have to spend a night or two at Blacklaw if they come from any distance."

"Of course they would. I remember times before your father died when there was not a single empty bedchamber. Our housekeeper and I can arrange everything. Magdalen and Adelaide will have nothing to do but plan their costumes."

Adelaide said hesitantly. "I could help write invitations, if Magdalen, Lady Blacklaw is not opposed to a ball. I have a tolerably good hand and would be happy to assist with anything else to save you effort."

Lord Blacklaw laughed. "Magdalen is fond of our entertainments, whether they are assemblies, harvest festivals, or dinners for our friends. She does not care a groat for town amusements. She will miss London this year but not miss it."

They all laughed at his little play on words. Adelaide hugged to herself the prospect of a masked ball, remembering the delight of the one at Lamburne Chase. Only when she began musing on how to costume herself did a problem occur to her.

"My lady, will it not be difficult to acquire costumes for the ball? There will not be much time between arrival of the invitations and the event. Towns of any size appear to be rare."

"This is Northumberland. We are accustomed to

making do. I venture to say our guests will surprise you with their ingenuity. Now, no discussing what you will wear. Everyone must devise his own garb and keep it a close secret from all. Except one's maid or manservant, of course, but they must be sworn to secrecy, too. A masked ball is most amusing when there is mystery about everyone's identity."

Adelaide hoped her own ingenuity might rise to the challenge.

****

Blacklaw Hall, a symmetrical rectangle of buff sandstone devoid of much interest, appeared capable of fending off an attack by border reivers or indeed, King George's army, though it had been built after the time of the border raids. Adelaide suspected its builder had not given a counterfeit ha'penny for style or fashion. At least it possessed windows of good size rather than arrow slits.

Inside, she understood why Gervase disliked gray and slate blue and certain other fashionable tints: the colors chilled the stately rooms. But in a month's time, she and Gervase could return to Dale Tower's cheerful informality.

As they arrived late in the day, she told Jenny to unpack only what she would need for the night and the morning. On returning to her chamber after breakfast, she found her maid beginning on the last of the trunks. Adelaide was pleased to see the riding habits and boots; perhaps Gervase would take her riding.

"Whatever is this, my lady? It looks like a casaquin but not really." She was holding up the gillyflower-embroidered jacket.

"Ohhh." Adelaide breathed out a sigh. The servant

who had cleared out her bedroom and dressing room at the Chase had taken Leonora's instructions literally. Adelaide had hidden the jacket, petticoat, matching cap, and mask she had worn to the ball, meaning to return them to the attics when she could. Jenny had never seen them because Adelaide had put them on without the maid's help.

"That will be my masquerade disguise." She explained how she had attended the Lamburne ball, though not her meeting with the mysterious man in the Venetian carnival costume. "Not a word to anyone about it, mind you. We are all to keep our costumes a secret."

The visit was proving less difficult than it might have been. Alison, Lady Blacklaw, had warmed to her and Magdalen Blacklaw possessed a great deal of good-humored common sense and accepted Adelaide unquestioningly. She came of a Northumberland baron's family, was somewhat younger than her husband, and rather plain.

"I will be well pleased to stay here when Blacklaw returns to town for Parliament, miss him as I will. London is tedious, dirty, and smelly, and I do not want to give birth there." She was also reluctant to leave her other children. She had taken Adelaide to the nursery wing, sure her guest would enjoy meeting her three daughters and her toddling son.

Adelaide concealed her reluctance. She knew little of children, having had no playmates from nearby manors. Looking back, she guessed the rumors about her mother and her own birth were to blame. Sometimes she had played with the sons and daughters of one of the tenants, until her father died. Afterward,

Edward must have discouraged them. The age difference between herself and her nieces and nephews had been too great for friendship, not that Leonora would have allowed it.

What did one say to children? Charlotte was a girl of about ten, Elizabeth seven, and Rosamunde three. Charles had been born just over a year ago. As she must speak, she chose to address them as if they were grown. She recalled disliking adults' nonsense talk.

The two older girls curtsied to their "new aunt, your uncle Ducane's wife" while the baby merely goggled at her. Rosamunde, the youngest girl, stood and stared.

"I beg your pardon on her behalf," Magdalen murmured. "She is somewhat shy with strangers. I have not tried to teach her to curtsy yet, as she can fall on her face while merely standing."

Then Rosamunde tottered forward to lean against Adelaide's knees and held up her arms.

"Rosie, your aunt will not want you on her lap. Come to me instead."

The little girl ignored this instruction, continuing to gaze up at Adelaide with pansy-blue eyes. What else could she do? She hoisted the child onto her lap, where she grinned up at her new aunt. Perhaps motherhood would not be as difficult as she had feared.

****

Jenny hummed as she put out Adelaide's night rail.

"What's made you so happy? Happier than you usually are, I mean."

The girl turned pink. "Oh…when Lord Blacklaw and Lady Blacklaw came to the Tower, there was the nicest outrider with them. He had such a friendly way about him. Then after a few days, he was gone. I was afeared he'd been turned off. But he's come back. He'd been sent to Newcastle with a letter."

"Which one was he?"

"Sandy Anderson, my lady, the one with the wheat-gold hair. Not the tallest, but he has such laughing eyes."

"I hope you won't grant him any liberties, Jenny. Not unless you're wed. Men can be very persuasive without being serious about marriage." So she understood though she'd never been courted, herself, unless one counted Ducane. "Do you know what I mean?"

Her maid sighed. "I know. Mr. Jenkins warned me, too. I don't think he cottons to Sandy."

Chapter 38

Gervase had ridden to the nearest village to visit an old retainer he recalled fondly from his youth, who now lived there with her son, and to purchase something at Magdalen's request, as Blacklaw was closeted in the estate office. As he prepared to depart, her husband whispered to Adelaide that it was for Magdalen's costume, and a great secret from Robert.

Part of the morning Adelaide assisted the Dowager Lady Blacklaw with housekeeping matters and preparations for the ball, as Magdalen was in the nursery, sewing furiously on her costume and enjoying time with her children.

"As she is breeding again, I don't wish her to exhaust herself before our guests arrive."

Adelaide was becoming almost fond of Gervase's mother. The elder Lady Blacklaw's intelligence impressed her; in London's beau monde she must rank as a social power. But she was not a warm-hearted woman. She had little time for her grandchildren, which supported Adelaide's suspicion that she had not doted on her own children. Of course, she had been busy and still was, in town and in court circles. Perhaps it was as well, for Magdalen was an affectionate mother but not interested in social success. She did her duty but no more than that.

In the early afternoon, her mother-in-law released

Adelaide and sent her to keep Magdalen company in the informal parlor. Adelaide enjoyed her company even though her conversation was mostly of her children. They were lucky to have her.

Magdalen said, "My mama-in-law thinks a more accomplished governess should be hired to teach my girls. The one we now employ instructs them in French, manners, ciphering so they can review the household accounts, dance, and needlework. She is also teaching them to play the harpsichord and sing, all the things girls usually learn, though I did not have harpsichord or French lessons myself. I do not see the use of natural philosophy, history, geography, and the like for young ladies." She hesitated. "I believe you were educated in at least some of those subjects, Lady Adelaide. Do you think they would be of value to my daughters?"

To have her advice sought on any subject rendered her speechless at first. "I did have a very good governess until my sister-in-law replaced her with the one who taught her daughters." How much had Magdalen been told of her history? Best to be discreet. "Until my marriage, I lived at Lamburne Chase all year. I found my old governess's instruction in subjects not usually taught to ladies a source of interest and consolation, and they have enabled me to converse with gentlemen without being considered a goosecap, and to make informed decisions."

"Oh, I see. If Blacklaw or his mother had explained the matter to me as you have, I should have had less doubt about its necessity. I confess, I sometimes feel quite stupid when they discuss London affairs. Thank you."

Before she could respond, Alison, Lady Blacklaw

entered. "Adelaide, Magdalen, please come to the drawing room. We have a guest."

As the footman sprang to open the door for them, her mother-in-law added, "I have such a surprise for you."

Adelaide had not taken in those words before the door opened and she beheld Edward standing by the fireplace. She was certain her face was as blank as his own.

"Addie. I rejoice to see you in good health. And in good spirits, I trust?"

"I am, thank you. Are Leonora and my nieces and nephews well?" As Lady Blacklaw had said "a guest," her half brother must be here by himself. To Magdalen, Adelaide said, "May I introduce my brother, Edward, Lord Lamburne?"

After a few civilities, Alison suggested Lamburne would like to go to his chamber as dinner would be ready within the hour. "By then, Blacklaw will be finished with his bailiff, and perhaps Ducane will have returned from his ride. We do not change for dinner when it is only the family present."

With a last glance at Adelaide, he allowed himself to be turned over to a footman and led upstairs.

"I am so glad your brother was able to arrive before the masquerade. At the time I wrote to him, there was no knowing whether he would be able to come north. I expect you will have much to discuss, though it is a pity Lady Lamburne and her daughters were unable to join him. Your nephews are at school, I think, so their absence is understandable." Which implied she wondered what kept Adelaide's sister-in-law from accompanying the earl.

Ducane did not return in time for dinner, to Adelaide's regret. When the Blacklaws, Edward, and she gathered in the drawing room before the meal, her brother was punctiliously polite. She hoped it might last.

Gervase had not returned by the time they had finished the meal. Adelaide was not altogether surprised, as tenants and people from the village tended to hold Ducane in conversation when she and her husband met them. He might have been stopped by acquaintances half a dozen times, consulted about some problem, and taken a simple meal with someone. So she was not worried…except by Edward's presence. They had been too successful at concealing her estrangement from her half brother. Of course Blacklaw, or the Dowager Lady Blacklaw, would think she must welcome a visit from him.

Well, she could endure his company when one or more of Gervase's family were with her, though she did wish her husband was present. But after they rose from the table, the marquess excused himself on the ground that he had not quite finished with his estate business. Magdalen, Lady Blacklaw, flitted away to the nursery to oversee her children's supper, leaving Adelaide with Edward and her mother-in-law, who said, "I am sure Lord Lamburne would enjoy the opportunity to walk in the garden, Adelaide. You must have much family news to talk about."

Trapped. She had no choice but to agree. "You will want to stretch your legs after so long a coach journey, Edward," she said because what else could she say?

"Thank you, Addie. I should like to talk to you."

Neither spoke until she had led him out to the

formal garden behind the house, walled like the kitchen garden to protect it from the wind. Magdalen cut flowers there with her daughters sometimes or sat enjoying the sun, without having any interest in gardening. She found nothing lacking in the garden, which was laid out to her mother-in-law's preferences: nature had been regimented into strict rows and beds, the plantings segregated by color and height. Adelaide preferred Dale Tower's cheerful riot of blooms. There were two or three flowers here she had not found at home, however. She would ask the gardener what they were and if seeds could be obtained.

Edward's "Ahem," drew her attention back to him.

"Did Ducane mention I'd written to him, Addie?"

"He did."

"I must apologize both to you and to him. Your elopement…" His mouth turned down.

"Yes, shocking, wasn't it? But I suspected you were on your way to town and it seemed best to remove myself, to avoid argument." Or worse. "I do not care to be spied on by servants."

He blew out an impatient breath. "I felt it justified, as you had not visited London for years and had been away longer than expected. I had a responsibility to make sure you did not fall into some difficulty."

"And embarrass you and your family?"

"Given your unusual behavior at the house party," he began.

"I conducted myself like a gentlewoman, Edward. Did any of your guests find anything odd about me?" Apart from the knife, of course.

"No. But you had always shunned company before. The change in you was so sudden and startling, we were alarmed."

She paused to rub the leaves of a sweet briar, releasing the apple fragrance. "I was encouraged never to show myself to your guests, Edward—"

"I never—"

"Leonora did. I preferred to spare myself her and your daughters' remarks about my ugliness and eccentricity."

He stood stock-still, mouth slightly open as if he had turned to stone on the point of responding. A satisfying sight: she had never seen him speechless before.

"I never noticed."

"You wouldn't. You hated my mother and me."

"I, er…" He frowned and began again. "I didn't hate you. I should have outgrown my resentment of you, however."

"I accept your apology." She would not mention that she knew he had written to Tate. Her brother had probably still been furious and had not yet considered that his family's estrangement from her might reflect badly on them. Too, if they healed the breach, they would still reap the advantages of a connection by marriage to Blacklaw.

"Thank you."

That should end their talk; no doubt Edward was as glad as she to be done with it. He would linger at Blacklaw long enough to forge a friendship of sorts with the marquess and not depart with rude haste as soon as his horses were rested. But Adelaide and he were done except for accidental meetings in London if she and Gervase ever went there. Adelaide was thinking the autumn gentian and the primrose should be allowed to spread as they chose rather than be boxed up in rectangular beds, when he spoke again.

"There is one thing more."

She gazed at him inquiringly.

"I do not understand why Ducane did not inform me of your intention to wed. He did not need my permission to court you, I know that, as you are of age." He laughed uneasily. "Or you could have told me."

She stooped to pluck a blossom from the mat of wild thyme to give herself a moment to compose her reply. "We knew neither family would favor the match. Ducane's mother hoped he would offer for Sophia, and I am perfectly sure Leonora and Sophia expected it. A fait accompli would prevent argument."

"Though not recriminations, tears, and megrims, unfortunately." His faint, sardonic amusement was perhaps the first time Adelaide had ever detected humor in her brother. "You've made a good marriage, Addie. I felicitate you."

And was relieved she was no longer his responsibility, as well, she supposed. "Thank you, Edward. How are Leonora and the girls? I hope Sophia has got over her disappointment."

"They are well. Sophia is betrothed."

"Is she?" Quick work; which of the neighboring gentlemen could it be?

"Ay, to Sir Martin Howe. He has property in Devon."

"My felicitations to her, not that I suppose she will welcome them."

He gave a short laugh. "A baronet is lower than I would have liked, and Leonora is distressed, but…" He grunted. "You may as well know. Howe was the best we could do as we could not wait for a better prospect. Sophia is enceinte and will not tell us who the father is. I don't suppose you know, when Charity doesn't."

They were walking slowly back to the house. "I wonder if I do? I think I might make a guess at least."

He stopped and turned toward her.

"If I am correct, one puzzling thing is explained. That night Sophia...ummm, approached Ducane in the garden...I told Sophia and the footman, Thomas, that Ducane and I were betrothed. Did neither of them ever mention that to you?"

"Betrothed? Then? A scurrilous bit in the newssheet alleged a clandestine engagement at Lamburne but not when it occurred."

She was quite in charity with Edward at the moment but could not help enjoying his astonishment.

"Yes. It was not actually true at the time, but I claimed we were because I did not like to see him forced to marry by a trick, as I told him later." She could almost read his mind as he pondered this new fact.

He asked cautiously, "What is your surmise?"

"As Thomas was her accomplice in attempting to compromise Ducane, I can't but wonder if he had taken advantage of her."

"One of our footmen? Thomas has always seemed very proper and obliging." Then chagrin replaced surprise; perhaps he was recalling the reason Adelaide had carried a knife.

"How could he deceive us all? Surely some of the other footmen noticed when he left their quarters to go to the garden. They would have told our butler, who would have informed me."

"Thomas is a sneaking wretch. He was not well liked by the other servants. They're probably all afraid of him. Who suggested you send him to London to spy on me?"

Edward flushed. "You knew?"

"My maid discovered he was staying at the house but not working there, only coming and going out of livery."

"Sophia heard I meant to send a man and put Thomas forth as being intelligent and devoted to our family, as I already knew. Thought I knew," he conceded. "He may well be a scoundrel, but I find it hard to believe Sophia would lie with a servant, no matter how well spoken he is."

Indeed. "Yet if she knew she was expecting his child, that would explain why she was so lost to propriety"—a sop to Edward's parental fondness, as propriety and Sophia were not even on nodding terms— "as to waylay Ducane and why Thomas would help her. She would not want you to know who seduced her, because the man being a servant would make the matter even more scandalous. Thomas tried to blackmail Ducane by threatening to tell you of our supposed engagement, which would destroy Ducane's chance of marrying for a dowry and informed the newssheets of our secret betrothal at the Chase when Gervase would not pay him." Or rather, was prevented from doing so by their sudden departure from London.

"By God, I'll…"

Whatever he had started to say, Adelaide saw his dawning awareness that punishing Thomas would be dangerous. "Edward, does he know Sophia is to marry?"

"We have not announced it, but we've corresponded with Sir Martin, the letters and settlement documents going by groom to save time, so he might have learned of it if one servant overheard something. Or Sophia might have told him. He may wish to keep his position which is safer and potentially more lucrative than blackmailing me. You may not know, Addie, but footmen often receive tips when they carry messages or packages or perform some other little service."

"And sometimes they take bribes," she said dryly.

"Ah...yes. So he will probably attempt extortion only if I dismiss him with no reference. But I won't keep a dishonest servant. Why, Leonora was thinking he should be made butler when Lowe is ready to retire. I know he aspires to it. But it's unthinkable now. The opportunities for a dishonest butler to feather his own nest are too great."

"There's Charity to consider, too. If he seduced one girl, one cannot assume the other is safe."

"I had not considered that. What a devilish coil." After a fraught pause, he went on, "I suppose there's nothing to be done at least until Sophia's married. Thank God for Sir Martin. He showed an interest in Sophia last season, but of course he knew he had no chance of winning her. He's a mere baronet, after all, with no fortune or connections worth having." Her brother smiled grimly. "Fortunately for us, he is still not married and has no vices I've discovered. He wants a wife, needs an heir, and is all of forty."

He must have read the thought in her face.

"I explained the situation to him. 'Twould be no use pretending I had suddenly changed my mind because she's almost on the shelf. I could still find some man of higher title who'd take her—if time were not of the essence. He's willing to accept her bastard."

"But if it's a boy, the child will be his heir."

"I do not like talking about this to a gently born female, but I feel I must explain. His first wife never conceived, and he has no by-blows he knows of. There are one or two who might be his but might not, and the women have never claimed they were. Who's to know for sure? Probably not even the wench if she was free with her favors." He turned red as a cooked lobster. "I beg your pardon! I am not raking up old scandal, Addie." He took a deep breath. "He's worried enough not to care whose get the baby is, and of course I will not tell him our suspicions. And if she conceives again, I dare swear he will be the happiest man in the kingdom."

"I hope he may make Sophia happy, or at least not unhappy."

"If she is not, it will be her own fault. His appearance is distinguished, he has polished manners, and is willing to court and indulge her to a certain extent. They will marry quietly at Lamburne, then rusticate in deepest Devon until well after the birth."

"I'm glad." Oddly, she really was, little as she liked her niece. Her conversation with Edward had wiped the slate clean between them, even if she was never able to forgive Leonora.

"I may have to leave Thomas's punishment to God, unless I can get him a better post elsewhere."

"It would be too bad to introduce such a blackguard into some other household. Or mayhap divine justice will overtake him sooner rather than later.

The press gangs are very active near the coast."

"Why, what do you know of such things, Addie?"

"According to the newspapers, they are always searching for recruits for our navy, and not too exacting in their requirements. Though they are supposed to take only men 'of sea-faring habit,' almost any working man who happened to be near the docks might be snatched up. I've heard they sometimes seize men they find incapable with drink," she remarked chirpily.

"Hmmm."

Chapter 39

They had not reached the door when Gervase burst through it.

"Ah, there you are, my dear." He strode to meet them and tucked Adelaide's arm through his own. Adelaide sensed he was scrutinizing her for signs of discomfort. She smiled at him, reassuringly, she hoped. Or was her expression too much like Tabby's when she had caught a mouse?

"Welcome to Blacklaw, Lamburne."

"Thank you. I have been making my apologies to my sister. There was a good deal I did not know or understand. I hope you will forgive me for the tone of my letter."

"Already forgotten. Misunderstandings sometimes happen in families."

"I congratulate you both on your marriage, and I have brought your wedding gift, a pair of silver candle branches."

"Thank you, Edward." Ducane echoed her.

"I also brought something that was left behind when your belongings were packed."

"How kind of you!" Adelaide hoped he failed to notice her surprise.

" 'Tis only a set of silver tableware and Chinese porcelain dishes, enough for twenty places, I think. They were given to my—our—father and your mother as wedding gifts. I don't think I ever knew they existed, and of course we have several other sets. It's only right they should come to you now. Lowe reminded me of them after I sent your belongings."

Tears welled up in her eyes. "There is no gift I would appreciate more, Edward. Thank you."

His eyes gleaming with amusement, he offered, "Leonora wishes you joy of them."

Adelaide caught the irony in his voice; her sister-in-law had not known of their existence either and must be mad as fire to lose them. She gave him a thoroughly unladylike grin. "Please thank her and assure her I will think of you both when we use them."

Beside her, Ducane swallowed a choke of laughter.

****

"Are you looking forward to your first masked ball, Addie?" Lamburne asked. "I think you never attended one before."

The family and those who were staying at Blacklaw Hall were eating a light supper early enough to give them time to put on their costumes before the guests from nearby arrived.

She almost answered that the Lamburne Chase ball had given her high expectations of tonight's entertainment. After only a second's hesitation, she murmured sedately that she was indeed looking forward to it. Edward and she had been on terms of perfect amity since they had spoken in the garden. She found it too pleasant to risk by mentioning her uninvited presence at that event, nor could she let the others know she had attended her family's event secretly.

Gervase laughed when she asked him to dress and go downstairs, leaving her to put on her costume in privacy.

"My dear, we shared a single room at all the inns from London to Dale Tower, and you are in your shift as we speak. Why this sudden modesty?"

"I want to surprise you and see if you recognize me among the ladies present."

"Adelaide, you always surprise me. 'Tis one of your attractions. I'll use the dressing room and go down by myself. You'll not see me again until you find me below. I misdoubt you'll know me." As he disappeared into the dressing room, she thought she heard him whisper something to Jenkins. Curious: she did not think he had more than a black domino and domino mask. Many men would probably be wearing similar costumes, but she felt sure she would recognize his jaw and chin, and his way of moving. She did not think Ducane would be able to identify her, but she intended to enter late, to lose herself among the guests.

As Jenny lifted the embroidered linen petticoat over her head, Adelaide saw that part of the front hem was coming down. Mayhap the thread had given way suddenly. It must be near a century old, after all, or more. She hoped only that part need be repaired. Examination convinced her that the entire hem should be reinforced. Fortunately, the petticoat was far narrower than the sweeping modern skirts.

Near an hour elapsed before the hem was tacked up and Adelaide was arrayed in the petticoat, jacket, and cap, and the black mask secured.

"Is anyone in the passage?" she asked. Jenny opened the door a few inches and peeked out.

"No, my lady."

"Then I'm ready." She sailed out, followed by

Jenny, but turned right rather than left.

"Lady Adelaide?"

"I'll go down the back staircase."

"But you could make such an entrance the other way, your ladyship."

She glanced back at her maid. At Lamburne Chase, Adelaide had avoided drawing anyone's attention to herself. Those last weeks at the Chase, she had cast off those habits…mostly. Some evidently persisted. The thought of fifty or sixty pairs of eyes skewering her made her shiver. "I wish to slip into the Great Hall inconspicuously."

"Oh! And just appear, like the spirit in the Aladdin story Mr. Jenkins told me!"

"Only less noticeably, Jenny." On their journey from London, Jenkins had read to her maid and taught her about caring for clothing, but Adelaide did not think that tale was in any of the books Ducane had brought. But the valet was surprisingly well-read. She noticed Jenny's diction had improved: she no longer sounded like a raw country girl, even if she did not sound as polished as a London lady's maid.

She entered the Great Hall through the servants' door that gave access to the kitchen passage. Food would arrive still warm, if a banquet were held there. Adelaide lingered at the edge of the room, taking in the scene. The sun would not set for some time yet, but the Great Hall, its windows on the east side of the house, was rather dim. The candles in the wall sconces and standing candle trees had not yet been lit.

Many of the guests wore enveloping silk cloaks and half masks, the sort of masquerade attire one might wear if one did not wish to bother with a real costume.

Others had raided their attics for their forebears' old clothes, as she herself had done at Lamburne Chase. One lady appeared to be emerging from a flowering bush: long, supple twigs, probably osiers, covered her from hem to bodice. The leaves and blossoms must be of stiffened silk, for nature could never have placed them so regularly or kept them from losing petals.

A minuet was in progress: a gentleman in brown velvet with the head of a bull partnered a Turkish lady, and an ancient Roman matron dipped and rose with some Anglo-Saxon king—Alfred, perhaps. Adelaide made her way around the edge of the room, watching for a man of average height and figure. She might recognize her husband by his suit, if his domino parted when he moved.

Some fifty or sixty people filled the Great Hall, some dancing, others standing or sitting around the edges, of whom a third of the number were staying at Blacklaw and the rest either lived near enough to go home at the end of the ball, or else were staying with friends nearby. She could not see anyone who might be Gervase.

She passed among those not dancing, acknowledging greetings and responding to comments. The guests apparently recognized friends they knew well; she should be able to identify her husband. A gentleman in the trunk hose and doublet of Queen Elizabeth's time invited her to join him in the country dance which was forming. Even after her ready acceptance at Dale Tower and almost three weeks at Blacklaw, the ease she felt in company surprised her.

The dance ending, she parted from the gentleman to search another section of the hall. Was he looking for her? The servants were lighting the candles in the candle trees. Perhaps she would not discover him until the unmasking. Who would have thought picking out one person would be so difficult?

She paused to speak for a few minutes with an older lady wearing a mask and domino sewn all over with silvery stars and a lady, perhaps her daughter, who was veiled in gauze dyed the colors of dawn or sunset. Lady Blacklaw was correct; her neighbors were inventive. She would wager the man in the yellow domino with a mask depicting the sun was a member of the same family. A sea captain joined them and requested the dawn lady's company for the next dance. Then in the eddy as others moved to the center of the room, a cluster of men dispersed from before the great fireplace, and Adelaide saw Tam Lin. How could he be here? Who was here tonight who had been at the Lamburne Chase masked ball apart from Gervase? She had not been privy to that guest list, so there was no way of knowing. But Tam Lin could not be her husband. The timbre of their voices and their manner were too different.

The stark white full-face mask was half turned away from her as if he were searching the far side of the room.

"Excuse me, please," she murmured to her companion. Without looking away from her goal, Adelaide weaved through the shifting crowd, heart pounding. If she glanced aside even for a moment, he would disappear, and she would know she was as mad as her nieces claimed. Had she really seen him at the Lamburne masquerade or was he an illusion? As she neared the fireplace, he stared down the Great Hall's length. Adelaide was no more than ten paces from him when his eyes met hers.

She stopped, frozen in place. She forgot the people around her, she forgot where she was, she forgot to breathe. Could it really be Tam Lin? Hadn't he told her the white mask and black cape was a common Venetian Carnivale costume? What if it concealed some other man? Then he held out a hand toward her. Despite her thrill of terror, she could no more resist the invitation than she could fly to the moon. She moved to rest her own hand in his. *The Devil came to court a maid and she was called Mad Adelaide…*

"Will you dance, Queen Mab?"

"Yes," she whispered, too breathless to speak more loudly.

He led her into a place in the line. Another country dance: she was able to perform the figures without thought. He spoke as they joined in one movement. "Do you know who I am?"

At the next opportunity, she murmured, "I think so." *The Devil came to court a maid…* Neither spoke again for the duration of the dance. As he led her away, he said close by her ear, "Shall we go out to the garden?"

She nodded and let him lead her out of the hall, wondering if anyone would notice.

Chapter 40

The Lady of the Gillyflowers, his Queen Mab, was suddenly before him, like some fantastickal apparition. A conviction washed over him: the world was a more magical and perilous place than this rational century believed. He had felt it twice before. First, when someone or something had bent over him as he lay half stunned in Lamburne Chase's park, then again when Queen Mab disappeared from the parterre.

They danced as they had once before. Wherever he was in the figures of Lord Canarvan's Jig, he was aware of her. At the end, it seemed inevitable they should reenact their last meeting. Would the magic remain if he led her out to the garden?

Luck or magic favored them for they saw no other couples. By the wall where a quince was espaliered, he halted.

"I think we have unfinished business, Queen Mab."

She nodded but did not speak.

"Where did you go when you vanished?"

A low laugh. "Back to my shadows."

"Now we meet again." Ducane wished he could discard the obvious, logical conclusion. The enchantment surrounding his Lady of the Gillyflowers and the cat-like female he had imagined in the dawn lingered in his thoughts. He hated to give up the magic of those experiences. "Did you feel the bewitchment, too?"

A sigh. "Yes."

"You need not disappear this time. Will you take off your mask?"

"It's not time for the unmasking."

"We're here alone. We can put them on again before we return to the house."

As he reached up to untie the ribbons of his own mask, she slowly mirrored his movements.

He pulled off his mask and dropped it; hers dangled from her hand by its ties.

"Well met by moonlight, Queen Mab." He bent to kiss her lightly. She was more lovely than he had known. Then his arms were around her and the affectionate meeting of their lips turned to something more, and she was clinging to him.

When he could speak, he murmured close to her ear, "After I left Lamburne Chase, I thought I'd returned to the commonplace world, my queen of the fairies. Now I'm not so certain. Were you not the mysterious cat-like lady who wiped the blood from my brow and invited me to her chamber for bacon or kippers?"

He had never heard her laugh delightedly before. "What a pretty compliment! Am I truly cat-like?"

"In all the best ways, sweetheart."

"However, I protest I did not ask you to breakfast in my chamber. That would have been shockingly improper when we had not even been introduced."

"Ha! I'm certain I heard you coaxing me to join you."

"I was addressing Tabby." Her voice filled with laughter, and he laughed with her.

He had his captivating Lady of the Gillyflowers, his strangely sensual cat lady, and his sensible wife, all in one. She pressed against him the way he had seen Tabby nestle in her arms. "I love you, Adelaide."

She gazed up at him with glowing eyes. Magic had not vanished after all.